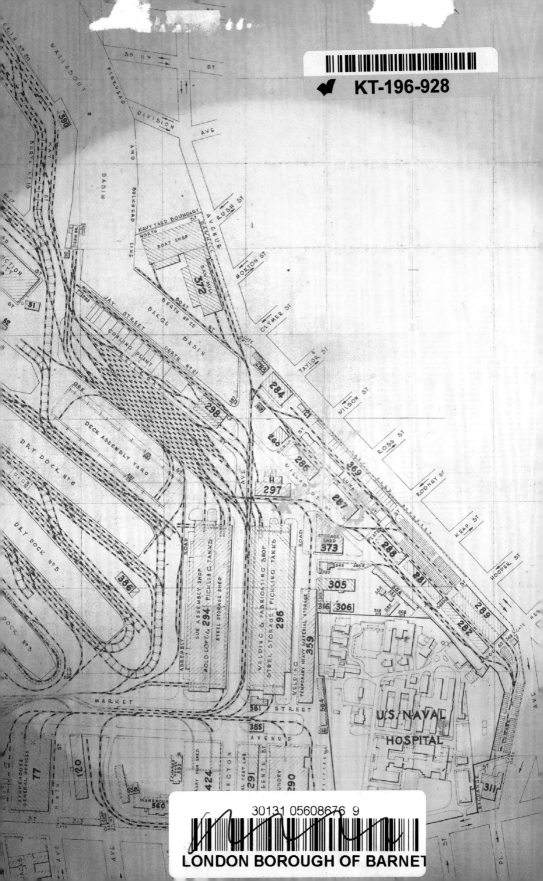

KT-196-928

MANHATTAN BEACH

MANHATTAN BEACH

JENNIFER EGAN

Signed by the author

This edition is 240 of 500

MANHATTAN BEACH

JENNIFER EGAN

corsair

CORSAIR

First published in the US in 2017 by Scribner
First published in Great Britain in 2017 by Corsair

1 3 5 7 9 10 8 6 4 2

Copyright © 2017 by Jennifer Egan

The moral right of the author has been asserted.

Interior design by Jill Putorti

Endpaper map courtesy of BNYDC Archives, SC/1, Brooklyn Navy Yard
Architectural Plans, Maps, and Drawings collection.

A CIP catalogue record for this book
is available from the British Library.

HB ISBN: 978-1-4721-5087-5
TPB ISBN: 978-1-4721-5088-2

Printed and bound in Great Britain by
Clays Ltd, St Ives plc

Papers used by Corsair are from well-managed forests
and other responsible sources.

MIX
Paper from
responsible sources
FSC® C104740

Corsair
An imprint of
Little, Brown Book Group
Carmelite House
50 Victoria Embankment
London EC4Y 0DZ

An Hachette UK Company
www.hachette.co.uk

www.littlebrown.co.uk

For Christina, Matthew, and Alexandra Egan,
and for Robert Egan—
our uncle Bob

Yes, as every one knows,
meditation and water are wedded for ever.

—HERMAN MELVILLE, *MOBY-DICK*

PART ONE

The Shore

CHAPTER ONE

They'd driven all the way to Mr. Styles's house before Anna realized that her father was nervous. First the ride had distracted her, sailing along Ocean Parkway as if they were headed for Coney Island, although it was four days past Christmas and impossibly cold for the beach. Then the house itself: a palace of golden brick three stories high, windows all the way around, a rowdy flapping of green-and-yellow-striped awnings. It was the last house on the street, which dead-ended at the sea.

Her father eased the Model J against the curb and turned off the motor. "Toots," he said. "Don't squint at Mr. Styles's house."

"Of course I won't squint at his house."

"You're doing it now."

"No," she said. "I'm making my eyes narrow."

"That's squinting," he said. "You've just defined it."

"Not for me."

He turned to her sharply. "Don't squint."

That was when she knew. She heard him swallow dryly and felt a chirp of worry in her stomach. She was not used to seeing her father nervous. Distracted, yes. Preoccupied, certainly.

"Why doesn't Mr. Styles like squinting?" she asked.

"No one does."

"You never told me that before."

"Would you like to go home?"

"No, thank you."

"I can take you home."

"If I squint?"

"If you give me the headache I'm starting to get."

"If you take me home," Anna said, "you'll be awfully late."

She thought he might slap her. He'd done it once, after she'd let fly a string of curses she'd heard on the docks, his hand finding her cheek invisibly as a whip. The specter of that slap still haunted Anna, with the odd effect of heightening her boldness, in defiance of it.

Her father rubbed the middle of his forehead, then looked back at her. His nerves were gone; she had cured them.

"Anna," he said. "You know what I need you to do."

"Of course."

"Be your charming self with Mr. Styles's children while I speak with Mr. Styles."

"I knew that, Papa."

"Of course you did."

She left the Model J with eyes wide and watering in the sun. It had been their own automobile until after the stock market crash. Now it belonged to the union, which lent it back for her father to do union business. Anna liked to go with him when she wasn't in school—to racetracks, Communion breakfasts and church events, office buildings where elevators lofted them to high floors, occasionally even a restaurant. But never before to a private home like this.

The door-pull was answered by Mrs. Styles, who had a movie star's sculpted eyebrows and a long mouth painted glossy red. Accustomed to judging her own mother prettier than every woman she encountered, Anna was disarmed by the evident glamour of Mrs. Styles.

"I was hoping to meet Mrs. Kerrigan," Mrs. Styles said in a husky voice, holding Anna's father's hand in both of hers. To which he replied that his younger daughter had taken sick that morning, and his wife had stayed at home to nurse her.

There was no sign of Mr. Styles.

Politely but (she hoped) without visible awe, Anna accepted a glass of lemonade from a silver tray carried by a Negro maid in a pale blue uniform. In the high polish of the entrance hall's wood floor, she caught the reflection of her own red dress, sewn by her mother. Beyond the windows of an adjacent front room, the sea tingled under a thin winter sun.

Mr. Styles's daughter, Tabatha, was only eight—three years younger than Anna. Still, Anna allowed the littler girl to tow her by the hand to a downstairs "nursery," a room dedicated purely to playing, filled with a shocking array of toys. A quick survey discovered a Flossie Flirt doll, several large teddy bears, and a rocking horse. There was a "Nurse" in the nursery, a freckled, raspy-voiced woman whose woolen dress strained like an overstacked bookshelf to repress her massive bust. Anna guessed from the broad lay of her face and the merry switch of her eyes that Nurse was Irish, and felt a danger of being seen through. She resolved to keep her distance.

Two small boys—twins, or at least interchangeable—were struggling to attach electric train tracks. Partly to avoid Nurse, who rebuffed the boys' pleas for help, Anna crouched beside the disjointed tracks and proffered her services. She could feel the logic of mechanical parts in her fingertips; this came so naturally that she could only think that other people didn't really try. They always *looked*, which was as useless when assembling things as studying a picture by touching it. Anna fastened the piece that was vexing the boys and took several more from the freshly opened box. It was a Lionel train, the quality of the tracks palpable in the resolve with which they interlocked. As she worked, Anna glanced occasionally at the Flossie Flirt doll wedged at the end of a shelf. She had wanted one so violently two years ago that some of her desperation seemed to have broken off and stayed inside her. It was strange and painful to discover that old longing now, in this place.

Tabatha cradled her new Christmas doll, a Shirley Temple in a fox-fur coat. She watched, entranced, as Anna built her brothers' train tracks. "Where do you live?" she asked.

"Not far."

"By the beach?"

"Near it."

"May I come to your house?"

"Of course," Anna said, fastening tracks as fast as the boys handed them to her. A figure eight was nearly complete.

"Have you any brothers?" Tabatha asked.

"A sister," Anna said. "She's eight, like you, but she's mean. Because of being so pretty."

Tabatha looked alarmed. "How pretty?"

"Extremely pretty," Anna said gravely, then added, "She looks like our mother, who danced with the Follies." The error of this boast accosted her a moment later. *Never part with a fact unless you've no choice.* Her father's voice in her ears.

Lunch was served by the same Negro maid at a table in the playroom. They sat like adults on their small chairs, cloth napkins in their laps. Anna glanced several times at the Flossie Flirt, searching for some pretext to hold the doll without admitting she was interested. If she could just feel it in her arms, she would be satisfied.

After lunch, as a reward for their fine behavior, Nurse allowed them to bundle into coats and hats and bolt from a back door along a path that ran behind Mr. Styles's house to a private beach. A long arc of snow-dusted sand tilted down to the sea. Anna had been to the docks in winter, many times, but never to a beach. Miniature waves shrugged up under skins of ice that crackled when she stomped them. Seagulls screamed and dove in the riotous wind, their bellies stark white. The twins had brought along Buck Rogers ray guns, but the wind turned their shots and death throes into pantomime.

Anna watched the sea. There was a feeling she had, standing at its edge: an electric mix of attraction and dread. What would be exposed if all that water should suddenly vanish? A landscape of lost objects: sunken ships, hidden treasure, gold and gems and the charm bracelet that had fallen from her wrist into a storm drain. *Dead bodies,* her father always added, with a laugh. To him, the ocean was a wasteland.

Anna looked at Tabby (as she was nicknamed), shivering beside her, and wanted to say what she felt. Strangers were often easier to say things to. Instead, she repeated what her father always said, confronted by a bare horizon: "Not a ship in sight."

The little boys dragged their ray guns over the sand toward the breaking waves, Nurse panting after them. "You'll go nowhere near that water, Phillip, John-Martin," she wheezed at a startling volume. "Is that perfectly clear?" She cast a hard look at Anna, who had led them there, and herded the twins toward the house.

"Your shoes are getting wet," Tabby said through chattering teeth.

"Should we take them off?" Anna asked. "To feel the cold?"

"I don't want to feel it!"

"I do."

Tabby watched Anna unbuckle the straps of the black patent-leather shoes she shared with Zara Klein, downstairs. She unrolled her wool stockings and placed her white, bony, long-for-her-age feet in the icy water. Each foot delivered an agony of sensation to her heart, one part of which was a flame of ache that felt unexpectedly pleasant.

"What's it like?" Tabby shrieked.

"Cold," Anna said. "Awful, awful cold." It took all of her strength to keep from recoiling, and her resistance added to the odd excitement. Glancing toward the house, she saw two men in dark overcoats following the paved path set back from the sand. Holding their hats in the wind, they looked like actors in a silent picture. "Are those our papas?"

"Daddy likes to have business talks outdoors," Tabby said. *"Away from prying ears."*

Anna felt benevolent compassion toward young Tabatha, excluded from her father's business affairs when Anna was allowed to listen in whenever she pleased. She heard little of interest. Her father's job was to pass greetings, or good wishes, between union men and other men who were their friends. These salutations included an envelope, sometimes a package, that he would deliver or receive casually—you wouldn't notice unless you were paying attention. Over the years, he'd talked to Anna a great deal without knowing he was talking, and she had listened without knowing what she heard.

She was surprised by the familiar, animated way her father was speaking to Mr. Styles. Apparently they were friends. After all that.

The men changed course and began crossing the sand toward Anna and Tabby. Anna stepped hurriedly out of the water, but she'd left her shoes too far away to put them back on in time. Mr. Styles was a broad, imposing man with brilliantined black hair showing under his hat brim. "Say, is this your daughter?" he asked. "Withstanding arctic temperatures without so much as a pair of stockings?"

Anna sensed her father's displeasure. "So it is," he said. "Anna, say good day to Mr. Styles."

"Very pleased to meet you," she said, shaking his hand firmly, as her father had taught her, and taking care not to squint as she peered up at him. Mr. Styles looked younger than her father, without shadows or creases in his face. She sensed an alertness about him, a humming tension perceptible even through his billowing overcoat. He seemed to await something to react to, or be amused by. Right now that something was Anna.

Mr. Styles crouched beside her on the sand and looked directly into her face. "Why the bare feet?" he asked. "Don't you feel the cold, or are you showing off?"

Anna had no ready answer. It was neither of those; more an instinct to keep Tabby awed and guessing. But even that she couldn't articulate. "Why would I show off?" she said. "I'm nearly twelve."

"Well, what's it feel like?"

She smelled mint and liquor on his breath even in the wind. It struck her that her father couldn't hear their conversation.

"It only hurts at first," she said. "After a while you can't feel anything."

Mr. Styles grinned as if her reply were a ball he'd taken physical pleasure in catching. "Words to live by," he said, then rose again to his immense height. "She's strong," he remarked to Anna's father.

"So she is." Her father avoided her eyes.

Mr. Styles brushed sand from his trousers and turned to go. He'd exhausted that moment and was looking for the next. "They're stronger than we are," Anna heard him say to her father. "Lucky for us, they don't know it." She thought he might turn and look back at her, but he must have forgotten.

Dexter Styles felt sand working its way inside his oxfords as he slogged back to the path. Sure enough, the toughness he'd sensed coiled in Ed Kerrigan had flowered into magnificence in the dark-eyed daughter. Proof of what he'd always believed: men's children gave them away. It was why Dexter rarely did business with any man before meeting his family. He wished his Tabby had gone barefoot, too.

Kerrigan drove a '28 Duesenberg Model J, Niagara blue, evidence both of fine taste and of bright prospects before the crash. He had an excellent tailor. Yet there was something obscure about the man, something that worked against the clothing and automobile and even his blunt, deft conversation. A shadow, a sorrow. Then again, who hadn't one? Or several?

By the time they reached the path, Dexter found himself decided upon hiring Kerrigan, assuming that suitable terms could be established.

"Say, have you time for a drive to meet an old friend of mine?" he asked.

"Certainly," Kerrigan said.

"Your wife isn't expecting you?"

"Not before supper."

"Your daughter? Will she worry?"

Kerrigan laughed. "Anna? It's her job to worry me."

*   *   *

Anna had expected any moment to be called off the beach by her father, but it was Nurse who eventually came, huffing indignantly, and ordered them out of the cold. The light had changed, and the playroom felt heavy and dark. It was warmed by its own woodstove. They ate walnut cookies and watched the electric train race around the figure eight Anna had built, real steam straggling from its miniature smokestack. She had never seen such a toy, could not imagine how much it might cost. She was sick of this adventure. It had lasted far longer than their sociable visits usually did, and playing a part for the other children had exhausted Anna. It felt like hours since she'd seen her father. Eventually, the boys left the train running and went to look at picture books. Nurse had nodded off in a rocking chair. Tabby lay on a braided rug, pointing her new kaleidoscope at the lamp.

Casually, Anna asked, "May I hold your Flossie Flirt?"

Tabby assented vaguely, and Anna carefully lifted the doll from the shelf. Flossie Flirts came in four sizes, and this was the second smallest—not the newborn baby but a somewhat larger baby with startled blue eyes. Anna turned the doll on her side. Sure enough, just as the newspaper ads had promised, the blue irises slid into the corners of the eyes as if keeping Anna in sight. She felt a burst of pure joy that nearly made her laugh. The doll's lips were drawn into a perfect "O." Below her top lip were two painted white teeth.

As if catching the scent of Anna's delight, Tabby jumped to her feet. "You can have her," she cried. "I never play with her anymore."

Anna absorbed the impact of this offer. Two Christmases ago, when she'd wanted the Flossie Flirt so acutely, she hadn't dared ask—ships had stopped coming in, and they hadn't any money. The extreme physical longing she'd felt for the doll scissored through her now, upsetting her deep knowledge that of course she must refuse.

"No, thank you," she said at last. "I've a bigger one at home. I just wanted to see what the small one was like." With wrenching effort, she forced herself to replace the Flossie Flirt on the shelf, keeping a hand on one rubbery leg until she felt Nurse's eyes upon her. Feigning indifference, she turned away.

Too late. Nurse had seen, and knew. When Tabby left the room to answer a call from her mother, Nurse seized the Flossie Flirt and half flung it at Anna. "Take it, dear," she whispered fiercely. "She doesn't care—she's more toys than she can ever play with. They all have."

Anna wavered, half believing there might be a way to take the doll without having anyone know. But the mere thought of her father's reaction hardened her reply. "No, thank you," she said coldly. "I'm too old for dolls, anyway." Without a backward glance, she left the play-room. But Nurse's sympathy had weakened her, and her knees shook as she climbed the stairs.

At the sight of her father in the front hall, Anna barely withstood an urge to run to him and hug his legs as she used to do. He had his coat on. Mrs. Styles was saying goodbye. "Next time you must bring your sister," she told Anna, kissing her cheek with a brush of musky perfume. Anna promised that she would. Outside, the Model J gleamed dully in the late-afternoon sun. It had been shinier when it was their car; the union boys polished it less.

As they drove away from Mr. Styles's house, Anna searched for the right clever remark to disarm her father—the kind she'd made thoughtlessly when she was smaller, his startled laughter her first indication she'd been funny. Lately, she often found herself trying to recapture an earlier state, as if some freshness or innocence had passed from her.

"I suppose Mr. Styles wasn't in stocks," she said finally.

He chuckled and pulled her to him. "Mr. Styles doesn't need stocks. He owns nightclubs. And other things."

"Is he with the union?"

"Oh no. He's nothing to do with the union."

This was a surprise. Generally speaking, union men wore hats, and longshoremen wore caps. Some, like her father, might wear either, depending on the day. Anna couldn't imagine her father with a long-shoreman's hook when he was dressed well, as now. Her mother saved exotic feathers from her piecework and used them to trim his hats. She retailored his suits to match the styles and flatter his ropy frame—he'd lost weight since the ships had stopped coming and he took less exercise.

Her father drove one-handed, a cigarette cocked between two fingers at the wheel, the other arm around Anna. She leaned against him. In the end it was always the two of them in motion, Anna drifting on a tide of sleepy satisfaction. She smelled something new in the car amid her father's cigarette smoke, a loamy, familiar odor she couldn't quite place.

"Why the bare feet, toots?" he asked, as she'd known he would.

"To feel the water."

"That's something little girls do."

"Tabatha is eight, and she didn't."

"She'd better sense."

"Mr. Styles liked that I did."

"You've no idea what Mr. Styles thought."

"I have. He talked to me when you couldn't hear."

"I noticed that," he said, glancing at her. "What did he say?"

Her mind reached back to the sand, the cold, the ache in her feet, and the man beside her, curious—all of it fused now with her longing for that Flossie Flirt. "He said I was strong," she said, a lump tightening her voice. Her eyes blurred.

"And so you are, toots," he said, kissing the top of her head. "Anyone can see that."

At a traffic light, he knocked another cigarette from his Raleigh packet. Anna checked inside, but she'd already taken the coupon. She wished her father would smoke more; she'd collected seventy-eight coupons, but the catalog items weren't even tempting until a hundred and twenty-five. For eight hundred you could get a six-serving plate-silver set in a customized chest, and there was an automatic toaster for seven hundred. But these numbers seemed unattainable. The B&W Premiums catalog was short on toys: just a Frank Buck panda bear or a Betsy Wetsy doll with a complete layette for two hundred fifty, but those items seemed beneath her. She was drawn to the dartboard, "for older children and adults," but couldn't imagine flinging sharp darts across their small apartment. Suppose one hit Lydia?

Smoke rose from the encampments inside Prospect Park. They were nearly home. "I almost forgot," her father said. "Look what I've here." He took a paper sack from inside his overcoat and gave it to Anna. It was filled with bright red tomatoes, their taut, earthen smell the very one she'd noticed.

"How," she marveled, "in winter?"

"Mr. Styles has a friend who grows them in a little house made of glass. He showed it to me. We'll surprise Mama, shall we?"

"You went away? While I was at Mr. Styles's house?" She felt a wounded astonishment. In all the years Anna had accompanied him on his errands, he had never left her anywhere. He had always been in sight.

"Just for a very short time, toots. You didn't even miss me."

"How far away?"

"Not far."

"I did miss you." It seemed to her now that she had known he was gone, had felt the void of his absence.

"Baloney," he said, kissing her again. "You were having the time of your life."

CHAPTER TWO

An *Evening Journal* folded under his arm, Eddie Kerrigan paused outside the door to his apartment, panting from the climb. He'd sent Anna upstairs while he bought the paper, largely to put off his homecoming. Heat from the tireless radiators leaked into the hall from around the door, amplifying a smell of liver and onions from the Feeneys', on three. His own apartment was on the sixth floor—ostensibly five—an illegality that some genius builder had gotten away with by calling the second floor the first. But the building's chief advantage more than compensated: a cellar furnace that pumped steam into a radiator in each room.

He was taken aback by the sound of his sister's brawny laugh from behind the door. Apparently, Brianne was back from Cuba sooner than expected. Eddie shoved open the door with a shriek of overpainted hinges. His wife, Agnes, sat at the kitchen table in a short-sleeved yellow dress (it was summer year-round on the sixth floor). Sure enough, Brianne sat across, lightly tanned and holding a nearly empty glass—as Brianne's glasses tended to be.

"Hi, lover," Agnes said, rising from a pile of sequined toques she'd been trimming. "You're so late."

She kissed him, and Eddie cupped her strong hip and felt the stirring she always roused in him, despite everything. He caught a whiff of the cloved oranges they'd hung from the Christmas tree in the front room and sensed Lydia's presence there, near the tree. He didn't turn. He needed to ready himself. Kissing his beautiful wife was a good start. Watching her shoot seltzer into a glass of the fancy Cuban rum Brianne had brought—that was an excellent start.

Agnes had stopped drinking in the evenings; she said it made her too tired. Eddie brought his sister her replenished highball glass with a fresh chip of ice and touched his glass to hers. "How was the trip?"

"Perfectly marvelous," Brianne said with a laugh, "until it went perfectly foul. I came back by steamer."

"Not so nice as a yacht. Say, that's delicious."

"The steamer was the best part! I made a new friend on board who's a much better sport."

"Has he work?"

"Trumpeter with the band," Brianne said. "I know, I know, save it, brother dear. He's awfully sweet."

Business as usual. His sister—half sister, for they'd different mothers and had grown up largely apart, Brianne three years older—was like a fine automobile whose rash owner was running it to the brink of collapse. She'd been a stunner once; now, in the wrong light, she looked thirty-nine going on fifty.

A groan issued from the front room, lodging in Eddie's stomach like a kick. *Now,* he thought, before Agnes had to prompt him. He rose from the table and went to where Lydia lay in the easy chair, propped like a dog or a cat—she hadn't enough strength to hold herself up. She smiled her lopsided smile at Eddie's approach, head lolling, wrists bent like birds' wings. Her bright blue eyes sought his: clear, perfect eyes that bore no trace of her affliction.

"Hello, Liddy," he said stiffly. "How was your day, kiddo?"

It was hard not to sound mocking, knowing she couldn't answer. When Lydia did talk, in her way, it was senseless babble—echolalia, the doctors called it. And yet it felt strange *not* to talk to her. What else could one do with an eight-year-old girl who couldn't sit up on her own, much less walk? Pet and greet her: that took all of fifteen seconds. And then? Agnes would be watching, hungry for a show of affection toward their younger daughter. Eddie knelt beside Lydia and kissed her cheek. Her hair was golden, soft with curls, fragrant with the exorbitant shampoo Agnes insisted upon buying for her. Her skin was velvety as an infant's. The bigger Lydia grew, the more tempting it was to picture what she might have looked like had she not been damaged. A beauty. Possibly more than Agnes—certainly more than Anna. A pointless reflection.

"How was your day, kiddo?" he whispered again. He scooped Lydia into his arms and lowered himself onto the chair, holding her weight to his chest. Anna leaned against him, trained by her mother to scrutinize these interactions. Her devotion to Lydia puzzled Eddie; why, when Lydia gave so little in return? Anna peeled off her sister's stockings and tickled her soft curled feet until she writhed in Eddie's arms and made the noise that was laughing for her. He hated it. He preferred to assume Lydia couldn't think or feel except as an animal did, attending to its own survival. But her laughter, in response to pleasure, rebutted this belief. It made Eddie angry—first with Lydia, then with himself for begrudging her a moment's delight. It was the same when she drooled, which of course she couldn't help: a flash of fury, even a wish to smack her, followed by a convulsion of guilt. Again and again, with his younger daughter, rage and self-loathing crossed in Eddie like riptides, leaving him numb and spent.

And yet it could still be so sweet. Dusk falling blue outside the windows, Brianne's rum pleasantly clouding his thoughts, his daughters nudging him like kittens. Ellington on the radio, the month's rent paid; things could be worse—*were* worse for many a man in the dregs of 1934. Eddie felt a lulling possibility of happiness pulling at him like sleep. But rebellion jerked him back to awareness: *No, I cannot accept this, I will not be made happy by this.* He rose to his feet suddenly, startling Lydia, who whimpered as he set her back down on the chair. Things were not as they should be—not remotely. He was a law-and-order man (Eddie often reminded himself ironically), and too many laws had been broken here. He withdrew, holding himself apart, and in swerving away from happiness, he reaped his reward: a lash of pain and solitude.

There was a special chair he needed to buy for Lydia, monstrously expensive. Having such a daughter required the riches of a man like Dexter Styles—but did such men *have* children like Lydia? In the first years of her life, when they'd still believed they were rich, Agnes had brought Lydia each week to a clinic at New York University where a woman gave her mineral baths and used leather straps and pulleys to strengthen her muscles. Now such care was beyond their reach. But the chair would allow her to sit up, look out, join the vertical world. Agnes believed in its transformative power, and Eddie believed in the need to appear to share her belief. And perhaps he did, a little. That chair was the reason he'd first sought out the acquaintance of Dexter Styles.

Agnes cleared the toques and sequin chains from the kitchen table and set four places for supper. She would have liked for Lydia to join them, would happily have cradled her in her own lap. But that would ruin the meal for Eddie. So Agnes left Lydia alone in the front room, compensating, as always, by keeping her own attention fixed upon her like a rope whose two ends she and her younger daughter were holding. Through this rope Agnes felt the quiver of Lydia's consciousness and curiosity, her trust that she wasn't alone. She hoped that Lydia could feel her own feverish love and assurance. Of course, holding the rope meant that Agnes was only half-present—distracted, as Eddie often remarked. But in caring so little, he left her no choice.

Over bean-and-sausage casserole, Brianne regaled them with the story of her smashup with Bert. Relations had already soured when she'd delivered an accidental coup de grâce by knocking him from the deck of his yacht into shark-infested waters off the Bahamas. "You've never seen a man swim faster," she said. "He was an Olympian, I tell you. And when he collapsed onto the deck and I pulled him to his feet and tried to throw my arms around him—it was the first amusing thing he'd done in days—what does he do? Tries to punch me in the nose."

"Then what happened?" Anna cried with more excitement than

Eddie would have liked. His sister was a rotten influence, but he was uncertain what to do about it, how to counter her.

"I ducked, of course, and he nearly toppled back in. Men who've grown up rich haven't the first idea how to fight. Only the scrappy ones can. Like you, brother dear."

"But we haven't yachts," he remarked.

"More's the pity," Brianne said. "You'd look very smart in a yachting cap."

"You forget, I don't like boats."

"Growing up rich turns them soft," Brianne said. "Next you know, they're soft everywhere, if you take my meaning. Soft in the head," she amended to his severe look.

"And the trumpeter?" he asked.

"Oh, he's a real lover boy. Curls like Rudy Vallee."

She would need money again soon enough. Brianne was long past her dancing days, and even then her chief resource had always been her beaus. But fewer men were flush now, and a girl with bags under her eyes and a boozy roll at the waist was less likely to land one. Eddie found a way to give his sister money whenever she asked, even if it meant borrowing from the shylock. He dreaded what she might become otherwise.

"Actually, the trumpeter is doing rather well," Brianne said. "He's been working at a couple of Dexter Styles's clubs."

The name blindsided Eddie. He'd never heard it uttered by Brianne or anyone else—hadn't even thought to gird himself against the possibility. From across the table, he sensed Anna's hesitation. Would she pipe up about having spent the day with that very man at his home in Manhattan Beach? Eddie didn't dare look at her. With his long silence, he willed Anna to be silent, too.

"I suppose that's something," he told his sister at last.

"Good old Eddie." Brianne sighed. "Always the optimist."

The clock chimed seven from the front room, which meant that it was nearly quarter past. "Papa," Anna said. "You forgot the surprise."

Eddie failed to take her meaning, still rattled by that close shave. Then he remembered, rose from the table, and went to the peg where his overcoat hung. She was good, his Anna, he marveled as he pretended to search his pockets while steadying his breath. Better than good. He tipped the sack onto the table and let the bright tomatoes tumble out. His wife and sister were duly staggered. "Where did you get these? How?" they asked in a welter. "From who?"

As Eddie groped for an explanation, Anna put in smoothly, "Someone from the union has a glass growing house."

"They live well, those union boys," Brianne remarked. "Even in a Depression."

"Especially," Agnes said dryly, but in fact she was pleased. Being on the receiving end of perks meant that Eddie was still needed—something they were never guaranteed. She took salt and a paring knife and began to slice the tomatoes on a cutting board. Juice and small seeds ran onto the oilcloth. Brianne and Agnes ate the tomato slices with moans of delight.

"Turkeys at Christmas, now this—there must be an election coming up," Brianne said, smacking juice from her fingers.

"Dunellen wants to be alderman," Agnes said.

"God help us, the skinflint. Go on, Eddie. Taste one."

He did at last, amazed by the twanging conjunction of salt and sour and sweet. Anna met his eyes without so much as a smirk of collusion. She'd done beautifully, better than he could have hoped, yet Eddie found himself preoccupied by some worry—or was he recalling a worry from earlier that day?

While Anna helped her mother clear the table and wash up, and Brianne helped herself to more rum, Eddie opened the front window that gave onto the fire escape and climbed outside for a smoke. He shut the window quickly behind him so Lydia wouldn't take a draft. The dark street was soaked in yellow lamplight. There was the beautiful Duesenberg he'd once owned. He recalled with some relief that he would have to return it. Dunellen never let him keep the car overnight.

As he smoked, Eddie returned to his worry about Anna as if it were a stone he'd placed in his pocket and now could remove and examine. He'd taught her to swim at Coney Island, taken her to *Public Enemy* and *Little Caesar* and *Scarface* (over the disapproving looks of ushers), bought her egg creams and charlotte russes and coffee, which he'd let her drink since the age of seven. She might as well have been a boy: dust in her stockings, her ordinary dresses not much different from short pants. She was a scrap, a weed that would thrive anywhere, survive anything. She pumped life into him as surely as Lydia drained it.

But what he'd witnessed just now, at the table, was deception. That wasn't good for a girl, would twist her the wrong way. Approaching Anna on the beach today with Styles, he'd been struck by the fact that she was, if not precisely pretty, arresting. She was nearly twelve—no longer small, though he still thought of her that way. The shadow of that perception had troubled him the rest of the day.

The conclusion was obvious: he must stop bringing Anna with him. Not immediately, but soon. The thought filled him with a spreading emptiness.

Back inside, Brianne administered a sloppy rum-scented kiss to his cheek and went to meet her trumpeter. His wife was changing Lydia's diaper on the plank that covered the kitchen tub. Eddie wrapped his arms around her from behind and rested his chin on her shoulder, reaching for a way they had been together easily, always, believing it for a moment. But Agnes wanted him to kiss *Lydia*, take the diaper and pin it, being careful not to prick her tender flesh. Eddie was on the verge of doing this—he would, he was just about to—but he didn't, and then the impulse passed. He let go of Agnes, disappointed in himself, and she finished changing the diaper alone. She, too, had felt the pull of their old life. Turn and kiss Eddie, surprise him; forget Lydia for a moment—where was the harm? She imagined herself doing this but could not. Her old way of being in the world was folded inside a box alongside her Follies costumes, gathering dust.

One day, perhaps, she would slide that box from under the bedsprings and open it again. But not now. Lydia needed her too much.

Eddie went to find Anna in the room she and Lydia shared. It faced the street; he and Agnes had taken the room facing the airshaft, whose unwholesome exhalations stank of mildew and wet ash. Anna was poring over her Premiums catalog. It bewildered Eddie, her fixation on this diminutive pamphlet full of overvalued prizes, but he sat beside her on the narrow bed and handed over the coupon from his fresh Raleigh packet. She was studying an inlaid bridge table that would "withstand constant usage."

"What do you think?" she asked.

"Seven hundred fifty coupons? Even Lydia will have to take up smoking if we're to afford that."

This made her laugh. She loved it when he included Lydia; he knew he should do it more often, seeing as it cost him nothing. She turned to another page: a man's wristwatch. "I could get that for you, Papa," she said. "Since you're doing all the smoking."

He was touched. "I've my pocket watch, remember. Why not something for you, since you're the collector?" He thumbed in search of children's items.

"A Betsy Wetsy doll?" she said disdainfully.

Stung by her tone, he turned to a page with compacts and silk hosiery.

"For Mama?" she asked.

"For you. Now you've outgrown dolls."

She guffawed, to his relief. "I'll never want that stuff," she said, and returned to glassware, a toaster, an electric lamp. "Let's pick something the whole family can use," she said expansively, as if their tiny family were like the Feeneys, whose eight healthy children crowded two apartments and gave them a monopoly on one of the third-floor toilets.

"You were right, toots," he said softly. "Not to mention Mr. Styles at supper. In fact, best not to say his name to anyone."

"Except you?"

"Not even me. And I won't say it, either. We can think it but not say it. Understand?" He braced himself for her inevitable guff.

But Anna seemed enlivened by this subterfuge. "Yes!"

"Now. Who were we talking about?"

There was a pause. "Mr. Whosis," she finally said.

"That's my girl."

"Married to Mrs. Whatsis."

"Bingo."

Anna felt herself beginning to forget, lulled by the satisfaction of sharing a secret with her father, of pleasing him uniquely. The day with Tabatha and Mr. Styles became like one of those dreams that shreds and melts even as you try to gather it up.

"And they lived in Who-knows-where-land." She imagined it: a castle by the sea disappearing under a fog of forgetfulness.

"So they did," her father said. "So they did. Beautiful, wasn't it?"

CHAPTER THREE

Eddie's relief at having departed his home was a precise inversion of the relief it once gave him to arrive there. For starters, he could smoke. On the ground floor, he struck a match on his shoe and lit up, pleased not to have met a single neighbor on his way down. He hated them for their reactions to Lydia, whatever those reactions might be. The Feeneys, devout and charitable: pity. Mrs. Baxter, whose slippers scuttled like cockroaches behind her door at the sound of feet on the stairs: ghoulish curiosity. Lutz and Boyle, ancient bachelors who shared a wall on two but hadn't spoken in a decade: revulsion (Boyle) and anger (Lutz). "Shouldn't she be in a home?" Lutz had gone so far as to demand. To which Eddie had countered, "Shouldn't you?"

Outside the building, he detected a rustling murmur in the cold, whistles exchanged around burning cigarette tips. At a cry of "Free all!" he realized these were boys playing Ringolevio: two teams trying to take each other prisoner. This was a mixed building on a mixed block— Italians, Poles, Jews, everything but Negroes—but the scene could as easily be happening at the Catholic protectory in the Bronx where he'd grown up. Anywhere you went, everywhere: a scrum of boys.

Eddie climbed inside the Duesenberg and turned the engine, listening for a whinnying vibration he'd noticed earlier and hadn't liked the sound of. Dunellen was running down the car, as he did everything he touched—including Eddie. Prodding the accelerator, listening to the whine, he glanced up at the lighted windows of his own front room. His family was in there. Sometimes, before coming inside, Eddie would stand in the hall and overhear a festive gaiety from behind the closed door. It always surprised him. *Did I imagine that?* he would ask himself later. Or had they been easier—happier—without him?

There was always a time, after Anna's father went out, when everything vital seemed to have gone with him. The ticking of the front-room clock made her teeth clench. An ache of uselessness, anger almost, throbbed in her wrists and fingers as she embroidered beads onto an elaborate feathered headdress. Her mother was sequining toques, fifty-five in all, but the hardest trimming jobs went to Anna. She took no pride in her sewing prowess. Working with your hands meant taking orders—in her mother's case, from Pearl Gratzky, a costumer she knew from the Follies who worked on Broadway shows and the occasional Hollywood picture. Mrs. Gratzky's husband was a shut-in. He'd a hole in his side from the Great War that hadn't healed in sixteen years—a fact that was often invoked to explain Pearl's screaming hysterics when jobs were not completed to her liking. Anna's mother had never seen Mr. Gratzky.

When Lydia woke from her doze, Anna and her mother shook off their lassitude. Anna held her sister in her lap, a bib tied across her chest, while their mother fed her the porridge she made each morning from soft vegetables and strained meat. Lydia emanated a prickling alertness; she saw and heard and understood. Anna whispered secrets to her sister at night. Only Lydia knew that Mr. Gratzky had shown Anna the hole in his side a few weeks ago, when she'd delivered a package of finished sewing and found Pearl Gratzky not at home. Impelled by daring that had seemed to come from somewhere outside her, Anna had pushed open the door to the room where he lay—a tall man with a handsome, ruined face—and asked to see his wound. Mr. Gratzky had lifted his pajama top, then a piece of gauze, and shown her a small round opening, pink and glistening as a baby's mouth.

When Lydia finished eating, Anna fiddled with the radio dial until the Martell Orchestra came on, playing standards. Tentatively, she and her mother began to dance, waiting to see if Mr. Praeger, directly below them on four, would jab at his ceiling with a broom handle. But he must have gone to a smoker fight, as he often did on Saturday nights. They turned up the volume, and Anna's mother danced with a reckless absorption quite unlike her usual self. It jogged faint memories in Anna of seeing her mother onstage when she was very small: a distant, shimmering vision, doused in colored light. Her mother could do any dance—the Baltimore Buzz, the tango, the Black Bottom, the cakewalk—but she never danced anymore except at home with Anna and Lydia.

Anna danced holding Lydia until her sister's floppiness became part of the dancing. All of them grew flushed; their mother's hair fell loose, and her dress came unbuttoned at the top. She cracked the fire escape window, and the hard winter air made them cough. The small apartment shook and rang with a cheer that seemed not to exist when her father was at home, like a language that turned to gibberish when he listened.

When they were all hot from dancing, Anna lifted away the plank covering the bathtub and filled it. They undressed Lydia quickly and eased her into the warm water. Released from gravity, her coiled, bent form luxuriated visibly. Their mother held her under the arms while Anna massaged her scalp and hair with the special lilac shampoo. Lydia's clear blue eyes gazed at them rapturously. Suds gathered in her temples. There was an aching satisfaction in saving the best for her, as if she were a secret princess deserving of their tribute.

It took both Anna and her mother to lift Lydia back out before the water cooled, bubbles gleaming on the unexpected twists of her body—beautiful in its strange way, like the inside of an ear. They wrapped her in a towel and carried her to bed and dried her on the counterpane, sprinkling Cashmere Bouquet talc over her skin. Her cotton nightie was trimmed with Belgian lace. Her wet curls smelled of lilac. When they'd tucked her in, Anna and her mother lay on either side of her, holding hands across her body to keep her from falling off the bed as she went to sleep.

Each time Anna moved from her father's world to her mother and Lydia's, she felt as if she'd shaken free of one life for a deeper one. And when she returned to her father, holding his hand as they ventured out into the city, it was her mother and Lydia she shook off, often forgetting them completely. Back and forth she went, deeper—deeper still—until it seemed there was no place further down she could go. But somehow there always was. She had never reached the bottom.

Eddie parked the Duesenberg outside Sonny's West Shore Bar and Grill, just shy of the piers. Saturday night, three days shy of New Year's Eve, and it was dead quiet outside—proof absolute that no ship had come in that week or the one before.

He saluted Matty Flynn, the snow-haired barkeep, and then crossed the sawdust to the back left corner where, under a placard of Jimmy Braddock kitted out for a fight, John Dunellen conducted his unofficial business. He was a big man with savage dock walloper's hands, though he hadn't worked the ships in over a decade. For all his natty attire, Dunellen gave a drooping, corroded impression, like a freighter gone to rust after being too long at anchor. He was surrounded by a gaggle of sycophants, suppliants, and minor racketeers delivering a cut in exchange for his blessing. Without ships, their rackets were booming—longshoremen were desperate.

"Ed," Dunellen muttered as Eddie slid onto a chair.

"Dunny."

Dunellen waved at Flynn to bring Eddie a Genesee and shot of rye. Then he sat, apparently abstracted but in fact attuned to the portable radio he carried with him everywhere (it folded into a suitcase) and played at low volume. Dunellen followed horse races, boxing matches, ball games—any event upon which bets might be placed.

But his special love was boxing. He was backing two boys in the junior lightweight class.

"You give the bride my regards?" Dunellen asked as Lonergan, a numbers man new to his circle, listened in.

"Too heavy," Eddie said. "I'll wait until after New Year's."

Dunellen grunted his approval. "Smooth and easy, nothing less."

The recipient of this particular delivery was a state senator. The plan had been to make the drop among the exodus from Saint Patrick's Cathedral earlier that day. The father of the bride was Dare Dooling, a banker close to Cardinal Hayes. The cardinal himself had performed the nuptials.

"Didn't feel heavy to me," Lonergan objected. "There was law, sure, but it was *our* law."

"You were there?" Eddie was taken aback. He disliked Lonergan; the man's long teeth gave him a sneering look.

"My ma was nanny to the bride," Lonergan said proudly. "Say, I didn't see you there, Kerrigan."

"That's Eddie." Dunellen chuckled. "You only see him when he wants you to." He slid his eyes Eddie's way, and Eddie felt a humid proximity to his old friend that was more familial than anything he'd ever felt for Brianne. Eddie had saved Dunellen's life, along with that of another protectory boy—pulled them bawling and puking out of a Rockaway riptide. This truth was never mentioned but ever present.

"I'll look harder next time," Lonergan said sourly. "Buy you a drink."

"In a pig's nose you will," Dunellen thundered, his abrupt fury rousing fleeting interest from the two loogans who accompanied him everywhere. Dunellen kept these snub-nosed giants at a distance; they undercut the avuncular impression he liked to make. "You don't *know* Eddie Kerrigan outside this bar—capeesh? How the hell does it look if he's hobnobbing with the high and mighty and jawing the next minute with a mutt like you? It's none of your fucking business where Eddie goes; quit sticking your snoot where it doesn't belong."

"Sorry, boss," Lonergan muttered, high crimson swarming his cheeks. Eddie felt the ooze of his envy and wanted to laugh. Lonergan envying him! Sure, Eddie dressed well (thanks to Agnes) and had Dunellen's ear, but he was a nobody of the highest order. "Bagman" meant exactly what it sounded like: the sap who ferried a sack containing something (money, of course, but it wasn't his business to know) between men who should not rightly associate. The ideal bagman was unaffiliated with either side, neutral in dress and deportment, and able to rid these exchanges of the underhanded feeling they naturally had. Eddie Kerrigan was that man. He looked comfortable everywhere—racetracks, dance halls, theaters, Holy Name Society meetings. He'd a pleasant face, a neutral American accent, and plenty of practice at moving between worlds. Eddie could turn the handoff into an afterthought—*Say, I nearly forgot, from our mutual friend—Why, thank you.*

For his pains, Dunellen kept him at subsistence wages: twenty dollars a week if he was lucky, which—combined with Agnes's piecework—barely kept them from having to hock the only valuables they hadn't already hocked: his pocket watch, which he would carry to his grave; the radio; and the French clock Brianne had given them at their wedding. A longshoreman's hook had never looked better.

"Anything in quarantine?" Eddie asked, meaning ships destined for one of the three piers Dunellen controlled.

"Maybe a day, two days, from Havana."

"To one of yours?"

"*Ours,*" Dunellen said. "Ours, Eddie. Why, you need a loan?"

"Not from him." Nat, the loan shark, who was throwing darts, charged twenty-five percent weekly.

"Eddie, Eddie," Dunellen chided. "I'll pay you for the week."

Eddie had meant to leave after one drink. Now, having been challenged by Lonergan, he thought it prudent to outstay him. That meant drinking alongside Dunellen, who was three times Eddie's girth and had a wooden leg. Eddie eyed the door, willing Maggie, Dunellen's harridan of a wife, to roust him out of the bar as if Dunellen were a loader blowing his pay, not president of the union local on his way to becoming an alderman. But Maggie didn't show, and eventually, Eddie found himself bawling out the words to "The Black Velvet Band" along with Dunellen and a few others, all of them wiping tears. At long last, Lonergan took his leave.

"You don't like him," Dunellen said when he'd gone—the very opening he would have given Lonergan had Eddie left first.

"He's all right."

"You think he's square?"

"I think his game is clean."

"You've a good nose for that," Dunellen said. "You should've been a copper."

Eddie shrugged, turning his cigarette between two fingers.

"You think like one."

"I'd have had to be crooked. And what kind of copper is that?"

From within the craggy topography of his head, Dunellen gave Eddie a sharp look. "Ain't crookedness in the eye of the beholder?"

"I suppose."

"They can't lay off cops, even in a Depression."

"There's something to that."

Dunellen seemed to fade out. His inattention led some men to take him lightly or act too freely in his presence—a mistake. He was like one of those poisonous fish Eddie had heard of that took on the look of a rock to fool its prey. Eddie was on the verge of rising to go when Dunellen turned to him, tamping Eddie with a wet, beseeching gaze. "Tancredo," he moaned. "Wop bastard likes the fights."

Stoking Dunellen's obsession with the wops would cost Eddie thirty minutes, at least. "How are your boys?" he asked, hoping to distract him.

At the mention of his boxers, Dunellen's face loosened like a cold roast warming over a flame. "Beautiful," he murmured, and to Eddie's alarm, he waved for another round. "Just beautiful. They're quick, they're smart, they listen. You should see them move, Ed."

Dunellen was childless, an oddity in this milieu, where the average man had between four and ten offspring. Opinion was divided on whether Maggie's shrewishness was the cause or the result of their unproductive union. One thing was certain: had Dunellen coddled sons as he did his middle lightweights (there were always two), he would have been openly derided. At their fights, he cringed and convulsed like an old maid watching her lapdog face off against a Doberman. The green sunshade he wore to the ring failed to conceal the freshets of tears that coursed from his small, cruel eyes.

"Tancredo's got his hands on them," he said in a trembling voice. "My boys. He'll fix it so they haven't a chance."

Even drunk, Eddie had no trouble deciphering Dunny's predicament: Tancredo, whoever the hell he was, was demanding a piece of Dunellen's lightweights in exchange for letting them fight—or possibly win—in certain rings the Syndicate controlled. The arrangement was identical to the one Dunellen imposed upon all manner of businesses around his piers: if you failed to pay, unemployment was the best you could hope for.

"They've my balls in a vise, Ed. The wops. Can't sleep for thinking of it."

It was Dunellen's cherished belief that the Wop Syndicate, as he liked to call it, had a design ulterior to its evident goals of profit and self-preservation: to exterminate Irishmen. This theory hinged on certain events he revisited like stations of the cross: the dissolution of Tammany by Mayor LaGuardia, the Valentine's Day Massacre in Chicago (seven Irishmen killed), and the more recent murders of Legs Diamond, Vincent Coll, and others. Never mind that those killed had all been killers. Never mind that the Syndicate was not all wops, or that Dunellen's personal enemies were, to a man, fellow micks: rival pier bosses, rogue hiring bosses, union holdouts—any one of whom might vanish, courtesy of Dunellen's loogans, until the spring thaw sent their bloated bodies wafting to the surface of the Hudson River like parade floats. For Dunellen, the threat of the Wop Syndicate was biblical, cosmic. And while normally this fixation posed no greater danger to Eddie than boring him silly, he'd spent today in the company of a Syndicate boss.

"You're thinking something," Dunellen said, peering at Eddie invasively. "Cough it up."

From within the abstracted, half-drunken heap that was John Dunellen, there prickled a supernatural awareness, as if his perceptions were routed through his radio and magnified. Here was the Dunellen most men failed to see until it was too late—the one who could read your thoughts. You lied to him at your peril.

"You're right, Dunny," Eddie said. "I would've liked to be a cop."

Dunellen eyed him a moment longer. Then, detecting the truth of the statement, he relaxed. "What would you do," he breathed, "about Tancredo?"

"I'd give him what he wants."

Dunellen reared back into a thunderhead of protest. "Why the fuck should I?"

"Sometimes fighting's no good," Eddie said. "Sometimes the best you can do is buy time, wait for an opening."

Occasionally, as now, the ocean rescue that had forged the bond between them and still radiated, allegorically, through all of their discourse, broke the surface and moved into the light. Dunellen and Sheehan were the older boys; Bart the brain, Dunny the mouth. When Eddie saw them thrashing, unable to get back to shore, he ran into the water and swam to them. He put an arm around each boy's neck and shouted into their terrified faces, "Stop fighting. Float and let the tide pull us out."

They were too tired not to obey. They floated, and when they'd caught their breath, Eddie led them swimming along the shore a half mile out. They were all water rats, having dived from city piers to escape the summer heat practically since they could walk. A mile down the beach, Eddie saw an opening in the breakers and herded Bart and Dunny back in.

"How do I buy time with an interfering wop?" Dunellen smoldered.

"Give him enough to keep him quiet," Eddie said. "Keep him satisfied. Then look for a way out."

He was aware of talking to himself as much as Dunellen—of talking *about* Dunellen. His old friend had moved very close, and Eddie was enveloped in a sour smell of the pickled onions he liked to suck. A corkscrew of nausea gyred through him.

"Some good advice, Ed," Dunellen said gruffly.

"Glad to help."

"You look after yourself."

Dunellen turned his chair away. In his cockeyed state, Eddie failed at first to perceive that he was being dismissed without the promised pay—punished for Dunellen's show of weakness. On the beach, it had been the same: Eddie yanked Dunellen by the hair onto the sand, where he lay keening and puking seawater for quite a while before he dried his tears and sauntered away. It was the other boy, Bart Sheehan, who had lifted Eddie into the air and kissed both his cheeks. But Eddie wasn't fooled by Dunellen then or now; he knew the bully would protect him after that. And so it had been: the stronger the bond, the more flagrant Dunellen's disregard. He loved Eddie deeply.

Dunellen pointedly turned his attention to several bookmakers who'd come to kiss his ring, now and then peeling bills from a roll and pushing them, with practiced intimacy, into fists, waving away murmured thanks. Eddie remained stubbornly seated. He waited even knowing he would go home empty-handed. In the byzantine calculus of their relations, waiting longer and receiving nothing would likely mean something extra from Dunellen down the line.

When he noticed Eddie still there, Dunellen scowled. Then his displeasure relented, and he asked softly during a lull, "How is the little one?"

"The same. As she always will be."

"I pray for her every day."

Eddie knew that he did. Dunellen was deeply devout, attending six-thirty morning Mass at Guardian Angel Church, sometimes without having slept, and returning for a second Mass at five. He carried a rosary in each pocket.

"I should pray for her more myself," Eddie said.

"Sometimes it's harder to ask God for your own."

Eddie was touched by this truth. He felt his intimacy with Dunellen, deep and primitive, as if their blood ran through each other's veins. "There's a chair I need to buy for her," he said. "It costs three hundred eighty dollars."

Dunellen looked flabbergasted. "Are they loony?"

"They have the chair," Eddie said, "and she needs it."

He hadn't intended to ask his friend for the money, but now he felt a sudden rise of hope that Dunellen might offer it. He had it, God knew. Might easily have the sum on him now, in his mammoth roll—warmed, like the rosaries, by his fierce body heat.

"Nat could help you with that," Dunellen said thoughtfully, after a long pause. "I'd have a word, buy you as much time as you need. Take it right off your pay if that would help any."

It took Eddie a moment, in his half-stupor, to absorb Dunellen's meaning. He was sending Eddie to the loan shark. And judging by the soft look in his eyes, Dunellen regarded the steer as an act of charity.

Eddie took great care not to react. "I'll think about it," he said mildly. If he remained at Sonny's another minute, Dunellen would read his displeasure and punish him for it. " 'Night, Dunny," he said, sliding the Duesenberg's key across the table. "Thanks."

They shook, and Eddie left the bar and stood outside for several minutes, waiting for the icy wind off the Hudson River to slap him sober. But he found himself staggering toward the IRT, drunker than he'd realized, and had to lean against Sonny's cold brick exterior. The groan and creak of ropes from the docks reached him like a grinding of teeth. He smelled rusty chains, planks sodden with fish oil: the very stench of corruption, it seemed to him now. Dunellen was beloved among the rank and file for handing bills around, but Eddie knew he controlled the shylocks, Nat included, taking his cut from the interest they collected, setting his loogans on debtors who failed to pay. A word from Dunellen and the hiring boss would choose a debtor for a day's work, so payments to the shylock could be deducted from his wages. The deeper you sank, the more fully *theirs* you became, the harder they worked to preserve you.

Ours, Dunellen had said. Our piers.

Eddie lurched to the curb and retched copiously onto the street. Then he wiped his mouth and looked around, relieved to find the block empty.

He was aware of having reached an end. He shut his eyes and remembered today: the beach, the cold, the excellent lunch. A white tablecloth. Brandy. He thought of the chair. But it wasn't just the chair that had driven him to Dexter Styles: it was a restless, desperate wish for something to change. Anything. Even if the change brought a certain danger. He'd take danger over sorrow every time.

CHAPTER FOUR

Two evenings each week, a charitable lady came to the New York Catholic Protectory and read aloud after supper from *Treasure Island*, *The Arabian Nights*, *20,000 Leagues Under the Sea*, and other tales of exotic adventure. As she looked out from the lectern at the swath of boys, Eddie tried to picture what she saw: row upon row of folded hands (as required when they'd finished eating), scores of faces interchangeable as pennies. The biggest, the ugliest, the sweetest might stand out (DeSoto; O'Brien; Macklemore, with his tiny angel's face), but not Eddie Kerrigan. His only noteworthy traits were an ability to slip through doors locked only with a chain and shimmy up streetlamp poles like a monkey. He could do accents but was too shy to show them off. He'd once stayed underwater longer than two minutes in Eastchester Bay.

His father had brought him here at age four, after his mother died of typhus. At that time, the protectory was still in the town of Van Nest, Westchester, but by the time Eddie was old enough to care, Van Nest had been absorbed by the East Bronx. A separate set of girls' buildings lay across Unionport Road, complete with an identical pond—but whether the girls were as adept at scooping wary, sulking carp into their hands, Eddie never knew. Brianne had gone to her mother's people in New Jersey, her own mother having died back in Ireland. His father would visit early on, bringing Eddie with him to the races, then a saloon. Eddie remembered little of these outings beyond clinging to his father's hand and trying, in short pants, to match his furious pace as he wove among horse carts and trolleys.

Lying in the vast dormitory, hearing his breath melt into the collective sigh of so many boys asleep, Eddie was shamed by his own meagerness: narrow hips; a sharp, unremarkable face; hair like dirty straw. Even more than the orphans' annual excursion to the circus, he thirsted for the moment each month when the protectory barber's hands would touch his scalp briefly, indifferently, yet capable of soothing him almost to sleep. He was of no more consequence than an empty cigarette packet. At times the brusque mass of everything that was *not* him seemed likely to crush Eddie into dust the way he crushed the dried-out moths that collected in piles on the protectory windowsills. At times he wanted to be crushed.

By nine or ten, the boys were expected, after lessons, to earn their pocket money at one of the myriad occupations advertised with BOY WANTED signs: delivering messages and packages; sealing boxes in one of the many Bronx piano factories. The more enterprising boys sold gum or buttons or candy at Van Nest Railway Station, working up sales pitches in groups of two or three involving songs and dance steps. Boys were watched closely near the protectory, everyone in the neighborhood aware that these were the very same boys who swiped caramels from their jars and sweet potatoes from their pushcarts. Eddie was not exempt from this thievery; no one wanted to be empty-handed when the spoils were divided. But he felt degraded by the crimes he was moved to commit, soiled by the suspicion that followed. He looked for work in other neighborhoods, clutching the rear of the West Farms Road trolley and riding it across the Bronx River past Crotona Park, where the houses were stone and brick. Although visibly poor in his orphanage-made breeches and shoes, when away from the scrum Eddie found he was able to straighten his spine and peer directly into the eyes of whomever he addressed.

One afternoon in early fall, when Eddie was eleven, an elderly gentleman in a wheeled chair called out to him as he crossed Clermont Park toward a bakery on Morris Avenue he'd been making deliveries for. The man asked to be rolled into the sun. He wore a double-breasted suit and a crisp orange feather in his hatband. Eddie pushed the gentleman's chair as directed, then fetched him a cigar and a *Mirror* from a newsstand on Belmont. He hovered nearby, awaiting dismissal, as the man read and smoked. At last, sensing he'd been forgotten, he declared himself, striving for the orotund speech of the charitable ladies' reading voices: "Alas, sir, the sun has forsaken you. Would you care to be moved yet again?"

The old man met his eyes, perplexed. "Can you play at cards?" he asked.

"I haven't any deck."

"What games?"

"Knuckles. Blackjack. Chuck-a-luck. Stutz. Poker." Eddie tossed out names as though pitching pennies—then knew, with poker, that he'd struck. The old man rustled under the plaid blanket covering his knees and handed Eddie a brand-new deck. "Seven-card stud," he said. "You deal. Honestly."

They introduced themselves and moved to a sunny bench so Eddie could sit down. They placed bets using small sticks he collected and broke into equal lengths, and their table was the blanket pulled taut across Mr. De Veer's shrunken thighs. The cards felt like glass. Eddie smelled their newness and had an urge to lick them, or slide them over his cheeks. He lost every hand, but he hardly cared—the sensation of those cards, of sitting in the sun, was transporting. Eventually, the gentleman fished a heavy silver watch from his pocket and announced that his sister would be coming soon to fetch him. He gave Eddie a nickel. "But I lost," Eddie said. Mr. De Veer replied that he was paying for the gift of Eddie's time and companionship, and asked him to come again the next afternoon.

That night Eddie lay sleepless, his whole body thrumming with certainty that something grand and new had begun. And he was right, in a way, for much of what had happened in the years since could be traced to that acquaintance. "Two men at poker ain't much of a game," Mr. De Veer told him on their second meeting, and proposed to give Eddie a stake to play as his proxy in a game where he was known. But his imprimatur had less weight than Mr. De Veer had hoped, and Eddie was turned away brusquely from the first several games he tried, once by a lady in curlers who swatted him with a broom. At last, in a cigar store across from the freight yard, he was grudgingly admitted by Sid, a chain-smoker of Old Golds who blinked at Eddie through a cumulus lazing under his green visor brim.

In the weeks that followed, weather permitting, Eddie joined Sid's game for an hour and a quarter—less, if he lost his stake before that time had elapsed. Afterward, he returned to Mr. De Veer and relayed the action card by card, bet by bet, a feat of memorization and recall that Eddie improved at with time. The old gentleman hung on his descriptions, interjecting at each error—"No, a high card won't do against Polsky, he can't bluff. You'll lose that one"—until Eddie began withholding outcomes until the end in order to further his employer's suspense and joy. On the rare occasions when Eddie came out ahead, Mr. De Veer gave him half the winnings. When he lost, he merely returned what was left. Eddie could have lied, of course—said he'd lost when he'd actually won, kept all the profits, but this thought occurred to him only in the negative: as something other boys might have done.

Mr. De Veer had been a "sporting man," which apparently meant a gambler and a connoisseur of horses. He'd played at Canfield's and the Metropole Hotel against Goulds, Fisks, and Vanderbilts, before "dogooders" like Reverend Parkhurst had hounded the best places out of business and closed the race track at Brighton Beach. Gentleman gamblers were a thing of the past, he told Eddie bitterly, drummed out by gangsters and crooks like Arnold Rothstein, the young sheenie who won by cheating. "Don't ever cheat, not even once," he warned Eddie, regarding him through faded eyes fringed with silver lashes. "Cheating is like a girl's maidenhead. Doesn't matter if she's done it once or a hundred times; she's ruined just the same."

These words lodged in Eddie's ears with the preternatural weight of a truth he'd already known. Cheating was a way of life at the protectory, but Eddie was different, had always been. Mr. De Veer saw that difference in him. He taught Eddie ways to spot loaded dice, crooked decks, signs of collusion between apparent strangers—anything that undermined the mystical activity of Lady Luck.

Mr. De Veer had a Civil War injury, but it was his "bum ticker" that had confined him to the chair two years before, and to the care of his maiden sister, Miss De Veer, who had put an immediate end to his gaming. She claimed it had ruined his health, but he suspected she'd designs on his military pension to augment her collection of porcelain dolls, which already numbered in the hundreds. One afternoon, having just resumed after a winter suspension, Eddie returned late from a card game. Mr. De Veer ordered him away harshly. Wounded, Eddie watched from inside the park as a heavyset lady in a wide-brimmed black hat moved toward Mr. De Veer with boxy determination. The old gentleman looked bowed and frail in her presence, and Eddie understood that he was afraid of his sister.

"Haven't you a timepiece?" he asked Eddie the next afternoon. When Eddie admitted he hadn't one, the gentleman unclipped his watch chain. "Use that," he said, pressing a silver pocket watch into Eddie's palm. It was heavy and engraved.

"I can't, sir," Eddie stammered. "They'll think I—"

"It is a loan, not a gift," Mr. De Veer said shortly.

In late May, Mr. De Veer failed to appear four days in succession. On the fourth, a Friday, Eddie waited all afternoon, checking the silver pocket watch at one-minute intervals. At last he entered Topping Avenue, from which Miss De Veer had emerged, and approached some girls carving potsy squares in the dust. "That old man in the chair, have you seen him?" he asked. To which a tiny girl with faded yellow braids said shrilly, "They took him in his coffin up to heaven."

"Or hell. We don't know his heart!" said a crafty-looking older girl, and all of them laughed at Eddie without mercy, exactly as his own scrum mocked any unknown child who bumbled into its midst. He felt the pocket watch against his thigh and knew he must find Miss De Veer, to return it. But that thought drew an internal rebuke: *No! Not to her,* and Eddie remembered the porcelain dolls and began walking back toward Clermont Park, keeping his pace at a saunter until he passed the iceman's dray, at which point he broke into a run. He'd turned twelve, tall and scrawny, fastened together with muscles like leather thongs. As he sprinted past the old Clermont casino and the elevated tracks, he realized that by maintaining this headlong pace, he could stay just ahead of the knowledge that he would not see Mr. De Veer again. He charged through Crotona Park and across the Bronx River, startling boys fishing on a bridge; he careened through empty farms divided into ghostly future streets, and finally across the railway tracks to what once was the faded town of Van Nest. In a state of near collapse, he gasped toward the Unionport nickelodeon, where the protectory boys were lined up for the cowboy flicker. It was an ordinary day. His friends knew nothing of Mr. De Veer. Eddie slumped in among them, and while they hissed and bawled at the train robbers with their devious mustaches, he allowed himself to sob. The boys' boisterous oblivion absorbed the racket of his grief and finally blunted the grief itself. Nothing had changed or disappeared.

After that, Eddie stayed close to his protectory brothers even when he drifted from them. He was the one who came and went, whom they never could quite figure, and their willingness to accept this partial version of him increased Eddie's tenderness toward them. They grew up and went their ways: several of the older ones to the Great War, where Paddy Cassidy died at Rheims; and a great many to the West Side docks, where they became stevedores or laborers (depending on how much they drank), police, saloonkeepers, aldermen, union officials, and outright hoods. It was possible to occupy more than one of these roles on the waterfront, and many did. Bart Sheehan, the boy whose life Eddie had saved along with Dunellen's, managed to com-

plete high school, then college, then *law school*: drastic achievements
that led to his being discussed in the same hushed tones as angelic
Kevin Macklemore, sliced in two by a loose railway car on Eleventh
Avenue. Sheehan worked for the state attorney's office now, although
Eddie hadn't seen him in many years. Dunellen had it from the kite—
a web of rumor and innuendo more omniscient than the *Shamrock*—
that Bart was investigating the Wop Syndicate. Eddie suspected this
was wishful thinking on Dunny's part.

To the bewilderment of his friends, Eddie gravitated to vaudeville,
where he danced, sang badly for comic effect, hung like a bat from theater rafters, and tricked his body into Houdini-like escapes. He booked
a season with the Follies, where he fell in love with a chorus girl newly
escaped (as Agnes put it) from a barley farm in Minnesota. After they
married, he managed a theater and studied to be a stockbroker. He
planned to buy a seat on the Curb Exchange, which was more afford-
able than the New York Exchange. Not that money was a problem.
Eddie had found his perfect game of chance and was buying stocks
on the margin, selling only to buy more—and to acquire the trappings
appropriate to his new wealth. He bought Agnes a Russian sable fur
and a string of pearls from Black, Starr & Frost. The kitchen sink of
their Fifth Avenue rental was afloat with Prince de Monaco cigarettes
they'd stubbed out into unfinished meals in their rush to the bedroom.
Eddie hired a maid to clean up in the afternoons. He engaged a tailor
and ordered suits from England and bought champagne for Agnes and
a dozen others at the Heigh-Ho and the Moritz after her shows. He'd
no idea how to be rich—so little, in fact, that he thought he *was* rich.
They brought Anna to parties and set her to sleep on mountains of fur
coats. Lydia was different, of course. They hired an Irish laundress to
care for her in the evenings while she did their washing.

Yet even in the pink of his delight, when Eddie barely noticed ships
hovering at the ends of Broadway side streets, he did just enough to
maintain his position in the scrum: attended Communion breakfasts
with the union brass at Guardian Angel and Knights of Columbus

meetings; bought costly tickets to the annual dinner dances where homage was paid to those who had ascended highest. Partly he wanted to show off Agnes, her starlet curls and lithe dancer's body. Irish girls turned dowdy on the wedding recessional, so the joke went, and Eddie enjoyed watching his brothers' faces pop a little with envy and shyness.

And thank God he'd maintained those ties—thank God! After the crash, when the accoutrements of a wealth Eddie discovered he'd never possessed vacated him one by one—sable, pearls, apartment, matching Cartier cigarette cases—when he lost his job (the theater closed), Dunellen had welcomed him back, bought the Duesenberg off him, and given him a union card. When Eddie joined one of the two daily shape-ups—a practice wherein those seeking work arrayed themselves before a hiring boss—Eddie placed a toothpick behind his left ear, which guaranteed he would get in the ship's hold, at the very least, and more likely one of the better loading jobs. His family would have starved otherwise. And when the shipping dried up in '32, Dunellen kept him on as a union lackey in pinstripes and lent him the Duesenberg to run his errands. Driving on Wall Street one afternoon, Eddie spotted a familiar-looking man selling apples on a corner. Only when he'd passed did he realize who it was: his stockbroker.

Anna heard her father's key in the lock and opened her eyes. From the density of silence outside the window, she knew it was very late. Not even the bell of a streetcar. She tiptoed around the Chinese screen they were keeping for Aunt Brianne into the dark front room. There she paused. Her father was shirtless at the kitchen sink, soaping up his torso. Anna watched him, mesmerized. He couldn't see her from the lighted kitchen, and for an eerie moment he appeared to be someone Anna didn't know and had no claim on. A gaunt, handsome stranger, turning something over in his mind.

When he left to use the hall toilet, Anna waited in the kitchen.

He jumped at the sight of her in her nightgown; then all of the worry seemed to leave him. He was himself again. And so was she.

"Toots," he said softly. "What are you doing awake?"

"Waiting for you."

He lifted her up, staggering almost to the point of losing his balance. From the medicine smell of his breath, she knew he'd been drinking.

"You're getting bigger," he said, steadying himself on the doorframe.

"You're getting smaller," she said.

He carried her, a bit unsteadily, through the front room to her bedroom door. The front room window shade was raised, and her father leaned against the frame, still holding her. They gazed together into the dark. Anna felt the city stretching around them, reaching its streets and avenues toward the rivers and harbor.

"Hear that quiet?" he said, speaking carefully, as if on tiptoe. "That is the sound of a harbor in a Depression."

"No ships," she said.

"No ships."

"I hear a bird."

"No birds, please. Not yet."

But a solitary bird had begun to chirp, a last holdout against winter. As if on cue, a tinge of light appeared in the eastern sky.

"You stayed out all night," she said wonderingly.

"We can sleep until church." But he waited another moment, leaning against the window frame with Anna in his arms. How many more times would he lift her? Even now, she was almost too tall.

"I'm sleeping here," she said, folding her arms around his neck. Her father's skin smelled of Ivory Flakes from its recent wash. She rested her cheek on his bare shoulder and shut her eyes.

PART TWO

Shadow World

CHAPTER FIVE

It all started with seeing the girl. Anna had gone outside to buy lunch over the disapproval of her supervisor, Mr. Voss, who liked them to bring their lunches from home and eat them on the same tall stools where they sat measuring all day. Anna sensed anxiety in his wish to keep them in sight, as if girls at large in the Naval Yard might scatter like chickens. True, their shop was pleasant to eat in, clean and brightly lit by a bank of second-story windows. It had conditioned air, a humming chill that had filled every corner during the hot September days when Anna first came to work there. Now she would have liked to open a window and let in the fresh October air, but the windows were permanently shut, sealing out dust and grime that might affect the measurements she and the other girls took—or was it that the tiny parts they were measuring needed to be pristine in order to function? No one knew, and Mr. Voss was not a man who welcomed questions. Early on, Anna had asked of the unrecognizable parts in her tray, "What are we measuring, exactly, and which ship are they for?"

Mr. Voss's pale eyebrows rose. "That information isn't necessary to do your job, Miss Kerrigan."

"It would help me to do it better."

"I'm afraid I don't follow."

"I would know what I was doing."

The marrieds hid their smiles. Anna had been cast—or cast herself—in the role of unruly kid sister, and was enjoying it immensely.

She found herself looking for little ways to challenge Mr. Voss without risking outright insubordination.

"You are measuring and inspecting parts to ensure that they are uniform," he said patiently, as if to a halfwit. "And you are setting aside any that are not."

Soon it came to be known that the parts they were inspecting were for the battleship *Missouri,* whose keel had been laid almost a year before Pearl Harbor in Dry Dock 4. Later, the *Missouri's* hull had been floated across Wallabout Bay to the building ways: vast iron enclosures whose zigzagging catwalks evoked the Coney Island Cyclone. Knowing that the parts she was inspecting would be adjoined to the most modern battleship ever built had indeed brought some additional zest to the work for Anna. But not enough.

When the lunch whistle blew at eleven-thirty, she was itching to get outside. In order to justify leaving the building, she didn't bring a lunch—a ploy she knew did not fool Mr. Voss. But he couldn't very well deny a girl food, so he watched grimly as she made for the door while the marrieds unwrapped sandwiches from waxed paper and talked about husbands in boot camp or overseas; who'd had a letter; clues or hunches or dreams as to where their beloveds might be; how desperately frightened they were. More than one girl had wept, describing her terror that a husband or fiancé would not return. Anna couldn't listen. The talk stirred in her an uncomfortable anger at these girls, who seemed so weak. Thankfully, Mr. Voss had put an end to that topic during working hours, prompting an unlikely trill of gratitude in Anna. Now they sang songs from their colleges while they worked: Hunter, St. Joseph's, Brooklyn College, whose song Anna finally learned—not having bothered to in the year she was a student there.

She synchronized her wristwatch with the large wall clock they all answered to, and stepped outdoors. After the sealed hush of her shop, the roar of Yard noise always shocked her: crane and truck and train engines; the caterwaul of steel being cut and chipped in the nearby structural shop; men hollering to be heard. The stench of coal and oil mingled with gusts of chocolate from the factory on Flushing Avenue. It wasn't making chocolate anymore, but something for soldiers to eat when they might otherwise starve. This chocolate cousin was supposed to taste like a boiled potato, Anna had heard, so that soldiers wouldn't be tempted to snack on it ahead of time. But the smell was still delicious.

As she hurried alongside Building 4, the structural shop, with its thousand dingy windows, she saw a girl climbing onto a bicycle. Anna didn't register at first that it was a girl; she wore the same plain blue work clothes they all did. But something in her bearing, the flair with which she mounted, caught Anna's eye, and she watched the girl glide away with a shiver of envy.

At a canteen near the piers, she bought her forty-cent boxed meal—today it was chicken, mashed potatoes, canned peas, and applesauce—and made her way toward Piers C and D, both close enough to her shop that she could eat (often while standing, even walking) and be back on her stool by twelve-fifteen. A ship had berthed at Pier C since the previous day, its sudden towering apparition almost otherworldly. With each step Anna took toward the ship, its height seemed to rise, until she had to tip her head fully back to follow the curved prow all the way up to the distant deck. It was thronged with sailors, identical-looking in their toylike uniforms and caps, all leaning over the rail to gawk at something below. In that same moment, a chorus of catcalls reached her. She went still, clutching her boxed lunch—then saw with relief that the object of their ardor was not her but the girl on the bicycle, who was riding back alongside the ship from the foot of the pier, a tousle of peroxide curls pried from her scarf by the wind. Anna watched her approach, trying to discern whether the girl was enjoying this attention or not. Before she could make up her mind, the bicycle hit a patch of gravel and skidded on its side, dumping its rider onto the brick-paved pier, to the jeering hilarity of the sailors. Had the men been within reach of the girl, they doubtless would have elbowed each other aside to rush to her aid. But at such a height, with only each other to show off for, they settled for an orgy of heckling:

"Aw, poor baby lost her balance."

"Shame she's not wearing a skirt."

"Say, you're pretty even when you're crying."

But the girl wasn't crying. She stood up angrily, humiliated but defiant, and Anna decided then that she liked her. She'd thought fleetingly of running to help the girl, but was glad she'd resisted—two girls struggling with a bicycle would be funnier than just one. And this girl would not have wanted help. She straightened her shoulders and walked the bicycle slowly to the top of the pier, where Anna was, giving no sign that she heard anything. Anna saw how pretty she was, with dimpled cheeks and flickering blue eyes, those Jean Harlow curls. Familiar, too—perhaps because she looked the way Lydia might have looked had she not been the way she was. The world was full of strangers (Betty Grable among them) for whom Anna felt a sisterly affection for that reason. But as the girl stalked past, ignoring Anna, she recognized her as one of the girls whom reporters had chosen to follow in September, on the first day girls had started working at the Naval Yard. Anna had seen her picture in the *Brooklyn Eagle*.

When she was safely past the ship, the girl mounted her bicycle and rode away. Anna checked her wristwatch and discovered with horror that she was almost thirteen minutes late. She sprinted toward her building, aware of creating a mild spectacle by running. She flew past the inspectors on the first floor—all men, using ladders to measure bigger parts—and resumed her stool at 12:37, sweat coursing from her armpits along the inside of her jumpsuit. She fixed her eyes on the tray of small parts she was given each day to measure and tried to quell her panting. Rose, a married she was friendly with, gave her a warning look from the next table.

The micrometer was stupidly easy to use: clasp, screw, read. Anna had been delighted with this assignment at first; girls in trades like welding and riveting had needed six weeks of instruction, whereas inspecting required just a week of aptitude tests. She was among college girls, and Mr. Voss had used the word "elite" in his introductory remarks, which had pleased her. Above all, she was tired of working with her hands. But after two days of reading the micrometer and then stamping a paper that came with her tray to certify that the parts were uniform, Anna found that she loathed the job. It was monotonous yet required concentration; numbingly mundane yet critical enough that it took place in a "clean room." Squinting at the micrometer made her head pound. She had an urge sometimes to try and use just her fingers to gauge whether the parts were correctly sized. But she could only guess, then had to measure to find out if her guess was correct. And the all-knowing Mr. Voss had spotted her working with her eyes closed. "May I ask what you're doing, Miss Kerrigan?" he'd remarked. When Anna told him (for the amusement of the marrieds), he'd said, "This is no time for whimsy. We've a war to fight."

Now, when the shift was done and they were back in street clothes, Mr. Voss asked Anna to step inside his office. No one had ever been called to his office; this was ominous.

"Shall I wait?" Rose asked as the other marrieds wished her luck and hurried away. But Anna demurred, knowing that Rose had a baby to get home to.

The snapper's office was bare and provisional, like most of the Naval Yard. After standing briefly when she entered, Mr. Voss resumed his seat behind a metal desk. "You were twenty minutes late returning from lunch," he said. "Twenty-two, in fact."

Anna stood before him, her heart pumping directly into her face. Mr. Voss was an important man in the Yard; the commandant had telephoned him more than once. He could have her dismissed. This was a prospect she hadn't fully considered in the weeks she'd spent gently galling him. But it struck her now with force: she had withdrawn from Brooklyn College. If she weren't here at work, she would be back at home with her mother, caring for Lydia.

"I'm sorry," she said. "It won't happen again."

"Have a seat," he said, and Anna lowered herself onto a chair. "If you've not had much experience in the working world, these rules and restrictions must seem like quite a bother."

"I've worked all my life," she said, but it sounded hollow. She was full of shame, as if she'd glimpsed her own reflection in a shopwindow and found it ridiculous. A college girl craving a taste of war work. An "elite." That was how he must see her. Slogans from the *Shipworker* drifted through her mind: MINUTES SAVED HERE MEAN LIVES SAVED THERE. WHEN YOU DON'T WORK, YOU WORK FOR THE ENEMY.

"You're aware that we may not win the war," he said.

She blinked. "Why, yes. Of course." Newspapers weren't allowed inside the Naval Yard for fear of damaging morale, but Anna bought a *Times* each evening outside the Sands Street gate.

"You realize that the Nazis have Stalingrad surrounded."

She nodded, head bowed in humiliation.

"And that the Japs control the Pacific theater from the Philippines to New Guinea?"

"Yes."

"You understand that the work we do here, building and repairing Allied ships, is what allows sailors, airplanes, bombs, and convoy escorts to reach the field of battle?"

A filament of annoyance waggled inside her. He'd made his point. "Yes."

"And that hundreds of Allied merchantmen have been torpedoed since the war began, with more going down each day?"

"We're losing fewer ships than before, and building more," she said quietly, having read this in the *Times* just recently. "Kaiser shipyard built a Liberty ship in ten days last month."

It sounded egregiously fresh, and Anna waited for the blow to fall. But Mr. Voss merely said after a pause, "I notice you don't bring a lunch. I presume you live at home?"

"Yes, I do," Anna said. "But my mother and I are awfully busy caring for my sister. She's badly crippled."

This was true. But also untrue. Her mother made breakfast and dinner for Anna; she easily could have packed a lunch, and had offered to. Anna had slipped into the unguarded manner she often found herself assuming with strangers, or virtual strangers. Her reward was a faint disturbance of surprise in Mr. Voss's face.

"Now, that's a shame," he said. "Can't your father help?"

"He's gone." She almost never revealed this fact, and hadn't planned to.

"In the service?" He looked dubious; surely a man with a nineteen-year-old daughter would be too old.

"Just—gone."

"He abandoned your family?"

"Five years ago."

Had Anna felt any emotion at this disclosure, she would have concealed it. But she did not. Her father had left the apartment as he would have on any day—she couldn't even recall it. The truth had arrived gradually, like nightfall: a recognition, when she caught herself awaiting his return, that she'd waited days, then weeks, then months—and he'd still not come. She was fourteen, then fifteen. Hope became the memory of hope: a numb, dead patch. She no longer could picture him clearly.

Mr. Voss took a long breath. "Well, that is difficult," he said. "Very difficult for you and your mother."

"And my sister," she said reflexively.

The silence that opened around them was uncomfortable but not unpleasant. It was a change. Mr. Voss's shirtsleeves were rolled; she noticed the blond hairs on his hands and strong rectangular wrists. Anna sensed his sympathy, but the tight aperture of their discourse afforded no channel through which sentiment might flow. And sympathy was not what she wanted. She wanted to go out at lunchtime.

The bustle of the shift change had settled; the night inspectors must be at work on their trays. Anna found herself recalling the girl on the bicycle. *Nell*—the name came to her suddenly, from the newspaper caption.

"Miss Kerrigan," Mr. Voss said at last. "You may go out for lunch, if you will carefully mind the time and work to your full capacity."

"Thank you," Anna cried, leaping to her feet. Mr. Voss looked startled, then stood as well. He smiled, something she hadn't seen before. It changed him, that smile, as if all the severity he displayed on the inspection floor were a hiding place from which this amiable man had just waved hello. Only his voice was the same.

"I expect your mother will be needing you at home," he said. "Good evening."

The next morning, Anna spotted Nell's pale froth of curls among the roil of hats and caps that flooded the Sands Street gate at a quarter to eight, barely in time to punch in before the cutoff. Once it had gone eight o'clock in your shop, you were docked an hour's pay whether you were late by thirty seconds or thirty minutes. There were dozens of sailors outside, dressed in the tailored skintight uniforms they bought for shore leave. Anna had heard there were zippers installed in the sides of the trousers so the boys could get them on and off. Judging by their ashen, squeamish looks, most of these sailors had spent their liberty in all-night benders. Two had lurched away from the crush and were leaning against the perimeter wall with greenish faces.

Nell was in line for Hardy, the middle marine. His line was always shortest because his nose had been seen to drip into thermoses he opened to check for alcohol. The marine guards opened packages, too, untying strings and prying apart layers of paper, checking for bombs. German spies and saboteurs would love to get inside the Naval Yard. And while the idea seemed far-fetched (Anna knew plenty of the fellows around her by sight), it was a fact that there were German spies at large in American cities. Thirty-three had gone to prison last January for telling the Reich the sailing date of an American merchant ship, the SS *Robin Moor*. The ship was sunk by torpedo off the coast of Africa.

Three men passed through the turnstile between Nell and Anna, but Nell's perfume lingered even as Anna showed her ID badge and opened her pocketbook for Hardy to look inside. Nell was not a married. Anna knew that just by the way she paused self-consciously beyond the gate to consult her wristwatch, and by the sculpted slant of her fingernails. Her hair looked done; this was a girl who'd slept in pins, which meant she must have a date after work, since the curls— which had to be covered inside the shops—would serve no purpose otherwise. Anna was not a flirt, but she didn't mind flirts the way some girls did. She rather enjoyed watching them take charge of men, even as the men believed *they* were in charge. Anna would have liked to flirt, but she was no good at it; her directness got in the way.

"You're Nell," she said, catching up. The girl nodded, as if being recognized were something she was well accustomed to. "I'm Anna." She put out her hand and they shook hurriedly, still walking. Anna caught irritation and bemusement in Nell's expression; like most flirts, she saw no reason to know other girls. Girls were either competitors or hangers-on, and Anna supposed Nell must be wondering which she was likely to be. "I saw you fall off the bicycle yesterday."

"Oh. That." Nell rolled her eyes, but Anna had her attention.

"Is it yours?"

"No, Roger's. He works in my shop."

"Do you think he might lend it to me?" Anna asked.

Nell glanced at her. "He'll lend it to me. I'll lend it to you."

Now that their talk had settled into Anna wanting something and Nell helping her acquire it, she seemed more at ease. As they hurried along Second Street, Anna asked, "Are there many girls in your shop?"

"A few with me in the mold loft, but they're drips."

"Married?"

"You said it. Most of the single girls are welders, but that's dirty work. I'd never do it."

"What happens in the mold loft?"

"We . . . we make molds," Nell said, the complexity of the topic apparently having exceeded her interest in explaining it.

"Of ships?"

"No, ice cream trucks. Don't be a boob."

Anna was glad they'd reached Nell's shop; she liked her less the longer they talked. "How can I get the bicycle?"

"Meet me at the entrance to Building 4 right after the whistle," Nell said. "I'll bring it."

"Your supervisor doesn't mind you going out?"

"He likes me," Nell said, an explanation Anna guessed she must employ—perhaps correctly—to account for much of what happened to her.

"Ours likes us to stay in," Anna said, aware that she was playacting a little, invoking a version of Mr. Voss that was slightly outdated. Hanger-on seemed to be the part she was auditioning for, perhaps the only one available.

"Try lipstick," Nell said. "Works wonders."

"He isn't that type."

Nell's face was all sunny curves; she looked perpetually on the verge of laughter. Yet her blue gaze was rife with calculation. "There's no other," she said.

At midday, when they met again, they were both wearing blue coveralls. Every last one of Nell's curls was swaddled inside a bulging scarf, and she wore the steel-toed safety boots they were all encouraged to buy. Though the *Shipworker* often ran little stories about disasters averted by those boots, Anna hadn't bought a pair. There seemed no point, when nothing she handled was larger than a quarter.

"You can leave it right here when you're done," Nell said, passing a beaten-looking black Schwinn to Anna. "I'll pick it up coming back. There's a lady just outside the Cumberland gate who sells swell egg salad sandwiches. Right out of her apartment—you'll see the line on Flushing."

"Thanks."

"You can't pack egg salad. Gets soggy."

"I wish there were two bikes," Anna said, feeling a rush of affection for this vain, generous girl.

"Not on your life. I'm all finished with that," Nell said. She added, smiling, "Besides, we'd cause a riot."

Anna had ridden bicycles before. You could rent them in Prospect Park for fifteen cents, and cycling there had been a popular weekend activity among boys and girls from Brooklyn College. This was different. It was a man's Schwinn, first of all, with a bar inconveniently placed so that Anna had to pedal standing up to be sure she wouldn't land on it. Maybe standing was what made the difference. Whatever it was, from the instant she pushed down on the pedals and the bike began to bump over the bricks, Anna felt as though lightning had touched her. Motion performed alchemy on her surroundings, transforming them from a disjointed array of scenes into a symphonic machine she could soar through invisibly as a seagull. She rode wildly, half laughing, the sooty wind filling her mouth. That first day she was too excited to eat, too worried about being late to take any chances on egg salad. She was back on her stool at 12:10 and starved the rest of the day, hands trembling as she held her micrometer, a strange electric joy swerving through her.

The next morning she worked furiously to make the time go faster, and had finished three quarters of her tray when the whistle blew. Nell was waiting with the bicycle. Anna rode that day in the direction of the building ways, cycling past their porous iron latticework several times and glimpsing, within shadowy vectors, a hull so vast it looked primordial. The USS *Missouri*. Having heard its name murmured since she'd arrived at the Yard, Anna found it uncanny, almost frightening, to actually see it. The thing itself.

Now that she was measuring more quickly, she began helping some of the slower girls to finish their trays when hers was done. One afternoon, Mr. Voss brought her a roll of blueprints and asked her to deliver them to the office of the captain of the Yard, in Building 77. Buoyed by the marrieds' pantomimed stupefaction, Anna hurried south along Morris Avenue and then Sixth Street to the faceless new building, which had no windows except at the very top. She rode an elevator to the fifteenth floor and found herself surrounded by walls imprinted with maps. The windows showed only sky, but a chilly glance from a secretary in street clothes stymied Anna's impulse to help herself to the view. The next afternoon, Mr. Voss sent her to the same office to retrieve a parcel. This ferrying of packages imbued Anna with a frisson of secrecy, even subterfuge, that she couldn't fully account for. She felt like a spy.

Without exchanging more than salutations as they passed the bicycle back and forth, Anna and Nell became friends of a sort. It was nothing like Anna's friendships with Stella Iovino or Lillian Feeney, girls from her building and block with whom she'd played paper dolls and jumped rope and helped to mind each other's younger siblings. Nor was it like her college friendships with studious girls from Crown Heights and Bay Ridge. Nell was not a good girl. Her secrets weren't for Anna to know, and this made her feel easy in Nell's presence— released from a scaffolding of pretense she'd been unaware of having to maintain with other girls.

When Nell was late, Anna waited by Building 4, dodging the cranes that slid in and out of its barnlike doors with giant metal flats suspended on ropes from their serrated jaws. She liked to peer inside at the welders with their heavy gloves and flaming rods. Sometimes, when a welder pulled off a protective mask, Anna was astonished to find that it was a girl. These girl welders ate their lunches sitting on the floor against a wall, steel-toed boots jutting into the room. Watching them, Anna felt her own grating distance from something urgent, elemental. Even before Pearl Harbor, this feeling had dogged her. It was what had drawn her to the Naval Yard last summer, when word first went around that girls would be hired. Yet even here the war seemed maddeningly abstract, at too great a distance to be felt. Anna longed somehow to touch it, and sensed she wasn't alone. Once she'd spotted Rose furtively scratching a nail file against a copper tube from her measuring tray. As they were changing back into street clothes in the locker room, Anna asked what she'd been doing. Rose flushed. "You sound like Mr. Voss."

"I didn't mean it like that," Anna said. "I'm just curious."

Rose confessed that she'd been scratching her baby son's initials onto the tube, moved by the thought of his name out at sea, a tiny part of an Allied ship.

Whatever direction Anna went—as far as she could go and still get back in forty-five minutes, allowing for a brief pause to wolf down lunch—she was drawn inevitably onto the piers: A to the west; G, J, and K across Wallabout Bay to the east, far from her own building. She bicycled onto them hesitantly at first, hair jammed under a cap, determined not to be singled out for mockery, as Nell had been. But it turned out that Anna's brown hair was unobtrusive even when it came loose. Her complexion was "Italian," and years of carrying Lydia had given her the flinty, taut-shouldered bearing of a man. With her eyes under the brim of a cap, she could cycle the piers incognito.

A familiar smell engulfed her: fish, salt, fuel oil—a brackish, industrial version of the sea that was so complicated, so specific, it was like the smell of a particular human being. It evoked an earlier time that she no longer quite remembered. Her father's suits still hung in his wardrobe, lapels sharp, shoulders brushed, painted neckties reinforced with whalebone. They looked like the suits of a man who would return at any moment to put them on. He'd left behind an envelope full of cash and a bankbook for an account her mother hadn't known about. These preparations had made them believe at first that he was merely girding them for a longer than usual trip—he'd begun to travel for work. For months his absence had remained volatile and alive, as if he were in the next room or down the block. Anna had awaited him acutely. She would sit on the fire escape, grinding her gaze over the street below, thinking she saw him—trusting that thinking so would force him to appear. How could he stay away when she was waiting so hard?

She had never cried. When she'd believed he was about to return, there had been nothing to cry about, and when at last she'd stopped believing, it was too late. His absence had calcified. When she caught herself wondering where he might be, doing what, she forced herself to stop. He didn't deserve it. That much, at least, she could deny him.

She presumed her mother had made a similar passage, but she wasn't even sure. Her father had slipped from their conversation as ineffably as he'd dropped from their lives. It would feel odd to mention him now. And there was no need to.

One lunchtime, as Anna was taking the bicycle from Nell, she said, "Say, you can keep it sometimes and ride it yourself."

"Not for all the tea in China."

"Because of one fall?"

"Have *you* fallen?"

"You looked as if it didn't bother you a bit."

"That was the idea."

Anna walked the bike alongside Nell toward Pier C, though whether she was following Nell or the reverse, she wasn't sure.

"So," Nell said with a sly look, "the snapper's letting you go out, even without lipstick."

"So long as I'm not late."

"Think what you might get if you wore some."

Men's voices fell away as they ambled past. It was very different, walking with Nell—what must it be like to *be* Nell? There was no ship berthed at Pier C today, and when they reached the end, Nell pulled a silver cigarette case from the pocket of her jumpsuit. It flashed in the sun; a gift from a beau, Anna supposed. "Is smoking allowed here?" she asked.

"Men smoke on the piers. I don't see any 'Danger' signs. I mean— mmm, good, you're blocking the wind—we're surrounded by water, for Pete's sake!"

With a coarse expertise that contrasted sharply with her general air of slinky refinement, Nell struck a match on the bottom of her boot and used it to light a narrow white cigarette pursed between her lips. The smoke she exhaled looked creamily delicious, as if she'd found a way to eat the chocolate wind. "If they're going to make us wear these plug-ugly outfits, they're going to have to let us smoke," she said. "Care for one?"

Only boys had smoked on Anna's block—the girls had thought it dirty. "Thank you," she said. "I will."

Nell placed a fresh cigarette between her lips, held the smoldering tip of her own against it, and drew on it until both tips crackled orange. The sight of her dewy face arrayed around the burning cigarette was jarring, exciting to Anna. The end of the fresh one Nell handed her was moist, red with her lipstick. "Don't inhale at first," Nell said. "You'll get dizzy. Although I like being dizzy."

Anna drew on the cigarette, enjoying the dry heat inside her mouth, and let the smoke scatter into the wind. It *was* dirty, but a dirtiness she liked—akin to the girl welders eating their lunches sitting on the floor. She and Nell smoked in silence. Anna looked across Wallabout Bay at the hammerhead crane bent against the sky. A few days before, she'd watched it lift a cement truck off the ground as if it were a die-cast toy. Beyond the crane sprawled the Williamsburg Bridge and then the low buildings on the shore of Manhattan, windows like gold flakes in the dusty sky.

"You should come out with me some night," Nell said.

"Where do you go?"

"Shows, pictures. Restaurants. Don't you ever go to supper in the City?"

Anna had sipped beer with Brooklyn College boys at the Fraternity House, on Third Avenue, but she sensed that college watering holes were not what Nell had in mind. "I've led a sheltered, virtuous life," she said.

Nell rolled her eyes. "Too bad. You won't know how to dress."

"I'll manage something. I won't damage your standing, I promise."

Nell's blue eyes curved with delight. "How about tonight?" she said, tossing the end of her cigarette into the bay. "It's Friday, after all—even if we have to work tomorrow."

As they walked back along Pier C, Anna noticed a barge off the end of Dry Dock 1 that was different from the usual dredging barges with their hooks and tackle and filthy lean-tos. This one was bare. At one end, two men were helping a third into a heavy canvas suit, like squires fitting a knight for battle. Nearby, two more men turned cranks on a large upright rectangular box.

"Say, what are they doing?" Anna asked.

"That one in the big suit is a diver, I think," Nell said. "They work on ships from underwater. Maybe he's learning—I think they train them on that barge."

"A diver!" Anna had never heard of such a thing. She watched, spellbound, as the helpers lifted a spherical metal helmet over the diver's head, encasing him within it. There was something primally familiar about the diving suit—as if from a dream or a myth. Nell watched, too, persuaded by Anna's riveted attention that something worthwhile was taking place.

"How did you know he was a diver?" Anna asked, not taking her eyes from him.

"Roger, from my shop. They're looking for civilian volunteers. He wants to do it for the hazard pay."

The diver rose onto his feet and moved hulkingly toward the edge of the barge, then stepped backward onto a ladder leading into the water. The bay looked impenetrable as stone, yet he lowered himself into it until only the bulbous helmet showed above the waterline. Then he was gone, leaving behind a coruscation of bubbles.

At some point, Nell had gone to the canteen and returned with two boxed lunches. She handed one to Anna. "You'd better eat fast."

Anna ate her spaghetti and meatballs with her eyes fixed on the water. She was waiting for the diver to surface, but he did not. He was breathing underwater. She tried to picture him at the bottom of the bay—would he walk or swim? What was down there? Jealousy and longing spasmed through her. "Would they ever let us do that?" she murmured.

"Would you want to?"

"Wouldn't you?"

Nell gave a disbelieving laugh. "They'd never *let* us. But they might just *make* us. If the men keep leaving in droves."

Anna's mind closed around this notion like a lucky coin. Two hundred seventy Naval Yard workers had been furloughed for the draft in September, according to the *Shipworker*. More men were leaving every week.

"That will be the day I walk out for good," Nell said. She'd removed a compact from her jumpsuit and was powdering her nose and applying lipstick.

As Anna returned their cutlery to the canteen, she felt a seismic rearrangement within herself. It was clear to her now she had always wanted to be a diver, to walk along the bottom of the sea. But this certainty was fraught with worry that she would be denied.

After lunch, Mr. Voss sent her to Building 77, so routine by now that the marrieds no longer even remarked upon it. On the fifteenth floor, Anna asked the captain's secretary whether she might look out the windows, in hopes of glimpsing the diving barge.

"Oh, of course," said the secretary, who had grown friendlier over their several encounters. "I take the view for granted; sometimes a whole week goes by and I've forgotten to look out."

Anna went to a window. In the rich late-October sunlight, the Naval Yard arrayed itself before her with the precision of a diagram: ships of all sizes berthed four deep on pronglike piers. In the dry docks, ships were held in place by hundreds of filament ropes, like Gulliver tied to the beach. The hammerhead crane brandished its fist to the east; to the west loomed the building ways cages. Around all of it, railroad tracks spiraled into whorls of paisley. The diving barge had gone.

"When I look out at all that," said the secretary, who had come to stand beside Anna, "I think: *How can we not win?*"

Mr. Voss was in his office when Anna returned to her shop. When she'd deposited the package on the desk, he said, "Come in, Miss Kerrigan. Have a seat. Shut the door."

They'd not exchanged a private word since their conversation of almost a month before. Anna sat in the same hard chair.

"I trust you've enjoyed your lunches out?"

"Very much," she said. "And I haven't been late."

"You have not. And you've become our most productive inspector, male or female."

"Thank you, sir."

In the pause that followed, Anna grew puzzled. Had he called her into his office for the sole purpose of making pleasant chat? "I've seen the *Missouri*," she said to break the silence. "Inside the building ways."

"Ah," he said. "Imagine that launching. You missed the *Iowa*, didn't you?"

"By three weeks." She hated to think of it. Mrs. Roosevelt had been present.

"It's tremendous, watching a battleship slide down the ways into the water. There wasn't a dry eye."

"Not even yours?" She had meant the question straightforwardly; it was impossible to imagine Mr. Voss weeping over a ship. But the remark tipped from her teasingly, and he laughed—a first.

"Even I may have shed a tear or two," he said. "Believe it or not."

She grinned at him. "They were cold tears, I'll bet."

"Frozen. They hit the bricks and shattered like glass."

Anna was still smiling when she resumed her stool. She began working quickly, feeling she'd been away too long. It was only after several minutes that she noticed an unusual silence around her. How long had that been there? She glanced at the other girls, but not a single married would meet her eye. Not even Rose. Yet Anna felt their keen awareness of her.

That was when she knew: the marrieds had started to talk.

CHAPTER SIX

Anna met Nell at the Roxy for the eight o'clock showing of *The Glass Key*, with Alan Ladd. But one look at Nell's creamy décolletage between the unbuttoned halves of her coat and she knew they weren't going inside.

"I've a different idea, if you're feeling open-minded," Nell said with an odd, singing gaiety. When Anna assured her of the open state of her mind, Nell went on, "A friend of mine takes a regular table at Moonshine—that's a nightclub. He's invited us to join."

"My dress won't be right."

"I warned him you'd look pokey."

Anna laughed. In fact, her dress—hidden under her coat—was not all that bad. When she'd told her mother that a girlfriend from the Naval Yard had invited her to the pictures but presumed her clothes would be dreadful, her mother had plunged into a frenzy of outraged alteration, adding shoulder pads and a peplum to a plain blue dress Anna had bought at S. Klein for Lydia's upcoming doctor visit. At the same time Anna had stitched a spray of turquoise beads onto the collar, hands flying alongside her mother's as if they were playing a duet. No one who really knew clothes would be fooled by these enhancements, but their sewing wasn't meant for scrutiny. As Pearl Gratzky liked to say, rather grandly, "We work in the realm of the impression."

Nell hailed a taxi and directed the driver to East Fifty-third Street. "We're six blocks away!" Anna protested. "Let's save our money and walk."

A somersault of artificial laughter greeted this suggestion. "Don't worry," Nell said. "This ride is the last dime we'll spend tonight."

Even dimmed out, the blocks north of Times Square were aglow with more light than seemed to issue from their half-blackened streetlights and murky marquees. Anna was rarely in Manhattan after dark, and the number of soldiers amazed her: officers in heavy coats, sailors and enlisted men, others in uniforms she didn't recognize—all hurrying, as if toward a single urgent event.

"One thing," Nell said, turning to Anna in the backseat. "Not a word about what we do."

"What we—"

"Shh!" Nell pressed a finger to her lips. Her nails had been lacquered scarlet since the afternoon.

"You mean the Nav—"

"Sh!"

"Why not?"

"Oh, come now," Nell chided in a merry falsetto. "Let's not play dumb."

"Which of us is playing dumb?"

There was a pause. "You know perfectly well what I mean," Nell said in her normal voice. She gazed seriously at Anna, dimples shadowed by the glow from outside the widow. "I need to be sure you'll behave."

"Don't worry," Anna said. "I promise not to embarrass you."

The taxi deposited them east of Madison Avenue before a gleaming white door whose top-hatted sentry greeted their arrival as if it were the single event necessary to complete his happiness. They stepped into a rumbling din that startled Anna like the Naval Yard noise did after the suctioned silence of her measuring shop.

"Better than I expected," Nell said, sizing up her dress when they'd checked their coats and hats. "Much."

"Well, that's a relief," Anna said, but Nell caught her teasing tone and cocked her head, smiling into Anna's eyes. "You're funny," she said.

"So are you," Anna said, and Nell took her hand, tugging her toward the boil of music and voices, and Anna supposed this exchange was as much a declaration of friendship as Nell made to any girl—like becoming blood sisters with Lillian Feeney when they were ten. What made it possible was that Nell looked so ravishing in her cream satin dress with its plunging cowl neck, it was inconceivable Anna would divert even a trace amount of male attention from her.

Descending the shallow flight of stairs into the nightclub felt clashingly unreal—as if she'd been thrust across an invisible barrier into a moving picture. She needed to prepare, to ease in slowly, but there wasn't time; she was engulfed by an orchestra, a fountain, a checkerboard floor, and a thousand small red tables humming like hives. Nell shimmied among these, pausing often to exchange shrill, passionate greetings with their occupants. Anna trailed anxiously behind.

Three men awaited them at a table beside a crowded oval dance floor. They registered as more or less identical, with silk handker-chiefs in their breast pockets and expensive-looking tiepins. Their only distinguishing traits were that one of the three was handsome, and one of the non-handsome ones looked older than the rest. Of the volley of shouted pleasantries that followed, only phrases managed to punch through the general roar.

". . . celebrate . . ."

". . . the Japs made . . ."

". . . sitting over there . . ."

". . . champagne . . ."

". . . be a darling . . ."

Anna tried to listen, well aware that she was coming off as stiff. She'd never been good at banter; it was like a skipping rope whose rhythm she couldn't master enough to jump in with confidence. The war seemed not to exist here, despite the presence of officers in uni-form. Why hadn't Nell's two younger suitors been called up?

Clams casino arrived, along with champagne. The waiter, a boy with a noticeable tremor (4-F, Anna thought), struggled to fill five shallow glasses. Anna had never tried champagne; at the Fraternity House she'd had only beer, and the liquor at home had always been whiskey. The pale gold potion snapped and frothed in her glass. When she took a sip, it crackled down her throat—sweet but with a tinge of bitterness, like a barely perceptible pin inside a cushion.

"Say, this is delicious!" she cried, and Nell rejoined breathlessly, "Isn't it grand? I could drink it all day long," and Anna was on the verge of kidding that they should bring some to work in a thermos, if they could get it past the marines. She remembered not to just in time.

Her glass emptied quickly, but the waiter was right there, refilling it. And from one moment to the next, as if turning an oven dial and feeling a hot gush of flame in reply, the scene around Anna softened into a smear of brightness—music, sparkle, laughter—an *impression*, as Pearl Gratzky would say, glimpsed from the corner of her eye, more than an actual place. And this change dissolved whatever barrier had been stranding Anna outside of it. She was vaulted into its midst, hot-cheeked, with a galloping heart.

A fast number began. The younger non-handsome suitor reintro-duced himself—Louie—and asked Anna to dance, cheerfully swat-ting away her demurral. "Stop fibbing, every girl dances. Up you go," he said, taking her hand and hauling her over the checkerboard tiles. Anna noticed he'd a slight limp. So that was it. She worried fleetingly that the twenties dances she'd learned from her mother—the Pea-body, the Texas Tommy, the Breakaway—would not be convertible to the Benny Goodman–style swing this orchestra played. But Louie made it easy, moving her around with a deft economy behind which she sensed a great deal of care—possibly to conceal his limp, which he managed flawlessly.

"Are you having fun?" he asked. "Are you sure?" Louie had appar-ently assigned himself the role of host, responsible for the happiness of their party. "What about Nell, is she having fun? You can never tell with that one."

"She is," Anna reassured him. "We all are."

Back at the table, their glasses had been filled again. Nell returned from dancing with the handsome suitor, and Anna supposed he must be her sweetheart. But as she and Nell pushed through the crowd toward the ladies', Nell whispered, "My date is a no-show, the swine."

"Oh," Anna said, confused. "Is he—"

"He looks like Clark Gable, that's what everyone says. Let's check the entrance."

When their checking turned up nothing, Nell grew fretful. "Damn that louse!"

"Is he unreliable?"

"He's—attached. He can't always get away."

"Attached meaning . . ."

Nell nodded. "But his wife is a shrew."

"Have they children?"

"Four. But he's hardly alive at home—he just counts the minutes until he can see me again."

"You sound like a girl in a love serial," Anna said.

"You shouldn't listen to those," Nell said. "You'll rot your brains."

"My mother puts them on."

"Why isn't he here? The whole point of those drips at our table is to give me a spot to perch until he arrives."

"Louie isn't a drip," Anna said. "He's a sweet man."

"They're one and the same," Nell said.

Anna returned to the table bent on dancing with the handsome suitor, now that she knew he wasn't attached to Nell. Instead, she found herself back on the floor with Louie, who kept her entertained by pointing out a brigadier general, a state senator, and a famous Negro scholar. There was Laird Cregar, whom she'd seen in *This Gun for Hire* last spring, and Joan Fontaine, who'd won an Academy Award for *Suspicion*, a picture Anna had loved. Shadowy tales of the city were always her favorites—the sort of pictures that made your stomach seize when you heard footsteps behind you after leaving the movie palace.

"You know everyone, Louie!" she said.

"I suppose I do," he said. "The shame of it is, they don't know me."

Anna studied him: a slight man, teeth overlarge in his narrow face. The limp. "What sort of work do you do?"

"Actuarial," he muttered, brushing past the topic before Anna could ask what it meant. "Yourself?"

Having barely avoided mention of the Naval Yard several times, Anna was ready. "Secretary," she said vaguely.

"I suppose the purpose of joints like this is to make us forget about jobs like ours," Louie said. "Moonshine has just the right naughty edge."

"Where?" Anna cried. "I don't see the naughty edge."

"Ah, you can't—that's the point. They've gaming upstairs, high rollers only. Baccarat, canasta, poker—so my sources tell me. And you've all types in here, including gangsters. You girls love the gangsters, of course."

"I've never met one!" Anna said. "Can you point one out?"

"Well, the owner's a gangster, so they say. Or was, during Prohibition. He generally sits over there." Louie squinted toward a back corner of the room. "Name of Dexter Styles. Owns a number of clubs, so he isn't always here."

"Dexter Styles," Anna said. She knew the name. "What does he look like?"

"Like a pugilist. Big strong fellow, dark hair. He may be there now, I can't tell."

Marco, the handsome suitor, finally asked Anna to dance. He looked like a screen heavy with his curly dark hair and brooding eyes, his scowling mouth. He was Italian—perhaps that was why he hadn't been called up. He pronounced Mussolini a pig perfunctorily, as if checking a box, then fell silent. His gaze roved the dance floor, and Anna soon realized he was keeping Nell in sight as she danced with the non-handsome suitor who wasn't Louie. Anna danced badly with

Marco, and he with her. The third time he stepped on her foot, she excused herself, smarting with disappointment. Rather than rejoin Louie, she made her way toward the corner where he'd said the club's owner liked to sit. Four men leaned around a table. Anna's champagne smear had given her a feeling of half-invisibility, and she walked straight to the table and looked down. The men noticed her as one. She knew immediately which was Mr. Styles—and realized, in that instant, that she had met him before.

"Powder room's all the way at the front," one of the men said.

"No, I— Excuse me," Anna said, and veered away. Dexter Styles was the man from the beach. This discovery arrived in a hot-cold rush, disorienting her as if the room had flipped on its side. A lost memory surfaced: riding in the car with her father. Playing with another girl. This man, Dexter Styles, on an icy beach. The coincidence felt miraculous. Without pausing to consider, Anna rushed back to the table to inform him of it.

The men glanced up a second time, a chill in their collective regard signaling that she'd outworn her welcome. The champagne blur abandoned her, and she felt exposed, unbuffered from the hostility of the youngest of Mr. Styles's associates, who had big jowls and bushy, uneven hair. "You're turning into a bad habit, baby," he said. "Scram."

Dexter Styles was on his feet instantly, standing between Anna and the table. "What can I do for you, miss?" he asked with remote politeness, his eyes barely grazing her face. He'd no memory of her, of course. The trip to Manhattan Beach faded into the distant past like an apple core flung from a train window. The very idea of invoking it seemed absurd. A silence opened between them and multiplied.

"I work at the Naval Yard, in Brooklyn," Anna blurted at last, the error of this choice assailing her before she'd finished the sentence.

"You don't say." She'd managed to snare the roving beam of his attention. "I read in the papers that girls had started working there. What do you do?"

"I measure parts with a micrometer," she said. "But girls do welding, riveting . . ."

"They *weld*?"

"Just like the men. You can't tell them apart until they take off the mask."

"Is it natural? Men and women working together like that?"

He was gazing at her directly. "I don't know," she said, flustered. "I mostly work with girls."

"Well, it was a pleasure talking with you, Miss . . ."

"Feeney," she said impulsively, extending her hand. "Anna Feeney."

"Dexter Styles."

They shook, and he touched the arm of a hovering waiter and said, "Gino, would you show Miss Feeney back to her table and send her party a bottle of champagne on the house? Good luck to you, Miss Feeney."

She was dismissed. Dexter Styles rejoined his companions, and Anna wandered through the crowd, ears ringing with the strangeness of all that had just transpired. It wasn't so much that she'd used Lillian Feeney's name—a phony name seemed all of a piece with this place—but that in doing so, she had obscured the connection between them. Why, when Mr. Styles might have recognized her name and remembered?

Back at the table, Anna remained pensive despite Louie's strenuous efforts to draw her out. She couldn't see Dexter Styles from where she sat—would likely never see him again. Only when she envisioned the conversation that might have followed the use of her real name did she understand her instinctive feint. *And how is your father? Where is he nowadays? What is he doing?* Those questions would surely have come, and the thought of trying to answer mortified her.

Their waiter arrived with the fresh bottle of champagne. Nell and Marco returned from the dance floor, Marco looking deeply satisfied.

"What's the matter?" Nell asked, dropping into a chair beside Anna. "Are you too tight?"

"Maybe." But she felt the opposite: that she'd not had enough champagne to quash the sudden dull sadness—emptiness, really—that had overwhelmed her.

"I'm ready to call it a night," Nell said.

For Louie, this prospect amounted to an emergency. "Aw, come on, girls," he cried. "Have some champagne—they've sent us a bottle on the house! I've been waiting all my life for a bottle on the house!"

"Sweet old Louie," Nell said.

"I aim to please. Sad faces mean I've failed."

Anna sensed a scurrying desperation beneath his cheer, and it pained her. "You've been wonderful, Louie," she said, putting an arm around his narrow shoulders. She kissed his cool, waxen cheek.

"Ooh-la-la," Louie cried.

Nell embraced him from the other side. Marco and the older non-handsome suitor both laughed. It was impossible not to wish Louie well.

"I'm going to faint," Louie said. "Catch me when I do, will you, girls?"

None of the furor within Moonshine leaked onto East Fifty-third Street; it was like passing from one world into another. Anna glanced at her watch and received a shock; it was after one A.M. "I have to get home," she said.

Nell made no answer; she was drooping to precisely the degree she'd been artificially enlivened at the start of the night. "Will you see him tomorrow?" Anna asked.

Nell shook her head. "He can't get away on weekends. That's why I'm so steaming mad that he didn't show, the rat."

"Did he buy you that dress?"

"In Palm Beach," Nell said. "He'd a business trip to Miami, and I went with him. Now I've shocked you, haven't I?" she added with reckless gloom.

"A little," Anna admitted. "It seems . . . dangerous."

"Only for him—I've nothing to lose. And he says I'm worth any risk." She smiled wanly. "Don't tell me you thought I was an angel."

"I didn't. Think that."

"There's no such thing, anyway."

Anna said nothing.

"Angels are the best liars, that's what I think," Nell said morosely. After a moment she asked, "Are you an angel, Anna?"

Anna was aware of the rattle of fall leaves over the pavement, the gardenia smell of Nell's perfume. No one had ever asked her that question before. Everyone simply presumed that she was.

"No," she said. "I'm not an angel." Her eyes met Nell's, and they understood each other.

Nell took Anna's arm, her spirits revived. They walked past town houses like handcrafted jewel boxes. "You hide it very well," she said softly.

"I suppose that's good."

"You could be a spy or a detective. No one would know who you really are, or who you work for."

"I want to be a diver," Anna said.

CHAPTER SEVEN

Driving along Eighty-sixth Street in Brooklyn, Dexter Styles saw Badger check his wristwatch and then extend a hairy hand toward the radio dial, presumably to turn on the five-thirty A.M. news. Dexter knocked the hand away.

"What'd you do that for?" Badger groused.

"You don't touch a man's car without his permission. Or did they not teach you that in Chicago?"

"Sorry, boss," Badger said meekly, but his stubborn, merry eyes told a different story. Sure enough, he went on, "It's just that . . . I'm touching the car by sitting in the car, if you take my meaning. I'm touching the seat when I lean back."

"If you want me to smack you, why not just ask."

"Say, you've been sore at me all night."

Dexter glanced at him. Among Badger's maddening traits was a fair degree of accuracy at reading Dexter's moods. He *was* sore—why, he couldn't recall. Maybe it was the fact that Badger was clogging up his car at what would soon be Dexter's favorite hour: the pause between night and dawn when you felt the possibility of light before any was visible.

"The girl," he said, remembering. "You were rude to the girl who approached my table. Miss Feeney."

Badger gaped incredulously.

"At Hell's Bells, that's one thing," Dexter said, referring to his roadhouse in the Flatlands, which they'd visited first after leaving Moonshine. "Even at the Pines, although you won't hear Mr. Healey talk that way to a customer. But not at Moonshine."

"Too high-class?"

"Something like that."

Badger heaved a sigh. "It was different in Chicago."

"So I'm told."

For seven nights running, Badger had yakked his ear off about Chicago's swell gin joints and incomparable dames and dishy lake; above all, the silken accord between Syndicate and Law. Badger loved Chicago, but Chicago did not love Badger. Something had gone very wrong in the Windy City, and a less lucky kid would be feeding fishes at the bottom of Lake Michigan. But Badger's mother was a favorite niece of Mr. Q.'s. Conversations had taken place, and Mr. Q. had secured his great-nephew's safe passage to Brooklyn, where he'd handed him over to Dexter for education and guidance. The normal thing would have been for Badger to drive him, but Dexter would sooner have made the kid his lawyer. He never let another man behind the wheel of his new Series 62 Cadillac, painted Norse Gray, one of the last to roll off the line before Detroit moved strictly into war production. Dexter loved to drive. He doubted there were ten men in New York who drove as much as he did, or went through more black-market gasoline.

"Say, you're going the wrong way, boss."

"That all depends where I'm trying to go."

"I thought you were taking me home." Badger meant Bensonhurst, where he was sleeping in the spare bedroom of Mr. Q.'s ancient maiden sister.

From Gravesend, where they'd just visited the Pines, Dexter had driven unthinkingly into Bay Ridge. He'd discovered an excellent view of the Narrows a few weeks ago, after visiting an associate on a hilly street above Fort Hamilton. He'd been about to get back in his car when he found himself staring into the dark of the Upper Bay, where boats and waterfront were blacked out. He'd perceived a new, dynamic density in the darkness. All at once his eyes had organized the mystery and he'd seen it: a procession of immense ships slipping from the harbor at regular intervals like beasts or ghosts. A convoy headed out to sea. There was something profound, unearthly, even, in its muted passage. Dexter waited until every ship passed—twenty-eight, he counted, but who knew how long the parade had gone on before he'd arrived. At last, the little gate boat had come along to close the anti-submarine net. After that, he'd made a habit of returning to this spot every few nights, hoping to catch sight of another convoy.

"You're young and healthy, Badger," he said as the engine idled. "Why haven't you signed up?"

"I'm not a soldier, that's why."

"A soldier is exactly what you are. As am I."

"Not that kind."

"Your great-uncle is our general."

"Not the marching kind."

Dexter turned to him sternly. "If Mr. Q. told us to march, we'd march. If he told us to wear monkey suits, we'd put them on. You wouldn't happen to be 4-F, would you, Badger?"

"Me?" Badger said shrilly. "Why, I've eyes like a Siamese. From the roof of the Drake Hotel, I could read blinker signals all the way from the middle of Lake Michigan."

Chicago again. Dexter watched the harbor while Badger rhapsodized, thinking over what he'd just heard at both Hell's Bells and the Pines: business was down. Men hadn't enough gasoline to drive to roadhouses. It would likely be the same story at the clubs on Long Island and the Palisades, which he would visit tonight and on Monday.

Heels, his man at the Pines, had told him something else: a former card dealer, name of Hugh Mackey, was making trouble. He'd gambled too much, borrowed too heavily, stuck his paws too deep in the till, and gotten canned. Now he was threatening Heels with blackmail if he didn't rehire him at a better salary. Claimed he'd seen enough in eight months to put them all in Sing Sing. Dexter tried to picture Hugh Mackey. He could always put a name to a face, but a name alone sometimes wasn't enough.

"What did she want in the end?" Badger asked lazily. "That twat who kept coming back."

"Watch your mouth."

"She can't hear me."

Dexter marveled at his insolence. It made him grasp something that had eluded him until that instant: Badger thought he was protected. He'd mistaken Mr. Q.'s helping hand for immunity of some kind—apparently unaware that Mr. Q.'s own brother had vanished in the course of his ascent, along with at least two cousins. This misapprehension explained Badger's exaggerated deference toward Dexter, the twist of mockery inside it.

"Get out," Dexter said.

Badger looked bewildered.

"Beat it. Now."

The kid sputtered a moment, but he must have known Dexter meant it. He opened the door and stepped into the dark. Dexter drove away quickly and quietly, glancing just once in the rearview mirror. He barely made out Badger gazing after the car in the cheap suit Dexter had bought him the week before at Crawford's. It would take him some doing to find his way back to Bensonhurst, if he even knew the address. Those squeaky new brogues would get broken in fast. With a kid like that, you'd no choice but to hit him hard, as many times as it took. Whatever Mr. Q. had saved him from in Chicago could not have been worse than the hellfire that would rain down on Badger here in New York if he failed to observe the chain of command. There was no such thing as immunity. Thinking you had it was suicide.

The good news was that Dexter would likely be free of the kid for a couple of days while Badger licked his wounds. Dexter preferred women, was the truth—they were easier to be around. He would have liked for women to run the whole of his business, if he could find any as tough as the speakeasy owners of his youth: Texas Guinan, Bell Livingstone, dames who'd run over rooftops to escape the dry agents. But modern girls seemed not to like weapons very much, and to be fair, it was hard to carry a gat inside a dress. Even Dexter didn't wear a shoulder holster; why bother having a suit tailored at F. L. Dunne only to spoil its line? As for keeping a gun in a pocketbook, that only happened in the pictures. A weapon needed to rest against the hide.

The magic hour struck as he approached Manhattan Beach: a swell of promise in the sky that Dexter experienced physically, an expansion inside his chest. He liked to await first light at the eastern end, where the grand hotels used to be. His pop had worked in the kitchen of the Oriental when Dexter was small, and although the hotel had been razed when he was eleven, he could call it to mind precisely—as if its ghost still faced the sea, arms outstretched, awnings, spires, flags snapping in the wind. Inside, miles of red-carpeted hallway were infused with a hum likely generated by the cast of hundreds—his pop included—who toiled just out of sight. Dexter had never been allowed on the Oriental's beach. Too exclusive.

Last February, just after Pearl Harbor, the Coast Guard had sealed off the eastern end of Manhattan Beach and built a training center amid the vacationers' cottages. Dexter idled by its gate, looking east as first light appeared. It was gradual, but it never felt like that. One second to the next, and it was day.

His house was on Manhattan Beach's western end. He kept the front door unlocked. In the kitchen, Milda had left him a pot of coffee, which he warmed on a burner. He poured himself a cup and raised the blackout curtains that covered the windows facing the sea. He only really knew what a day looked like when he'd seen it through these windows. With each quarter turn of dawn, the density of boats was more fully revealed: lighters, barges, tankers, some quarantined at anchor. Wooden-hulled minesweepers moved back and forth across the width of the Ambrose Channel. Tugboats gadflied like circus clowns alongside ships headed into the Upper Bay.

He brought his coffee and binoculars onto the back porch, which overlooked the sea. Tabatha appeared a few minutes later, sleepy-eyed in her frilly lavender robe. Dexter was pleased; normally, his daughter slept late on Saturdays. Her auburn hair—the exact shade of her mother's—was still indented from the pins she must have yanked from it moments before, to prevent him teasing her. "Tabby cat," he said, kissing her proffered cheek. "What's this, you're drinking my coffee?"

"It's mostly milk." She curled into the chair beside his, hugging her knees. Her flimsy chemise was no match for the wind.

"No slumber party last night?"

Lately, it seemed she was always with a girlfriend (often Natalie, whom he didn't trust), or else two or three girls were over here, making lapel pins out of melted wax or "broomstick skirts," which involved dipping the skirt in a pot of dye and twisting it around a stick to dry. The result was nothing short of hideous.

"Any picture stars last night?" she asked.

"Well, let's see. Aline MacMahon was there, Wendy Barrie. Joan Fontaine, she won the Academy Award." He was teasing her, mentioning only girls.

"No one else?"

"Well, I did catch a glimpse of Gary Cooper. Very late."

She clapped her hands. "What was he doing?"

"Sitting happily beside his wife and keeping her in martinis."

"You always say that!"

"It's always true." But it was practically never true. Dexter told no one what he saw through the hidden window on the club's second floor. He left that to Mr. Winchell, his friend and regular, who was a genius at the art of saying something and nothing at the same time.

"Anyone else?" She was hoping for news of Victor Mature. She had gone with Natalie to *I Wake Up Screaming* last year, and the sight of Mature in a swimming rig had proved a conversion experience. Now his sappy stills decorated her schoolbooks under cellophane.

"No sign of Victor, if that's who you mean," he said.

"I didn't," she said piously. "He has more important things to do than go to nightclubs. He's joined the Coast Guard."

In the old days, when she'd been a regular early riser, Tabby had joined Dexter out here most mornings with her cup of milk. He'd been impressed by her shrewdness, by the grave thought she gave to small topics, and had imagined going into business with her one day—legitimate, of course. But his hopes for Tabby had dimmed over the past year, when she'd begun styling her hair like Veronica Lake and devoting herself to the Ouija board. Yet every couple of weeks she still appeared out here in the morning, as if observing a ritual.

"What's on tap for today, Tabs?"

"Something with Natalie."

"Something like what?"

"A picture. Maybe the drugstore." The studied way she avoided his eyes told him boys would be present. Natalie was boy-crazy, and Tabby had grown prettier than Dexter would have liked. Not that he wished ugliness on his only daughter, but showy beauty was an invitation to dependence. He'd have liked her to have the hidden kind, visible only to those who looked closely. She'd made a lapel pin out of an aspirin box painted over with red nail varnish, and called it a Wish Box. Apparently, there was a secret wish inside, written on a slip of paper. The idea of Tabby maintaining a secret vexed him a little.

"Care for a look?" he asked, offering the binoculars. She shook her head. She'd produced an emery board and was filing her nails into perfect ovals. "English, if you please," he said.

"No, thank you, Daddy."

"Lots of ships."

"I see them."

"How, when you're staring at your fingernails?"

"I see them every day."

He raised the binoculars, scanning the nervous gray water for the conning tower of a submarine. The net across the Narrows protected the Upper Bay, but as far as Dexter knew, there was nothing to stop a

U-boat from slipping around the corner of Breezy Point, where Fort Tilden was, and coming right to where sea met rocks below his house. Watching the sea in dread of a submarine felt at times like anticipating one—hoping for it, even.

"Here," he said, thrusting the binoculars at Tabby to break the spell of her self-absorption. "Make sure no Germans are coming ashore like they did on Amagansett Beach."

"Why would they, Daddy? There's nothing important here."

"To help with your fingernails? Those seem to be very important."

She yanked her fragment of a robe around her and stalked back indoors. Dexter seethed at her vanity and his own impulsiveness. It was a weakness.

He tossed his cold coffee onto the rocks and went inside. In his dressing room, he removed his gat from its ankle holster and locked it in the cabinet he kept for that purpose. He hung his trousers and jacket in the closet, threw his shirt into a corner to be laundered, and stood at the sink in his Sulka undershorts, washing with cold water. Then he entered his musky, sunken bedroom. The lush expanse of the bed he and Harriet shared was a repudiation of the barracks-style sleeping arrangements favored by her Puritan forebears. He heard her breathing and slipped into bed beside her. The light from the dressing room caught on the wingspan of her cheekbones, her sultry mouth. Very pretty, his Harriet. Distractingly pretty—why had he supposed her daughter would be any less so? She was composed even in sleep; it was Dexter's job to discompose her. He'd been doing it since she was sixteen, begging to come along on his liquor runs, which he'd interrupted to fuck her by moonlight in Long Island pumpkin fields, her debutante dresses bunched over her head, full of leaves. A night's worth of aggravation had gathered inside him like racehorses twitching at a starting gate. This would do for action, it always would. He was on top of Harriet before she was even awake.

"Morning, baby," she said in the husky voice that had been so unnerving in her youth, before she'd grown into it. "Rude awakening."

"Long night," Dexter said.

*   *   *

Before Mass the next morning, the new deacon took Dexter aside to discuss the bell. It had an "invisible crack" that not only compromised its sound but might result in a break, a fall, a crushed parishioner. Clergy always assumed Dexter would be an easy mark for church improvements, sin being inherent to his livelihood. Already there had been a chipped altar slab, new robes for the choirboys, and now this bell, which sounded fine to him. In fact, he wouldn't have minded if they'd rung it less.

"I'm surprised, Deacon," he said as they stood in a bushy nook outside of Saint Maggie's. "A church not twenty-five years old."

"During the Depression, we made no improvements at all," the deacon murmured.

"Not so. Your predecessor, Deacon Bertoli, tapped me for vestments and a new chalice, not to mention those stations of the cross wall hangings in the apse."

"Your generosity has sustained us," the deacon intoned, eyes downcast.

Dexter studied him in the frank sunlight: a young man, pouches under his eyes, a flush at odds with the season: booze, probably. Less common in wop clergy than Irish but certainly not unheard of, especially in a celibate. Having built his career on the force of human appetites, Dexter could only shake his head at Rome's mad insistence that its priests leave unsatisfied the most primal urge of all. Bertoli played the ponies; Dexter had run into him twice at Belmont and once at Saratoga during his "faith retreat." He'd been transferred to a city without a racetrack. And now his replacement, a wino, wanted higher-quality ink than he could afford on the pittance they paid him. Who could blame him?

Dexter paid no attention to the sermon. He didn't give a fig about religion; he'd tethered himself to Saint Maggie's to fend off any possibility of being roped into Episcopal worship with his in-laws. All those Puritans, God help him. If you had to spend an hour in church, let it be gory, incense-drenched Catholicism. He found Mass a good time to mull over business. Today he wondered what to do about Hugh Mackey, the debt-ridden dealer who was trying to blackmail Heels. Heels was the most genial gee in the world until he got sore, and he was starting to get sore.

After Mass, when the requisite neighborly mixing had taken place outside the church, Dexter piled his family into the Cadillac for the long drive to his in-laws' house on Sutton Place. He'd barely pulled the car away when the twins began fencing with twigs. "Daddy!" Tabby shrieked. "Make them stop!"

"Boys," Dexter said sharply, and the twins fell still. A current of amusement flickered between them always, like a telegraph.

"At the hunt club yesterday," Tabby said, "they hit their jai alais by the terrace until people made them stop."

"Don't be a tattletale," Harriet said.

"We were quiet," John-Martin said resentfully.

For reasons that eluded Dexter, his sons liked to enter promotional contests, usually at picture theaters. They tap-danced, turned somersaults, hung from bars upside down, and whistled through their teeth. When successful, they brought home bugles or harmonicas or roller skates—items they already owned or could easily afford. Dexter feared they were constitutionally unserious.

"The hunt club doesn't consider jai-alai-ing a sport, eh?" he couldn't resist needling his wife. "Not in the same category as the steeplechase?"

"There haven't been races in years," she said. "As you know."

As a girl, she'd gone to those steeplechases with her mother, who had hoped Harriet would find a husband of suitable pedigree—ideally, a Brit visiting for the Oxford-Cambridge-Rockaway team matches. "It's just a bunch of old stoves getting stinko and leering at polo players" had been Harriet's early description of the Rockaway Hunting Club, and she and Dexter had made a point, on their rare visits, of exercising their marriage vows in at least one new location. But in recent years, Harriet had grown inexplicably fond of the place. Now she went often, sipping pink ladies with the same old stoves she once mocked, listening to their doddering tales of meeting Queen Victoria as debutantes. She'd taken up golf. All of it bothered Dexter in some indefinable way.

"We should never have gone," John-Martin grumbled. "We don't fit in."

"Play polo," Dexter said. "You'll fit in just fine."

"We don't have horses," Phillip reminded him.

Harriet's parents faced each other at opposite ends of a long table in a dining room overlooking the East River just south of Hell Gate, where it joined the Long Island Sound. Beth Berringer had the classic old stove's face: a drought-stricken delta of cracks and tributaries affixed to the reactive jaws of a Doberman. She alone could move or halt the old man with a flick of her fair blue eyes. Their son and three daughters were always present, along with spouses and some complement of the fourteen grandchildren they had collectively produced, the older boys being away at school. A roast was carved and served by two of the Romanian servants Beth Berringer favored. Arthur said grace, and there was a pause of quiet chewing, filled with the churn of East River boat traffic, before children's voices raided the silence.

When an apple crisp had been doused in cream and consumed, the women drifted from the table into the kitchen and library, the children to the nursery and bedrooms. The men remained, positioning themselves around Arthur in the usual formation: his only son, Arthur Jr. (known as Cooper), on his right, Dexter on his left, each flanked by another son-in-law: George Porter, a surgeon, on Dexter's other side; Henry Foster, a schoolmaster, on Cooper's. Thus began an hour of conversation that Dexter looked forward to all week.

He noticed Tabby idling by the pocket doors to the dining room.

"Come on over, Tabs," he called to her, having first received a nod of approval from the old man. "Sit with us a minute."

He moved an extra chair to the corner between himself and Arthur. Tabby sat, coughing gently in the spiraling smoke from Cooper's cigarette, the old man's pipe, and George Porter's cigar. Dexter and Henry Foster didn't smoke—the one trait he'd in common with the schoolmaster, who wore patched tweed and drove a decomposing tin lizzie.

Arthur poured each of them a glass of port. He'd retired from the navy as a rear admiral after the Great War and gone into banking, but even military posture couldn't raise him above middling height. He'd small pink hands, thinning white hair, was well tailored (Brooks Brothers), but not as well as he might have been (Savile Row). He drove a mud-colored '39 Plymouth. Yet what emanated from these nondescript trappings was a more potent distillation of *life* than Dexter had encountered in any man. He admired his father-in-law without reservation.

"So, my boys," the old man said, ignoring Tabby. "What do you hear?"

He didn't mean from newspapers. The old man had come to know Roosevelt as governor and went often to Washington, where he'd worked on war bond issues and helped to craft lend-lease. His navy intimates commanded fleets. Arthur Berringer knew a great many things, in other words, but he recognized that his rarefied connections lofted him above the better part of human experience.

Henry Foster began with news from the Westchester town where his prep school, Alton Academy, was situated: a local woman had grown convinced that the family next door—neighbors of eight years—were German spies disguised as Americans. "She thought they were hiding their accents, even the children," he said. "She could *hear the German poking through.* They had to commit her to a sanitarium."

"What do you make of it?" the old man asked George Porter, the surgeon.

"The stress of war working on a weak mind," George said. "She may well recover."

Dexter watched for Tabby's reaction, but she kept her eyes down, pulling the rind from a lemon slice.

"Suppose the neighbors really are German," Cooper suggested, causing his father to wince.

"We'll have to keep Alton Academy open through Thanksgiving," Henry went on. "Husbands overseas, mothers taking jobs . . . some boys haven't anywhere else to go."

Hoping to engage Tabby, Dexter said, "We've had girls in the club who work at the Naval Yard, right in Brooklyn. Welding, plumbing . . . apparently, there are hundreds of them."

The old man looked skeptical. "Hundreds?"

"Sounds dangerous," Cooper said with a glance at his father, although it wasn't clear whether he meant dangerous to the girls or to the world. Likely Cooper didn't know. He was a weaker, far less intelligent version of his father, the embodiment of the limitations of their breed. The old man saw this; there was no way not to, with Cooper working for him at the bank. In moments of disappointment between father and son, Dexter felt the ease and strength of his own bond with his father-in-law. Cooper would never tell Arthur Berringer anything he didn't know, whereas Dexter saw and knew things the old man couldn't afford to, without personal compromise. He was nearer the earth, its salts and minerals, than any Berringer had been in several generations. And he was the only son-in-law not to require a penny of the old man's dough.

"Oh, I don't know, Coop," his father said gently. "Dangerous?"

"Girls haven't any practice at building ships."

Tabby watched her grandfather, but the old man's gaze never touched her. A weakness of his generation: they'd no idea of the worth of women.

"Were the girls masculine?" George Porter asked Dexter with a chuckle. He came often to Moonshine with his wife, Regina, Harriet's battle-ax of an older sister, in their refurbished '23 Duesenberg, painted chiffon yellow. Thanks to Dexter's hidden window, he knew that the dapper doctor brought other women, too. George knew that Dexter knew, and this made for a warm understanding between them.

"Just ordinary girls," Dexter said. "The kind you see in Automats at lunchtime."

"I don't go to Automats," said the old man. "Paint us a picture."

The task of multiplying Miss Feeney into several girls was becoming onerous. The duplication had been instinctive—a long-standing wish to head off even the faintest speculation about his fidelity. It was one thing for George Porter, a minister's son from an old family, to cheat discreetly. Dexter had no such leeway. His fealty to Harriet had been a condition of the old man's blessing, and Dexter had given it gladly. In this way, as in so many others, his father-in-law had done him a favor. Womanizing was as bad as being a hophead or a cokie, for all the mayhem Dexter had seen it wreak in men's lives.

"Early twenties . . . dark-haired, Irish names," he said. "Nice wholesome girls. Not fashionable."

"Fashionable enough to be at Moonshine," said Henry Foster, who disapproved of nightclubs.

"They did look a bit out of place," Dexter reflected. "Someone brought them, I suppose."

"They sound identical," his father-in-law said, with a laugh. "You're sure they weren't twins?"

Dexter flushed. "I suppose I didn't look closely."

"Say, why don't I phone the Naval Yard's commandant," the old man said. "We were together in the Philippines. Arrange for a tour when Grady comes home from Annapolis."

"Yes!" Tabby cried, catching everyone off guard. "Please, Grandpa! I'd like to see the Naval Yard."

Dexter nearly swooned from astonishment and pride.

"When will Grady be home for Thanksgiving?" the old man asked Cooper.

They all inclined toward the name: Cooper because Grady was the lustrous jewel of his bland existence, the rest of them—why? There was a radiance about Grady, the eldest of the Berringer grandchildren, as if all of the old man's wit and mischief, his easy touch with other men, had bypassed Cooper and resurged, thrillingly, in his eldest child. Grady seemed destined for great things, as the saying went, and Dexter was not above envying Cooper such a son.

"Tuesday before Thanksgiving," Cooper said, puffing up a little, as he always did when discussing Grady. "But he's awfully busy with early graduation—I'll have to ask Marsha."

"Wednesday before Thanksgiving then," the old man said, ignoring his son's equivocation. "I'll telephone the admiral tomorrow morning. You'll come, too, Tabatha?" Her name sounded oddly formal on his lips.

"Yes, Grandpa," she said, subdued in the aftermath of her outburst. "I'd like to come."

"I'm afraid I'll have to stay at Alton," Henry said. "But I'm sure Bitsy would like to come, if someone would fetch her at the station."

"Of course," Dexter said, to Henry's obvious relief. Bitsy, Harriet's younger sister, had been the ideal schoolmaster's wife until eight months ago, when she'd become "overwrought," as Henry put it, after the birth of their fourth child. She'd begun studying Russian with a tutor and chanting passages from Pushkin. She spoke of wanting to travel the world and live in a yurt. Poor Henry hadn't any idea what to do.

George's drab daughters, Edith and Olive, hovered in the doorway, skeins of mud-colored wool dripping from their knitting needles. Something for soldiers. "We've been waiting," Olive said to Tabby reproachfully, and she rose and went with them, Dexter basking in the wonderful knowledge that she'd done well.

"And you, Arthur?" he asked his father-in-law when the girls had gone. "What do you hear?"

"Well. Unlike you gentlemen, I don't actually *do* anything other than listen at doors," the old man said. "But my listening tells me that something is imminent. With us at the fore."

It took all of them a moment to absorb this. Even Cooper understood that the old man meant an aggression. "In Europe or Asia, Pop?" he asked.

"No self-respecting commander would ever let such a thing slip," the old man said gruffly. "Of course, there are more possibilities than just those two."

Dexter guessed then that he meant North Africa, where the Brits were finally mustering some grit against Rommel. "We need the battle experience," he said, working it out in his mind.

The old man grazed his eyes. "Precisely."

If true, it was a staggering thing to know in advance. So far, what Arthur Berringer told them had always proved true. Dexter used to puzzle over why the old man would share sensitive facts with the likes of Cooper, who lacked intelligence or judgment, or Dexter, whose business took place on both sides of the law. It had occurred to him that his father-in-law might be feeding them false facts—either to test them or to use them as mouthpieces for rumors he wanted spread. But Dexter had never repeated a word; such was the old man's power. And that was the answer. Arthur Berringer confided freely in his son and sons-in-law for the same reason Dexter left his front door unlocked: he'd the power to *make* them trustworthy. But while Dexter's power derived from physical force, the old man's had been distilled into abstraction. The Berringers were wearing top hats to the opera when Dexter's people were still copulating behind hay bales in the old land. He liked the thought that his own power would one day be refined into translucence, with no memory of the blood and earth that had generated it.

"The Allies will win this war," the old man said.

"Isn't that . . . premature?" George asked.

"Well, I wouldn't say it to just anyone," the old man said. "But it is a fact."

"I doubt the navy sees it that way, Dad," said Cooper.

"It's not the navy's job to think that way, son. Or the army's. Or the Coast Guard's. Their job is to win. It is the *bankers'* job to anticipate— second job, that is, after we've paid for the war itself."

For Arthur Berringer, all of human achievement—be it the Roman conquests or American independence—was a mere sideshow of the machinations of bankers (taxation in the first instance; the Louisiana Purchase in the second). Like any hobbyhorse, this one occasioned its share of weary sighs from family members. Not Dexter. For him, the existence of an obscure truth recessed behind an obvious one, and emanating through it allegorically, was mesmerizing. It was what had first intrigued him, at age fifteen, about the two men who came every third Monday to see his father at his Coney Island restaurant. Another man came less often, always in brand-new spats, a red handkerchief gushing from his breast pocket. Dexter's father always went behind the bar to pour this man's brandy rather than have the barkeep do it.

The blank face his pop wore after these visitations betrayed humiliation and anger, and Dexter knew better than to ask what they meant. But he was drawn to the men—a smoldering of dim feeling behind their eyes, a heaviness to their hands when they gave him a pat or a swat. He curried their favor, refilling their glasses, lingering at their tables when his father wasn't watching. They took notice of him gradually, with a mute animal awareness. Later, when men who'd fought the Great War returned, Dexter recognized, in their fractured gazes and somnolent movements, something of what he'd first admired in Mr. Q.'s men. By then he knew what it meant: intimacy with violence.

"Of course," Arthur added with a laugh, "since the Depression, we bankers have had the leisure and . . . solitude, you might say, to think about the future. The Civil War left us with a federal government. The Great War made us a creditor nation. As bankers, we must anticipate what changes this war will thrust upon us."

"What do you anticipate?" asked Henry, who distrusted Roosevelt.

The old man leaned forward and took a long breath. "I see the rise of this country to a height no country has occupied, ever," he said quietly. "Not the Romans. Not the Carolingians. Not Genghis Khan or the Tatars or Napoleon's France. Hah! You're all looking at me like I've one foot in the funny farm. How is that possible? you ask.

Because our dominance won't arise from subjugating peoples. We'll emerge from this war victorious and unscathed, and become bankers to the world. We'll export our dreams, our language, our culture, our way of life. And it will prove irresistible."

Dexter listened, a dark umbrella of worry opening slowly inside him. He'd been a soldier for over two decades, observing a chain of command to ensure the prosperity and vigor of the organization he served: a shadow government, a shadow country. A tribe. A clan. Now, suddenly, everyone was an American. A common enemy had made for strange bedfellows; rumor had it that the great Lucky Luciano had struck a deal with the feds from his jail cell to root out Mussolini sympathizers from the waterfront. What would Dexter's own place be when the war ended?

"I won't have much part in all this," Arthur Berringer said. "I'll be too old to see it fructify." He waved away their rustle of demurral. "It will belong to you, my boys, you and yours. Make certain you're ready."

He spoke casually, as if reminding them of a departing ferry. In the stillness that followed, Dexter heard a rapid, flickering pulse, like a clock run amok. His own pulse, he supposed.

The old man slapped his hands on the table and rose. Lunch was concluded. The room was foggy with smoke. The men shook hands and dispersed into the din of femininity and childhood.

The conversation left Dexter full of unease and a corresponding wish to speed along empty roads toward his home. A light supper of soup and toast, then *Crime Drama*, which they listened to all together, a Sunday ritual. And then sleep: a long, deep, annihilating sleep to compensate for the little he got all week.

He was hunting for Harriet when her younger sister, Bitsy, bolted from the library and flung the door shut, nearly colliding with Dexter as she ran past. Harriet and Regina emerged a moment later, looking shaken.

"She needs to be taken in hand," Regina said. "Poor Henry can't do it."

"She's volunteered to have dates with servicemen," Harriet told Dexter.

"*What?*"

"You know, show them around town," Regina said. "The sort of thing certain kinds of girls are doing at twenty. Not Westchester wives with four children!"

"We must find a way to stop her," Harriet said.

It was strange to hear his wife clucking with her bossy older sister when, for so long, Harriet had been the one clucked about. She looked almost prim in her high-collared dress. It was not a thought he was accustomed to have about his wife.

"To the car," he said.

Tabby, knitting wanly with Olive and Edith, leaped to her feet in eagerness to go. That left the twins, whom no one had seen for hours. Grandchildren joined in a search, tumbling through the house, prying open splotchy-mirrored armoires and peering under beds. "Phil-lip . . . John-Mar-tin . . ." It was entirely possible they were hiding, and Dexter half looked forward to the spanking he would give them if this proved to be the case.

On the top floor, he glanced out a back window at a tanker plying its way south from the Long Island Sound. Again he heard that nervous patter, like a panicked heartbeat. He hadn't imagined it; it was a real sound. Dexter followed it to the front of the house and peered down through a round window at York Avenue.

There were the twins, faces vacant with concentration as they walloped small red balls attached to paddles.

Pat-a-pat-a-pat-a-pat-a-pat-a-pat-a-pat-a-pat-a . . .

They'd been jai-alai-ing all this time.

Despite himself, Dexter smiled.

CHAPTER EIGHT

As he drove toward his own house, the last and largest on a cul-de-sac ending at the sea, Dexter passed a worn-out Dodge coupe, dove gray, parked at the curb. A lone man sat at the wheel. It was not a car he knew.

He didn't so much as turn his head or glance in the rearview mirror, but some part of Dexter recoiled instantly, tense and alert. Strange cars didn't park on this block. Children didn't play on this block. And no man visited Dexter's home without bringing his family.

"What is it?" Harriet asked.

"Not a thing."

Her reply was a single raised eyebrow. She didn't turn, either.

Inside, Dexter went straight to his dressing room, unlocked the cabinet where he kept his gat, slipped it into his ankle holster, and secured the holster to his calf. Then he went back upstairs. The front door-pull would sound shortly, and he wanted to assemble a tableau of familial absorption to illustrate to the caller that this was neither the time nor the place for whatever business he'd brought.

The twins were building with Lincoln Logs on the parlor floor. Dexter settled hastily into an easy chair with the *Journal-American* and its fat sheaf of Sunday comics. "Boys, come here," he said. "I'll read you the funnies."

They approached looking perplexed, and Dexter realized, as they loomed above his chair, that it had been quite a while since he'd read them funnies—possibly over a year. In that time they'd grown much larger, John-Martin especially. Well, it was only until the bell rang. Dexter pulled the boys onto him, and they toppled heavily against his chest, briefly depriving him of breath. It was difficult to hold both boys and the *Journal-American*; impossible to see the funnies once he'd managed it. But Dexter persisted, squinting at *Prince Valiant* through a keyhole between their necks. They began to squirm and snicker, the closed circuit of their hilarity irritating Dexter, as always. He ordered them quiet, then strained for a lively funnies-reading voice for *Bringing Up Father*. The twins went sullen, suffering him and no more. Dexter glanced at the front door, his ire at this interloper for encroaching upon his Sunday compounded by impatience at how long the man was taking to show.

At last the bell rang and Harriet answered, her timing and tone flawless. Dexter had the small satisfaction of presenting exactly the picture he'd wished to. It hardly mattered; even from the threshold, the man's blinkered affect was manifest. The scene of paternal absorption was lost on him.

Dexter released his sons, who dispersed with relief, and went to greet his guest. The man was gaunt, almost skeletal, with an odd stretched-looking face that might have seemed more at home in clown makeup: a wide mouth and crescent-shaped eyes. Dexter placed him instantly.

"What an unfathomable surprise, Mr. Mackey," he said in a tone that anyone who knew him would recognize as a reprimand and a warning. He shook Hugh Mackey's heavy hand. "What could possibly have induced you to come without your wife?"

"She's visiting her mother," Mackey said with effort.

"We'll be having our Sunday supper soon," Dexter said coldly. "I don't suppose you'd like to join us."

Mackey gave him a strained, haunted glance—the look of a man whose desperation had trumped his ability to play along. He was still wearing his hat. "No, no, I can't stay," he said. "I just need a word. I tried to see you in the Manhattan club last week, but they stopped me at the door."

Dexter's only thought was of getting Mackey out of his house. The man's very presence was a defilement—he might as well have been pissing on the parlor floor. "Say, I've promised my daughter a walk on the beach," Dexter managed. "Why don't you join us?"

Mackey regarded him balefully. His mournful rejection of the sleight of hand whereby the shadow world blended with the one everyone could see infuriated Dexter. Maintaining an appearance mattered as much—more—than what was underneath. The deeper things could come and go, but what broke the surface would be lodged in everyone's memory.

He could put Mackey out; send him away like a scalded dog. Judging by the man's woebegone aspect, he expected as much. But who knew what Hugh Mackey would do next. No. A walk was the best solution; get him away from the house. It was nearly sunset.

Dexter left him in the front room with Harriet and went upstairs to knock on Tabby's bedroom door. She was seated at her new vanity, a sixteenth-birthday present. A ring of small electric lightbulbs surrounded its mirror, creating the impression of a Hollywood starlet in her dressing room. What better name for a device that encouraged all the wrong elements of the female personality?

"Tabby," Dexter said brusquely. "Let's take a walk."

"I don't care to, Daddy."

He took a long breath, muzzled his impatience, and crouched beside her chair. Heat from the mirror bulbs magnified the dusty floral scent of the powder she'd received with the vanity: Charles of the Ritz, if he remembered correctly.

"I'm asking a favor," he said. "I need your help."

Her curiosity was a well whose waterline often seemed a long way down. But at the word "help," Dexter heard the splash.

"There's a gentleman here, an associate of mine, who's—who's sore about something. If you come with us to the beach, he won't beef about it."

"Because I'll be there?"

"That's it."

She rose from her vanity and disappeared inside her closet— "dressing room," as she'd taken to calling it. After several minutes she reappeared in a colorful patchwork skirt, cable-knit sweater, and sailor hat. Apparently, she presumed that comeliness would be part of her assignment.

They found Harriet and Hugh Mackey sitting in silence in the parlor, Mackey staring out the windows at the sea. "My daughter, Tabatha," Dexter said, introducing them. Mackey trained upon Tabby a look of exhausted appraisal, as if sizing up a burden he'd no choice but to heft. He could not—would not—play his part.

They left the house and walked along the path toward the beach, Dexter taking care to keep Tabby positioned between himself and Mackey. The sand looked unusually white, almost lunar under the changing sky. Normally, Dexter would have remained on the path, but Tabby went nearer the sea, and he followed her onto the sand.

"Daddy, take off your shoes," she said. "It's not so cold."

She'd slipped off her own, barely more than slippers, and Dexter realized that one of her goals in changing clothes had been to remove her wool stockings so she could go barefoot. It was the beach, after all. Her slender feet glowed a whiter shade of white against the sand, and seeing them sparked in Dexter a wish to take off his oxfords. Then he remembered the ankle holster. "That's all right, Tabs," he said. "I'll leave mine on."

Tabby didn't suggest that Mackey remove his shoes; it was hard to believe, from his weary clown's face, that Mackey had feet.

There was no such thing as silence on a beach; wind, gulls, and splashing waves filled the void of conversation. Ships were visible toward Breezy Point, their lights already snuffed. Dexter began to relax. He sensed Mackey longing for some way to begin, but the obstacle of Tabby prevented him. They walked east, toward the dusk. Tabby skipped a little, which took her a few paces ahead.

Mackey seized his chance. "My position has become quite difficult, Mr. Styles," he said in a high, peevish voice.

"I'm sorry to hear it."

Tabby paused to wait, and Dexter hastened to rejoin her. He could feel Mackey straining to channel the enormity of his discontent into language that would not disturb the placid surface of this beach walk. That effort, at least, he was making.

"I don't see that things can continue this way, Mr. Styles," he began again in a pleasanter tone, this time in full hearing of Tabby.

"I should say not," Dexter rejoined.

"I'm telling you," Mackey said. "They cannot."

Dexter was briefly silenced by this affront. With Tabby there, he'd no choice but to respond in the same affable tone Mackey had used. "I'm afraid it's out of my hands, Mr. Mackey," he said. "You and Mr. Healey must sort this out."

"Mr. Healey and I don't understand each other."

His voice, at once wheedling, injured, and menacing, revolted Dexter. "I've known Mr. Healey for twenty years," he said. "And he's never—not once, in all that time—turned up at my house on a Sunday."

"What else could I do?"

The exchange had an offhand quality, as if they were discussing baseball scores. Dexter moved between his daughter and Mackey and said, in a hard clear tone intended to end the discussion, "I can't help you, Mr. Mackey."

"It might be worth your while to try," Mackey said. "To save yourself trouble later on."

"Trouble?" Dexter asked lightly. Tabby had taken his hand. It felt cool and delicate as a bracelet.

"I know what I know," Mackey said. "But I don't know what other people might say if they knew it, too."

The man's sheepish, hooded eyes were fixed straight ahead, to the east, where darkness was falling. Dexter's ears began to ring. He had an urge to spit into the sand. Through the twilight, he saw the dregs of sunset glittering on the fences of the Coast Guard training station. He understood then what would have to happen.

"I'll see what I can do," he managed to say.

"Why, I'm glad to hear that. I'm—relieved," Mackey said. "Thank you, Mr. Styles."

"Don't mention it." Dexter, too, was relieved. The only difficulty now was finding himself still on the beach with Mackey. Had he foreseen this outcome, he would have handled the matter differently. He never would have involved Tabby.

"Look what I found," she said, holding up a scallop shell. It was pale orange. She positioned it against the sky and examined its ruffled edge in silhouette.

"Say, that's a beauty," Mackey said.

"Let's turn back," Dexter said.

Reversing directions, they confronted wild celebration in the western sky: streaks of gaudy pink like the delayed aftermath of a fireworks show. The sand was pink, too, as if it had absorbed the sunset and was releasing it slowly.

"Son of a gun, would you look at that," Mackey said to the sky. He seemed a different man now that he'd unburdened himself and been reassured.

"Isn't it grand?" Tabby cried.

Dexter tried to move between them. He no longer wished them to speak. But Tabby stuck to Mackey, seeming heartened by his improved spirits.

"Have you children, Mr. Mackey?" she asked.

"I've a daughter, Liza, she's around your age," he said. "She likes Tyrone Power. He's got a new picture coming soon, *The Black Swan*, I promised I'd take her to see. You like Tyrone Power?"

"Sure I do," Tabby said. "And Victor Mature has a new one opening this month, *Seven Days' Leave*. He made it right before he joined the Coast Guard."

Dexter listened as if from a great distance, his eyes on the eerie, festive sky. Mackey's mention of a daughter elicited no pity from him—the opposite. A family man was doubly reckless to have broken rules that everyone in the shadow world knew like a catechism. There were no exceptions. Amazing what trouble men had, believing that. Everyone thought he was the exception.

Mackey was a louse. His family was better off without him, for all the care he'd taken to protect them. Dexter would leave this one to Heels and his boys. His own distance from what would follow made it seem as though it had already happened. It had happened the moment he'd decided it would.

"I've a cousin, Grady, at the Naval Academy," Tabby was saying.

"Ho, college boy. My son is in the army."

"He was supposed to graduate next June, but now it's moved to December. Because the navy needs more officers."

"Why, sure they do, all those boys in the Solomons."

Dexter wanted Tabby away from this terrible, prattling man. The house was still at a maddening distance. Harriet had closed the black-out curtains, and it looked as though nobody lived there.

"Say, you know what I'll do?" Mackey said suddenly to Tabby. "I think I'll take off my shoes, too."

"Oh, yes!" Tabby cried, clapping her hands.

"We need to get back," Dexter muttered, but his daughter and Mackey had formed an alliance he couldn't breach.

Mackey sat down on the sand and rolled up his trouser legs, then unrolled his socks carefully, methodically, as if stalling for time. Tabby grinned at Dexter. She must have thought she'd succeeded brilliantly, for there had been no argument.

In the long minutes Mackey spent unrolling his socks, the pink streaks faded from the sky as if someone had brushed them from a table. What remained was an aquamarine so glassy and pure it looked as though it would chime if you tapped it with a spoon.

"I haven't done this sort of thing enough," Mackey said with a sigh. He looked up at Dexter with his spent clown's face. "Have you, Mr. Styles?"

It wasn't clear what he meant. The shoes? The beach?

"Probably not," Dexter allowed.

Mackey stood, shoes dangling from one hand, the other holding his hat to his head. His big white feet splayed obscenely against the sand. Dexter couldn't look.

"Let's run, Mr. Mackey," Tabby said. "Let's run in the sand."

"Goodness, run?" Mackey asked, and then he laughed—a light, hollow sound that landed in Dexter's ears like a death rattle. "All right, if you say so. We'll run in the sand. Why not?"

And they ran, kicking up sprays of white, sending up a shout as they faded into the twilight.

PART THREE

See the Sea

CHAPTER NINE

It took Anna and her mother both to wrestle Lydia into a floral-print tea dress with a Peter Pan collar and a neckerchief to camouflage her drooping spine. Dressing up for Dr. Deerwood was a matter of tradition and pride—Park Avenue women bought made-to-order dresses at Bergdorf's and $125 shoes at Lieberman's. But Lydia chafed against women's clothing, and her mute resistance to the brassiere and slip and stockings and garters seemed to Anna to express what all of them felt.

Inspired by Nell, Anna had pinned her sister's curls while she slept. Now she combed the golden hair so it fell across Lydia's face peekaboo-style from under a blue beret. "Oh, Anna, that's wonderful," her mother said, dabbing Mille Fleurs behind Lydia's ears. "She looks just like Veronica Lake."

Children from the block played carefully on the sidewalk in their church outfits as Anna walked to Fourth Avenue to hail a taxi. Riding back, she stopped at Mr. Mucciarone's grocery to pick up Silvio, who waited with hair combed and sleeves rolled. Silvio was simpleminded, couldn't even make change at his father's cash register. With a look of devout concentration, he carried Lydia down the six flights from their apartment. Most of his expression resided in his biceps, which trembled above his rolled sleeves as Lydia moaned and kicked. She hated being carried by Silvio. Anna suspected the problem was his smell: oniony, mineral, more pronounced at each turn of the stairs. It was the smell of a sixteen-year-old boy—the only one who had ever held Lydia, or likely would.

The children pecked like pigeons around Silvio's legs when he emerged from the building with Lydia and placed her inside the taxi. Anna had run ahead and installed herself in the backseat to ensure that the cabbie couldn't flee. Her mother anchored Lydia from the other side while the cabbie placed her folded chair in the trunk. A perfect mid-November day. The taxi crossed the Brooklyn Bridge and turned up the East River Drive, and there was Wallabout Bay across the river—ships and smokestacks and hammerhead crane. "Mama, look!" Anna cried. "It's the Naval Yard!"

By the time her mother turned, the Yard was behind them. It didn't matter; she'd little interest in it. She hardly seemed to care about the war, dutiful though she was about saving fat for the butcher and helping to sew blood pressure cuffs. It seemed to Anna that their mother spent her days listening to serials, *Guiding Light, Against the Storm,* and *Young Doctor Malone,* in the company of various neighbors. It was Anna who turned the radio to *The New York Times News Bulletin* at suppertime, eager for news of the U.S. landings in French North Africa. In the week since they'd taken place, the Yard had fizzed with new optimism. Anna had even heard talk of a turning point in the war, the long-awaited second front.

Anna's own nervous excitement had a different origin: Dexter Styles. In the two weeks since she'd encountered the nightclub owner, her imagination had begun tiptoeing into dire, thrilling scenarios. Suppose her father hadn't left home at all. Suppose he'd been obliterated by a hail of gangland bullets, Anna's name on his dying lips like "Rosebud" in *Citizen Kane?* She read an awful lot of Ellery Queens. The winnowing of diffuse danger to a single corrupt soul had always been an inexhaustible pleasure for Anna. Now her own life seemed to have tipped into the world of those mysteries; the long November shadows leaned suggestively, and the sheen of streetlight on Naval Yard brick sent an ominous ripple through her belly. There was dynamism in this new foreboding, a stinging vitality, as if she'd wakened from drugged sleep.

Dr. Deerwood's office was on the first floor of an apartment house on Park Avenue. His waiting room was "Victorian," according to Anna's mother, layered with Oriental carpets and brocade-upholstered sofas. There were gold tassels on the curtains, and the walls were a patchwork of small paintings overwhelmed by heavy frames. Other patients sometimes waited here, crunched or folded into chairs, walking with canes, their resemblance to Lydia familial, as if they were cousins in affliction. Today being Sunday, the room was empty. Anna and her mother sat side by side on a settee, Lydia in her chair. Waiting for Dr. Deerwood, knowing he would come, was the high point for Anna of these biannual visits. Anticipation effervesced under her ribs. *The doctor will come! The doctor will come!*

The whisper of a door, then his voice: "Good day, good day. Welcome, all of you." He was a round man whose waxed white mustache looked better suited to a top hat than a gray medical coat. He greeted Lydia first, gently pushing aside her peekaboo hair. "Hello, Miss Kerrigan," he said. "Lovely to see you again. And the elder Miss Kerrigan," he added, shaking Anna's hand. "And, of course, Mrs. Kerrigan." The whereabouts of Mr. Kerrigan in recent years had never been addressed.

The examination took place in an adjacent room, plainer in decor but comfortably warm. A cascade of pulleys and leather straps occupied one corner, but these were never invoked for Lydia. The doctor lifted her from the wheeled chair and stepped with her onto a scale. Anna, who had been excited by this job as a younger girl, adjusted the weights until the bar was suspended. Then the doctor set Lydia down on a soft examining couch, took her head in his hands, and moved it gently from side to side. She lay still, almost sleepy, while he looked inside her mouth and smelled her breath and listened to her heart and lungs with a stethoscope. He examined her hair and fingernails. He manipulated her body: arms, legs, torso, feet, and hands, which he carefully uncurled to their full size and measured. Lydia would have been taller than Anna by some two inches.

"Is she more restless in the evenings?" he asked. "I'll give you camphor drops that should calm her. Is it harder for her to swallow? Eating can become a trial, I know. I'm impressed that she hasn't lost weight; many of my patients begin to at about this point. Don't be alarmed if she starts to look thinner; that's perfectly natural."

Lydia used to laugh. She used to look out the window. She used to repeat what was said around her in a babbling, nonsensical form. She used to be alert for long periods. One by one, these pleasures and habits had fallen away. Each time another one disappeared, Anna and her mother would adjust to a new state in which they no longer expected that thing—hardly remembered it.

Now, in her awakened state, Anna found herself thinking differently about her sister. Wouldn't listening to love serials all day send anyone into a stupor? What did Lydia have to stay alert *for*?

The examination complete, Dr. Deerwood pulled a chair close to Lydia, making her a part of their colloquy. "I must commend you both," he said to Anna and her mother. "Your efforts continue to bear wondrous fruit."

Tears streaked from their mother's eyes, as they often did at this juncture, although she never cried. "Do you think she's happy?" she asked.

"My goodness, yes. Lydia has been surrounded by love and care the whole of her life. Few people in her position enjoy that luxury, I'm afraid."

Anna had sometimes thought she might be in love with Dr. Deerwood, this magician who could transform their long struggle into something luminous. But today, perhaps because she'd noticed he wore riding boots under his medical coat and she wondered if he kept a horse in Central Park, she found herself thinking, *We're paying him an awful lot of money to tell us we're wonderful.* And then, as if another voice had interposed itself, *Nice work if you can get it.*

"Why is she getting worse?" Anna asked, and felt her mother flinch.

"There is no cure for Lydia's condition," Dr. Deerwood said. "You know that."

"Yes," Anna admitted.

"She is following a course that is natural to her. What we might consider 'better' or 'worse' does not apply to your sister in quite the same way."

"Can we do more with her?" Anna asked. "Take her outdoors more often? She's never even seen the ocean—not once in her whole life."

"Novelty and stimulation are good for everyone, Lydia included," the doctor said. "And sea air is full of minerals."

"Suppose she catches cold," Anna's mother said tightly.

"Well, I wouldn't take her in winter. But a day like today would be fine, if she's properly dressed."

"I'd rather wait until spring."

"Why?" Anna asked her mother. "Why wait?"

"Why rush?"

They stared at each other.

"I would tend to agree with Miss Kerrigan," Dr. Deerwood said gently. "Tempus fugit, after all. Before we know it, we'll be meeting again next May. Why wait?"

Normally, visits to Dr. Deerwood left Anna and her mother swathed in a gauze of well-being that lasted hours—some of the loveliest they spent together. Now they avoided each other's eyes as they pushed Lydia back to Park Avenue. Outside, Anna adjusted her sister's hair while their mother retied the kerchief at her neck.

"Well. The park?" her mother asked.

"Why not the beach?"

"What beach, Anna?"

Anna was incredulous—had her mother not heard a word the doctor had just said? "Coney Island or Brighton Beach! We can hail a taxi."

"It will take forever and cost a fortune," her mother said. "We haven't enough diapers or food. And why this sudden fixation on Lydia seeing the ocean? She can hardly see at all."

"Maybe she hasn't enough to look at."

In the rich autumn light, her mother's face appeared terribly faded—the more so for the bright green feathers she'd sewn onto her hat the night before. "What's gotten into you, Anna?" she asked sadly. "Can't we enjoy our day like we usually do?"

Anna relented. Her mother was right about the food and diapers; it was too much to attempt without more planning. They walked to Central Park, full of mothers with their children and soldiers eating frankfurters carefully, so as not to soil their uniforms with mustard. Anna tried to snatch the pleasures of the day as if she were biting into candies. The huff and snort of horses. The smell of popcorn. Leaves floating from the trees. Lydia fell asleep, her head forward. With her shining hair covering her face, she looked like a girl with trouble in her legs, no more. This vision elicited a more benign pity than what her true condition provoked. Anna could almost hear soldiers murmuring to each other, *What a shame, such a pretty girl.*

But Anna's thoughts strayed stubbornly to the beach and then to Dexter Styles. As they looked down the steps to the Bethesda Fountain, she said, "Do you think Papa will come back?"

It had been a year, easily, since they had mentioned him, but her mother showed no surprise. Perhaps she, too, had been thinking of him. "Yes," she said. "I've a feeling he will."

"Did you look for him? On the piers? Or at the union hall?"

"Of course. You knew it at the time. But the Irish never tell. 'So sorry, Aggie dear, shame of a thing . . .' Those twinkly blue eyes. You've no idea what they're thinking."

"Suppose there was an accident. On the piers."

"Oh, they wouldn't hide that! Widows and orphans are their specialty. It's wives they've trouble with."

"What if—someone hurt him?" Anna's heart accelerated as she said these words. She saw amazement in her mother's face.

"Anna," she said. "He hadn't an enemy ever, in all the years I knew him."

"How can you be sure?"

Her mother seemed to grope for a reply. At last she said, "He left his affairs in perfect order. Cash, bankbooks . . . not a loose end anywhere. People who—who disappear the way you mean, they've no warning."

Anna had lost sight of these facts. Recalling them now, she was gutted by disappointment so profound it made her lean against the balustrade. After a long silence, she said, "Do you think he's far away?"

"I don't think he could be nearby and not be with us."

"Doing what?"

"I've no idea."

"What do you *think*?"

Her mother glanced at her. "I don't think about him, Anna. That's the truth."

"What do you think about?"

A spot of red had appeared on each of her mother's cheeks. She was angry. Anna was, too, and the anger strengthened her, as if she were bracing herself against it.

"You know perfectly well what I think about," her mother said.

Shortly after Silvio carried Lydia back upstairs (always calmer on the return climb), there was a perfunctory knock, and Brianne shoved open the door. She heaved herself onto a chair, gasping from the climb, and flung off her coat, swamping the room with a smell of roses and jasmine tinctured with something medicinal, like witch hazel. Lady of the Lake. For as long as Anna could remember, her aunt had worn that perfume. *No man can resist it,* she liked to say—sardonically, even when it was still somewhat true.

Having caught her breath, she rose and kissed Anna and her mother hello and cocked her head fondly at Lydia. "How's life in the salt mines?" she asked Anna. "Still oiling the machine for our war-mongering president?"

"Well, I'm hoping to sell you a war bond."

"Certainly. When pigs fly."

"We're behind Philadelphia and Charleston. Mama won't let me join the Ten Percent Club."

"She's speaking War," Brianne remarked to Anna's mother, who was feeding Lydia. "I'm afraid I'm unfamiliar with that tongue."

"She'd like to be paid ten percent of her wages in war bonds," her mother said flatly. She and Anna had hardly spoken in hours.

"I'll bet they give you some sort of gewgaw if you buy enough bonds. Eh?" Brianne said. "Tell the truth."

"I signed a scroll that will go to sea on the USS *Iowa*." Anna took pride in saying this, even knowing her aunt would find it silly.

"Listen to her! They've bewitched you, dearie. It wasn't even our war. The Japs played right into Roosevelt's hands—I'd not be surprised if he paid them to do it, the weasel."

"You sound like Father Coughlin," her mother said.

"They should have left Father on the air. And Lindy should have run against Roosevelt and given him the drubbing he deserves."

"Lindbergh supports the war now, Auntie."

"Hah! Knows they'll run him out of town if he speaks his mind."

"Father Coughlin is a rabid dog," her mother said.

"Hitler needs a good spanking is all," Brianne said. "He's a bully in a sandlot, and our boys have to die for that? I don't just mean the soldiers and sailors—how about the boys in the merchant marine? They're all over Sheepshead Bay—they've a new maritime training station there. Food, weapons, blankets, tents—who do you suppose brings all that to the field of battle? Merchant ships are being torpedoed by the dozen, and those boys haven't even proper guns to defend themselves." She'd gone red in the face.

"That's what war bonds are for, Auntie. To give Hitler a spanking."

"Fine. How much?"

"One dollar? Two?"

"Make it five. And when are you going back to college?"

"Thank you, Auntie!"

Brianne unearthed a five-dollar bill from her pocketbook, along with a bottle of Chartreuse. For several years she'd had a "special friend"—a wholesale lobsterman who was flush enough to keep her shopping at Abraham & Straus and buying Chartreuse at ten dollars a pop. But she was ashamed for Anna and her mother to meet him.

Anna exchanged a tentative smile with her mother; Brianne made them feel their likeness to each other. She was forty-seven, stout and raspy, her crimson lipstick a memento of old times like the Cheshire cat's disembodied grin. At seventeen, she'd rechristened herself "Brianne Belaire" and joined the Follies; Anna's mother had come eight years later, but they'd hardly overlapped before Brianne fell out with "Mr. Z." and moved on to more risqué revues: George White's *Scandals* and Earl Carroll's *Vanities*. By her own account, Brianne's life had been one long fever of love affairs, narrow escapes, failed marriages, small parts in seven moving pictures, and various scrapes with the law arising from booze, or nudity onstage. None of it had stuck except the Scotch, she liked to say: an indictment of the world's thin and fickle offerings that not one could compete with the reliable satisfaction of a whiskey soda. Men were the biggest failures: rats, lice, good-for-nothings—you couldn't blame them; they'd been bumly manufactured. The best possible outcome of marriage was a wealthy, childless widowhood. Brianne had managed only to be childless.

She fixed the drinks and slid a glass toward Anna's mother. "Say, isn't it time you had one of these?" she said to Anna. "God knows I was drinking them by nineteen."

"You were married at nineteen," Anna's mother pointed out.

"Divorced!"

"No, thank you, Auntie."

Brianne sighed. "So virtuous. Must be your influence, Agnes."

"We know it wasn't yours."

Anna was tempted sometimes to accept the drink—just to see her aunt and mother react. Her role, so firmly established that she no longer recalled its origins, was to be impervious to the vices around her—*good,* despite everything, in her bones, heart, teeth. The fact that she was not good in the way they thought—hadn't been since age fourteen—should have been easy to forget in their company. But Anna never quite forgot.

Her mother put a hand on her shoulder: a peace offering. Anna touched it with her own. "Let's get her changed and into bed," her mother said.

"Sit down and have your drink, Aggie," Brianne commanded. "Lydia isn't going to run away."

Her mother sat, oddly docile, and they raised their glasses. Across the table, Lydia drooped in her chair. Brianne took no part in her physical care—that was out of her line. Anna guessed her aunt thought it madness to keep Lydia in the apartment in diapers—a grown woman, practically. But if her mother sensed this opinion, she was unperturbed by it.

"Sad story," Brianne said after a first long pull on her drink. "Remember that usher, Milford Wilkins? With the toupee? Who wanted to be an opera singer?"

"Why, sure," Anna's mother said.

"Saw him at the Apollo the other day, taking tickets. Hooked on dope."

"No!"

"The eyes. There's no mistaking it."

"Oh, that's terrible," her mother said. "He'd such a beautiful voice."

"Was he a singing usher?" Anna asked.

"No, but he would sing for us sometimes, after the show," her mother said.

Brianne shook her head, eyes downcast, but Anna could practically hear her rummaging for the next tragic tale about fellow dancers or others they'd known in their Follies years. When fresh mishaps had been exhausted, there were old standbys to fall back on: Olive Thomas, who drank mercury bichloride after a fight with her ne'er-do-well husband, Jack Pickford—Mary Pickford's brother. Allyn King, who jumped from a fifth-story window when she got too fat for her costume. Lillian Lorraine, legendary temptress and longtime mistress of Mr. Z., now a hopeless drunk who still washed up in this or that bar, making a cluck of herself. As a child, Anna had imagined these doomed beauties occupying the same magical sphere as Little Miss Muffet, Queen Guinevere, and Sleeping Beauty. A separate intelligence had revealed itself more slowly: the storied girls had been stars, whereas Brianne and her mother were ordinary chorus girls, whispering in their wakes.

"I went to a nightclub two weeks ago," Anna said. "With a girl from the Naval Yard." She spoke nonchalantly, although she'd been longing for a chance to discuss Dexter Styles with her aunt. "It's called Moonshine. Have you been?"

"It's illegal to enter a nightclub looking like I do," Brianne said. "They'd cuff me at the door."

"Stop it, Auntie."

"It's run by a racketeer, that I do know. The best ones usually are— remember Owney Madden's club, the Silver Slipper? Or El Fay?" She was asking Anna's mother, who had made Lydia her own cocktail of the new camphor drops in warm milk and was helping her drink it.

"With Texas Guinan emceeing the floor show?" Brianne went on. *"Hello Suckers!"* She hove a sigh. "Poor Texas. Dysentery, of all things."

Anna was growing impatient. "What racketeer?"

"Dexter Styles. You ever come across him, Aggie?" her aunt asked. "He's younger than we are."

"I'm younger than you are," Anna's mother reminded her. "By eight years."

"Fine, then. He's your age, more or less. I'd a beau years ago who played trumpet at one of his clubs."

"Dexter Styles," her mother said, and shook her head.

"What does 'racketeer' mean, exactly?" Anna asked.

"Well, it used to mean you moved liquor," Brianne said. "Now that's a government racket."

Anna's mother rose and took the handles of Lydia's chair. "I'll get her to bed," she told Anna. "You do supper."

Her mother had made spare ribs and sauerkraut the night before and left them in the icebox under a towel. Anna turned on the oven and slipped the dish inside, then emptied two cans of green beans into a pan to warm. Speaking softly so her mother wouldn't hear, she asked, "Did Papa know him?"

"Who—Styles? I doubt it."

"They didn't have business together? Something with the union?"

"The union, not a chance. They're all micks, and Styles is a wop."

"But his name. It's—not Italian." Anna felt a curious reluctance to say it.

Brianne laughed. "Styles is a wop, trust me. Or part wop. Names were made to be changed, dearie; haven't I taught you that much? Although here's what a dope I was: I didn't want a mick name, and Brianne is more mick than Kerrigan. That's the one I should have changed!"

"To what?"

"Betty. Sally. Peggy. One of those American names. Anna's not bad, but Ann would be better—better still, Annie."

"Ugh."

"Say, why all these questions?"

Her aunt's shrewd gaze gave an impression of having seen everything in the world at least once; it was purely a matter of recognizing it. Anna turned to check on the ribs. Facing the oven, she said, "I thought I'd heard of him."

"He's in the society columns," Brianne said. "Styles is one of the four hundred, practically. But not really—people just want him to seat them near the picture stars."

Anna's mother returned, having changed into a shift without girdle or stockings. "Who's this?"

"Careful, Aggie. Your daughter's taken an interest in gangsters." Anna's mother laughed. "She does need a vice," Brianne mused. "Beyond warmongering."

Anna tried over dinner to reason through the ferment of her thoughts. Her father had known Dexter Styles—that was a fact. Yet neither her mother nor Brianne had been aware of the acquaintance, nor was there any obvious reason for it. That meant it must have been a secret. Why had they met?

Brianne dredged up a new tale of woe: the great Evelyn Nesbit was reduced to making clay pots in California. "What a comedown," she groaned.

"Suppose she enjoys making clay pots," Anna's mother said.

"Aggie," Brianne said, setting down her drink. "Evelyn Nesbit? The legendary beauty? The reason Harry Thaw murdered Stanford White? A *potter*?"

"It is a surprise." Anna's mother always said just enough to keep Brianne talking; she was the maypole around which Anna's aunt braided the ribbons of her knowledge and gossip and ghoulish revelations.

"Someone must have turned out well," Anna said. "Out of all those girls you danced with."

"Adele Astaire is Lady Cavendish in Scotland now," her mother said. "I imagine that's fun."

"I hear Scotland is cold and dark," Brianne said, sucking a rib. "And the people are odd."

"Well, there's Peggy Hopkins Joyce. Doesn't she get richer with every divorce?"

"Fat and desperate," Brianne said happily. "Almost a prostitute."

"Ruby Keeler married Al Jolson."

"Divorced. Raising brats with a nobody."

Her mother thought a moment while Brianne polished off the sauerkraut. "Say, aren't Marion Davies and Bill Hearst still together?"

"In seclusion. Scandal hanging over them," Brianne fairly sang.

The Lobster King, as her "special friend" was affectionately known, had allowed Brianne to give sums of money to Anna and her mother— if they were to believe her sworn promise that her beau knew and approved of these gifts. Wittingly or not, he had paid Anna's fees at

Brooklyn College and bought Lydia a new chair when she'd outgrown the last. Brianne offered more help than Anna's mother would accept.

"Please bring him to supper," Anna's mother implored while they ate their canned crushed pineapple. "I'll make spare ribs again. Weren't these nice?"

"He's a fisherman," Brianne said, as if that were demurral enough.

"Doesn't 'wholesale' mean he doesn't actually fish?" her mother asked.

"He smells like fish." Brianne had always been sly about her beaus, disappearing with them on yachts and private railway cars and introducing them, years later, as "old friends." "I promise, it's all very ordinary," she said. "Not the den of iniquity this one is picturing." She meant Anna, of course.

"I'm not, Auntie."

"Only because you've no idea what to picture!"

Before getting into bed, Anna lay beside Lydia in hers. From the kitchen, she could dimly hear her mother and aunt discussing Ann Pennington's famous dimpled knees over fresh highballs. ". . . dead broke," she heard her aunt murmur. "Lost everything at the racetrack, poor thing . . ."

"Liddy," Anna said softly. "I'm going to take you to the beach."

In the faint illumination that leaked around the window shade, she saw that her sister's eyes were open. Her lips moved as if to reply.

"We're going to see the sea," Anna whispered.

See the sea the sea the sea the sea

A vibration seemed to flow from inside Lydia, as if she were a radio tuned to a distant frequency. She knew all of Anna's secrets; Anna had dropped them into her ears like coins down a well. It was Lydia she'd turned to when their father first stopped bringing her with him on union business. Anna tried to force him to surrender with arguments and threats of misbehavior, but at night she clung to her sister and wept into her hair. She hated being stranded among the neighborhood children, with nowhere special to go anymore. At twelve, there was little of interest to do; the girls gaggled at the sidelines while the boys played stickball or stoopball or football (the "ball" being a block of wood tied inside newspaper). Anna used the excuse of Lydia to absent herself from these dull proceedings and waited for their father to come to his senses—to recognize that she was indispensable. She pretended not to care. And gradually, over months, then a year, she did care less.

Ringolevio—hide-and-go-seek with prisons and teams—was the one game that still united girls and boys on the block, even into high school. In March of her eighth-grade year, Anna was crouching among barrels of fall apples in someone's cellar when she heard a whisper: "They'll find you there."

It came from inside a storage paddock with high wooden sides. The door was sealed with a padlock, but Anna managed to vault from a barrel over one of its sides onto what felt like a pile of logs but was actually—she knew by touch, it was too dark to see—a heap of rolled carpets.

"Shut up. They're coming."

It was a boy, she realized then. Peeking through a sliver between planks, Anna made out three members of the opposing team. One was Seamus, Lillian's older brother, who was sweet on her. He went to the apple barrels where she'd been, then to the paddock where she was now. He felt the planks, looking for a way in. Anna smelled mothballs from his clothing and Juicy Fruit on his breath—and feared he could smell her, too. She lay rigid with alarm at being discovered with a boy in an enclosed space, fodder for merciless teasing. She had just turned fourteen. When the seekers moved to other parts of the cellar, Anna breathed her relief. A thick silence fell. She waited for the boy to engineer their exit as he had their entrance. But the longer she lay still, the less urgent her departure seemed to be. It was rather nice to lie in the warm dark, hearing the distant thrum of the furnace and the boy breathing beside her.

Eventually, he took her hand. Anna waited, not wanting to overreact; then, not having withdrawn it, she thought it awkward to do so. Was she afraid to have her hand held? Obviously not. The boy's warm grip pulsed around her fingers like a heart. *I might not be here,* Anna thought as he moved her hand to his trousers, where the fabric strained against the buttons. She could withdraw her hand, of course, but she waited, thinking, *This might not be me.* A boozy apple smell mingled with a dusty, wheaty scent from the carpets. As the boy moved her hand, Anna's curiosity about what would happen became knowing what it was and wanting it. Eventually, he convulsed as though he'd touched an electric wire. He curled onto his side and seemed to think that would be the end of it. But there he was wrong, for whatever was at work between them had entered Anna, too. She took his hand and held it against her pleated skirt, moving over his warm fingers until a violent pleasure shuddered through her.

The boy was Leon, she realized then. Perhaps had known all along. "I'll go out first," he said.

They rejoined the game separately. He was sixteen. That would be the end of it, Anna thought. But it was not.

Leon worked for his father carving tombstones after school, but business stank, as everywhere, and often he could get away. Occasionally, Anna would notice him missing from a game he'd been playing outside just moments before, and find him waiting in the paddock. Sometimes she would wait in vain or learn that he had. Once inside it, they moved with the stealthy rapacity of burglars—initially, to repeat the raptures of their first encounter. But soon enough, layers of clothing began to yield to the marvel of bare flesh. Leon stole a feather blanket from his mother's linen chest and spread it over the carpets. After each small advance, Anna promised herself they had done enough; now they would merely repeat. But the greater logic they were yielding to contained an inexorable will to progress. Anna couldn't picture what they were doing: proof of her innocence. Even as she spent her days aching to renew their dark dream, she felt as if it were happening somewhere else, to a different girl. In the dark paddock, she slipped from her life like a pin dropping between floorboards. *I don't know what you mean, I haven't done those things,* she imagined saying, truthfully, to a faceless accuser. *I don't even know what they are.*

There were close calls, inconvenient visits to the cellar by the building landlord; by a washerwoman; by members of the Italian family whose apples were stored in the barrels to make fruit wine. But the very extremity of what they were doing made it relatively easy to conceal; no one would have fathomed it. There had been gropings on the block, kisses stolen and coerced, three boys and two girls in a closet at Michael Fasso's—an interlude no one stopped talking about for weeks. There were sweethearts monitored by wary parents, not left alone for a minute. But planned assignations over months; lying fully naked in the summer heat? It was unthinkable. Had Anna tried to tell Lillian and Stella, they would have thought she was lying or loony. She told only Lydia.

The day she lost her virginity, Anna brought along a ruler. She knew from Stella, who had it from her married sister, that it hurt like the devil. When the pain began, she fastened the ruler in her mouth like a dog and let her molars cut into the wood. She never made a sound.

He knew to pull out, of course. All boys knew that.

At times her secret clanged inside her so loudly that she wanted to cover her ears and scream. Her father would disown her. Anna sensed him watching her with wary attention and feared he might somehow have guessed. But he couldn't *know*. His work consumed him, often taking him away overnight. Occasionally, he tried to talk to Anna in their old way, but she'd lost the habit of talking with her father and no longer wanted to. She felt his disappointment but couldn't help it. He'd disappointed her first.

When he vanished, Anna felt only relief. And a week or two later, when the gravity of his absence began to press upon her in queasy bouts, she went to the paddock with Leon to forget it.

There were rumors at the high school of girls who'd had to depart suddenly to "live with relations." One of these, Loretta Stone, was now a year behind her peers: a chastened solitary girl whose alleged ruin was a succulent dish the other children feasted upon. But Anna was lucky: she was the only one of her friends not to have the curse yet.

In November, eight months after her first visit to the paddock, the landlord brought in a brigade of cousins to dig out that cellar and make way for a saloon—the only way left to make money, he said. They filled sheets of burlap with stones and soil and broken barrels and parts of coal stoves and carried them into the street. Anna watched with the other children who happened to be outdoors. In the unforgiving daylight, she saw a pile of moth-infested carpets crowned by a filthy bloodstained coverlet. She walked into her building, latched herself inside a first-floor toilet, and vomited.

She and Leon were beset by the cringing intimacy of strangers who had appeared in each other's dreams. She noticed his dirty fingernails, the gaps between his teeth. Her father had been gone two months by then, but Anna couldn't shake the feeling that Leon would appall him. They never touched again. Rather, they continued not to know each other, and the following year Leon's father moved the family west.

The saloon was never built.

For the rest of high school and during her year at Brooklyn College, Anna tried to impersonate a girl who knew nothing. How would that girl react when a boy backed her against a wall and tried to kiss her? Would she be frightened when he ran his palms over her breasts through her sweater-blouse? The breadth of her experience was perilous; if boys had an inkling of all she'd done, she would be cast out like Loretta Stone. So much caution made Anna stiff, and boys called her cold, even frigid. "I can see you're scared, but I won't hurt you," said one of her dates. "I just want to give you your first real kiss." But a real kiss, Anna knew, could unleash so much. These encounters often ended with the boy stalking away mad. Long after she'd given up on her father's return, Anna still occasionally invoked him: an abstract witness to her virtue. *See?* she would say. *I'm not a floozy after all.*

But her only real witness, then and now, was Lydia. And her sister could only listen. She could not advise, or answer the questions that troubled Anna most: When would she be allowed to know what she knew? Or when would she have forgotten it?

CHAPTER TEN

The Wednesday morning before Thanksgiving, Dexter waited with Henry Foster under the balding trees of Alton Academy. Boys' voices jingled in the air, although none was in sight. "Sorry for the wait," his brother-in-law said, glancing nervously at his ramshackle wood-frame house on its modest lawn, surrounded by dormitories. "Bitsy has been taking longer than usual with her toilette."

Like most of his Protestant brethren, Henry was constitutionally unable to express feeling. But Dexter saw from his pained expression that things hadn't improved at home. "Don't give it a thought," he said, patting Henry's shoulder while surreptitiously checking his watch. The old man had been quite clear: the Naval Yard commandant must not be kept waiting. "How is the baby?"

"Beautiful little thing," Henry said. "She cries a lot. Bitsy can't bear it." Dexter noticed the schoolmaster's shaking hands.

"It will all come right," he said.

"Do you think so?" Henry's gentle blue eyes fixed upon Dexter with unusual energy, as if he hung on the reply.

"Of course," Dexter said.

At last Bitsy emerged in a getup that—were she Tabby—would have had Dexter marching her back indoors to change. Her low-cut angora sweater and ruffled silk skirt made her look like a stenographer having an affair with the boss, or hoping to. She'd the same russet hair and catlike eyes as Harriet, but Bitsy's fastidiousness had always prevented the sisters from looking alike. Now her hair spilled, unpinned, from under a small hat. Dexter exchanged a look with Henry—poor, prudish Henry—in which he tried both to acknowledge Bitsy's impropriety and reassure him that he couldn't care less. Why should he? They were meeting the old man; let him discipline his daughter if he saw fit.

The bitter musk of Bitsy's perfume half choked Dexter when the Cadillac's doors were shut. As he sped along the parkway trying to make up the time they'd lost, she stupefied him by lighting a cigarette. Were she a man, Dexter would have plucked it from her mouth and flicked it straight out the window. You didn't light up in a man's automobile without permission, certainly not a new Series 62 with cream-colored lambskin upholstery. He shook his head curtly when she offered the packet.

"You've quit?" She sounded disappointed.

"Years ago."

"You disapprove. Henry has spoken to you."

"Not a word."

"I suppose he wouldn't."

"Henry adores you, you know."

"He deserves better," she said, sighing out a cloud of smoke.

"Then why not give it to him?"

Bitsy made no reply. When Dexter glanced at her, he was taken aback to see tears running from her eyes, staining her face with mascara. "Bitsy," he said.

"I've spoiled everything."

"Don't be silly."

"I'm a horrid mother. All I want is to be left alone. I wish I could run away and start over again as someone else."

She began to sob. Dexter heard a trill of hysterics in her weeping and wanted to pull off the parkway and try to calm her. But they hadn't the time. When the crying failed to abate after several minutes, he said sternly, "Listen to me, Bitsy. You must pull yourself together and try to think clearly. You're a marvelous girl; you've the world by the tail. You're just . . ."

She went silent and seemed to listen acutely. Dexter felt her awaiting his diagnosis much as Henry had. The trouble was, he hadn't the first idea what was the matter with Bitsy. ". . . overwrought," he finished disappointingly.

She gave a bitter laugh. "That's what Henry says. You've grown like him, Dexter; I couldn't have dreamed it. You and Hattie both. I suppose you were never as wild as you seemed."

"It doesn't wear well," he said, but her remark had cut him. As he drove, its sting intensified, and he found himself arguing theoretically (while also flooring the gas pedal): a schoolmaster's wife accusing him of insufficient wildness? Had she forgotten whom she was talking to? Christ!

They hardly spoke for the rest of the ride. Bitsy smoked Lucky Strikes—fourteen in all, but who was counting—and restored her face painstakingly with a compact. By the time Dexter parked outside the Naval Yard gate with three minutes to spare, he felt as if he'd smoked a packet himself. He was certain his upholstery had darkened a shade.

Four marines met them at the gate and divided them into touring cars. Dexter lost no time maneuvering Bitsy into a different car from his own. He rode with the old man, who sat in the front seat with Tabby and the marine driver. Tabby's eagerness for this visit, which she'd mentioned excitedly several times, had restored Dexter's faith in her gravitas. Comparisons were a sucker's game, but he thought her every bit as impressive, with her grown-up roll of hair and sober, interested face, as Grady in his dress blues, sitting to Dexter's right in the backseat.

They began at the Naval Yard hospital, where a line of men and girls waited outdoors to give blood. A shipfitter's band played "Remember Pearl Harbor." Dexter scanned the girls, wondering whether he might see the one he'd met at the club a few weeks back, but either she wasn't here or he didn't recall her well enough to pick her out. Next they left the cars to watch a hammerhead crane seize a gun turret the size of a streetcar, swing it over the water, and tweeze it onto the deck of a battleship floating below. Bitsy clung to the arm of George Porter, who had come without Regina, thank God. Let George take over Bitsy duty for a while.

"Graduation in what, three weeks?" Dexter asked Grady as they watched the crane.

"Yes, sir. Three and a half."

"When you 'sir' me, Grades, I think I've an officer standing behind me."

"I keep telling him that," Cooper said giddily.

"Force of habit, s—" Grady stopped himself with a grin. He was tall and beautifully made, an impish sparkle to his wide-set eyes.

"Any idea when you might be shipping out?" Dexter asked.

"The sooner the better," Grady said. "I'm fed up with writing essays on the Punic Wars when we've our own war to fight."

"We're in no hurry to see you go," Cooper drawled, slinging an arm around his son's shoulders, visibly broader than his own. "There will be plenty of war left to fight."

Grady stiffened at his father's touch. "It's what I've been trained to do, Dad," he said.

Building 128, their next stop, was a vast machine shop housing a gristle of pistons and turbines and pulleys all juddering toward some mysterious purpose. Wind tunneled through from the river, whirling a confetti of dry leaves. Tabby was shivering. Dexter hadn't worn a topcoat, but Grady, who carried his grandfather's coat over one arm (the old man being bizarrely impervious to weather), went to Tabby and tucked it around her shoulders. He seemed to linger there an extra moment, holding the coat around Tabby—holding Tabby—and she tipped her face to look up at him, a private smile at her lips. Dexter went very still, eyes on his daughter and nephew, machine sounds bludgeoning his ears. *What am I seeing?* he thought. An image of her Wish Box pin returned to him, lacquered red, a secret curled inside it.

Back in the car, he tried to put the question from his thoughts. Grady was nearly twenty-one, had lived away from home for the better part of seven years, since he'd left for Choate. He was effectively a man, whereas Tabby was a girl of barely sixteen. But they'd been together at Newport last summer, sailing on Cooper's yacht, lounging at the club after tennis. What might have happened between them? Grady was dutiful, yes, but also mischievous—it was all part of his charm. Dexter struggled to pull himself out of this spiral of thought. Kissing cousins was nothing new, so long as kissing was the extent of it.

Was the whole thing a trick of his mind?

Eight hundred girls worked inside Building 4, a structural shop, their last stop. It was hard to separate them from the men—the welders especially, with their thick gloves and face shields. You had to go by stature, and as their group moved from bay to bay, Dexter got better at this. Girls holding blowtorches. Girls cutting metal into pieces; girls building molds of ship parts from wood. A matter-of-factness about even the pretty ones; *look or don't look.* Scarves tied over their hair. Dexter often lamented the softness of modern-day girls, but these dames looked more than capable of packing a revolver. Hell, you could wear a shoulder holster under one of those jumpsuits without anyone the wiser.

"Impressive, eh?" he remarked to Tabby.

She turned, flushed. "What?"

"The girls. Wasn't that what you wanted to see?" he asked pointedly. "Isn't that the reason we're all here today?" But they were empty words. He knew the answer: Tabby's excitement had been to see Grady, not the Naval Yard. It had all been for him.

"I don't remember, Daddy," she said, touching her hair distractedly. "I thought you were the one who wanted to come."

When Anna reached the front of the blood donation line, she heard Deborah, a married whom Rose had nicknamed "the faucet," ask if there was a way to ensure that her blood would go directly to her husband.

"I'm sorry, that isn't possible," the nurse said. "Besides, you may not have the same blood type."

"I have," Deborah wailed. "I'm certain I have."

"Thar she blows," Rose whispered.

"Are you quite sure?" the nurse asked soothingly while inserting the needle into Deborah's arm. "One thing you must never, ever do is give somebody the wrong type of blood. That would be terribly dangerous. Unless his type is AB, which can take any kind. Do you happen to know your husband's blood type?"

Deborah's answer was muffled in sobs. The nurse held her arm deftly as blood twirled from it through a clear plastic tube. The shipfitters' band was playing "Don't Sit Under the Apple Tree."

"Five years of marriage," Rose said softly to Anna. "She'll stop her blubbering, I promise." Rose was twenty-eight, older than most of the marrieds, and had the lush dark curls that everyone envied in Jewish girls. She spoke of her husband with eye rolls and wisecracks and said she was getting more sleep with him gone. She called Melvin, their little boy, "the nuisance," but with such a smitten look that Anna understood she'd no choice but to make light of her feeling.

As Anna watched her own blood coil through the tube, she asked, "Is it supposed to be so red?"

The nurse laughed. "What other color would it be?"

"It's very . . . bright."

"That's the oxygen. You wouldn't want it any other way."

Anna glanced along the row of chairs at identical scarlet skeins spiraling from arms of varying plumpness. She was looking for Nell. Her friend had disappeared without warning the week before. Anna waited beside Building 4 through five straight lunchtimes before going up to the mold loft to inquire. She was embarrassed not to know her friend's last name, but everyone knew who Nell was. Mention of her prompted a crackling silence among the girls that was all too familiar to Anna from her own shop. The snapper said Nell hadn't shown up for work that week. He wasn't expecting her back.

There was nothing terribly surprising in this, but Anna couldn't seem to get over it. Perhaps the bicycle had spoiled her. Now she felt trapped in the Yard's brick alleys, angular sunlight barely clearing the rooftops even at lunchtime. Perhaps it was the dreariness of her own shop now that the marrieds had turned on her. With the exception of Rose, they treated her with bruised politeness, as if their husbands had whispered her name in their sleep. Anna consoled herself with the thought of escaping her shop and becoming a diver. Each evening, she ran to Pier C after work to look for the barge before the light failed. She wanted to ask Mr. Voss about volunteering to dive, but couldn't think how to do it without seeming ungrateful.

When they'd given blood and had their mandatory rest, Anna and Rose boarded a bus back to the Sands Street gate. They were already in street clothes; girls were allowed to leave work for the day after donating blood. They were encouraged to drink fruit juice, and Rose had decided this meant she and Anna should have a glass of wine together over lunch. "It is fruit juice, fair and square," she said.

Anna proposed Sands Street, whose sailor haunts intrigued her, but Rose subscribed to the general view that nice girls could not walk there safely, even in daylight. They took a streetcar to the Hotel St. George, on Henry Street, and rode an elevator to the Bermuda Terrace, which over-looked all of Brooklyn and had dancing at night. They ordered plates of spaghetti—the cheapest item—and a small carafe of red wine. Anna dis-liked the wine she'd tasted at Stella Iovino's, but she sensed that drinking some with Rose might make a different sort of conversation possible. Sure enough, when the waiter topped off their glasses, Rose said, "You must know what the girls are saying. About you and Mr. Voss."

"I guess I can imagine."

"They say he's left his wife and you're the reason why."

"He hasn't any ring."

"He did at first—that's what they say. I never noticed. Is it true, Anna?"

"Of course not."

"I knew it! I told them: 'She isn't that kind of a girl.'"

"I wonder if Mr. Voss knows about the rumors," Anna said.

"He's done everything to cause them!"

"Could they get him in trouble?"

Rose stared at her in a way that made Anna feel both naive and disingenuous. "You're the one who's likely to get in trouble, Anna," she said. "Calling you into his office, sending you on special errands; it won't stop there. He'll expect something in return—I'm surprised it hasn't already come to that. I heard this same story a dozen times when I worked for the telephone company: sooner or later he'll want his reward, and then you'll be in an awful fix. If you turn him down, he'll be sore—he might dismiss you or start some nasty rumors of his own. And if you give in, well. Then you're a different kind of girl."

"How can the rumors hurt me if they aren't true?"

Rose looked shocked. "It doesn't matter whether they're true or not," she said. "If a girl gets a reputation, nice boys won't want her."

"Because they'll think she's sinned?"

"In your words, yes, I suppose. Oh, this is hard to talk about, Anna."

"I'll look the other way." She turned to the windows, where the crowded East River was mute from this height. There was something she wanted to tell Rose, but she couldn't think how to say it without sounding dangerously experienced or hopelessly dimwitted. Mr. Voss wasn't interested in her that way. There was none of that feeling between them; Anna was certain of this.

"If a girl isn't nice, people will think she's trouble," came Rose's soft voice as Anna watched the river. "They'll look at the two of them and think: *He's married trouble.* No self-respecting man will stand for that."

"But practically all the men are away in the service," Anna said. "How will anyone remember who's supposedly nice and not nice when it's all over?"

"A reputation lasts," Rose said. "It follows you. It can interfere when you least expect, and there's no way to erase it. After the war, the world will be small again. Everyone will know everything, just like before."

Their gazes had drifted back together. Anna saw earnestness and effort in Rose's face and felt a deep pull of affection for her. "You mustn't worry," she said. "I already have a nice boy."

"Oh!"

"From my neighborhood," Anna went on. "We went to school together. It's been clear between us for a long time."

"Oh, Anna. You never mentioned him."

It had been years since she'd fabricated a story from whole cloth. It brought a sense of returning to an earlier time when she was questioned more often and had fewer evasions at her disposal. Besides, she thought, looking into Rose's relieved and joyful face, people practically told you the lies they wanted to hear.

"He must be overseas," Rose said, and Anna nodded, on the verge of adding "Navy" when her throat tightened and her eyes inexplicably ached. She fastened them to the single red carnation on their table and watched it smear.

"You're private about him, I can see that," Rose said, taking Anna's hand. "I won't say a word to the other girls."

She excused herself to the ladies', and Anna hastily dabbed at her eyes with her napkin, mystified by that rise of emotion. The wine, it must be.

They waited for a streetcar to Rose's apartment so that Anna could meet little Melvin. During the ride, she thought about Mr. Voss. He'd made a point of singling her out, but not for the reason everyone thought. What was the real reason? As Anna turned this question over, it came to her that the answer made no difference. He wanted something from her. And she wanted something from him.

Lunch was served in the oval dining room of the commandant's quarters, a grand yellow colonial and greenhouse set upon a grassy hill that once must have overlooked a pristine shore and now afforded a lavish vista of churning smokestacks. Sliced lemon in the water pitchers, curls of butter on ice, individual saltcellars: the navy brass knew how to throw a lunch. Arthur Berringer sat at the commandant's right; they'd served together in the Philippines in '02. Every word of their conversation was aimed outward for the edification of the twenty-odd luncheon guests: a smattering of bankers and state officials and a few wives.

"Say, it would be nice to have those islands back again," the old man said with a chuckle. He meant the Philippines.

"Oh, I trust we shall," the commandant said. He was a rear admiral recalled from retirement, voluble and rotund. Dexter noted that his vast new responsibilities hadn't dampened his ability to enjoy a capon.

"General MacArthur rarely takes no for an answer, it's true," the old man rejoined.

Dexter and George Porter exchanged a glance. Both knew that their father-in-law disdained MacArthur, whom he'd been referring to as "Dugout Doug" since the Japs had sent him packing from the Philippines last March.

Tabby and Grady sat across from Dexter, ignoring each other a bit too pointedly. He suspected their feet were intertwined under the table and considered dropping his napkin for a look, like a man in a comedy.

"November has been the Allies' best month yet, thanks in large part to boys like this one," the commandant said, raising his glass to Grady. "We've an encirclement in Stalingrad and landings in North Africa. Our enemies have begun to suffer in earnest: twenty thousand Japs dead on the Kokoda Trail in New Guinea! Malaria, jungle rot . . . that putrid flesh swells so they can't even pull on their boots. They're marching barefoot through the mud."

"Mud is a petri dish for parasites," said George Porter, offering his surgeon's perspective. "Bacteria enters through a tiny opening in the skin, and before you know it, you've dysentery, tapeworm . . ."

Several guests set down their forks, but the old man added with relish, "How about those biting flies in Tobruk? The Krauts are used to forests; they've never seen a desert fly. The bites become infected, and pretty soon they're dragging gangrenous limbs across the sand!"

"Winter in Russia," boomed the commandant, waving for another capon. "The Krauts' frostbitten fingers are snapping off like plaster of paris!"

Mrs. Hart, one of the few ladies present, had gone very white. Sensing the need of a fresh topic, Dexter said, "Say, I was pleased to see so many girls at work in your Naval Yard, Admiral."

"Ah, I'm glad you noticed," the commandant said. "The girls have surpassed our highest expectations. You'd be surprised—I know I was—they actually have some advantages. They're smaller, more limber; they can fit inside spaces the men can't. And housework makes them dexterous, all that knitting and sewing, darning socks, mincing vegetables . . ."

"We treat our girls too gently, that's a fact," declared a dyspeptic-looking man at the far end of the table. "In the Red Army, girls work as medics—they carry the wounded off the battlefields on their backs."

"They fly planes, too," someone said. "Bombers."

"Is that true?" Tabby asked.

The old man chuckled. "Soviet girls have been raised a little differently from you, Tabatha."

"Let's not forget," said the commandant, "the Red Army has a whole division whose job is to stand behind the soldiers and shoot them if they try to desert. These are not gentle people."

"I hope you don't let girls do everything the men do, Admiral," Cooper said.

"Of course not," the commandant said. "Jobs requiring physical strength or sustaining of extreme conditions, those are all off-limits. In the trades the girls are what we call 'helpers'—they assist a man senior to them. And we keep them off the ships."

Bitsy, who hadn't uttered a word so far, suddenly spoke up. "Girls can't go on ships?" she asked. "Is that a rule?"

"Oh yes. We're quite firm about that."

"Girls can't go on ships in a *naval yard*?"

Everyone turned to look at Bitsy. With her high color and wind-blown hair, she looked beautiful, as if her restless unhappiness had amplified some fire in her. Dexter watched the old man, wondering if he would rein her in, but Arthur looked on impassively while the commandant sputtered about close quarters and tight spaces. "You understand," he said more than once, to which his guests—all except Bitsy, who regarded him bitterly—wagged their heads like jack-in-the-boxes.

After bowls of peach melba, the commandant's wife offered a tour of the house, where Commodore Perry had lived a hundred years before. Tabby and Grady accepted, along with several others. Dexter meant to join but changed his mind when Cooper rose; more preening over Grady he could live without. The commandant broke out brandy and cigars, and the talk returned to quashing the Philippine uprising, several guests making an avid audience.

Dexter was logy from the heavy lunch; he wanted to splash cold water on his face. An elderly Negro steward showed him to a powder room that proved occupied; then to a second one farther away, near the kitchen. When that door proved to be locked as well, Dexter told the steward he would wait. He was about to push open a pair of casement doors leading outside to the greenhouse when he heard noises behind him. He moved back to the bathroom door and stood near it, listening. Whispers, groans, sighs—there was no mistaking what was taking place behind that door. His first thought—of his daughter and Grady—made the blood drain from his skull.

"Ohhh . . . ohhhh . . . ohhh . . ."

Rhythmic female moans rose in volume and urgency from inside the bathroom. Dexter lurched away and staggered through the casement doors onto the dry grass. Vertigo made a fun-house riot of the Naval Yard below, and he sagged against the greenhouse, gasping. At last he bent over, elbows on his knees, and let the blood flow back into his head. He'd come close to passing out.

"Daddy?"

He straightened up hastily, blinking. Tabby's voice had come from above, and he threw back his head to look up. There she was, waving from a window at the uppermost part of the house. The intensity of Dexter's relief induced a fresh wave of faintness. His knees felt watery. Something must be wrong with him to have thought such a hideous thing.

"Daddy, what's the matter?"

"Nothing," he called weakly. "I'm right as rain."

"Come look. The view goes all the way 'round."

"I shall," he cried, and bounded back inside at the same moment that the bathroom door opened and George Porter emerged half-smiling, adjusting his waistcoat with hands still damp from washing. He looked as startled as Dexter was. Hastily George shut the bathroom door, the woman presumably still inside. Dexter suddenly knew that it was Bitsy—as if he'd recognized the timbre of her hysterics in those moans he'd heard through the door. His violent astonishment was impossible to hide, and George saw it. He smiled uneasily and Dexter smiled back, straining for the hale neutrality he'd always brought to his brother-in-law's indiscretions. As they walked in silence toward the dining room, Dexter felt a need to say something to blunt the appalling thing he'd witnessed. Nothing came to mind.

They sat apart. A while later Bitsy reappeared, looking peaceful for the first time all day. She sat beside her father and put her arm around him, resting her cheek on the old man's shoulder. Gradually, Dexter's woozy relief over Tabby's innocence yielded to foreboding. For George to betray their father-in-law in this way—to compromise the eldest and youngest daughters right under his nose, in the home of an admiral who'd made him the guest of honor—was a transgression so egregious that it seemed to imperil all of them. What would happen if Arthur Berringer found out? How would he not find out, when he'd known of the North African landings weeks before they took place? And the thought came to Dexter that George Porter was a dead man.

But he was mixing up his realms. Only in the shadow world did men die for such things. Not in the old man's sphere—except perhaps metaphorically. Yet Dexter couldn't shake the sense of a menace near at hand. He remembered the moans he'd heard through the bathroom door. To his shame and confusion, their cadence aroused him now, and he found himself calling it to mind again and again: a pleasure so explosive, so transporting, that it justified even the risk of annihilation.

Dexter knew the danger of chasing a forbidden pleasure. A woman on a train to St. Louis had taught him, which was to say that he hadn't learned it yet eight years ago, when she tapped very lightly on the door to his first-class sleeper after midnight. They had noticed each other in the dining car, exchanged a few words in the corridor. She wore a wedding ring (as did he) and a small gold cross at her neck, but a current of wayward sensuality had been unmistakable in her, making these symbols seem apotropaic. Her nocturnal visit launched an interval of debauchery that extended into the following day—fused in Dexter's memory with the frozen farmland slipping past outside the parted window curtains. Even now, driving in January through New Jersey or Long Island, he often found himself stirred by the flickering vanishing points of the frosted fields.

They disembarked that afternoon in Angel, Indiana, intending— what? Intending to continue. They checked into a grand old hotel near the station as Mr. and Mrs. Jones. Immediately, Dexter felt a change: now that the bleak winter landscape was all around him, rather than sliding picturesquely past, he liked it less. Other irritants followed: a sudden dislike of her perfume; a sudden dislike of her laugh, the dry pork chop he was served in the hotel restaurant, a cobweb dangling from the light fixture above the bed. After making love, she fell into a torporous sleep. But Dexter lay awake, listening to the howling dogs, or was it wolves, wind clattering the loose windowpanes. Everything he knew seemed irrevocably distant: Harriet, his children, the business he'd been charged to transact for Mr. Q.—too far gone for him ever to reclaim them. He felt how easily a man's life could slip away, separated from him by thousands of miles of empty space.

In the shorn light of predawn, he dressed, buckled his suitcase, and quietly closed the door to the hotel room. He walked to the station under drooping telephone lines and swinging traffic lights and bought a ticket for the next train. It was going the wrong direction, toward Cincinnati, but he got on anyway. He'd left a twenty-dollar bill on the bureau, a move he regretted by the time he reached the street and regretted still when he thought of it. She wasn't a prostitute. She was someone like him.

When he'd arrived in St. Louis, nearly two days late, he found urgent telegrams from Harriet: Phillip had nearly died from appendicitis. Mr. Q.'s associate had come and gone without finding him; the trip was in vain. Dexter pleaded a sudden high fever: hallucinations on the train, unconsciousness, removal to a hospital. It was the sort of story you might get away with once in your life, at long distance, if no one had any reason to doubt you. In fact, he reflected later, it wasn't far from the truth.

Marines in touring cars waited in the circular driveway of the commandant's residence to ferry guests back to the gate ahead of the shift change. Ships bore down blankly from the piers. Bitsy had decided to spend the night at Sutton Place, meaning that Dexter was free of her, thank God. Of course, George and Regina lived just a few doors down from the old man—that would be convenient. *You've grown like Henry,* Bitsy had said. Perhaps he had.

Tabby wanted to go to Sutton Place and bake for tomorrow's Thanksgiving feast. Dexter readily agreed and kissed her goodbye. Her flirtation with Grady seemed so innocent now—wholesome, compared with what he'd just witnessed—that he felt a kind of fondness for it.

Standing alone outside the Sands Street gate, Dexter had a need to unburden himself. He decided to telephone Harriet before driving to the club, and ducked inside Richard's Bar and Grill, on the corner. A sailor was feeding nickels into the telephone, pleading for a date. Dexter fidgeted, looking out through a window. All at once, a mass of humanity surged from the gates: thousands of men in work clothes and the occasional girl in a dress thronging Sands Street like fans leaving Ebbets Field after a game. Dexter watched invisibly, envying their camaraderie. They were working on the war. An awareness of this fact was visible in the loose, easy way they walked. Perhaps they sensed the shimmering future the old man had described at lunch, felt their part in it.

As quickly as the crowd had amassed, it scattered. The sailor was gone, the telephone liberated. But Dexter's wish to speak with his wife had passed. Harriet had a cool head—back in his rum-running days, she'd crouched in his automobile giggling through exchanges of gunfire. But telling her about Bitsy and George would force her to keep a monstrous secret or spill its poison. No. Telling Harriet was exactly the wrong thing—what in Christ had he been thinking? Tell no one. Let the affair run its course and hope it ended soon, without excess cuts or bruises on either side. Dexter was well accustomed to keeping secrets.

Dusk was falling when he left the bar. As he approached his car, a familiar girl passed on the sidewalk, walking quickly in the other direction. "Miss Feeney," he called after her. It was the girl he'd been looking for, the one who had told him about the Naval Yard in the first place.

She spun around, looking spooked.

"Dexter Styles," he said. "Are you going to work?"

"No," she said, smiling at last. "I gave blood and left early."

"Can I drive you home?" He was eager for the company.

Anna looked up at Dexter Styles. She'd thought of him so often since their last meeting that he seemed eerily familiar, imbued with dark significance. He stood beside his gangster's car.

"Thanks just the same. I need to speak with my supervisor," she said, grateful for an excuse that also happened to be true. She was going to ask Mr. Voss about volunteering to dive. She'd been waiting for the shift change.

"Don't mention it. Good evening, Miss Feeney."

As he tipped his hat, Anna was impelled by a sudden, visceral wish to keep him in her sights. "Would it be possible," she blurted, "to accept your offer at another time?"

Dexter nearly groaned aloud. Being in possession of a healthy automobile he insisted on driving himself meant that he often was called into service nowadays. He'd driven a neighbor's boy with toothache to a dentist; taken Heels to an all-night pharmacy when his mother needed blood pressure pills. Once a request had been made he found it difficult to refuse; he needed to feint at an earlier point. "Why, certainly, I'd be happy to if we meet again," he said, preparing to open his door.

"My sister isn't well. I've promised to take her to the beach."

"Best wait until spring, if she's sickly."

"Not ill. Crippled. There's a boy who carries her downstairs."

Cripple. Boy. Stairs. Dexter felt the elements of this dreary tale falling around him like stones. Miss Feeney wore a plain wool coat, frayed at the cuffs. It was a weakness in him, this awareness of others' misfortunes.

"When were you hoping to do this?" he asked heavily.

"Sunday. Any Sunday. I've that day off." Her mother had been spending Sundays out, leaving Anna on her own with Lydia.

Dexter's mind was already working: if they helped the cripple in lieu of church, he could avoid the new deacon (now hitting him up for pew repairs) and still be done in time for lunch. And helping a cripple might be just the thing to remind his spoiled children of their own good luck.

"How about this Sunday?" he said. "Before winter sets in."

"Perfect!" she said. "We haven't a telephone, but if you'll tell me what time, I can have the boy ready to carry her down."

"Miss Feeney," he said chidingly, and waited.

She looked up at him, but his silhouette blocked the streetlamp, leaving his face in shadow.

"Do I look like I need a boy to carry her down?"

CHAPTER ELEVEN

"You're interested," Lieutenant Axel said, gazing up at Anna as she stood before his desk. He'd not risen when the marine had shown her into his office.

"Yes, sir," she said. "Extremely interested."

"And what gave you the impression that diving would be *interesting*?"

She hesitated, not entirely sure. "I've watched divers on the barge," she said. "From Pier C. At lunchtime. And after my shift." She followed each utterance with a pause, awaiting some indication that he had understood.

"You've watched the divers at lunchtime," he finally said.

As this was not a question, and as her words, reverberated through Lieutenant Axel, had a way of sounding ridiculous, Anna remained quiet. In that silence, she became aware that she was looking down at the lieutenant. Perhaps he felt this, too, for he rose suddenly to his feet: a petite barrel-chested man in naval uniform, his face both weather-beaten and strangely boyish, with no suggestion of a beard. "If you don't mind my asking, Miss Kerrigan, whose idea was this?"

"Mine," she said. "Entirely mine."

"Entirely yours. But entirely your idea didn't get the commandant to telephone me yesterday and ask me to see you."

"My supervisor, Mr. Voss—"

"Ah. Your supervisor. Mr. . . . . Voss." He drew out the name as though its syllables were the last bits of meat he was sucking from a bone. Then he grinned. "I imagine he's just as eager to please you as you are to please him."

The mockery blindsided Anna, but the crude power of the insult expressed itself more slowly, like a burn. It made the lieutenant seem unhinged. She noticed an unnatural hush quivering around them in the small building, and wondered if he was performing for a hidden audience.

Coldly, she said, "Is there a test you give people to see if they can dive?"

"No test. Just the dress. Let's try it on for size."

"On me?"

"No, on that Eskimo over there."

Mr. Voss had tried to dissuade her from coming. "They don't want you," he'd said after telephoning the commandant. "I'm afraid it won't be pleasant." Anna had assumed, stupidly, that he didn't want to lose her.

She followed the lieutenant down a hallway pocked with doors suggestively canted, and then outside. Building 569 was wedged against a perimeter wall to the west of the building ways, part of the Yard she hadn't seen, even on the bike. The Edison plant was directly overhead, its five stacks disgorging wet-looking smoke.

Lieutenant Axel led the way to a bench at the top of the West Street Pier, where a diving suit lay folded. Its bulk and stiffness made it appear sentient, like a person doubled over. Anna quickened at the sight of it.

"Mr. Greer and Mr. Katz will be your tenders," Lieutenant Axel said, indicating two men who idled nearby with marked nonchalance, having likely dashed from their eavesdropping posts just moments ahead of the lieutenant. "Gentlemen, Miss Kerrigan is *interested* in diving. Please get her dressed."

The directive sounded perfectly straightforward, yet something about the terms—tenders, dress—made Anna wonder whether they were genuine or coined purely to confuse her. She was relieved when Lieutenant Axel went back indoors.

"We'll put the dress right over what you're wearing now, dear," said the man called Greer. He was slight and weak-chinned, with thinning hair and a wedding band. "Just take off your shoes."

The other man, Katz, had a swaggering aspect. "Is this a one?" he asked as they held up the diving suit in front of Anna, now in her stocking feet. "What do you know, Greer? She wears the same size as you."

Greer rolled his eyes. The rubberized canvas gave off a grainy smell tinged with an earthen sourness that made Anna think of her grandparents' farm in Minnesota. She stepped through the wide black rubber collar and pushed her feet along the stiff legs into socklike shapes at the bottoms. She had to hold on to the men in order to do this, an awkward business that Katz and Greer seemed to take as a matter of course. They hoisted the rubber collar over her torso and shoulders, and she shimmied her arms through the sleeves, which ended in attached three-fingered gloves. They buckled narrow leather straps around her wrists.

"Straps should be tighter," Katz remarked. "Her wrists are so small the gloves might still blow off. Although you seem to manage, Greer, with those ladylike hands of yours."

"Mr. Katz is proud of his stature," Greer told Anna conspiratorially. "Makes him feel better about being 4-F."

Anna was horrified, but Katz faltered only briefly. "Greer likes to mention that. He envies my chin."

"Even with the chin, he can't find a girl who'll marry him," Greer retorted.

"If you saw how henpecked Greer is, you'd know why I'm taking my time."

Anna tried to look cheerful amid this volley of insults, but the men hardly seemed to notice. They were behind her, pulling tight the laces that ran along the back of each canvas leg. "Why are you 4-F, by the way?" Greer asked Katz.

"Busted eardrum. Teacher boxed my ears in the second grade."

"Talked too much then, too, eh?"

"That's awful," Anna said, but sensed immediately that she shouldn't have spoken. For the first time, Katz looked ashamed. "It's an advantage for diving," he said after a moment. "No pressure on that side."

They guided Anna's feet into "shoes": blocks of wood and metal and leather. There was an intimacy to their utilitarian touch; Katz actually went on his hands and knees to fasten buckles over one of the laced shoes. "The shoes weigh thirty-five pounds," he told Anna. "The whole dress weighs two hundred. How much do you weigh?"

"No wonder you can't get a girl," Greer muttered, shaking his head.

"Half that, I'm guessing," Katz went on, ignoring his partner. "Give you an idea, I weigh two forty, and I can barely walk in the dress."

"You've rotten balance," Greer said. "Must be that eardrum."

"I weigh well over a hundred pounds, actually," Anna said, but it sounded fussy, and again she regretted speaking. She was sitting down. The men lifted a copper breastplate over her head, its sharp edges digging into the soft tissue between her shoulders and neck.

"Uh-oh," Greer said. "We didn't give her . . ."

An evil grin glittered on Katz's face. "What's that?"

"You know . . ." Greer pinkened to his receding hairline. "Come on, Katz. Have a heart."

"Oh, the *pussy cushion*," Katz said at last. "You're right, we forgot. That's a special kind of pillow"—he spoke toward Anna without actually meeting her eyes—"that blunts those sharp collar edges. You'll want it when we get the hat on; the two together weigh fifty-six pounds."

Anna had no intention of asking for a pussy cushion—certainly not by name. Greer's scalp had gone scarlet. Now the men began wrestling the rubber collar of the canvas dress over the breastplate, threading a series of holes in the rubber over long copper studs. When each rubber hole had a stud through it, they slipped copper clamps over these studs and anchored them in place with wing nuts. They used T wrenches to tighten the nuts, Greer in front of Anna, Katz behind, calling out to each other as they moved around the collar until the rubber made a tight seal between copper and canvas.

"Now the belt," Katz said with a smile. "Eighty-four pounds."

The belt had blocks of lead attached. They draped it around Anna's hips while she was sitting down and buckled it against her back. Then they crossed two leather straps at her chest and lifted them over her shoulders. "Stand up and lean over so we can jock you up," Katz said.

Rising was harder now, with the breastplate and belt weighing her down. She leaned over, aware of straps passing between her legs and jerking up at her groin. She'd no idea if this was the usual way or some humiliating adjustment concocted just for her. Greer hadn't met her eyes since invoking the pussy cushion.

"Take a seat," Katz said. "It's time for the hat."

The "hat" was the spherical brass helmet, which at close range looked more like plumbing or a piece of machinery than something a human being would wear. Anna felt a thrill of disbelief when Katz and Greer each took half and lifted it over her head. Then she was inside, encased in a humid metallic smell that was almost a taste. They screwed the base of the helmet into the breastplate like a lightbulb fitting a socket. A crushing weight bore down upon Anna through the collar's sharp edges. She writhed under it, trying to move away or unseat it. There were two raps on top of the helmet, and the round front window popped open, admitting a shock of cool air. Greer was there. "You must tell us if you feel faint," he said.

"I feel fine," she said.

"Stand up," Katz said.

She tried to stand, but the breastplate and helmet and leaden belt fused her to the bench. The only way to rise was to force her weight against those two spots where the collar cleaved her shoulders. Anna did this with a sensation of nails being pounded into her flesh. The pain made her eyes swim, and the weight threatened to buckle her knees, but she heaved herself upright, each instant bringing a fresh negotiation over whether she would be able to bear the weight another second. Yes. And yes. Yes again. Yes, yes, yes.

Katz peered through the faceplate opening. She noticed a thin white scar bisecting his right upper lip and felt an itch of hatred for him that partook of the vicious pain in her shoulders. Katz was enjoying this. "Walk," he said.

"She'll faint."

"Let her."

"I don't faint," Anna said. "I've never fainted in my life."

Balancing the helmet's weight on those two ravaged points of pain, she took a step, dragging a shoe over the bricks as if she were manacled in chains. Then another step. Sweat crawled over her scalp. Two hundred pounds. The hat and collar weighed fifty-six, the shoes thirty-five, the belt eighty-four. Or was each shoe thirty-five, making a total of seventy?

Another step. And then another. Sliding the shoes with no idea where she was going or why. Pain had wiped away those facts.

Someone pressed an object into her three-fingered gloves. "Untie that."

"While I'm walking?" she shouted.

Greer appeared in front of the face opening. "You can stop walking," he said gently. He looked worried; she supposed her expression must be contorted. Anna raised the object to where she could see it: a rope, elaborately knotted. She rearranged her hands in the three-fingered gloves—pinkie and ring fingers in one slot, pointer and index in a second, thumbs in the third—and pushed against the knot with all ten fingertips. Through the hot, slightly damp insides of the gloves, her fingers explored its contours, and the pain in her shoulders felt suddenly at a remove. There was an area in every knot that would yield when you pushed on it hard and long enough. Anna closed her eyes, her hands delivering her to a purely tactile realm that seemed to exist outside the rest of life. It was like pushing through a wall to find a hidden chamber just beyond it. She felt the knot's weakness, like the faint, incipient bruise on an apple, and dug her fingers in. Loosening a knot always seemed impossible until it was inevitable; Anna knew this from years of rat's nests and cat's cradles, shoelaces, jumping ropes, slingshots—things children on the block had always brought her to unscramble. The knot made a last clutching effort to preserve itself, its reluctance to yield making it seem almost alive. Then it surrendered, the cords loose in her hands.

She held them out and someone took them. Katz looked in through the window. Anna expected hostility, but he spoke with evident wonder. "Well done." More surprising than his palpable admiration was Anna's swoon of pride; she hadn't wanted to defeat Katz after all, it seemed, but to impress him.

They unscrewed the helmet and lifted it from her shoulders, followed by the belt and breastplate. Released from their weight, Anna felt as if she were floating, even flying. Her buoyancy infected the tenders, as if her success belonged to them, too—or placed her in a category nearer their own. They helped her from the shoes and belt and dress in the same high spirits they'd started out with, except that those high spirits had been at her expense, and these included her. Soon she was standing on the pier in her jumpsuit, as before. It had gone dark without her noticing.

"You want to tell him?" Greer asked Katz.

"You think he'll blame us?"

"He'll blame someone."

"You do it," Katz said. "He likes you better."

"Most people do," Greer said with a wink at Anna.

Lieutenant Axel listened wincingly to Greer's account of Anna's achievements, then dismissed him curtly from the office. Greer tipped his cap at Anna, making her part of a conspiracy.

"Have a seat, Miss Kerrigan," the lieutenant said.

Anna's soaring lightness made it hard to keep from smiling, but she mastered the urge, determined not to seem smug. The lieutenant watched her a long moment, drumming his fingers on his desk. "You wore the dress," he said, using a conciliatory tone that alarmed her. "But that isn't the same as diving."

"You said that was the test."

He took a long, patient breath. "It is enormously taxing for the human body to perform underwater," he said. "I understand that may be hard to believe; you see the pretty waves, the nice sea foam. You like to swim. But it isn't like that underneath. Water is heavy. The pressure of that weight is something ferocious. We've no idea how the female body would react."

"Let me try," she said, her mouth suddenly dry.

"You're a strong girl, Miss Kerrigan, you've proved that. But in good conscience, I can't let you go down there any more than I would my own daughter."

He was protective, sympathetic, sorry—unrecognizable as the snide man who had greeted her. Anna liked the first one better. With him, it seemed, she'd had a chance.

"Let me try," she said again. "If I fail, then we'll know."

"Have you ever seen a man with the bends?" the lieutenant asked, leaning forward as if to share an intimacy. "The nitrogen bubbles trapped in his blood must find a way out, so they push through the soft tissues. Men bleed from their eyes and nose and ears. Or the squeeze? The entire diver—I mean to say a whole man—is squashed by the ocean's pressure into just that helmet you wore. So when you say, *If I fail,* failing underneath fifty feet of water ain't the same as failing topside."

"Those things could happen to anyone who makes a mistake," Anna said. "Not just a girl." But she felt snuffed by a sense of foregone failure.

The lieutenant smiled: white teeth, tanned, beardless skin. "I like you, Miss Kerrigan," he said. "You're full of spirit. My advice is, go back to your shop—whatever it is you do here at the Yard—and give that work everything you have. Help us win this war so we're not eating Wiener schnitzel and dried octopus for Sunday dinner when it's over."

He slapped the desk, apparently believing this to be the last word. But Anna couldn't seem to move. She was so close. She had untied the knot! Time seemed to elongate, allowing her to consider every possible course and know its result. Anger would revolt him; tears would prompt sympathy but prove her weak; flirtation would put her back where she'd started.

He was waiting for her to go.

"Lieutenant Axel," she said at last in a flat, neutral voice. "Everything you've asked me to do, I've done. How can you turn me away? There's no basis for it."

"Since we're speaking frankly, Miss Kerrigan, I'll tell you that there was never any chance of your diving." Gone was the avuncular cajoler. Now he spoke in a plain, unvarnished manner much like Anna's own. "Your Mr. Voss must be blind with love if he thought I'd put a girl underwater. I told the commandant when he telephoned that it was out of the question. Said I'd put you in the dress and give you a chance to see for yourself."

"But I wore the dress," Anna said. "And I walked. And I untied the knot."

"You surprised me, I'll admit that," he said. "But your diving was never a possibility, so it isn't one now. I'm sorry; I can well imagine that this is frustrating. But those are the facts."

They regarded each other across the desk in a state of perfect understanding. Anna rose from her chair.

She found herself back outside Building 569 with no memory of having put on her coat or whether she'd seen Katz and Greer again on her way out. In the dark, she began the long walk back to the Sands Street gate. Cold wind scrubbed away the memory of the dizzy pleasure she'd felt at her victory. She passed the building ways, clusters of artificial light exaggerating the dead ships' hulls within.

The answer was no.

Never in her life had Anna been obstructed by such naked prejudice. *Those are the facts,* the lieutenant had said, but there weren't any.

As Anna walked, her disappointment and wretchedness hardened into a stony opposition that partook of the hatred she'd felt earlier for Katz. The lieutenant wouldn't break her; she would break him. He was her enemy. It seemed to Anna now that she had always wanted one.

She imagined the knot in her hands, the clenched aliveness of it. There was always a weakness, it was just a matter of finding it.

Those are the facts.

There were no facts. There was just him. One man. And not even a beard.

CHAPTER TWELVE

In the four days that passed between agreeing to chauffeur Miss Feeney's crippled sister to the beach and the appointed Sunday morning, Dexter's minimal enthusiasm for the adventure dissipated entirely. His children would not be there. At Thanksgiving dinner, Beth Berringer had unveiled a plan for the entire family to attend church at Saint Monica's, on York Avenue, as a prelude to volunteering with Bundles for Britain. Bundles was the project of a Park Avenue girl; Dexter dismissed it as society dressed up as war work. There was a lot of that going around.

The old man seemed as eager as he to dodge the proceedings, and invited Dexter instead to lunch and billiards at the Knickerbocker. This was a tempting offer, for both the gorgeous mural at the bar and the aghast looks of the Puritans who recognized him. Had Miss Feeney a telephone, he'd have deferred the appointment as a first step toward making it vanish. But she hadn't one, and with the holiday, a letter might not arrive in time. The only way out would be not to show up at all, and whatever Dexter might be, he wasn't a heel. So he told his father-in-law that he'd promised to drive an employee's crippled sister to the beach that morning, and vowed to join him at the club as soon as he'd finished.

Therefore: No Tabby. No twins or Harriet. A mild day, unseasonably warm for the end of November, eliminating foul weather as an excuse. Miss Feeney's street looked much as he'd expected, children buzzing around the Cadillac even before he'd parked it. They wouldn't have seen a Series 62 very often, if ever. Stepping from his automobile, Dexter anchored his hat and tipped back his head, squinting into the glare. A waving hand in an upper window banished his last hope: that Miss Feeney herself might have forgotten.

He pushed through a squeaky front door into a vestibule still fragrant with Friday's fish. Everything about the place was familiar; above all, the echoey clatter of his footsteps in the stairwell. Christ, how many floors were there? Barbaric to have a cripple living all the way up.

The apartment was small, crowded, close. Femininity breathed from every surface down to the cheap wainscoting. Perfume, women's hair, fingernails, their monthly time—all of it enclosed him in a gamy, intimate cloud that made his head swim. It was almost a surprise to find Miss Feeney, with her arched eyebrows and man's handshake, standing in this female miasma. She seemed to have nothing to do with it.

She led him past the gloomy kitchen to the front room, where every pretty thing her family had managed to hold on to through the Depression was on display. There wasn't much. A stained glass aureole of Saint Patrick banishing snakes, a feathered fan pinned to the wall beside a calendar of the Dionne quintuplets. Several empty rectangles where pictures had been removed from hooks. He nearly asked why, but the answer arrived in that feminine cloud: there was no man here. Dead or gone away. Likely the latter, judging by those empty patches on the walls. Everyone liked to remember the dead.

Shouts of children from the street mingled with the ticking of an old clock, gold angels at its base, the time off by twenty minutes. The treasure of the house: the thing that everyone would lunge for in a fire. Like his mother's bell. "Check for me my bell," she would say, and Dexter would run to fetch it, holding the clapper. She'd brought it with her from Poland, and its silver stream of sound evoked her descriptions of girlhood: churches, snowdrifts, skating on ice-covered ponds in the dark. Warm bread pulled from howling red ovens. He

was not accustomed to thinking of his mother. The familiar apartment, the sound of his footsteps in the stairwell, had done it. Or perhaps the presence of an invalid.

"Where is your sister?" he asked.

She led him into a room barely large enough to hold two narrow
beds. The shade was drawn on the single window. A beautiful girl lay
splayed on one of the beds in what appeared to be an erotic faint, pale
curls scattered in the half-light like spilled coins. The vision discon-
certed Dexter. He moved closer, blinking to dispel it, and saw that her
face was like that of someone very frightened or in a death throe. Her
limbs jerked as he watched: a lack of control that was permanent. She
wore a blue velvet dress and wool stockings and appeared to be asleep.
Dexter imagined the effort that must have gone into dressing her and
was relieved he'd fulfilled his promise to show.

"She looks . . . well," he said, feeling that some remark was expected.

"Doesn't she?" The sister gazed with such love and pride at the
malformed creature before them that Dexter doubted himself for
blundering into this family's pain. But then it hadn't been his choice.
She had engineered it.

"So. What next?" he asked, eager to be moving again.

"I'll get our coats."

He nearly followed her from the room, so reluctant was he to be
left alone with the cripple. He went to the window and lifted the
shade to check on the Cadillac. Then he glanced at the bed, reassured to find the prone girl's eyes still shut. He thought of the father,
Feeney, having to look upon this daughter day after day. The agony
of it. A whisper of what might have been in that beautiful hair. Was
that why he'd gone—if he'd gone? Dexter liked the Irish, was drawn
to them, although time and again they had proved untrustworthy. It
wasn't duplicity so much as a constitutional weakness that might have
been the booze or might have been what drove them to it. You wanted
a mick to help you dream up schemes, but in the end you needed a
wop or a Jew or a Polack to bring them off.

Miss Feeney returned, leaned over the bed, and shimmied her sister's crimped limbs into a smartly trimmed navy blue wool coat. Her expertise left no doubt as to how much time she'd spent caring for her. All her life, Dexter guessed.

He scooped the cripple from the bed and hefted her into his arms. Only when her smell reached him did he realize he'd been dreading it, expecting that rank odor of bodies in rooms without much air. But she smelled fresh, wonderful, even, that version of flowers that inheres in feminine creams and shampoos. She smelled like a girl who had bathed that very morning, pointing toes from the suds to shave her legs smooth. He shielded her head from the doorframe and angled her into the front room, her golden hair dousing his sleeves.

"What is her name?" he asked.

"I'm sorry, it's Lydia. Lydia, this is Mr. Styles. He's kindly offered to take us to the beach."

Not exactly, Dexter thought, permitting himself a wry smile as he followed her to the front door, carrying her sister. When he looked back down at Lydia, her eyes had opened and were fixed upon his face. The engagement startled him physically, as if a pair of hands had seized him. Her eyes were luminous blue, unblinking, like the eyes of the dolls Tabby used to play with.

Descending, he watched the soiled walls, feeling with his feet for turns in the stairs. It was awkward work. "She's so calm," marveled the healthy sister from behind. She was carrying a folded wheelchair that looked heavier than Lydia. "She whimpers and cries when Silvio carries her."

"I'm flattered."

Outside, she greeted one or two children by name. He shifted the cripple in his arms and began opening the door to the backseat, but the sister said in a rush, "We'd like to ride in front, if that's all right."

"You'll have more room in back."

"I want her to see."

"Suit yourself." Her hurry had infected him, and he came around quickly to open the passenger door. She slipped in, and Dexter carefully placed the cripple in her arms. It was a tight fit, even in the Series 62. Only as he closed them inside did he realize how much he'd counted on retreating into the role of chauffeur rather than companion to these girls.

A good deed needs no excuse. So his pop used to reassure Dexter when he would resist, embarrassed, carrying a covered dish of leftover meatballs to the bums and hoboes who haunted the carny houses near his restaurant. Dexter muttered the phrase to himself as he lifted the heavy folded chair into his trunk. *A good deed needs no excuse.*

He drove away from the children and headed back toward Flatbush, enlivened by the thought that at this rate, he'd have no trouble reaching the Knickerbocker by lunchtime. He heard whispering across the seat. "Can she talk?" he asked.

"She used to. Not talk, but repeat things."

"That's talking, isn't it? How much can she understand?"

"We don't really know."

We. The mother, presumably; how else could the healthy sister hold a job at the Naval Yard and turn up at Moonshine of an evening? A cripple like this would need constant care—would normally be in a home, he suspected. Recalling her hurry at the curb, he bit back an impulse to ask whether her mother was aware of today's escapade. Not his lookout. He was as deep inside this family as he meant to go.

They sped past Grand Army Plaza and alongside Prospect Park toward Ocean Avenue. Dexter's mother hovered in his thoughts— as if, having been summoned by the bell, she was reluctant to sign off just yet. There had been a time when she was healthy, before his brother's stillbirth, when Dexter was seven. It had damaged his mother's heart, so that something once solid inside her became terribly fragile: a clock made from sugar. Her inner frailty distinguished her from other mothers, whose many squalling children they were often ignoring or backhanding across the face. She would have to leave him prematurely: this was the secret they both pretended not to know.

She withdrew from the restaurant Dexter's father had opened—his own, at long last—and saved herself for Dexter. Mostly, she slept. Dexter's lunchtime was her dawn, and it broke with the sound of his shoes mauling the stairs as he ran up four flights to their apartment. Other children came home to bread and milk and ham left out, but Dexter enjoyed a full meal his father had brought from the restaurant the night before, warmed in the oven. His mother greeted him fresh and full of questions, laughing and kissing him until it was time for him to return to school, at which point she sank back into her bower, lined with pillows his father had had specially made for her, to renew herself for his return.

Dexter had adored her to a degree that was unheard of among neighborhood boys. She was a person who might disappear at any time, yet she was always there: an enthralling blend of unattainability and complete possession. How had she done it? Witchcraft? Fairy dust? Later, he learned from his father that they'd been told her heart would not last a year past the stillbirth. Yet six years after, when Dexter turned thirteen, she was still there. He began to resent her, and stayed out playing stickball until after dark. He stole apples and peppermints and chalk: little acts of subterfuge that he feared she could actually see when she cupped his guilty face in her delicate hands. She declined with a merciless speed that seemed retroactive, as if the clock had already crumbled long before, and her body had only just realized.

"Say, I never asked," Anna said after a long silence. "Where are we going, exactly?"

"Manhattan Beach," he told her. "It's near Coney Island but cleaner, private. My house is right on the water—in fact, you could take her on the back porch and avoid the sand altogether."

"That sounds swell," Anna strained to say lightly. Returning to Manhattan Beach put an intolerable pressure on the question she'd been agonizing over since they had made their plan four days ago: should she tell Dexter Styles about the connection between them? At the last minute she'd decided not to; her goal was to gather information, not give it away. Hastily, she'd removed from the walls photographs of her mother and Brianne in their dancing costumes; her parents on their wedding day; a movie still from *Let a Bullet Fly* that showed Brianne cowering in a doorway as a man's shadow fell across her.

Yet riding in Dexter Styles's automobile to the very place where she'd met him years ago was a duplicity too egregious to sustain. She wanted to tell him, to have it out in the open. But that wasn't true—she dreaded telling him. What she wanted was already to have told him.

She held Lydia's slender body against her own, hands around her sister's midriff, where the heart nudged the soft bones of her chest. Lydia's eyes were open. She seemed to look through the window at the spiky gray trees of Prospect Park. Anna felt her sister's alertness, and it roused in her a rush of anticipation: They were going to the sea! They would see it together! She had made the request of Dexter Styles unthinkingly, snatching at any excuse to keep him in sight. But now that they were underway, her mother and Brianne out for a day of shopping and Schrafft's and a matinee of *Star and Garter,* she felt the richness of what she'd set in motion. She must not jeopardize it. That meant not telling him who she was until their day had ended.

"How do you like working at the Naval Yard?" Mr. Styles asked suddenly. "What exactly do you do?"

"I measure tiny parts that go on ships," Anna began, every word threatening to burst under the pressure of all she was withholding. But he seemed interested, or perhaps just tired of driving in silence. The longer she talked, the more natural it came to seem. She told him about her hatred of measuring, her wish to become a diver. Eventually, prodded by his questions, she found herself recounting what had happened with Lieutenant Axel the evening before.

"That crumbum," he said, sounding genuinely angry. "What a bunch of screwballs. Tell them to jump in the river."

"Then I wouldn't have a job."

"To hell with their lousy job. Come work for me."

Anna held very still, her arms around Lydia, who seemed also to be listening. "Quit the Naval Yard?"

"Why not? I'd pay you better than they do."

"I make forty-two a week before overtime."

He seemed impressed. "Well, I'd match it."

Anna felt a sudden uncanny proximity to her father. Not that she pictured him, exactly—she still couldn't call him to mind. It was more like standing in a station she knew he'd passed through at an earlier point, trying to guess which train he had boarded. For the first time in years, the air was enlivened by a faint tingling trace of him.

"What do people do? Who work for you," she asked carefully.

"Well, I've many businesses. One of them you've seen, the night-club, and there are more in that line here and in other cities. And then there are businesses that . . . interact with those. Flow through them, you might say."

"I see," Anna said, though she didn't.

"Not all of those businesses are legal, in the strictest sense of that word. I'm of a mind that people should decide for themselves how they like to be amused, rather than have the law decide for them. You may feel differently, of course. Not everyone has the stomach for that sort of thing."

"I've a strong stomach," Anna said. She felt like Alice in Wonderland, fitting herself through smaller and smaller doors with no idea where they might lead.

"That's why I made the offer," he said. "Consider it a standing offer. If you're interested, I'll work you in."

Anna remembered Mr. Styles's home as a castle on an outcropping of cliff surrounded by snow and sea. What she saw when he parked his car was a city block lined with freestanding homes—grand, yes, but no grander than houses she'd seen near Brooklyn College. She felt a dig of disappointment.

"I'll bring the chair," he said. The car rocked as he lifted it from the trunk.

"We're here, Liddy," Anna said softly. "We're almost at the sea."

The car door swung wide, and Mr. Styles lifted Lydia from her arms. Anna stepped out of the car. At the end of the street, under a gray expanse of sky, she sensed the ocean, like someone asleep. Wind yanked pins from her rolled hair, and they twinkled onto the pavement. Carrying the chair, she followed Mr. Styles to his house. He turned the front door handle, Lydia still in his arms, and pushed open the door.

The cripple lay quietly against him while her sister opened and prepared the wheeled chair in the front hall. Dexter was growing accustomed to the contortion of her face, her unblinking stare. When the chair was ready, he placed her in it, and the sister anchored her with belts and straps. There was a U-shaped stand to hold her head upright. Her hands were bent and folded at the wrists; he'd a powerful urge to press them flat. "How did she become this way?" he asked.

"It happened when she was born."

"I'm asking what caused it."

"She hadn't enough air."

"But why? Why hadn't she enough?" He could not repress his impatience. Problems he couldn't solve made him angry.

"No one knows."

"Someone knows. You can be certain of that. She must have a doctor."

"The same one for years." She was doing the very thing he'd wanted to do: straightening out those bent wrists enough to cuff them to the chair, her touch brisk and gentle at once.

"Has he helped her? This doctor?"

"There's no cure."

"What kind of doctor accepts that his patient will get worse?"

"I suppose he makes us feel better."

"Nice work if you can get it," he muttered, and saw her start. These must be old arguments.

"Can we take her outdoors?" she asked.

"Yes, of course," he said, chastened. "The porch is right over here."

He led her into the front room, toward the porch door. Beyond the windows, the sea was a flat gray iridescence. It appeared calm, but the moment he opened the door, a rigid wind assailed them. The cripple jolted in the chair as if she'd been slapped.

"It's too cold," cried the sister, stricken. "I didn't dress her warmly enough."

"Relax. We've plenty of blankets."

He wasn't entirely sure where Milda kept them. As always, she'd gone to spend Sunday with her family in Harlem, from whence she would return in time to fix their breakfast Monday morning. As he swung open closets and riffled through drawers in search of blankets, he experienced a moment of appreciation that his family was not at home. The situation was too painful, Lydia too troubling. He didn't want his children exposed to her.

He'd been unaware of the existence of a second-floor linen closet, but there it was, blankets folded neatly within. He saw the enormous Landrace wool that George Porter had brought them as a gift after a hunting trip to Lapland. He seized that, along with four others, and sprinted back downstairs. He and the sister set to tucking blankets tightly around Lydia. Her hat was laughably insufficient—Dexter wrapped one of the smaller blankets around her shoulders and used the Landrace to swaddle her head, hat and all. In order to do this, he had to lift her head from its stand and hold it in his hands. It had that surprising weight of all heads, her hair impossibly soft, the skull inside it knobby and raw. Holding her head, Dexter felt the protesting part of himself—angry, eager to be done—slide abruptly away. He settled into the project of providing this accursed creature an experience of the sea. He absorbed the importance of it, the singleness of the task. It was a relief.

When Lydia was fully bundled, Anna wheeled her onto the porch for the second time. Her sister's eyes snapped open at the first blast of wind. Anna leaned down so their heads were level and looked out, tethering her gaze to her sister's. Water and sky were all she saw. No convergence of ocean with land; the stone-and-concrete barrier was too far below. No beach, in other words.

"Mr. Styles," she said, "I'd like to take her onto the sand, if that's all right. I can do it alone."

"Nonsense. There's a path at the bottom of these steps that leads to a private beach."

They each took half of Lydia's chair and carried it down the steps. The path was pressed gravel, wide and well maintained enough that Anna could push the chair along it easily. Her sister's eyes were shut— perhaps she'd gone to sleep. Anna wondered if, after all this effort, Lydia would even be able to take in the beach; whether she would drift through the interlude in the drowsy limbo where she spent so much of her time. Anna experienced a throe of frustration: a wish that her sister would do more, be more.

Several steps led from the path down to the sand. Dexter lifted the chair and carried it, taking big draws of sea air. The chair was heavy and cumbersome with Lydia in it, but he liked having his muscles tested. The sand was the gray-white of bones. It seemed to rise up, encompassing the bottoms of the wheels when he set down the chair. "I'll take half," she said, although he doubted she could carry it far in the sand. The water was some distance away. She did, though. He was impressed by her physical strength.

Anna called for him to wait and took off her pumps, setting them side by side in the sand. Her hat was useless; she anchored it under her shoes. Quickly, she plaited her hair and slipped the plait inside the collar of her coat. She felt the cold gritty sand through her stocking feet as they resumed their march. The wind teased and bludgeoned, as if daring them to continue.

They stopped once more, to rest. Dexter wrapped the Landrace more securely around Lydia's lower face, so that only her eyes met the wind. They were open but empty-looking, like the windows of a house no one lived in.

At last they set down the chair near the water. Panting from the walk, Anna leaned her head against her sister's and watched a long wave form, stretching until it achieved translucence, then somersaulting forward and collapsing into creamy suds that eked toward them over the sand, nearly touching the wheels of Lydia's chair. Then another wave gathered, reaching, stretching, a streak of silver dashing along its surface where the weak sunlight touched it. The strange, violent, beautiful sea: this was what she had wanted Lydia to see. It touched every part of the world, a glittering curtain drawn across a mystery. Anna wrapped her arms around her sister. "Liddy," she said, speaking into the blankets where she thought her sister's ear must be. "Can you see the sea? Can you hear it? It's right in front of you—this is your chance. Now, Liddy. Now!"

See the sea the sea

Rinfronyoo. Liddy! Liddy!

Canyeerit?

Hrasha   Hrasha   Hrasha   the sea

"Look at that ship," Mr. Styles said, gesturing at the water. "Look at the size of her."

Still holding her sister, Anna looked. She saw the usual tugs and lighters, a few freighters and tankers that appeared to be stationary. And behind them, on such a scale that her eye didn't register it at first, a mammoth ship, pale gray, moving with fantastic speed past Breezy Point. Anna was certain it hadn't been there a minute before. "What is it?" she asked.

"Troopship," he said. "A liner. The *Queen Mary*, is my guess. They covered up all that fancy woodwork and packed her full of soldiers. Fifteen thousand she can hold, a whole division."

He'd crossed the Atlantic in the *Queen Mary* with Harriet after their wedding—steamed to Southampton in three days to meet the old man, whose aunt, Lady Hewitt, bred racehorses in Kent. Dexter's job had been to win her blessing, and he'd done it.

"She's too fast for convoy," he went on, although she must know these things, working at the Naval Yard. He wanted to explain it—to talk about the liner while she was still in sight. "Convoys have to sail at the speed of the slowest ship: that means eleven knots if it includes a Liberty, even slower for coal burners. But the *Queen Mary* can make thirty knots. The Gray Ghost, they call her. U-boats can't catch her."

He felt an odd yearning toward the ship, as if wishing himself on board. Not with soldiers, though. Before the war? But that wasn't it, either. Perhaps with soldiers after all.

"Are your businesses doing any war work?" she asked after the ship had steamed out of sight.

"If you include keeping the brass amused and easing the pain of rationing, we're doing more than our share," he said.

She laughed. "You're a profiteer," she said, apparently without judgment. But he didn't like the word.

"I prefer 'morale booster,'" he said. "I keep people's spirits up, despite the war."

"Would you like to do more?"

It appeared to be that rare thing: a genuine question asked from curiosity, nothing else. She stood straight, hands on her sister's shoulders, and watched him from under those arched eyebrows. Her gaze was bright and clear.

"Yes," he said. "Yes, I would like that." It seemed to him now that this wish was long-standing. He was filled with impatience at not yet having achieved it.

Anna felt a jolt under her hands, like a drawer slamming shut. Alarmed, she looked into Lydia's face and found her sister's eyes wide-open, registering the rise and fall of the waves. "Liddy," she cried. "Do you know where you are?"

See the sea. Sea the sea the sea the sea

"She's talking," Anna cried. "Listen!"

Dexter had briefly forgotten Lydia, lost in the question her sister had posed about war work. Now he looked again at Lydia.

With just her blue eyes showing above the Landrace, a few strands of hair whirling from its folds, she looked like a veiled beauty, a woman of mystery. He leaned close and heard murmuring through the wool.

"I felt her wake up," her sister said. "She started, as if someone had shaken her."

Dexter looked out at the silvery swells. Wind lashed his overcoat and gulls cried overhead. "It is beautiful," he said. "No wonder she's paying attention. Everyone should see this once in their lives."

"I think so, too," she said.

I wanted you to see the sea. See the sea the sea the ishywarmenuf?

Bird ree ree rawk reek rawk you know what birds are, remember the little birds that camrwindosill, remember?

Cree cree   Bird

That wind is picking up.

You can tell she's watching

Oh yes, she sees. She laughed a minute ago

shelafdamingo. Flamingo. Bird cree cree.

Kiss

Oh, Liddy!

Kiss

My darling you haven't done that in suchalontym.   Look, she kisses me if I pull the blanket aside.

Shekissississ.

This is a kiss. Do you see?

I suppose I do. Poor kid.

Her lips are so soft.

Anna

Listen, she's talking. She's trying to talk. Being outside is making her well.

Anna   Papa   Mama   Liddy

She's talking to you. She's looking at you.

She hasn't any idea who I am. Probably wondering who this stranger is.

Whothistrangris Wholyam Papa

"Thank you for bringing us, Mr. Styles," Anna cried, suddenly overcome. No one had done this, ever—taken them to the beach together. "Thank you for bringing us. We're so terribly grateful." She clasped his hands and stood on tiptoe to kiss his cheek. But she only reached his jaw.

"It's nothing," he muttered, though he felt strangely moved. The change in the crippled girl was extraordinary. He'd found her sprawled unconscious, as if she'd been dropped from a height, but now she sat up independently, holding her head away from the stand. The Landrace fell from her face as she confronted the sea, lips moving, like a mythical creature whose imprecations could summon storms and winged gods, her wild blue eyes fixed on eternity.

He'd lost track of the time. Twelve-thirty. Not as late as he'd feared, but too late to meet the old man. Ah well. He didn't really care—was glad not to have to hurry anywhere else. He stood beside the girls and watched the sea. It was never the same on any two days, not if you really looked. Smart, taking the poor kid to the beach. Good for anyone to breathe this air.

Kiss Anna

Bird Cree cree

See the waves   hrasha   hrasha   hrasha

Seetheseatheseethesea

Kiss Anna

Blue Bird Shhh

Breathe

Faaaah laaaaah

Seethseethseathsee thusea seethe

I don't want to . . . when will she babeltu

Papa

Wholyam Whothistrangris

Kiss Anna
Kiss Liddy
Papa   Whothistrangris
Afraid to leave she might
Hrasha   hrasha   hrasha
In no hurry. Stay here as long as you like.

PART FOUR

The Dark

CHAPTER THIRTEEN

Anna's mother returned from her own Sunday expedition in the late afternoon. She flung open the door and ran to Lydia, her visible alarm leaving no doubt that she'd been informed, in the course of ascending five flights, of the car, the strange man, and the lengthy absence. Lydia sat by the window, watching a bird on the fire escape. She turned to their mother and smiled.

"My Lord," her mother cried, throwing her arms around her. "Where in heaven did you take her?"

"Look," Anna said.

Her mother's wonder at the change in Lydia made it easier to unpack, like crockery from a picnic basket, the untruths Anna had spent the ride home carefully assembling: that her supervisor, Mr. Voss, had made an unexpected visit in his car. That he'd taken them for a drive to Prospect Park, where Lydia (well bundled, of course) had sat outdoors. And then a flourish, appended spontaneously: Mr. Voss had a sister like Lydia! That was why he'd cared to come and see her, and why Anna had entrusted him to carry her downstairs.

"It's cold for the park," their mother said, touching Lydia's forehead. "But she seems so alert."

"Maybe she likes the cold."

Lydia's gaze was full of perception—not just of the falsehoods Anna was uttering now, but of her broken resolve to disclose to Mr. Styles the connection between them. During the drive back from

Manhattan Beach, he'd switched on the news. The scuttling of the French fleet in Toulon was overshadowed by a horrific conflagration the previous night in a Boston nightclub, the Cocoanut Grove, after an artificial palm tree caught fire. Mr. Styles seemed already to know of the disaster, but the details agitated him: three hundred dead, hundreds more in hospitals. All the result of panicked chorus girls and patrons stampeding toward blocked exits.

"Idiots," he muttered. "Criminals. Christ, who needs the Krauts when we're burning our own people alive?"

"Was it one of your nightclubs?" Anna asked.

He replied with a withering look. "No one has ever died in one of my clubs," he said.

After carrying Lydia upstairs, he'd seemed in a hurry to go. And so Anna had said nothing about their father. She'd no regrets—was proud, in fact, of having given nothing away. Still Lydia watched her. She didn't feel embarrassment, like other people; it was up to Anna to look away. Finally, she did, waiting for her sister's attention to wander. When she looked back, Lydia was still watching her.

On that Monday and Tuesday, while Anna was at work, Silvio carried Lydia downstairs, and their mother pushed her all the way to Prospect Park and back—a sojourn of hours in brisk and windy weather, she reported. At night, Lydia maintained a steady patter about birds and kisses and Anna and Mama. "She keeps mentioning the sea," their mother said. "I wonder what she means by it." Anna and Lydia exchanged a smile.

On Wednesday, Anna returned from work to find her mother and Aunt Brianne drinking highballs in the front room with a man called Walter Lipp, whom Brianne introduced as an "old friend." His sallow complexion and pencil mustache reminded Anna of Louie, Nell's friend at the Moonshine Club. It emerged that Walter Lipp had driven Agnes, Brianne, and Lydia in his Ford sedan to a picnic spot under the George Washington Bridge. Lydia had sat up in her chair, muffled in coats, and watched a brisk parade of boat traffic. She had laughed and prattled and eaten most of a sweet potato from a stand. Walter Lipp listened with grave attention while Anna's mother described these events, nodding occasionally as if squaring her account with his own. He lacked the celebratory air of most of Brianne's "old friends," and left his highball unfinished.

"Not a moment too soon," Brianne stage-whispered as Walter Lipp's steps faded down the stairs.

"I liked him," her mother said. "He'd a quiet sense of humor."

"That's like saying, *What a terribly interesting girl.*"

"Why did you invite him?" Anna asked.

Men who were the best company were the worst drivers, her aunt explained. "Now, with the war, they can't get new whitewalls, so they're patching their old ones." Walter was a man she could depend upon not to wreck his car with Lydia in it.

Lydia sat in her chair in a state of lively bloom. Clearly, her second waterfront visit had agreed with her. They stayed up very late, all four of them, the windows open to the December chill, the dim, smoldering city sidling in alongside Benny Goodman's snaking clarinet. Lydia craved stimulation, that was clear; now it was a matter of sustaining it. Brianne had other snores and pills in mind for further chauffeuring. They spoke of what might be possible if things continued in this vein: Suppose Lydia could learn to walk and to talk? Suppose she could marry and have children? Anna watched her aunt, wondering if she really believed these things, then wondering why she wondered. The answer came to her gradually: she and her mother were the ones imagining and elaborating, while Brianne said just enough to spur them on. Her aunt had become the maypole. She believed in having fun, and they were having it.

Lydia had retreated a little by the next morning, and Anna and her mother agreed they'd let her stay up too late. No more of that! But when Anna arrived home from work that evening, her sister was even more lethargic; they had trouble coaxing her to eat. She didn't cough or shiver or sneeze. She hadn't a fever. She was just still, far away.

"I'm afraid," her mother said. "She doesn't seem right."

"Why don't you take her out tomorrow?"

"I'm afraid we've hurt her, doing that."

"She isn't hurt, Mama." But a feather of panic tickled Anna's heart.

The next morning Lydia was difficult to wake. At the Yard, Anna was too anxious to go out at lunchtime; even the barbed familiarity of the marrieds felt less foreboding than eating alone among the long December shadows. She hurried home after work, uttering feverish prayers that her mother would meet her with a smile; that Lydia would be back in her chair, smiling, too. But before she'd reached the last turn of stairs, the door flew open and her mother ran into the hall. "She's worse," she hissed at Anna over the railing. "I don't know what to do!"

Anna's heart clenched. But she managed to say calmly, once they were inside their apartment, "We must call Dr. Deerwood."

"He doesn't make house calls to Brooklyn," her mother shrieked.

Trembling, Anna went to her bedroom, where Lydia lay. Their mother wavered briefly in the doorway, then retreated. Anna heard her sobbing. She lay beside Lydia as she had so many nights—thousands of nights since they were little girls. "Liddy," she whispered. "You must wake up."

Lydia's eyes opened halfway. They had a lazy glow. She seemed unnaturally still, as if her breathing and heartbeat had slowed.

"Liddy," Anna said with quiet urgency. "Mama needs you and I need you."

Every word rang with her panicked awareness that whatever had gone wrong was her fault. She felt close to vomiting from fear. But Lydia was alive. She was breathing, her heart was beating. Anna curled around her sister and concentrated on the life moving inside her as if she were anchoring it in place—absorbing Lydia, or being absorbed by her. She drifted among memories: their grandparents' farm in Minnesota, where she and their mother had taken Lydia twice in summer while their father stayed behind. A rabble of boy cousins had shrunk from her as from a freakish curiosity, and Anna had felt marooned with Lydia while they chased each other through the woods, whooping like Indians. They seemed to exist in the plural: addressed as one, scolded and whipped and rewarded collectively, at which point they had to fight each other for the reward itself. They pushed close to Lydia as one mass, studying her hair, the lace collar Anna had sewn on her dress. "Does she *do* anything?" they asked.

"No," Anna said, hating her sister. "She doesn't do anything at all."

But in the following weeks, an unexpected thing began to happen: individual boys separated themselves from the group, as if for the first time, and came to sit quietly with Lydia. They begged for extra time, and Anna began to feel important, arranging these visits. The boys claimed that Lydia had told them things: she liked pie; was afraid of spiders; loved rabbits best of all animals. No, goats. Chickens. Horses. Pigs. *She's never even seen a pig, you oaf!*

"She misses her home," said Freddie, the smallest boy, after holding Lydia's hand for a quarter of an hour.

"What does she miss?" Anna asked, and waited for Freddie to say, *Her papa.* But although Freddie lived fifty miles from the nearest lake, he said, "She misses the sea." It was the first time Anna realized that her sister had never seen it.

Anna's mother ran a bath that night, and Anna washed Lydia's hair. They hoped the pleasure of the warm water would jolt her into awareness, but it was the opposite: Lydia floated with eyes shut, the faintest smile on her lips. Anna had an eerie impression that the crumpled body she was holding no longer contained her sister, or not entirely. It was as if Lydia were fading into the mystery she had always partly inhabited, as if its pull were too great to resist.

The next morning Anna overslept and had to rush to get to her shop before eight o'clock. The sight of Lydia unmoving in bed haunted her through the day. She measured parts in a state of trance-like absorption very like prayer, dread and hope twining in a burning

nimbus around her heart. *Please let today be a turning point. Please let
her get better today.*

She arrived home to find an unfamiliar coat and hat hanging
inside the apartment door, a walking stick poised against the wall.
Anna set down her purse, slipped off her shoes, and went quietly into
her bedroom in stocking feet. Dr. Deerwood sat on a kitchen chair
just inside the door. Her mother sat on Anna's bed. Lydia lay in her
own bed, her body unnaturally straight. There was a new hollowness
around her closed eyes. The blanket rose and fell on her chest like a
pendulum swinging very, very slowly.

Dr. Deerwood stood up from his chair and shook Anna's hand.
Removed from his opulent office, he looked like any doctor making a
house call. Although his stiff black bag was closed and nothing especially doctorly was taking place, his presence imparted a sense of order
and safety. Anna's faith in him was instantly restored. Nothing could
go wrong while the doctor was present.

She knelt in the narrow space between the beds and laid her head
beside Lydia's, breathing the flowery scent of last night's shampoo.

"I should never have taken her out," her mother said. "There was
too much wind."

"Nonsense," Dr. Deerwood said.

"It's made her worse."

"You must put that thought from your mind, Mrs. Kerrigan," he
said with quiet authority. "It is not just wrong but damaging. You've
given Lydia one more pleasant experience in a life that has been full
of them."

"How do you know?" her mother pressed. "How can you tell?"

"Look at her," the doctor said, and they did, Anna lifting her head
to take in her sister's radiant flesh, the delicate bones of her face, her
luxuriant hair. Her eyes seemed to flicker under their long lashes as if
she were watching them through the silken drapery of her lids.

Something broke in Anna's mother. She doubled over and began
to howl like an animal. Anna had never heard her make such a sound,

and it terrified her—as if her mother might go mad or throw herself
out the window. Panic sprang up in her; she had done this! But no,
she'd done nothing wrong. The doctor had said so, and his presence
made it true.

Dr. Deerwood took her mother's hands in both of his. He'd large
hands, broad and worn like a workingman's. Anna watched them in
fascination—how had she never noticed those oversize hands?

"You must believe me, Mrs. Kerrigan," he said. "You've done everything it is possible to do."

"It isn't enough," her mother wept.

"It was more than enough."

His words hung in the air like an echo. Even when he'd forgone
the usual cup of coffee that followed a house call and taken up his
coat and hat and stick, Anna seizing upon the unruliness of his silver
eyebrows; when he'd shaken their hands, all of them understanding
they would not meet again, and the sound of his tread had faded
downstairs; when Anna and her mother were back in the bedroom
watching over Lydia, still she could hear the doctor's voice: *It was
more than enough.*

Her mother wore a vacant expression. "He never opened his bag,"
she said.

The funeral took place on a cold Sunday the week before Christmas.
Anna sat in a front pew between Stella Iovino and Lillian Feeney; her
mother between Aunt Brianne and Pearl Gratzky, who had become
more friend than boss since Mr. Gratzky's passing two years before. It
was Pearl who had purchased the arrangement of white lilies for the
altar. Their smell peppered the air as Father McBride likened Lydia
to lambs and angels and other deserving innocents.

A merciful numbness had engulfed Anna since her sister's death,
enabling her to fulfill the many logistical tasks that had followed: taking a short leave from the Naval Yard; arranging the funeral, burial,

and lunch to follow; purchasing a coffin and a plot. The question of where Lydia should rest had briefly paralyzed Anna and her mother. Her mother's people were all buried in Minnesota, and the thought of Lydia alone here among strangers was intolerable. As a last resort they chose New Calvary, where Pearl Gratzky bequeathed to Lydia the plot she had purchased beside her husband, and where there was extra room on both sides for Agnes and Anna. Pearl was euphoric at this arrangement. "They can visit together," she cried, with the greedy relief of one who believed she had thereby extended her own earthly tenure.

As they followed Lydia's coffin from the church, Anna was amazed to see how crowded the pews had become during the Mass. Who were all of these people? She'd expected a handful, the Mucciarones, the Iovinos, the Feeneys, but there were dozens of other faces, familiar but hard to place. The old ladies from the building across the street who rested their elbows on bath towels to spy down on the block. Neighbors Anna knew only to say good morning. Silvio Mucciarone sobbed in his mother's arms. Mr. White, the druggist, wept unabashedly into a handkerchief. Dozens of women lifted the netting from their church hats and blotted their eyes. The neighborhood boys were absent, of course, enlisted or called up, and a great many fathers were traveling for war work or taking Sunday shifts. Standing under the gray sky among so many women, Anna began to understand the collective grief: Lydia had been a last still point amid so much wrenching change.

Brianne oversaw the funeral lunch, arranging covered dishes brought by neighbors and doling out liberal amounts of beer and whiskey she'd brought herself. Guests overflowed the apartment into the hall and down the stairs, holding food in paper cocktail napkins Brianne had apparently filched from a bar in Sheepshead Bay called the Dizzy Swain. Each napkin was emblazoned with a cartoon shepherd: hearts in his eyes, sheep at his feet, a crook in one hand, and a cocktail shaker in the other.

Anna climbed onto the fire escape with Lillian and Stella, all of them huddling together in their coats and hats on the freezing iron grille. It felt good to be squeezed between her old friends, with whom she'd hidden in cupboards and shared a single mattress on hot nights when their families took to the roofs. They had braided each other's hair and administered Toni Home Permanent waves and used Mr. Iovino's razor to shave one another's underarms. Lillian, whose round freckled face made her look fourteen, was working as a stenographer and living with an aunt in Manhattan. Stella, the beauty, had just become engaged. She kept stretching out her long fingers to admire the tiny tear-shaped diamond her fiancé had presented, on bended knee, before departing for boot camp.

"I owe Seamus a letter," Anna told Lillian.

"My brother thinks you'll marry him if he comes back a hero," Lillian said.

"I will," Anna said. "Anything for a hero."

Mrs. Feeney had organized the letter-writing project when Seamus enlisted, and now Anna found herself corresponding at length with neighborhood boys she'd hardly known when they were still home.

"Mother wants us not to mention Stella's engagement in our letters," Lillian said, assuming one of those lockjawed moving-picture accents they often mimicked together. "Give the boys something to live for."

"We mustn't rob a soldier of his dreams," Anna said in the same tone, but halfheartedly.

"Honestly, girls, you'll make my head swell up like a great big balloon," Stella drawled, but the routine fizzled, and they looked down at the street in silence.

"Anything from your papa?" Lillian asked.

Anna shook her head.

"Awful for him not to know," Stella murmured.

"I think he must be dead," Anna said.

They turned to her, mystified. "Did you hear something?" Lillian asked.

Anna searched for an answer. She'd hardly seen her friends in the months since she'd begun working at the Naval Yard—the war had made all of them so busy. It felt impossible to tell them about Dexter Styles or explain the change in her thinking. There were too many steps to retrace.

"Why else would he not come back?" she said at last. "How could he just . . . forget?"

Stella took her hand. Anna felt the new engagement ring like a sliver of ice against her friend's warm skin.

"He's dead to you, is what you mean," Stella said.

In the middle of the night, Anna's mother shook her awake. "We don't know Mr. Gratzky!" she hissed into Anna's ear. *"What if he's not nice?"*

"He is nice," Anna said groggily.

"You're taking Pearl's word for it, but we haven't met the man. He never left his bed!"

"I met him once," Anna said.

Her mother was dumbfounded out of extremis. "You met Mr. Gratzky?"

"He showed me his wound," Anna said.

The next morning, a Monday, she pried herself awake in the War Time dark. The kitchen counter was strewn with Dizzy Swain cocktail napkins. Brianne had slept over, and Anna heard the raucous snores from her mother's bed.

Her limbs felt wobbly and peculiar as she boarded the streetcar, but by the time she joined the crowd outside the Sands Street gate, Anna felt stronger. The winter sunrise shearing into her eyes down Flushing Avenue and blasts of salty wind were fortifying. Lydia had never been to the Naval Yard. Apart from Mr. Voss and Rose, no one there knew of her existence.

Returning home that evening, she found her key no longer fit the lock. Her mother let her in and gave her a new key flecked with metal filings. "If your father happens to return," she said, "he is no longer welcome in this house."

Anna was incredulous. "Are you expecting him?"

"Not anymore."

Her mother spent the next two days emptying the armoire and bureau of every piece of her father's clothing. The exquisite suits Anna had helped tailor and adjust, the fine shoes and coats and painted neckties and silk handkerchiefs—all were folded ignominiously into boxes for H-O oats and Bosco chocolate-flavored syrup. Anna lifted a suit jacket from one of the boxes before her mother tied it shut. It had gone out of fashion, lacking the squared shoulders and military cut that everyone favored nowadays. Silvio carried the boxes to church for Father McBride to give to the poor.

On the surface, Anna's life hardly changed. She left for work in the dark (her mother still asleep) and returned in twilight. Christmas came and went, and the year turned to 1943. They sewed to keep busy at night: a housecoat with embroidered lapels for Stella's wedding present; christening gowns for Anna's eldest cousins—those muddy, rowdy boys from the farm, all in the service now—some of whose wives were already expecting. They listened to *Counterspy, Manhattan at Midnight, Doc Savage.* Neighbors brought food, which they warmed for supper. This routine formed a fragile, makeshift bridge across an abyss. Anna's mother spent her days inside that abyss; there was a deadness about her, a torpor that Anna was frightened of feeling herself. What saved her from it was going to work. She performed her measurements in a state of hushed withdrawal. Everyone knew there had been a death in her family, and the marrieds were being nice to her again. But the unruly kid sister Anna had played with them before could not be resurrected.

Curiously, the apartment felt smaller without Lydia in it. Anna and her mother collided as they moved between rooms, both veering at once toward the icebox, the window, the sink. Some evenings she came home to find her mother still asleep, with no evidence that she'd risen from bed to do anything more than visit the hall toilet. Once her mother wasn't at home, and Anna walked among the small rooms taking deep breaths, relieved to find herself alone, then guilty over her relief. It turned out her mother had been using the public telephone at White's Drugstore to call her sisters in Minnesota. She began calling often, collecting coins in a coffee tin to satisfy the voracious operators.

One night Anna noticed a few of her mother's old dancing costumes spread out across the bed: a short skirt made of yellow feathers; a bodice with a pair of green wings; a red waistcoat spangled with sequins. By the next night, they were gone. "Pearl is going to sell them for me," her mother said as they dined on Mrs. Mucciarone's cannelloni and listened to *Easy Aces*. "They've value, apparently, now that the Follies are finished. Someone might put them in a museum." She gave a disbelieving laugh.

"Did you try them on?"

"Too fat."

"You'd get thinner if you danced."

"At forty-one? Anyone can see I'm washed up."

There was a way Anna knew she should feel, beholding her mother's anguish, a cloud of tenderness and pity that seemed to hover just beyond her reach. Instead, she recoiled. Her mother was weak, but Anna was not. In the mornings she rushed to work, welcoming the indifference that enfolded her as she passed through the Sands Street gate. She tried to forget the apartment and everything in it.

In January, three weeks after her return to work, Mr. Voss called her into his office and asked if she was still interested in learning to dive.

"Why, yes," she said slowly. "Of course."

Lieutenant Axel needed more civilian volunteers; too many had failed to complete the training. "He remembered you," Mr. Voss said. "You must have made an impression."

"I remember him," Anna said.

Climbing the stairs a few nights later, she smelled real cooking from behind her apartment door for the first time since early December. Opening it, she looked instinctively toward the front windows, where Lydia would have been. The empty chair was folded against a wall. Anna's stomach clenched as if someone had kneed her.

"Hello, Mama," she called, but it came out a sob. Her mother wrapped Anna in her arms and held her a long time.

She had prepared a feast: steak and mashed potatoes, carrots and string beans and grapefruit juice. "Our neighbors have been feeding us for so long, we're swimming in ration coupons," she said. "I brought some to the Feeneys and the Iovinos this afternoon."

"What's happened, Mama?"

"Let's enjoy our meal first."

Eating in the warm kitchen made Anna sleepy. When they'd finished their canned cherries with vanilla ice cream, her mother set down her spoon and said, "I think it's time we went back home."

"Home . . . ?"

"Minnesota. Spend some time with my parents and sisters. And your cousins, of course."

"The *farm*?"

"You've been carrying an enormous weight, Anna. I'm so grateful. But it's time you had a chance to set it down. Let our family take care of us for a while. Not that there isn't plenty to do on a farm," she added under her breath.

"You hate the farm!"

"That was long ago. And you've always loved it."

"Why sure, to visit, but that's— I can't leave, Mama," she said, clawing free of her sleepy contentment. "They're going to let me dive."

"They're what?"

But Anna had never mentioned diving to her mother—to protect it from the chill of her indifference. "I can't leave," she said again.

The appearance of an obstacle, even one she couldn't identify,

roused instant consternation in her mother. "I've spoken with everyone there," she said in a high, thin voice. "They're all very eager to
have us."

"You go. I'll stay here."

Her mother leaped to her feet, knocking her chair backward.
"That is out of the question," she said, and Anna understood that her
dread of an objection was what underlay the steak and potatoes and
cherries, perhaps even the long embrace.

Had Anna *ever* known of an unmarried girl living alone, not
counting old maids like Miss DeWitt, on two, whom the children
believed was a witch? No, she hadn't, because unmarried girls didn't
live alone—unless they were a different sort of girl, which Anna was
not. What would the neighbors think? Who would meet her at the
end of each day? Fix her breakfast and supper? Suppose an intruder
climbed in from the fire escape? Suppose she fell sick or got hurt?
Anna pointed out that she could move into a women's hotel, as her
mother had done when she came to New York. Yes, but those were
different times; now the Germans might begin a blitz, and how would
Anna escape? Suppose there was a sea invasion—hadn't the harbor
been closed over some scare last November? Hadn't Germans landed
on Amagansett Beach just last summer? And besides, more went on
in those women's hotels than you might think.

Because her mother was desperate to go and Anna determined
to stay, the outcome of the debate was never in serious doubt. Anna
perceived this from the outset, and it made her sufficiently calm to
reassure her mother on every count: she had the Feeneys on three,
the Iovinos and Mucciarones down the block, Pearl Gratzky near
Borough Hall, and Lillian Feeney in Manhattan. She could leave a
message for Aunt Brianne in her apartment house in Sheepshead
Bay. Her supervisor, Mr. Voss, would help if she needed help. Diving
would mean longer days; she would come home mostly to sleep. And
anyway, Brooklyn was full of girls with husbands overseas—how was
Anna living alone any different?

And so, on a Sunday afternoon in late January, five weeks after burying Lydia, Anna helped her mother load two suitcases into a taxi. She would take the Broadway Limited overnight to Chicago and transfer to the 400 (a splurge courtesy of the Lobster King) to Minneapolis late the next day.

Pennsylvania Station swarmed with soldiers carrying identical brown duffels. Anna welcomed the din of their voices and the whorls of their cigarette smoke. She sat beside her mother in the Grand Hall and watched pigeons flapping against the honeycombed ceiling. There was something they should say to each other, Anna felt, but everything she thought of seemed to go without saying. They lingered, both waiting, then had to hurry into the drafty concourse where stairs led down to the platforms. Two soldiers carried their suitcases. Anna followed them down with mounting anticipation, as if she, too, were about to board a train. Did she want to go to Minnesota after all? No. She wanted her mother to go.

Agnes, too, craved some meaningful exchange—it was the reason she'd said goodbye to Pearl and Brianne the night before and come to the station just with Anna. "I can't bear to think of you lonely," she fumbled on the platform.

"I won't be," Anna said, and it was hard to imagine her lonely; she was so self-contained.

"I'll write every day. I'll post the first letter tomorrow, from Chicago."

"All right, Mama."

"Telephone any time; I've left the can full of coins. The telephone is in the main house, but they'll ring the bell if I'm not there."

"I remember."

None of this was right, but Agnes couldn't seem to stop. "Mrs. Mucciarone is more than pleased to cook for you. I've already paid for this week. You can pick up the dish on your way home tomorrow."

"Fine, Mama."

"And return it in the morning."

"Yes."

"You must give her your ration coupons."

"Of course."

"And you'll visit Lydia?"

"Every Sunday."

The train's whistle blew. Agnes felt her daughter's impatience that she go, and it made her want to cleave, as if holding Anna would somehow awaken in her daughter the need to be held. Agnes clasped her fiercely, trying through sheer force to open the folded part of Anna, so deeply recessed. For a hallucinatory moment, the sinewy shoulders she held seemed to be Eddie's. Agnes was hugging goodbye the whole of her life: husband, daughter, and fragile younger daughter whom she'd loved the most. She climbed aboard the second-class sleeper and waved to Anna from the window. The train began to move, raising a flock of flapping arms. It came to Agnes that this was the very station—perhaps the very platform—where she had arrived, at seventeen, to seek her fortune. As she waved, she thought, *This is the end of the story.*

The train rounded a corner, and everyone's arms dropped as though a string holding them aloft had been cut. People left quickly to make room for new travelers boarding the train across the platform, new loved ones sending them off. Anna stayed where she was, watching the empty track. At last she climbed the steps to the concourse, turning sideways to let soldiers and families rush past. A novel awareness began to assert itself: there was nowhere she needed to be. Just minutes ago, she'd been rushing like the people on those steps, but now she'd no reason to rush or even to walk. The weirdness of this sensation strengthened when Anna found herself back on Seventh Avenue. She stood in the twilight, wondering whether to turn left or right. Uptown or downtown? She'd money in her pocketbook; she could go wherever she wanted. How she'd craved the freedom of not having to worry about her mother! Yet it arrived as a kind of slackness, like the fall of those waving arms when the train turned.

She began walking north, toward Forty-second Street, resolved to
see a picture at the New Amsterdam. *Shadow of a Doubt* was only ten
minutes in when she reached the theater; she could sit in the very
hall—perhaps the very seat—where, as a little girl, she'd watched her
mother dance. But Anna no longer wanted to sit and watch a scary
picture. She wanted to mirror the purpose that seemed to fuel everyone else on Forty-second Street: clutches of laughing sailors; girls
with hair pinned and sprayed; elderly couples, the ladies in fur, all
moving in haste through the murky half-light. Anna watched them
searchingly. How did they know where to go?

She decided to head back home. Walking toward the IND on Sixth
Avenue, she passed a flea circus, a chow-meinery, a sign advertising
lectures on what killed Rudolph Valentino. Gradually she began to
notice other solitary figures lingering in doorways and under awnings:
people with no obvious place they needed to be. Through the plate-
glass window of Grant's at the corner of Sixth, she saw soldiers and
sailors eating alone, even a girl or two. Anna watched them through
the glass while, behind her, newspaper vendors bawled out the evening headlines: "Tripoli falls!" "Russians gaining on Rostov!" "Nazis
say the Reich is threatened!" To Anna, these sounded like captions to
the solitary diners. The war had shaken people loose. These isolated
people in Grant's had been shaken loose. And now she, too, had been
shaken loose. She sensed how easily she might slide into a cranny of
the dimmed-out city and vanish. The possibility touched her physically, like the faint coaxing suction of an undertow. It frightened her,
and she hurried toward the subway entrance.

But when she reached the stairs to the IND, curiosity about her
new state kept Anna from descending just yet. She continued to Fifth
Avenue, where faint streetlights smoldered along its dusky cavern.
The public library hulked like a morgue. Her father had watched that
library being built on the site of a reservoir when he was a boy. This
fact returned to Anna a moment ahead of her father's voice, which
murmured so casually that it seemed always to have been there: *Top*

hats up and down the street . . . pampered horses too good for a carrot if you held one up . . . a single mansion where the whole Plaza Hotel is now, can you feature that? His voice: offhand, confiding, dry from weariness and smoke. His voice in the car, even when she wasn't listening.

After years of distance, Anna's father returned to her. She couldn't see him, but she felt the knotty pain of his hands in her armpits as he slung her off the ground to carry her. She heard the muffled jingle of coins in his trouser pockets. His hand was a socket she affixed hers to always, wherever they went, even when she didn't care to. Anna stopped walking, stunned by the power of these impressions. Without thinking, she lifted her fingers to her face, half expecting the warm, bitter smell of his tobacco.

CHAPTER FOURTEEN

One of the queer facts of Dexter's long association with Mr. Q.—nearly thirty years, if you counted from when he first become enamored of the minions in his father's restaurant—was how rarely he saw the man. Four times a year at most, unless there was trouble. Yet Mr. Q. was omnipresent: the silent partner and primary investor in all of Dexter's schemes, the first to profit from them. The transit of money between them was ongoing and intricate. It took the form of legitimate checks and surreptitious bundles that moved in both directions—Dexter's ultimate job being the protection of his boss's gargantuan illegal earnings from the arachnid appetite of the Bureau of Internal Revenue. No man had the power to intimidate Mr. Q., but the mechanistic forces of taxation and audit were another story. Even the great Al Capone had succumbed. It was the syndicate no syndicate could beat.

To the naked eye, Mr. Q. still partook of an agricultural economy that dated back to the previous century, when he'd arrived by clipper ship as a young man and found Brooklyn teeming with farms. He made wine, preserves, milk, and cheeses at home in Bensonhurst and sold them from an unprepossessing storefront a half mile away, operated by his four sons.

Dexter pulled up in front of this storefront now, as he did every Monday morning (the only day he arose with the rest of the world), a checkbook in his breast pocket and neatly wrapped bundles of cash in several others. A bell jingled as he pushed open the door. Frankie, Mr. Q.'s eldest son, who looked close to sixty (though no one really knew), sat at the counter. Like his brothers, Giulio, Johnny, and Joey, Frankie had thin brilliantined hair and an expressionless face. All of them smelled like cloves or pepper, a dry-goods smell, although it might have been the shop itself. Dexter rarely saw them outside it.

"Good morning, Frankie."

"Morning yourself."

"Enjoy your weekend?"

"Oh, sure."

"Awful cold, wasn't it?"

"Why, yes, it was, now you mention it."

"The missus well?"

"She is at that."

"And the grandchildren?"

"Oh, sure, they're swell."

"Getting big, I imagine."

"You can say that again."

With occasional variations for temperature, season, and family configuration (Joey, the youngest, hadn't any grandchildren yet), this conversation was indistinguishable from those Dexter held every Monday morning with whichever of Mr. Q.'s sons he happened to encounter at the shop. All were such perfect proxies for their father that it was tempting to regard them as drones: men whose every movement was controlled from afar. Yet occasionally, Dexter thought he glimpsed, in the vacancy of their faces, stores of memory, knowledge, and savvy opinion.

He wrote a check to Mr. Q. for eighteen thousand dollars: his legitimate earnings for the previous week. Waving dry the ink, he said, "War is good for nightclubs, and that's a fact."

"Pa will be happy to know it."

"The roadhouses aren't quite as flush, with gasoline in such short supply. But the city clubs more than compensate."

"Son of a gun."

"Say, I'd like to speak with your pa this afternoon, if he's a minute to spare."

"You know where to look."

"Why don't I stop by around three."

This plan, so casually made that it hardly qualified as an appointment, could not have been more ironclad had it been typed into an executive diary by a secretarial school graduate fluent in stenography.

Before saying goodbye, Dexter slipped Frankie three envelopes fat with cash: the week's undocumented profits. The thickest, always, were the gaming proceeds, marked "No. 1" in pencil on the outside.

"Say, you haven't seen Badger lately," he said, turning to go.

"Why, he's in here most days," Frankie said.

"Making out okay, new to the city and all?"

"Well enough, I'd say," Frankie said, with a chuckle that could only mean Badger was bringing in money. How—picking pockets at the racetrack? Even that seemed over his head. The kid had surprised Dexter by not returning after he'd put him out of the car last October. Word had reached him later that Badger had affixed himself to Aldo Roma, an old-school racketeer and one of Mr. Q.'s lesser chiefs, with whom Dexter maintained a cordial, wary distance.

Back in the Cadillac on his way to Heels's place, he began preparing for his visit to Mr. Q. Other bosses whiled away their days in social clubs, gossiping with their lieutenants—not this one. For as long as Dexter could remember, there had been rumors that Mr. Q. was finished, a doddering loony fiddling with cucumber seeds, driving a horse cart packed with jars of tomato jam in his bedroom slippers. Yet the tendons of his power stretched from Bensonhurst to Albany to Niagara Falls, Kansas City, New Orleans, Miami. The coherent functioning of this corpus was a neat trick that required not a little hocus-pocus. Did the thing run itself? When—how—did Mr. Q., who was surely pushing ninety, oversee it? Was there another man behind the man—a deeper potentate whose proxy Mr. Q. had secretly become? How did he spend his money? Was it true he'd purchased a small South American country?

Dexter had had a vision—the sort of revelation that gobsmacked him once every few years, and that Mr. Q. counted on him to provide. It had come while he was standing on the beach with the crippled girl, right after Thanksgiving, and had strengthened and ramified in the weeks since: an unforeseen dividend of that charitable act.

Heels lived with his ailing mother in the same Dyker Heights house where he'd grown up: knickknacks and cut crystal, lace curtains indistinguishable from their embellishment of cobwebs. He was a committed bachelor, as they said. He appeared at the door in a Rangoon dressing gown with velvet lapels, his last shock of yellow-white hair brilliantined to filigree over a ceramically shiny pate. He carried a cigarette in a long ivory holder. "Apologies, boss," he said. "Mother's been fussy this morning; I haven't had time to dress."

"Those from Sulka?" Dexter asked, gesturing at the pajamas with turquoise piping visible under his dressing gown. Heels had a good eye—one of many things Dexter liked about him. He owned several vicuña coats.

"Custom," Heels said. "I find Sulkas just a shade too rough."

"You're a tender flower," Dexter rejoined dryly.

"Coffee, boss?"

While Heels went to get it, Dexter settled onto a couch in the parlor. Music was open on the upright: Chopin. Dexter had always assumed Heels's mother played, but she'd taken to her bed in recent weeks. "Heels," Dexter said when he returned with the coffee. "Don't tell me you can play Chopin."

"Only when I'm tight."

Heels ran the Pines directly, but in the past couple of years he'd become Dexter's all-around man at the New York clubs. Every midmorning, when they'd both had a few hours' sleep, they reviewed a list of concerns—or headaches, as Dexter had come to think of them. Today the first order of business was a police raid the night before at

Hell's Bells, in the Flatlands. Three dealers and a croupier were in the Tombs; Heels would bail them out.

"Same lieutenant?" Dexter asked.

"The very one."

"You've talked to him?"

"Tried. He claims not to speak our mother tongue."

"Holding out or showing off?"

"The latter, I'd say, seeing as he made no demands. And there was mention of 'cleaning house,' 'moral turpitude,' and 'scum of the earth.'"

Dexter rolled his eyes. "A mick?"

"Phelan." Heels grinned. His own name was Healey.

"I'll fix it," Dexter said.

Understandings with the law were axiomatic, of course, and by far his greatest business expense. Arrangements were required at every level, from the beat cops who enjoyed a regular bottle and the occasional envelope to district commanders and beyond. It was in this realm, where police brass kept company with union leaders and state politicos, that Dexter's business and family lives came closest to touching. Undoubtedly, his father-in-law's blue blood and known intimacy with the president afforded Dexter a degree of protection beyond what he paid for. He was as close to untouchable as any man could be in his line of work, yet there would always be idealistic young lieutenants wanting to make a name. Most could be turned with the right combination of blandishments. Purists, like Phelan, were transferred by their superiors to other districts.

Next problem: Mrs. Hugh Mackey. She had come around the Pines twice, with police, loudly demanding an inquiry into her husband's disappearance.

"Men skip town every day of the week," Dexter said. "Even when they aren't trying to blackmail their former employers."

"She says her Mackey would never walk. Devoted husband, adoring father. Tears."

"What does she want?"

"Same thing he did, is my guess."

"That's easy. Pay her off."

A maître d' who appeared to be skimming off the house. A manager who might have fallen into dope. Fighting among the girls who worked the gaming tables at the Wheel, in the Palisades. "Screaming, clawing, pulling of hair," Heels said. "We should charge a supplement."

"Their beef?"

"Stealing each other's gamblers, so they say. But there's a fancy man in there somewhere."

"You'll take care of them?" He was growing restless.

"I've chocolates and champagne in the car. If that doesn't work, I'll knock their heads together."

"What else."

After thirty more minutes, Dexter returned to the Cadillac in a state of clamoring impatience. The girls, the bulls, the wheedling Mrs. Mackey—all of it was petty and pointless when measured against his new vision. He hungered for a sense of progress, of new things approaching while old familiar ones receded. It seemed far too long since he'd had that sensation.

At three o'clock, he parked the Cadillac outside a modest yellow wood-frame house that sagged, knock-kneed, against the one beside it. It had been many years since Mr. Q. had given away brides and kissed squalling wet babies at their christenings. Nowadays he left home only to visit his store. He'd no doorbell, no telephone, and was fond of saying he had never sent—or accepted—a telegram. If you wanted to talk to Mr. Q., you knocked at this door and waited while his Scotch terrier, Lolly, amplified the news of your arrival.

Three minutes after her yapping commenced, Mr. Q. opened the door and sealed Dexter in his warm, fruit-smelling embrace. He was hulking and cavernous at once, browned to mahogany. Time had enlarged him in an organic, mineral way, like a tree trunk, or salts accreting in a cave. The frailty of his advanced age showed itself in the silty, tidal labors of his breath.

"Have a seat," he whispered as the excitable Lolly buzzed at their feet, white ribbons twitching in the fur on her head. "I'll make . . . the coffee."

From the time Dexter had first managed, at almost sixteen, to read the coded signals in his father's restaurant with enough precision to trace their source to this house; when he'd turned up on Mr. Q.'s doorstep with no more right than a stray dog, each visit had begun with the brewing of coffee on this same coal stove. The operation seemed to require a more delicate touch than Mr. Q.'s floppy, glove-like hands could manage, but Dexter had never seen him spill a drop.

During the silent interval while Mr. Q. stooped over the stove, Dexter (and every other visitor, presumably) gazed through the back window and gathered his thoughts. The stone birdbath was full of last week's snow, and the swaddled peach and pear trees—vestiges of an orchard—looked like boxers petrified mid-blow. Even more thickly cosseted were the six grapevines Mr. Q. had brought with him on the ship to New York, roots inside soil inside clay inside burlap inside layers of Sicilian newspaper. The vines of his youth. Only men he regarded as family were asked to assist in harvesting his grapes. Dexter had done so many times. Even now he could conjure the dry, sour smell the stems released when cut, the velvety sun-warmed weight of the grapes in his palm. The yield was symbolic; the wine Mr. Q. aged in pine barrels in his cellar was an alloy consisting mostly of grapes he purchased, delivered by the crate.

When the coffee hissed on the stove, Mr. Q. poured it into two small cups and brought them to the table. "You look good," he said softly, patting Dexter's cheek. "But that's the luck of . . . being a handsome fella. How you feel?"

"Good," Dexter said. "Very good."

"You strong? You look strong."

"Yes. Strong."

Though barely more than a whisper, Mr. Q.'s voice broke with the rumbling, soupy force of a primeval exhalation. He managed to emanate volcanic warmth while almost never smiling—a habit those around him tended to mirror in his presence. When Mr. Q. made an observation, or acknowledged one, it became immediately true. Dexter *was* strong. He knew that always, and he knew it now especially.

"You're my . . . strongest man," Mr. Q. said, pausing for breath between sentence halves. "I hope you won't mind a . . . little canning . . ."

"My pleasure, boss."

He had canned once before with Mr. Q.: peaches from his trees. On the spectrum of possible chores, canning fell in the middle: more laborious than harvesting vegetables from the large greenhouse (whether by rental or fiat, Mr. Q. controlled the land behind all of the houses on his block, making for a farm of some three acres); preferable to shoveling manure from Apple, his dray. The worst chores involved milking—either his cow, Angelina, whose rubbery udders throbbed with veins and horseflies, or—worse—his goats, who kicked, nibbled neckties, and produced almost nothing for one's pains. Mr. Q.'s chores were a source of gentle mirth among his chiefs on the rare occasions when they met, but cautious mirth—no one wanting to laugh harder than anyone else.

Today they would be canning yellow pole beans from the greenhouse. "Try one," Mr. Q. urged as Dexter began cutting off the tough ends on a worn marble slab. It tasted like a bean, more or less, but he pronounced it capital and finished it off. "You may have heard," he began as he worked, "I gave Badger some necessary hell a few months back."

"Badger," Mr. Q. breathed, "has energy."

"Never saw him again."

"Chutzpah. To quote my Jewish friends."

"If you say so."

"He's put together a little . . . numbers game."

Dexter was glad to have the beans to look at, for this news surprised him. Badger had his own numbers game after three months in New York? Not likely; he must be overseeing one of Aldo Roma's

games. Mr. Q. permitted favored chiefs an unusual degree of auton-
omy and independence. Dexter relished the distance from his coun-
terparts—he wanted nothing to do with the Red Hook piers, for
example, where men behaved like animals. But the sprawling, "blind"
nature of Mr. Q.'s empire allowed for little mutual curiosity among
chiefs, let alone gossip. For that reason Dexter was gratified when his
boss said, "I'd like Badger to . . . bring his game into a . . . couple of
the clubs."

"Of course. Which ones?"

"You decide."

Dexter nodded, satisfied. He wanted to keep an eye on Badger.

A large pot simmered on the stove, steaming the air in the small
kitchen. Mr. Q. gathered the beans in his shaking hands and dropped
them in.

"I've a new idea, boss," Dexter said. "The next step, as I see it."

A shudder of liveliness moved through Mr. Q. like a roll of thun-
der and settled in his moist brown eyes. "You know I . . . count on you
for that," he said.

It was Dexter who had divined, even before Prohibition ended in
'33, that rather than howl like scalded dogs, as so many in the underworld were doing, they should open a series of legitimate clubs that
would cleanse Mr. Q.'s gargantuan liquor trade earnings. Aside from
inoculating his fortune against the Bureau of Internal Revenue, the
arrangement had allowed them to profit from an array of ancillary
rackets both legal and illegal—everything from hat-checking to cigarettes to love matching, as Dexter thought of it. His own role as fig-
urehead had been essential: not once arrested; pedigreed by marriage,
with the foresight to have shed his tongue-twisting name in favor of a
short, stylish one (you might say) long before anyone cared to know it.

And oh, how the plan had worked! Buoyed them both on a tide of
legitimacy that swept Dexter into the presence of picture stars and news-
papermen and elected officials, state and national, into whose pockets
Mr. Q.'s influence had then been pressed. A beauteous arrangement

all around. There had been one mistake: Ed Kerrigan, Dexter's sole misjudgment in twenty-seven years of employment. People had gotten hurt, as the parlance went. But in the end, the trouble had brought down a rival and left Mr. Q. unscathed. This felicitous outcome was surely what had prompted Mr. Q. to declare three years ago, in his primordial hush, "It is forgotten. We won't speak of it again." Afterward, in the privacy of his automobile, Dexter had wept with relief.

When the beans were sufficiently boiled (something Mr. Q. seemed to know innately), it fell to Dexter to ladle them, upright, into mason jars. When each jar looked like an overcrowded elevator, Mr. Q. instructed him to pour scalding water over the beans, filling every jar to the neck.

"Now we screw these lids on tight . . . but not too tight . . . and we . . . put them into the pressure canner," Mr. Q. said, sounding overly winded for the little they'd done. "And then . . . you tell me our . . . idea."

Dexter had wanted to lead up to it gradually, like steps in a waltz, until there was nowhere left to move except his inevitable conclusion. But the broiling beanwork had cleared his mind of those steps, as perhaps it was meant to. In this atmosphere of heat and truth, preambles fell away and you ended up just saying the thing. He helped Mr. Q. screw the mason jars closed and place them carefully in a tarred pot that looked as if it had been dredged from the bottom of the sea. Mr. Q. covered the pot and hefted the flame underneath it. Then he sank onto a chair, breathing hard.

Dexter mopped his face with his handkerchief, resumed the seat across the small table, and began. "I'd like to approach Uncle and offer our services, and our businesses, for the war effort."

No immediate response; there never was. The onus was on Dexter to illuminate the bedrock layers underneath.

"The Allies will win, it's only a question of time," he said. "At that point, the U.S. will be more powerful than it has ever been. More powerful than any country ever, in the history of the world."

He quoted Arthur Berringer knowingly; it pleased Dexter to feel adjacency between the two. He'd been too lowly at the time of his wedding to warrant Mr. Q.'s attendance; as far as he knew, his boss and father-in-law had never met. But he'd sensed in each an oblique curiosity about the other, and it was conceivable that their paths might have crossed without his knowledge. He rather liked the thought.

"Mr. Stalin won't . . . expect a reward?" Mr. Q. asked.

"He'll get it. But his country will be wrecked."

Mr. Q. lowered his chin, his version of a nod.

"The Europeans," Dexter went on. "Broke and broken. That leaves Uncle. I want us—you—to have a legitimate part in the victory. A seat at the table."

Mr. Q. roused himself for the Socratic rumble that inevitably followed, sometimes extending over a subsequent visit. "As long as we've . . . money in hand," he said, "we'll have our . . . seat."

"At the table," Dexter said. "Not underneath it."

"The advantage?"

"Power. Legitimate power."

"All power is . . . legitimate."

"All right, then, legitimacy. Which would let us use our power in ways we can't now."

He was tempted to air his suspicion that a newly strengthened United States might use the rule of law to make their way of life extinct. Tammany had already gone—something no one had believed possible. But Mr. Q. didn't like worries. And Dexter sensed the idea already working on him.

"Lucky made a deal," Mr. Q. said, meaning Luciano. "Helped Uncle seal . . . up the port."

"And it'll likely get him sprung from Comstock."

"They came to him."

"We'll go to them."

"And offer . . . what?"

Here was the leap. Dexter took a long breath and leaned across the table. "We buy an issue of war bonds at a discount and resell them through every arm and leg of our business. Put everything liquid into the purchase. Sell off what we don't want and put that in, too. Our business becomes the war bond business."

"We're . . . a bank."

"In a manner of speaking, yes. Temporarily. When the war ends, our money is clean. We take it anywhere we want."

The pressure canner had begun to hiss, steam mounting behind a pin-size hole in the top. Mr. Q. tottered from his chair and clamped down a weight, sealing off this vent and anchoring the lid into place. A needle gauge on the side of the pot began to jump. He turned his soft brown eyes back to Dexter, who sensed that the moment had come to play his trump.

"If you work for Uncle, boss, Internal Revenue can't touch you. Probably ever again." The sealed pot began to shudder on the stove directly behind Dexter's head. "How long does it have to stay on?" he asked mildly.

"Long enough to . . . kill the botulism spores," Mr. Q. said. "Boiling isn't enough. The jar has to . . . stand a certain pressure." He remained upright, steadying the canner with a floral pot holder that was an artifact of Annalisa, his late wife.

"You're a . . . patriot," Mr. Q. said, regarding Dexter fondly.

"It's the right thing to do," Dexter said. "How often can we say that?"

"Our interests and . . . Uncle's are . . . aligned."

Dexter was surprised at how easy Mr. Q. was making this. Had he already been thinking along the same lines? The canner thrashed like a trapped squirrel against the cast-iron stove, threatening to wrest free of Mr. Q.'s quavering pressure. Dexter stood up, lest the pot disgorge its scalding contents over his head.

"We all want to win," Mr. Q. said softly amid the racket.

Dexter found himself grinning, he couldn't help it. And Mr. Q. grinned back. There was something wrong with his smile, something missing—teeth, was always one's first thought, but he had his teeth;

they were just very, very small. The result was a dark, asymmetrical void, more gash than face. Dexter's own smile wilted at the sight of it.

"Have you . . . spoken to . . . Uncle about this?" Mr. Q. asked.

"Of course not," Dexter exclaimed, grateful for the shrieking canner to mask his astonishment. Could Mr. Q. possibly think him stupid enough—disloyal or crazy enough—to talk to the feds without his blessing?

Mr. Q. covered the flame, and the cacophony collapsed into silence so profound that it made Dexter want to pop his eardrums.

"Trouble is," Mr. Q. breathed, "you open a channel . . . now it exists. Hard to regulate what . . . passes through or . . . what direction it . . . moves."

Dexter said nothing. What the hell was he getting at?

"This may be your . . . blind spot."

Kerrigan. It was the first allusion Mr. Q. had made to that mistake since assuring Dexter it had been forgotten. Apparently, it was not forgotten.

And now his boss was holding Dexter's cheeks, his hands soft and clumsy and full of blood. "We have many plans in our future," he said. "Many, many plans."

Dexter went rigid. There was a code to Mr. Q.'s utterances: repetition invoked a law of opposites. "Many plans," uttered twice, meant: not this plan.

"Many plans," Mr. Q. said again, drawing out the words as he gazed tenderly into Dexter's eyes.

No plans.

Meetings with Mr. Q. hewed to a stealthy efficiency, and Dexter found himself outside the front door just moments later. His boss embraced him as when he'd first arrived, affection undiminished—magnified, even. He favored Dexter, adored him. Dexter knew this.

"Ah! Slipped my . . . mind," Mr. Q. said, knocking his forehead with the hull of his hand. "How many . . . ripe tomatoes you . . . had this week?"

"They haven't any taste," Dexter mouthed. He was trying to absorb what had just happened. He stood on the porch while his boss disappeared back inside the house. Weak sunlight glistened on piles of shoveled snow. The local children played far away from this block; aside from the bawling of Mr. Q.'s livestock, there was no sound but distant harbor noises. Mr. Q.'s horse cart was parked at the curb. He still used it to deliver produce to his store—a rarity nowadays except for milkmen, who'd yet to find an automobile that would advance to their next stop while they delivered bottles at the last.

Eventually, Mr. Q. returned and pressed a small brown bag full of ripe tomatoes into Dexter's hands, along with a jar of peach jam, unlabeled. If Dexter wasn't mistaken, it was the very jam he'd helped his boss scoop into jars years before. Christ, how long did botulism prevention last? "Thank you, boss," he said.

"Good to see you, son," Mr. Q. wheezed. He leaned in the doorframe, gasping from his errand. It seemed to Dexter he'd declined markedly in the months since his last visit. In the bald winter light, he looked almost pale. "You should visit . . . more often. Come more . . . often. Don't . . . leave an old man alone."

Meaning: he'd exhausted his time with Mr. Q. for several months. Dexter took the fruit and preserves, kissed his boss on both cheeks, and walked to his car.

He drove with little idea where he was going. He wanted to think, but his need to move—to act—made it difficult to think unless he was driving. He was dumbfounded that Mr. Q. had rejected his idea out of hand. Had he really? Was that entirely clear? Was a wait of several months—the soonest he could conceive of returning unless asked—the same as a rejection? Had Mr. Q. fully understood what he was proposing?

He soon found himself at Coney Island, everything closed for winter, the clam and hot dog joints shuttered over. As a kid, Dexter had liked this time of year best; no more day-trippers. Just the people who lived here—or came, from all over, to eat at his pop's restaurant.

He parked and climbed onto the deserted boardwalk. Coast Guard sentries patrolled the waterfront. Muddy brown waves shoved in from the Lower Bay against the snowy sand. He thought of his pop: a man with a passion to cook—to serve. Dexter had revered him until around the time his mother died, when he was fourteen. At that point his adulation had reversed itself without warning, yielding a caricature of his father as cringing and servile. Dexter couldn't dispel it.

He'd said nothing to his pop about his first visit to Mr. Q.'s yellow house, but the memory of it lived in Dexter's belly like a snake, luxuriantly rearranging its coils. When his pop had learned of it some months later, he'd yanked Dexter by the ear into his office, although by then Dexter was sixteen and bigger than his pop. His father stared at him, nostrils flaring. "This is the single thing on God's earth I've most feared," he said.

"More than Ma dying?" Dexter countered, wriggling his feet in the stiff new spats he'd been flush enough to buy.

"More."

"More than going broke?"

"More. You take money from that man, you belong to him for life."

"I'd rather take his money than give him mine."

Such bald disrespect normally would have earned Dexter a cuff. But his pop leaned toward him urgently. "You're not of age," he said. "If you pull away now, he'll let you go."

"Pull away!"

"Do it now and do it clean. Put the blame on me."

Dexter saw that his father was frightened—for him. And out of some crude wish to reassure him, he said, "Mr. Q. is an old man, Pop. He won't live forever."

His father slapped his face with such force that tears sprayed from Dexter's eyes like juice from an apple smashed between the jaws of a horse.

"I'm not going to say don't talk that way," his pop said very softly. "Don't *think* that way. Or he'll guess it. He'll sniff you out."

"You don't know him, Pop." His voice shook.

"Mr. Q. has been around here a long time. I've seen people disappear like they were never born. One day to the next. You think I'm kidding? You think he's an old man, helping his wife can the fresh fruit? Hah!"

"You've never met him."

"One day to the next. And no one mentions their name. Like God never made them."

"Maybe *you* should be careful."

"I don't take his money."

"He might read *your* thoughts."

"I'd tell him to his face."

"You might disappear, Pop. You ever thought about that?"

He wanted his father to feel the magnitude of Mr. Q.'s power, his own comparative frailty. But his pop's fear had gone, leaving only disgust. "Get out."

Dexter left the restaurant and in some sense never returned, although of course he came and went. And those were mythical years to work for Mr. Q., thanks to Congressman Andrew Volstead of Minnesota and his ilk, who believed that drink would bring ruination upon the United States. Dexter was barely nineteen when the legislation passed, and defying it was a delirious kick. He loved driving fine automobiles on country roads and was good at giving chase. In the worst case, there were always woods, and he could run like hell. Flattening himself by a brook to mask the sound of his panting, smelling moss and pine and ash, a splatter of stars overhead—beauty and exhilaration beyond anything he could have fathomed.

Dexter got back in his automobile and drove a few blocks north, to the corner of Mermaid and West Nineteenth. The restaurant had closed in '34. Dexter could have saved it, but his pop would accept no more than relief from his own protection payments. The cancer got him at fifty-eight, although Dexter had never really heard him cough before the bank took his restaurant away.

It had been years since he'd stood on this corner, yet the place looked eerily unchanged: the cockeyed window shades and dusty bar, the gold lettering of his own unpronounceable name flaking away inside the window glass. A single broken table, upended. Dexter must have served his father's famous pescatore at that table, a white linen napkin hung crisply over his forearm as he poured the wine. Electrified by the invisible landscape he'd discovered: a latticework of codes and connections that shrank the everyday world into nonexistence. At times he'd thought he could actually *hear* Mr. Q.'s power pulsing through ordinary life inaudibly as a dog whistle. Nothing could have stopped him from finding his way to its source.

"What I want for you, Dexter," Mr. Q. had told him on that first visit, "is that you be your own man. Your *own* man." Cupping Dexter's peach-fuzzed cheeks in his hot, heavy hands, gazing into his lovestruck eyes: "Your own man, you understand?"

Dexter had understood his words and believed them. Only now, reading the code of repetitions and opposites, did he know what Mr. Q. had really meant.

He's an old man, Dexter thought, recalling his boss's labored breathing on the stoop this afternoon. *He won't live forever.* And felt again the sting of his father's slap, the wet ache in his eyes.

CHAPTER FIFTEEN

Lieutenant Axel's reason for calling Anna back became clear on the first morning of training, when he hollered at the group of thirty-five volunteers, "The dress weighs two hundred pounds. The hat alone weighs fifty-six. The shoes together are thirty-five. Now, before you start rolling your eyes about carrying all that weight, you should know that that *girl* standing over there—she's on the tall side, but she's no Sherman tank, like a lot of the females you see around here—she not only wore the dress without bellyaching, walked in the dress without bellyaching, but she also untied a bowline on a bight wearing three-fingered gloves. How many of you gents can even tie a bowline on a bight?"

Two hands rose. The other men glanced warily at Anna. She felt herself blush—from embarrassment but also from false pretenses. She hadn't known the name of the knot she'd untied, much less how to tie one. Nor had any of these volunteers—mostly from the trades, by the burly look of them—appeared to cower at the prospect of shouldering two hundred pounds. Lieutenant Axel was a man who rejoiced in discomfiting others; with his wizened, beardless face, he brought to mind a sadistic child. In the course of that day, he managed to call attention to DelBanco's fatness, Greer's slightness, Hammerstein's asthma, Majorne's "four eyes," Karetzky's flat feet, Fantano's slight limp, McBride's poor balance, Hogan's flatulence, and so on. Most of the men were too old for the service, but to Lieutenant Axel, a master naval diver at the time of his retirement, they might as well have been

4-F. And what better way to rattle them than with the threat of failing where a girl had succeeded?

Everyone except Anna had to wear the dress. For each wearer there were two tenders, just as Katz and Greer had been for her. Lieutenant Axel stood on a bench, bellowing instructions into a snowfall outside Building 569. Anna was back tender to a machinist called Olmstead, whose wrists were almost too bulky for the straps to buckle around the sleeves of his size-three dress. When at last Anna managed to fasten one, Olmstead brayed an ostentatious groan of relief, followed by a sly look. She kept her head down and feigned oblivion, relieved that the other tender—fair-haired, with a blank, dyspeptic face—seemed genuinely oblivious. Together he and Anna buckled the belt onto Olmstead, who then stood to be "jocked up."

"Tighter, darlin'," Olmstead crooned as Anna hiked the straps under his groin for the other tender to fasten to the front of the belt. "One more good pull. Ohhh, there you go, darlin'. That's it, just a little . . . uh . . ."

"Call me 'darlin'' one more time, pal," said the front tender in an inflectionless drawl, "you'll get it in the puss."

"Not you! Her!" Olmstead was mortified.

"It ain't her pulling." The tender's eyes were narrow and metallic, like fishhooks. He never glanced at Anna.

Olmstead spat on the pier and fell silent. When Anna and the other tender hoisted the enormous helmet to lower it over his head, he said, "Wait." Turning to Anna, he asked, "Can I breathe inside there?"

"Of course," she said coolly, fighting a tremble in her arms as she and the front tender held the helmet aloft. "It's a little musty, but you'll breathe just fine."

"Wait," Olmstead said again.

"We're falling behind," the front tender said. "On it goes."

They lowered the helmet, matching its threads to those in the breastplate collar and screwing it on. The front tender tapped the top of the helmet, meaning that Olmstead should stand and be inspected by Lieutenant Axel. He rose from the bench and began to thrash. The dress baffled his movements and the shoes rooted him to the pier, giving the impression of a tree harried by a gale. Only when the front tender managed to open his faceplate did a roar yaw through the premises: "I can't breathe. Get me out! I can't breathe in here!"

Lieutenant Axel was there with Greer a moment later, expertly removing the helmet, releasing Olmstead from the belt, collar, shoes, and dress. The machinist slunk away from the pier. With pleasure verging on glee, Lieutenant Axel informed the group, "That, gentlemen, was what they call claustrophobia: fear of enclosed spaces. There's usually one claustrophobic in every group, and I like to flush him out early. Such men have no business trying to become divers."

"What a bum," the front tender muttered—to himself, Anna supposed, since he seemed unaware of her. "We dressed him perfect, and we've no credit for it."

A second test involved the recompression chamber, whose purpose was to simulate the pressure of being underwater. Men whose eustachian tubes were blocked by ear damage or infection would have trouble equalizing the pressure on their eardrums. These unfortunates would experience piercing pain and even ruptured eardrums, should they decide to "play the hero" (the lieutenant warned, chuckling) and suffer in silence. Those with lung problems might just find themselves unable to breathe inside the tank. And then there were the men whose bodies responded to pure oxygen under pressure by going into seizures, no one quite knew why.

When they were suitably jittery, Lieutenant Axel admitted them to the recompression chamber in groups of six. It was a room-size cylinder divided into sections, the largest of which contained a bench where five men crammed together like pigeons on a wire to leave space around Anna. The expressionless front tender was among them; Paul Bascombe, she learned when all of them introduced themselves.

"You pass this one with flying colors, too?" Bascombe asked, glancing in Anna's general direction.

"No, it's my first time," she said, sounding overly bubbly to herself. "And I wasn't so very good in the dress. They're just using me to needle you."

"I figured."

This irked her. "I did untie the knot."

A silence overtook the group as the air warmed and grew close. "Try to whistle," Bascombe said.

They all tried, including Anna, but no one could make a sound. "What the hell," someone said.

"It's the pressure. Listen to our voices," Bascombe said. "I promise mine ain't always this squeaky."

Anna tested her own voice softly while the men drowned her out with impressions of Tweety Bird and Bugs Bunny. The more they were able to forget her, the easier they seemed.

The recompression chamber reduced their overall ranks by four more—so reported a euphoric Lieutenant Axel before dismissing them at the end of the first day. Sacco and Mohele had ear pain; Hammerstein began to wheeze; and McBride "felt funny in the head" and was quickly removed.

The next four days were spent in the classroom, where the lieutenant lectured them on diving physics, standard equipment and maintenance, air composition, and depth charts. For every hour spent at a depth of thirty-three feet or more, they would have to spend eight hours topside in order to be considered "clean" to dive again. "There's no shortcut, boys," he admonished them. "Don't go playing the tough guy unless you want nitrogen bubbles coming out through your ears and eyes and nostrils until every soft tissue in your body is hemorrhaging. The longest you can spend at a depth of forty feet without recompression is two hours. At fifty feet it's seventy-eight minutes. These shouldn't be numbers you have to think about—they should be as familiar as your birthday, your anniversary, or December seventh, 1941."

There was a lesson on potential hazards. "As divers, you'll earn two dollars and eighty-five cents an hour," Lieutenant Axel said. "But I've noticed civilian divers sometimes forget that 'hazard pay' means the work is dangerous." With the lip-smacking relish of a man reading off a dessert menu, he described fouled airlines; being dragged by a boat, "blowing up," and flying to the surface like a cork; nitrogen narcosis; and of course, the infamous "squeeze." Littenberg and Maloney, both married with several children, did not return the next morning. "Went home and spoke with their wives," Lieutenant Axel gloated. "We lose a couple that way every time."

Then a troubling reflection passed visibly over his childish brow. "Say, Katz," he said in an undertone. "How many have we left?"

There was one Negro: a welder called Marle who looked close to Anna's age and completed each challenge with ease. She was keenly aware of Marle but also eager to avoid him—a wish that shamed her, although she sensed Marle shared it. They sat at opposite corners of the classroom—Anna in back, where she wouldn't feel watched from behind; Marle in front, where he took tiny, meticulous notes with his left hand. On the rare occasions when they crossed paths, recognition flared between them, and they both slid their eyes away.

At the end of each day, the divers already trained returned to Building 569 from their jobs in Wallabout Bay or from working on the freshwater pipeline that ran from Staten Island to a navy monitoring center elsewhere in the harbor. Anna and the other trainees dispersed into the dusk, some through a small gate near the diving tank, others the long way, through the Sands Street gate. Anna always took the longer route to look for Nell, although she no longer really expected to find her.

On the fifth night of diving school, she spotted Rose leaving the inspection building. They embraced and walked arm in arm out the Sands Street gate. "The shop isn't the same without you," Rose said. "All the girls say so."

"No one to gossip about," Anna said.

"They say Mr. Voss is pining. He looks pale and slightly thinner."

"Sounds like they're the ones in love with him."

Rose chortled. Anna walked her to Flushing Avenue and waited with her for the streetcar, hoping her friend would ask her to supper. But when the crowded car arrived, Rose hopped aboard and seized an overhead strap, waving goodbye to Anna through the window.

Anna watched the streetcar slide east toward Clinton Hill. Only when she turned to walk toward her own streetcar stop on Hudson did solitude engulf her. In daylight it retreated; she'd tried in vain, during diving school, even to remember what it felt like. But at dusk it closed back around her with macabre comfort. It had a pulse and a heartbeat. Its clutch removed Anna from the realm of mothers pulling children by the hand, and men hurrying home with evening papers under their arms. She climbed onto her streetcar, accordion doors knocking shut behind her, and watched the night slide past outside the window. It quivered with a danger against which her lonely routine formed a last thin line of defense. But what was the threat?

Supper awaited her, still warm, at Mr. Mucciarone's grocery counter. As Anna took the covered dish from Silvio, a memory brushed her like a cat circling her shins: Lydia, whimpering in Silvio's arms. In her own building, she opened the mail slot and found the usual letter from her mother, along with V-mails from two neighborhood boys. She climbed the stairs, mail in one hand and supper in the other, passing the Feeneys' two apartments, which had been like an extension of her own when she was small. In her solitude, she couldn't bring herself to knock. *You mustn't,* she thought. *They aren't expecting you.*

The same thing happened when she imagined using the public telephone at White's to call Stella or Lillian or Aunt Brianne. She'd gone to *Casablanca* with Brianne and skated with her friends at the Empire Roller Dome. But at the end of these interludes, the others returned to their homes and Anna to her isolation. No one could protect her from it.

She bolted the apartment door, pulled down the shades, and turned on every light and the radio. First news, then music. She'd abandoned her favorites, Count Basie and Benny Goodman; their boiling sound was too suggestive of the city's furrowed darkness. Instead, she turned the dial in search of Tommy Dorsey, Glenn Miller, even the Andrews

Sisters, whose syrupy crooning used to gag her. Now it had the reassuring effect of whistling as you walked on a dark street. She read her mother's letter. Her missives were short and stuck mostly to facts: the punishing Minnesota winter, the health of the cows and sheep, news of Anna's cousins in training or overseas.

In each letter, her mother seemed at one point to forget herself—or Anna—and wander into more introspective territory: *I keep expecting to wake up one morning and know what to do, the way I knew to come to New York after high school. But any decision I make seems to last about twenty-four hours, if that.*

And another time:

The boys of my youth are fat, balding, and in three cases dead (1 turned tractor, 1 riding accident, 1 throat cancer). I look at my face and see no real change; obviously I am kidding myself!

And once:

The moon out here is too bright.

When she'd finished eating, Anna cleaned and dried Mrs. Mucciarone's dish and set it aside to return the following morning. She began a letter to her mother, taking satisfaction in relaying details that would not have interested her had she been here. Tonight she wrote about Lieutenant Axel's glee at frightening them. She wrote until she felt tired enough to sleep, then sealed the letter and turned off the radio and all of the lights except the one in her bedroom. She lay in her bed and hugged Lydia's pillow. For as long as she could remember, there had been another creature nearby at night, breathing, radiating warmth. She clutched the pillow as if plugging a wound, and inhaled the faint essence of her sister that still clung to it.

Last, she opened her Ellery Queen. For all their varied and exotic settings, mystery novels seemed to happen in a single realm—a landscape vaguely familiar to Anna from long ago. Finishing one always left her disappointed, as if something about it had been wrong, an expectation unfulfilled. Her dissatisfaction accounted for the number of mysteries she read, often returning several to the library in a week.

Since her mother's departure, these novels had become trapdoors leading Anna to memories of accompanying her father as a little girl. Holding his hand on an elevator while an old man with mussed hair sleepily turned a crank. Walking beside him down an empty corridor lined with doors, gold lettering on pebbled glass panes, the sound of their footsteps twanging the walls. Looking down from a skyscraper window at yellow taxicabs buzzing like bees under greenish thunderclouds. Anna knew to keep her back turned until she heard the rustle of paper, the weight of a parcel sliding across a desk. A drawer whispering shut. Afterward there would be a rush of ease, everyone suddenly jolly.

What had he been doing, exactly? Was it dangerous? Here was the mystery that seemed now to have been flashing coded signals at Anna from behind every Agatha Christie and Rex Stout and Raymond Chandler she'd read. Becoming aware of this deeper story made it burn through the allegorical surface of whatever plot she was reading until she found herself not reading at all, but holding the book and remembering. Puzzling. Mr. Styles was part of the mystery. But *that* Mr. Styles—who had known her father—seemed a different man from the one who had taken her with Lydia to Manhattan Beach. His act of kindness had left Anna with one of her happiest memories. Reverting to Mr. Styles the nightclub owner, the gangster—or former gangster—felt like forfeiting their exalted, mystical day. She refused. She returned to her book and read herself to sleep. In the middle of the night, she woke and turned out the light.

In class the next morning she heard a faint murmur, distinct from the voice of Lieutenant Axel. To her left, Bascombe sat looking straight ahead. His expression was blank, yet somehow Anna knew the murmuring issued from him. Was he talking to himself? The topic was rules and regulations—the importance of abstaining from beer twenty-four hours before a dive.

"They tell you all kinds of bunk that ain't true," the patter continued. "Bubbles in the blood got nothing to do with bubbly drinks. Not that I give a damn—I'm a teetotaler."

She stared straight ahead, certain that Lieutenant Axel would hear him and blame her.

"Don't let 'em fill up your head with that crud. They think you'll believe anything because you're a girl. They've no intention of letting you dive, by the way."

"What do you mean?" Anna hissed despite herself.

"They expect you'll wash out when we get in the water next week," he reported in a monotone. "Overheard 'em."

Anna's pulse began to race. She stared at Lieutenant Axel and remembered their earlier meeting—the hopelessness of trying to persuade him even after she'd worn the dress. Did he still plan to thwart her?

In her distraction, she forgot to put on her coat before leaving Building 569 to walk to the building ways cafeteria for lunch. Bascombe brought the coat and caught up with her. "Climbing the ladder in the wet dress is the hardest part," he muttered as if still in the classroom, falling into step beside her. "Especially for lightweight divers."

"You've dived before?" she asked, keeping her own eyes forward.

"Nah. I worked as a tender in Puget Sound."

"Canada?"

"West Coast. Near Seattle, Washington. It was a body job: a contract diver was pulling corpses out of two carriers before they went into dry dock. January 1942. Yep, you're thinking right, you're thinking right: they'd towed 'em all the way from Hawaii."

She glanced at him, disbelieving.

"Top-secret. Not one of us navy."

"Was there a second tender?"

"No, ma'am. Just me. Diver taught me what to do. He bagged the bodies underwater, and I pulled 'em up. His air supply came direct from the dock."

Anna liked this way of talking: an exchange of information without having to witness the wet depth of another person's gaze. "Is that why you want to dive?" she asked.

"I suppose," he said. "Keep trying to join the navy. Tried in Seattle, tried again in Frisco, then San Diego, but I can't get my goddamn eyes to read those itty-bitty letters on the chart. They say if you're good enough, you can cross over from civilian diving into navy."

Anna glanced at Bascombe's face. For the first time, his scowling impatience and fuming concentration were legible as striving. "You came all the way out here," she said.

"You bet I came. No better place for civilian diving than New York City. We've had the *Normandie* belly-up at Pier 88 since she caught fire a year ago—that's a thousand-foot-long training ground. They've opened up a whole salvage school to get her righted, and you know where she'll come to be refitted when they finally do? This Naval Yard right here. And something else," he added as they approached the entrance to Building 81. "Doesn't make a damn bit of difference about your eyesight; you can't see a thing underwater." With that, he left her side so abruptly, it was as if they hadn't been speaking at all.

In their second week of training, some of the younger diving students began leaving the Yard together at day's end. Anna heard them discussing bars—Leo's, Joe Romanelli's, the Oval Bar, and the Square Bar—the latter two kitty-corner from each other on Sands Street and owned by rival brothers. Now that the Germans had finally surrendered Stalingrad, morale was running high. Whenever a cluster of camaraderie began to form near Anna, she fell back, fading from the scene at just the moment when it might have seemed rude not to invite her. It was uncanny, given the distraction of her presence, how easily she could vanish. Marle, the Negro, had perfected this art. Though physically imposing, he'd a way of detaching himself from the general flow until it rushed on without him. Only Anna noticed, but she hid her awareness; an allegiance between her and Marle would jeopardize what slender ties fastened each of them to the larger group. And so the estrangement they had in common estranged them doubly from each other.

Most nights, a girl with thin blond hair awaited Bascombe outside the Sands Street gate. Anna gleaned from his conversation with the other divers that she was his fiancée, Ruby, whom he'd met after arriving in Brooklyn last summer. For a Brooklyn girl, Ruby was bizarrely ill-equipped for winter, shivering in a thin coat, then lassoing Bascombe in a lariat of sinewy arms and hanging at his neck, her forehead pressed to his. Anna liked Bascombe, which was partly to say that she liked herself in his company. Their flat, unvalenced exchanges were the closest she had ever come to feeling like a man. Bascombe in the grip of those greedy arms would be another matter, but Anna felt no envy. She had the Bascombe she wanted.

On the morning of their first dive, twelve divers loaded up the barge, and Lieutenant Axel steered it around the building ways, jostling waxy-looking ice cakes and hugging the piers to avoid boat traffic. Men watched from the piers, just as Anna had once done. She was nervous, knowing that Lieutenant Axel expected her to fail. But then he wanted all of them to fail. That was no secret.

Lieutenant Axel anchored the barge off the foot of Dry Dock 1. Two divers would go down at once, he explained, each with two tenders, while the rest would turn the massive flywheels on the two air compressors, one supplying air to each diver. They would rotate positions through the day until everyone had dived.

With a show of randomness, he chose Anna and Newmann to go down first. But Anna had spent enough time studying his baby ancient's face to recognize mischief spidering across it. The lieutenant was up to something. Perhaps her job would be to shame the others, as before— Anna half hoped for this, since it meant succeeding. He selected Bascombe and Marle, the Negro, to be her tenders. Only then did Anna catch something amiss: Marle, a welder, should not have been on the barge at all. Welders and burners were making their first dives back on the West Street Pier in the new diving tank: a twenty-by-seventeen-foot cylinder with portholes for Katz and Greer to look in. Now she understood. The devilry lay in forcing proximity upon herself and Marle, the two outsiders who had worked so hard to stay apart. The intent was to rattle them and thereby worsen their chances.

Anna saw her own disquiet reflected in Marle's face. Bascombe's expression yielded nothing, but his jaw muscles flexed like the gills of a gasping fish. Failure was Bascombe's enemy; he wanted no part of it. An agony of unease engulfed all three of them as the men held the canvas envelope for Anna and she stepped gingerly inside, trying not to touch them. A tender's job was to hold and guide the diver, but being handled by these men, one a Negro, awakened in Anna a balking shyness she was certain they could detect. All of them lurched through the early steps: wrist straps and shoes and tightening of leg laces. But as Bascombe and Marle were pulling the rubber collar over the brass studs, routine began to neutralize discomfort. They tightened wing nuts over the studs, calling back and forth across Anna's shoulders. At last they lifted the hat over her head, and she was surrounded by its tinny odor. Two hundred pounds bore down upon her when she stood. She'd remembered the fact of this weight but not the brutal sensation of being crushed by it. Could she sustain it? She could. And now? Yes. It was like someone knocking continually at a door, awaiting a new reply. And now?

Bascombe glanced through the faceplate, as pleased as she'd ever seen him—which was to say not frowning. "Under five minutes," he said. "Newmann's collar ain't even fully sealed."

Trying not to stagger, Anna shuffled toward the diving ladder. Marle checked her umbilical cord—air hose and lifeline, bound together—and she heard the hiss of air entering the helmet. At the ladder, they turned her around so her back was to the water. Marle looked in at her, his eyes engaging Anna's with a lively, antic gaze. "Pleasure to meet you, Miss Kerrigan."

"Likewise, Mr. Marle."

"Good luck down there."

"Why, thank you."

Marle closed the faceplate and sealed it. They'd had their first conversation.

Holding the curled rails of the diving ladder, she began taking careful backward steps, finding each rung with the metal tip of her shoe before resting her weight there. Water contracted around her legs with cold energy, suctioning the wrinkles in her jumpsuit pinchingly to her skin. Ice cakes nudged at the dress. Soon the water was at her chest, then lapping the bottom of the faceplate. Anna took a last look up and saw Bascombe and Marle watching her from the ladder. Two more rungs and she was submerged, the green-brown water of Wallabout Bay visible through her four windows. No sound but the hiss of air.

On the last of the ladder's fourteen rungs, she paused to increase her air supply. Sure enough: the dress inflated slightly, easing the water's pressure on her legs. She felt for the descending line, swung her left leg around its manila cord, and let it slide through her left glove as she drifted down, the weight of the dress lulling her toward the bottom, the water darkening as she left the surface behind. At last her shoes met the bottom of Wallabout Bay. Anna couldn't see it: just the wisps of her legs disappearing into dark. She felt a rush of well-being whose source was not instantly clear. Then she realized: the pain of the dress had vanished. The air pressure from within it was just enough to balance the pressure from outside while maintaining negative buoyancy—i.e., holding her down. And the weight that had been so punishing on land now allowed her to stand and walk under thirty feet of water that otherwise would have spat her out like a seed.

There was a single pull on her umbilical cord: *Are you all right?* She repeated the pull to indicate that she understood and was fine. *All is well.* She found herself smiling. The air in her nostrils was delicious; even the hiss of its arrival, which Lieutenant Axel had described as "a mosquito you can't swat," was welcome and sweet. They'd been told they wouldn't need to adjust their exhaust valve from the two and a half turns it had been set at, but Anna couldn't resist tightening the star-shaped nozzle a hair to let more air gather inside the dress. She began just slightly to rise, mud sucking at the bottoms of her shoes as they pulled away. A burst of pleasure broke inside her. This was like flying, like magic—like being inside a dream. She opened the exhaust valve and flushed out the excess air until her feet settled again on the floor of the bay.

A tool bag, perforated with holes that looked comical on land, floated into her grasp by a lanyard attached to the descending line. Inside were hammer, nails, and the five pieces of wood she was expected to hammer together into a box. The challenge would be keeping the wood—and the box itself—from shooting to the surface prematurely. Every diver would be timed, of course. "The clock ticks more loudly underwater," Lieutenant Axel had warned. "If you have to surface to retrieve your wood, you've wasted precious bottom time."

Anna opened the mouth of the tool bag wide enough to insert a hand. The wood pieces clamored at her wrist, eager to escape, but she managed to remove just two before realizing she'd left hammer and nails inside. She secured the loose pieces under her left arm and felt inside the bag for the hammer. A piece of wood shot from the bag, and in trying to seize it, she released the two from under her arm. She was barely able to block and snatch the three errant pieces before they lofted out of reach. Her heart stammered, and she felt light-headed. Panic, or any exertion underwater, made you exhale more carbon dioxide, which then weakened you when you breathed it back in. Anna returned everything to the bag and closed it. She took a long breath and shut her eyes and immediately felt a new responsiveness in her fingertips, as if they'd suddenly wakened from sleep. Of course. She would keep her eyes closed. Anna loosened the mouth of the bag and let two wood pieces nudge their way into her right hand. With her left, she prised free the hammer and a single nail. She hung the bag on her shoulder and braced the wood pieces at a right angle against the lead blocks of her belt. With a somnolent underwater motion, she hammered the nail until it perforated the soft wood and joined the two slats. Her hands were in charge; she hardly looked. Soon she was hammering the bottom onto the box, wishing it had taken longer to complete. She didn't want to surface.

Without signaling the tenders, she stowed the box inside the tool bag and tightened her exhaust valve just enough to allow for a sequence of buoyant, floating steps. She felt debris under her shoes, the hidden topography of Wallabout Bay. What exactly was down there? She wished she could kneel and feel it with her hands. Holding up her umbilical cord so as not to get tangled, she turned all the way around, feeling the pressure of tides and currents from the river and the ocean beyond.

Three sharp tugs on her umbilical cord put an end to these antics. *Stand by to come up.* Her bubbles must have betrayed her; she imagined Bascombe's annoyance at the sight of them straying from the ladder. His concern would be timing and performance, completing the job before the other team. She looked for the descending line, but the three-inch manila rope had disappeared. She'd hardly moved, it seemed, yet somehow she'd gone far enough for the line to be outside the reach of her extended arms in every direction she walked.

Seven pulls: they'd perceived the problem and were switching to searching signals to guide her. Anna echoed the seven, then received three pulls, which meant *turn right*. But how could they know which way she was facing? Dutifully, she turned and began to walk, sweeping her arms in hopes of intercepting the line. Her heartbeat squelched in her ears as she imagined the shame of having to be hauled up by her lifeline.

Then it came to her that she could surface without using the descending line at all, simply by adjusting her control and exhaust valves. She let the dress inflate just enough to rise gently, shoes plucking away from the mud. She kept her hands on the two valves, air supply and exhaust, inflating the dress enough to lift her through the brightening water without "blowing up" and flying spread-eagled to the surface.

Her hat broke the water, and daylight poured through her faceplate. The hammerhead crane was in front of her, which meant she was facing away from the barge. By paddling her arms underwater, she swiveled herself around and saw the barge only twenty feet away. She could not swim in the dress, but by pedaling her legs as if she were riding a bicycle, she was able to propel herself slowly forward. Cycling the boots was exhausting; sweat streamed between her breasts, and her faceplate fogged. She knew she should pause and vent her carbon dioxide, but she gave the last of her energy to closing the gap between herself and the ladder. At last she clutched a rail in each glove and let herself submerge again, resting her metal shoes on the lowest rung and trying to catch her breath.

Gasping in the overheated hat, Anna recognized the price of her innovation: she'd no strength left. She tried to climb the ladder, but once her hat was exposed, she had to pause again, reckoning with the weight that five inches at sea level visited upon her spine and shoulders. At last she mustered the energy to drag herself up another rung. She managed three more, bringing the water to her waist, but could go no farther.

Her faceplate jerked open, and Bascombe peered in from above her on the ladder. His face was every bit as grim as she'd expected. "Squat and let water run off the dress," he told her. "That'll lighten it."

Anna gulped cold fresh air through the open faceplate. "I need to . . . go back down," she panted.

"Don't tell me that. Squat."

Anna squatted and felt water being forced off the dress. But the hat and collar were still too heavy.

"Take a step," Bascombe said, withdrawing to give her room. She managed to get her left shoe onto the next rung, but when she tried to hoist the remainder of her body up the next five inches, her knee buckled and she nearly fell in backward. Bascombe seized her forearms and pinned them, hard, to the ladder rails. Together they absorbed what had almost happened: falling into the water with her faceplate open would have meant plunging straight to the bottom.

"You want Marle and me to pull you up?" Bascombe said. "Fine, we'll pull you up. And those mugs will say, *Good riddance. Send her back home to Mama.* Fuck that." He jabbed his gaze through the faceplate into her eyes. His own were very blue, hard as quartz. Anna felt as if she'd never really seen them before. "Find the strength, Kerrigan," he told her. "Find. The. Strength."

She saw that he was desperate. "It won't count against you," she breathed, "if I can't."

He made a disdainful noise. "It won't touch me," he said. "Newmann blew up, Savino nailed a hole through the leg of his dress, Fantano's wood is floating down the river. Morrissey's on his way up, but I doubt he's built the box. At this rate, Marle and I are the only ones who'll pass."

"I made the box," Anna panted.

Surprise flickered in his eyes. "All right, then," he said. "Get up this goddamn ladder and take the credit. Lift your shoe! Good. Now the other. Up. Up." He was still securing her wrists to the ladder, leaning down from the rungs above her like a bat. "I'll see you topside," he said, and sealed her faceplate.

His hectoring worked upon Anna like smelling salts. Or maybe it was having rested. Or breathed fresh air. Whatever the reason, she climbed the ladder. One step, then another. She was stronger than she knew.

Back on the barge, Marle steered her toward the diving bench, and she sank onto it. When Marle opened her faceplate, she saw Lieutenant Axel holding two completed boxes. Everyone paused to listen, Anna and Morrissey still in their helmets.

"We've had our share of tribulations this morning," the lieutenant told the group coyly. "But I'm pleased to say we've two boys here who are honest-to-God divers."

"One is Kerrigan, sir," Marle shouted over the wind.

Even in her exhaustion, Anna knew she would not forget the look of appalled bewilderment that blighted the lieutenant's childish face. Shaking his head, he peered at the diving benches.

"No," he said. "No, no." And then, "Which one?"

CHAPTER SIXTEEN

In bruising terms, Lieutenant Axel expelled from the program the three men who had failed their dives in Wallabout Bay. But as there was nowhere for them immediately to go (the barge being surrounded by water), and as their services—as both tenders and flywheel turners on the air compressors—were still required, they remained on board, the lieutenant eyeing them warily as the day progressed. He'd fewer divers than he needed. Of his two irreconcilable wishes—to amass a robust diving program and sack every diver in it—the latter had gained an edge.

When everyone else had dived successfully, the lieutenant grudgingly offered Newmann, Savino, and Fantano a chance to redeem themselves. This time all three managed to assemble their boxes and haul themselves back onto the barge. Celebration crested among the group as they steamed back to the West End Pier. It gathered force as they unloaded diving chests and air compressors and heavy wet diving dresses and carried them back into Building 569.

"We did a good job weeding out the bad apples early," Lieutenant Axel told the group in subdued approval. "What we've left now are the strongest men, the ablest men, for diving. Some of you will fall away yet," he said, a catch of excitement in his voice. "Accidents, injuries, mishaps—those are inevitable. But for now, congratulations, men."

His eyes seemed to graze Anna each time he used the word "men," as if he were conjuring her disappearance. In the lieutenant's eyes, she was the inconvenient residue of a failed experiment—Anna knew this. Building 569 hadn't even a ladies' room. In order for her to use the toilet, Katz or Greer had to clear the men's room and stand awkward guard outside it. She dreaded the arrival of her monthly. Back in her old shop, the marrieds had groused about marine guards glimpsing their Kotex during inspections of pocketbooks at the Sands Street gate. She'd have liked to see them react to this arrangement!

Her makeshift locker room was a broom closet. As she changed back into her street clothes, she overheard the male divers clowning in their locker room down the hall. A plan was afoot to meet at the Eagle's Nest. It was Saturday night; tomorrow would be a day off. Anna stayed hidden as they passed her closet in boisterous packs on their way out.

When the building was quiet, she peeked from the closet and saw Marle walking alone toward the exit. Like her, he must have been waiting for the others to go. Anna had an impulse to join him. She was about to step from her closet when she heard Bascombe call from outside: "Say, Marle, you still in there?"

"Still here," Marle called back, slowing his steps.

"The boys are walking over now. I'll wait for you."

Marle hesitated, glancing at his wristwatch. Anna had an uncanny sensation of being inside his mind—feeling hesitant, shy of the awkwardness of joining but eager to be included. Bowing out now, with Bascombe waiting, would look churlish; he might not be invited again. "All right," Marle said, and moved toward the door with purpose.

Anna heard the crunch of their boots on the brick pier as their voices faded into the faint din of construction noise and boat traffic. Silence reverberated around her, prelude to the streetcar, the covered dish, the empty apartment. The prospect repelled her. All day she'd handled other divers and been handled by them in a way reminiscent of childhood: jostling with other kids, the feel of their breath, their sticky hands, the bready smell of their scalps. Having been nourished by so much proximity, she couldn't bear to return to her solitude.

She hurried to the inspection building to look for Rose, intending to ask her to supper. If Rose demurred—as she likely would, with little Melvin at home—she might at least invite Anna with her. But she'd missed the shift change, and when she reached the second floor, she found Rose and the other marrieds gone, strangers on their stools.

The supervisor's door was ajar. Anna knocked, uncertain whether it would be Mr. Voss or the night snapper.

"Come in."

"Mr. Voss!" she cried.

He'd his coat on, hat in hand. "Miss Kerrigan," he said, smiling. "What a lovely surprise."

"I was—I came—" she stammered, trying to account for her presence. "I dove in Wallabout Bay this morning."

"In the great big suit?"

"Two hundred pounds."

"Wonderful. Was the lieutenant pleased?"

"Not at all," she said. "He was hoping I would fail, and it was my pleasure to disappoint him." The voice was not entirely her own—a return to the bantering rhythm she and Mr. Voss had fallen into before.

"This calls for celebration," he said. "May I take you to dinner?"

"I'll need to bathe." She was caked with dried sweat. Mr. Voss wore a fine gray suit.

"Why don't I take you home and wait outside while you freshen up."

Now that he wasn't her supervisor, Anna saw no harm in being seen with Mr. Voss; the *Shipworker* routinely carried small items on the weddings of couples employed at the Yard. She walked beside him along Sands Street, able at last to satisfy her curiosity about its uniform shops and tattoo parlors and dusty windows with small signs advertising "rooms." But her solitude leered at her from behind the bustle like a mastiff at a window. On the streetcar, she kept her eyes on Mr. Voss and avoided looking at the dark.

In her apartment, she ran a bath. Nell had told her about department stores where girls could go after work to bathe and be styled and made up before their dates. The idea of transformation appealed to Anna. She was tired of herself. She rifled through the frocks her mother had left and found an off-the-shoulder strapless dress of sea-green satin. She adjusted the seams before the tub had even filled. Then she scrubbed herself with soap flakes in the hot bath and shaved under her arms. After drying, she powdered her breasts and neck, painted her lips, and rouged her cheekbones with her mother's cosmetics. She added a string of pearls and diamond drop earrings—all paste, of course, but good from a distance. She found a pair of silver faux-satin gloves that reached her elbows. Lifting the hair from her neck, she pinned it as best she could—it was heavy and shiny for pins—then added a small round hat to match the dress. When she looked in the kitchen mirror, the glamour girl gazing back at her made her laugh. A disguise! Why hadn't she thought of this before? She exchanged a wink with her dashing new partner in crime.

Mr. Voss leaned against a wall in the chilly vestibule, reading his evening *Tribune*. "Miss Kerrigan," he said when she reached the bottom of the stairs in her mother's beaded cloak. "I am staggered."

"And why is that, Mr. Voss?"

"Charlie. Please."

"Only if you'll call me Anna." She felt a niggle of worry; was she certain he didn't care for her that way?

"I'd been planning to take you to Michael's, on Flatbush," he said. "Now I think nothing short of a taxi ride to Manhattan will do."

"I don't know whether to be flattered or insulted." She'd lapsed into one of the moving-picture voices she and Lillian and Stella liked to use.

They hailed a taxi on Fourth Avenue and soon were crossing the Manhattan Bridge. The East River was a blue-black void, ticks of light suggesting a density of boats. Anna took a long breath. Without the familiar ballast of her loneliness, she felt unmoored, as if she might fall off the bridge into the dark river.

"Tell me something, Charlie," she said. "Is there a woman at home right now, wondering where you might be?"

He turned to her, serious. "There is no woman waiting for me," he said. "You have my word."

"The girls in the office . . ."

"Ah, they love to talk."

"Could it have hurt you? What they said?"

"Only if it were true."

She'd been right; they were friends, no more. "Not even a daughter?" she asked. "Waiting at home?"

"I am, so far, childless."

"A handsome fellow like you, Charlie," she chided, tumbling back into banter like a bed of feathers. "How can that be?"

"Bad luck, I suppose. Until tonight. Providence has smiled upon me at last."

"You've used that line a hundred times. And you got it from a fortune cookie."

"Seventy, eighty times at most."

They were laughing together, reveling in each absurd escalation of their repartee. Anna had always wanted to flirt; now, suddenly, it was effortless.

At Chandler's, on East Forty-sixth, they ate hamburger steaks with smothered onions and french-fried potatoes, followed by slices of apple pie. They drank champagne. Charlie Voss had a way of asking questions that kept the conversation safely in the realm Anna wished to inhabit: her diving test, Lieutenant Axel's eccentricities, the progress of the Russians against the Krauts in the Ukraine. The darkness surrounding this well-lighted patch went unmentioned. Anna sensed in Charlie Voss a symmetrical darkness. In moments she felt at the brink of understanding it—some truth about him that was practically in view. But she was left merely baffled.

After supper, as they walked toward Fifth Avenue, Anna took his arm. She felt as she had this morning underwater—unwilling to surface. Charlie Voss must have felt this, too, for he said, "Let's not call it a night so soon. Have you a favorite nightclub?"

"I've only been to one," she said.

*   *   *

Moonshine's top-hatted doorman was cherry-picking entrants from a crowd that had massed outside the lacquered door. It occurred to Anna that she could say, with some small truth, that she knew Dexter Styles, but it turned out not to be necessary. The gatekeeper admitted them, and Anna's first impression was that nothing about the place had changed—that this night was a continuation of the last. In the glittering checkerboard arena, she sought out the table she and Nell had occupied. Strangers sat there now, and Dexter Styles was nowhere in sight. After a flash of disappointment, Anna was relieved not to find him. The day with Lydia at Manhattan Beach could remain intact.

A maître d' showed them to a table at the room's outer edge, and Charlie ordered champagne. The orchestra's ominous horns and snares sounded like the approach of a thunderstorm or an army. A wastrel-looking singer briefly silenced the room with her temblor of a voice. Anna and Charlie rushed the dance floor with dozens of other couples. Anna was nervous, recalling how badly she'd danced with Marco last October, but Charlie Voss made it easy. "Thank God you're such a good dancer," she said.

"You've summoned it forth."

"Hah! A good liar, too." She was dizzy from champagne and the pleasure of holding another person. Warm currents of air hummed on her collarbones.

"Anna? Is that possibly you?"

She turned and saw Nell, in strapless peach chiffon, dancing with an older man in a dinner suit. Anna broke from Charlie and threw her arms around her friend. "I can't believe it," she cried. "I looked for you everywhere."

"I hardly recognized you," Nell said. "What happened? You're gorgeous!"

Nell looked bewitching, as always, if slightly more affected. Her curls had a new reddish tint and her skin was impossibly white, as if she never went outdoors. "I'm sure you two are seated in Siberia; we've room at our table," she said. "This is Hammond, my fiancé."

Hammond gave a pinched smile, his aquiline nostrils flaring under a pair of inert green eyes. Anna supposed he was handsome. She introduced Charlie Voss, and the four of them threaded among dancing couples away from the orchestra. "We're not really engaged," Nell whispered. "I just say that to rattle his cage."

"Is he . . . that one?"

"The same. He's put me up in the most beautiful little apartment on Gramercy Park South. I've a key to the park! You should come visit. Number twenty-one. Say it, so I know you'll remember. Twenty. One."

"Twenty-one," Anna duly repeated. Her friend seemed jumpy, possibly drunk. "Did you find a better job?"

"I haven't any job at all," Nell said. "Unless you count trying to look smashing all the time so Hammond doesn't toss me out."

They seated themselves among a group who occupied several tables near the dance floor. Anna noticed Marco and reddened when he looked in her direction. But he was watching Nell.

"Would he really throw you out?" Anna whispered.

"Hammond is a pig," Nell said, which dumbfounded Anna, Hammond himself being inches away, his arm around Nell's shoulders. Anna averted her gaze as if she'd been guilty of an indiscretion. "Then why do you—"

"Money," Nell said brightly. "He's loaded with money, and he pays for everything. He lives in an eight-bedroom mansion in Rye, New York, with his wife and four children. He'll never leave them—I was nuts to think he would. Isn't that right, darling," she called to Hammond. "Anna worked with me at the Naval Yard. Hammond doesn't like to hear about that. He thinks girls shouldn't work at all; they should just dream up new ways to entrance him."

She kissed the side of Hammond's pale cheek, leaving behind a lesion of fuchsia lipstick. As though he could see it, Hammond wiped it away with his hand, going over the spot several times. He seemed unnaturally still, like a man walking stiffly to hide drunkenness. But he wasn't drunk; there was some other dissolution Hammond was fending off.

"We're going to the ladies'," Nell cried, seizing Anna's hand and tugging her onto her feet. "Grab your pocketbook, Anna, we girls must powder up!"

Anna found it difficult to keep a straight face, Nell's act was so overdone. Who was the audience? Not Charlie Voss, with whom Anna had already exchanged a wry look across the table. That left only Hammond. But Hammond, paralyzed somewhere between rage and panic, was too preoccupied to wonder why his mistress was play-acting.

"We're not going to the powder room at all," Nell said as soon as they were away from the table. "Everyone eavesdrops in there, and the girls are snakes. Plenty of them would like to get their hooks into Hammond."

They paused in an eddy beside a column. A tincture of dread had begun to infect Anna's vision of her friend. "Are you happy?" she asked. "In the apartment?"

"More or less," Nell said. "Hammond works too hard to come around all that often." She gave a secret smile. "I've someone else who visits me."

"Marco?"

Aghast, Nell took Anna's shoulders in her hot, trembling hands. "If someone told you that, I need to know exactly who it was," she said.

Anna swallowed, spooked by Nell's disjointedness. "It was a guess," she said. "Marco sat with us before, remember? When we came last October?"

Nell gave her a long look, then released her. "I'm sorry. I get a little . . . I don't know what."

"You're afraid of Hammond finding out?"

"I am. Although I shouldn't be. If he cut me off, I would telephone his wife and tell her everything. Then he would get thrown out, too. But the question is, what would Hammond do then? That would be interesting to know."

"You don't seem to like Hammond much."

"I hate him. And he hates me, too. It's like a soiled, awful marriage, except without children—well, we might have had a child, but we won't."

Anna stared at Nell's sweet face and marveled that it had come to that. "I'm sorry," she said.

"I've no regrets. I didn't want the child of a pig—I could never love it. I'd lose my figure over nothing."

"Oh, Nell," Anna said. The dread was upon her, a sense of foreboding for her friend. The sad tales she'd heard all her life—Olive Thomas, Lillian Lorraine—seemed real to her for the first time. Those doomed girls had been just girls at first, like Nell. "Why not give all of it up—the apartment, Hammond, Marco? Come back to the Naval Yard! I'm a diver now. Maybe you could dive, too. In the big dress, remember? We saw them training on the barge?"

Nell let out a cry of laughter, but Anna persisted, even knowing she sounded like a sap. "What about the war, Nell? Do you think of it?"

"Mine with Hammond or the great big one?"

Anna laughed despite herself.

"What can I do about it? Hammond won't let me work; he said he could smell the Yard on me even when I'd bathed twice and sprayed myself from head to toe with Sirocco."

Anna smiled helplessly at her friend. Nell embraced her suddenly, their bare shoulders and arms making the gesture feel startling, intimate. Anna caught the briny tang of Nell's armpits and the animal flux of her ribs. "You're different," Nell breathed into her ear. "It's awfully nice."

"That's funny. I'd have said you were different."

"That means we can be friends," Nell said, drawing away and gazing into Anna's eyes. "True friends, not like the serpents around this place. You work hard and come home exhausted, but I'm allergic to that sort of life. My ma says I think I'm too good for it, but it isn't that. I'm just trying to live a different way. Even if it looks like nonsense."

"It looks . . . dangerous."

"I like not knowing what will happen, not waking up at any certain time, drinking champagne at ten in the morning if I've a mind to. And don't think this is the end for me—I've big plans, make no mistake."

Anna noticed that sped-up quality in her friend. She wanted to say, *What plans?* but was concerned about getting back to Charlie Voss.

"Now that we've settled everything, we can go to the ladies'," Nell concluded, weaving her fingers among Anna's and tugging her through the crowd.

The long mirror in the powder room was jammed with the faces of girls appraising their own looks of astonished delight as if they'd never expected to meet themselves in such a place. Nell traded eager greetings with several. Anna gave her friend a wink and a wave and slipped back out.

Before she'd reached her table, an elderly waiter intercepted her. "Miss Feeney?"

The name, familiar and unfamiliar, seemed to wend its way toward Anna across a tortuous expanse. "Yes . . ." she finally said.

"Mr. Styles would like to see you in his office."

"Well, I—I can't right now. I need to—"

But the waiter had already turned, intending that she follow. She saw Charlie Voss across the room and tried to wave but couldn't catch his eye. Anna felt a thud of inevitability. Of course Mr. Styles was here. Of course she would see him. She had made that choice by walking through the lacquered door.

She followed the waiter into the turbulent clatter of a kitchen, then up a flight of narrow steps, scuffed and bare, which led through another door into a hushed corridor. This felt like a different establishment: thick soft carpet, oil paintings lit by small lamps attached to their frames. Anna heard muted laughter from behind closed doors. The air was gamy with cigar and pipe smoke.

Her escort knocked at a door at the end of this hall and pushed it open. Anna stepped inside a wood-paneled office and found Mr. Styles reposed behind an expensive-looking desk. "Miss Feeney," he said in a hale, mannered voice, rising to his feet. "Swell of you to pay us a visit."

Anna felt accused, as if she'd been caught trying to avoid him. "I looked for you," she said. "I thought you weren't here."

"But I'm always here," he said. "If I'm not, the whole place goes up in smoke. Right, boys?"

Four young men with the unfriendly faces of hoods had been lounging about the room like gargoyles. They murmured assent, apparently recognizing the rhetorical nature of their conversational role.

"In that case," Anna said, "I suppose we're lucky you stayed."

The bantering channel remained open in her; she angled her discourse toward it and listened with pleasure as it jingled through.

Mr. Styles watched her with a gravity that bore no relation to his jocund tone. "Boys," he said, "say hello to the exceptionally charming Miss Feeney."

Mumbled hellos. Her guide had left, shutting the door behind him. Anna watched the handsome gangster in his beautifully cut suit and felt their day with Lydia at Manhattan Beach dissolving like an aspirin into a tumbler of water. She longed to withdraw, to leave the memory intact, but the power to summon and dismiss seemed to lie entirely with Mr. Styles. She was suddenly angry.

"Go on ahead, boys," he said as they took up their hats. "I'll see Miss Feeney out."

When they'd gone, he stood at his desk, glancing at a page or two that lay there. Then he turned back to Anna and spoke in an altogether different voice. "I'm glad to see you. How is your sister?"

She froze, staring at her empty hands. As lightly as she could manage, she replied, "That's a story for another day. I need to get back to my date."

"To hell with your date." He was smiling.

"He might feel otherwise."

"No doubt."

A buzzing filled Anna's head. She was furious with Dexter Styles and could feel that he was angry, too. She'd no idea why.

"I'll drive you home," he said.

"Thank you, but I've no plans to leave at the moment, and I don't need a ride. Besides," she added mockingly, "won't the whole place go up in smoke?"

"That's an added incentive!" he said with a laugh.

She pushed past him through the door into the carpeted hallway. Making no effort to follow her or even raise his voice, he said, "My car is outside. Someone will meet you by the coat check."

She pretended not to hear. But as she wended her way along hushed turns of hall, she found herself planning her excuse to Charlie Voss. This discovery further enraged her. Who did Mr. Styles think he was?

She fumbled through a warren of corridors and stairs and burst into the dining room through a different door than the one she'd left by. Hammond sat alone at their table, eyeing the dance floor with a look of pale fury. Following his gaze, Anna made out Nell and Marco pressed together.

She was relieved to find Charlie Voss a few tables over with several men he seemed to know. "I've run into an old friend of my mother's," she told him. "He disapproves of my being out and insists on driving me home. I hope that's all right."

If Charlie was surprised, much less hurt, he managed to iron every trace of it from his voice. "As long as I've your word that you'll be in good hands."

"Thank you, Charlie, for a wonderful evening. Let's do it again."

"I shall count the hours."

There were lines for the coat and hatcheck, but the elderly waiter who had brought her to Mr. Styles's office was waiting. He took Anna's claim checks and joined her a few moments later with her coat and hat. They left the club through an exit that deposited them a few doors down the block from the lacquered entrance. Mr. Styles's Cadillac idled there discreetly.

As the waiter was opening the passenger door, a man approached the driver's window. Mr. Styles rolled it down. "Hello, George," he said, shaking hands through the window as Anna slid into the front seat beside him.

"Leaving early?" George asked.

"Just to drive Miss Feeney home. Miss Feeney, this is Dr. Porter, my brother-in-law. Miss Feeney works for me."

The doctor peered into the dark car at Anna. She caught a mirthful gaze over glints of mustache. A ladies' man.

"Ask for a bottle on the house," Mr. Styles told him. "I'll look for you shortly. If we miss each other, I'll see you at Sutton Place tomorrow."

He rolled up his window and pulled away. As the big car drifted uptown, headlights misting the icy air, he said, "Tell me what happened."

Anna explained what had followed their day at Manhattan Beach. It was the first time she'd told the story, and she told it carefully. The leather smell of the car transported her back to the day itself: holding Lydia's warm weight, the heartbeat fanning out from somewhere deep. She was stricken by loss, as if her sister had just been torn from her arms. She remembered the roar of life under Lydia's skin even in her stillness, and hungered for that life in a way that left her weak.

When she finished, Mr. Styles said in a tight voice, "I'm sick to hear it."

They drove uptown and then back down. On Fifth Avenue, they floated past the public library, where Anna had walked after seeing her mother off at Pennsylvania Station. It was here she'd first perceived the suctioning dark and felt its danger. She'd been fending off that danger ever since. *A different kind of girl.* How did you know what kind of girl you were, with no one around you? Maybe *those kinds of girls* were simply girls who'd no one to tell them they were *not* those kinds of girls.

The night was everywhere, reaching and black; it filled the car and surrounded Anna. But her dread of the dark had vanished. Without knowing when or how, she had released herself to it—disappeared through a crack in the night. Not a soul knew where to find her. Not even Dexter Styles.

He looked straight ahead as he drove, but Anna sensed his febrile restlessness from across the seat. The bones of his throat moved like knuckles when he swallowed. He must have felt her eyes on him, but he waited a long time before returning the gaze. A new understanding opened between them.

"You look different," he said softly. "In green."

"That's why I wore it," she said.

CHAPTER SEVENTEEN

Dexter cracked the car window and let the winter wind rake his face. An intelligent person sat beside him, a girl who was not silly, who would understand whatever he gave her to understand, who intrigued him through some combination of physical attributes and mental toughness, but really it was the latter, because physical attributes surrounded him daily and prompted little feeling. And yet there was a problem with the girl in his car—this smart, modern girl with correct values, joined to the war effort, a girl matured by hard times and familial tragedy—and that problem was that all he could think of doing, in a concrete way, was fucking her. The rest—vague notions that she might work for him, that her toughness could be of use, that she was likely a good shot (taut slender arms, visible in the dress she was wearing tonight); confusion about how they had originally met (had someone introduced them?)—flickered at a middle distance, well behind his need to *have* her. And even as that need made it hard to drive the goddamn car, he was also thinking: this was the problem of men and women, what made the professional harmony he envisaged so difficult to achieve. Men ran the world, and they wanted to fuck the women. Men said "Girls are weak" when in fact girls made *them* weak. At the same time, another line of thought was unspooling: Why this? Why now? Why her? Why take the risk when George Porter had just seen them? But those questions were theoretical, to be debated at some future point. For now, the explosive discontent that had been mounting in Dexter since his visit to Mr. Q. two weeks before had at last found an object. And another line of thinking: Where could they go? Somewhere private, somewhere indoors. Lust made an idiot of everyone it touched—Dexter felt stupidity shrouding his head like a hood in the shape of a dunce's cap. Where? Where? Where?

The queer part was, he'd given hardly a thought to Miss Feeney since driving her to Manhattan Beach right after Thanksgiving. The crippled sister had haunted him a bit, her lustrous eyes above billowing scarves returning to him at odd times for perhaps a week. The healthy one, no. Yet glimpsing her tonight in that green dress had brought a tightness to his chest. He'd watched her through his hidden window and waited for it to pass. But the feeling only ratcheted as he formed his disapproval of the company she kept: that cokie girl, mistress to another woman's husband, and the date: a fruit, he'd put money on it. Watching her in that dress, he'd found himself recalling Bitsy's moans through the bathroom door.

As they crossed the Brooklyn Bridge, she told him she'd become a diver. She said it in a relaxed way—to break the silence, he supposed, and appreciated. It happened to be interesting, both the topic and the sensation of talking to the same girl in the same car, but with an entirely different object before them. He asked about the equipment, how she breathed underwater, whether she'd bumped up against any dead bodies. But they might have been saying anything.

As he followed the curved shore toward Bay Ridge, Dexter knotted his fingers with hers, which were slender and warm. She pushed her thumb into the flesh of his palm, and a sensation like lightning tore through him, as if her hand were inside his trousers. The air in the car rang and shook. There was one cure for this, and that was to exhaust it.

The old boathouse was an unlikely choice for a tryst, having been the site of a number of Dexter's business dealings over the years, not all of them pleasant. But the same advantages recommended it in both cases: it was isolated, private, padlocked. Not a mile east of his home, it had so far been spared the Coast Guard's wartime reconfigurations. Dexter wondered each time he approached whether he would find it razed to the ground.

He parked on an empty street, and the car clicked and sighed into stillness. The dark was absolute. He leaned over and kissed her for the first time, his mind emptying at the lush taste of her mouth. Apparently, she was the last girl in New York who didn't smoke. He sensed appetite beating inside her like a second heart, larger and softer than her real one, and his impulse—adolescent, surely—was to begin right here, right now. But that was too dangerous. He opened his door and came around and opened hers.

"Let's look," she said, and he realized she meant the sea, noticing only then how loud it was. They walked to the dead end and looked out at a ghostly procession of waves, like rows of people in white hats holding hands as they dove into oblivion. Dexter did what he'd promised himself he wouldn't do: kissed her in the wide open. If it were warmer, he'd have liked to pull her down right here, as he'd done under the Coney Island boardwalk with more than one girl of his youth, bathers' feet dropping grains of sand over them through gaps between planks. But there was no rush. They'd left the club before one; War-Time sunrise was not until eight. Time enough to do all that needed to be done.

The boathouse was a block over, beside a short pier. Dexter opened the padlock with his key and shoved the sticky door, sensing immediately that the place had been occupied since his last visit a few months before. He struck a match on his shoe and lit the wick of the hurricane lamp that was always just inside the door. Its rippling light confirmed his hunch: a whiskey bottle, cigarette butts. This hardly touched him in his present state. He needed to warm the place up. There was no electricity, just a squat stove that heated efficiently once it got going. He shoved in wood. The kindling was gone, but he found a newspaper and lit that, realizing too late that he should have checked the date to get a notion of when exactly someone had been here without his knowledge or approval.

He turned from the blazing stove, half expecting her to have disappeared in the time he'd spent absorbed in that housekeeping. But she was still there, pulling pins from her dark hair. Its lavish weight spilled over his hands when he held her. He put aside further practical concerns: should they lie on their coats; climb into one of the rowboats suspended from brackets on the walls? He braided his hands under her backside and lifted her off the floor, carrying her to a table pushed against the wall behind the stove. He perched her on its edge. There was almost no light here. He kissed her mouth and neck, then opened her coat and peeled up her dress and slip, exposing hose and garters. He kicked off his trousers and flattened himself along her bare belly, logs cracking in the stove behind them.

"Do you want this?" he whispered.

"Yes," she said, at which the dumb, blind part of his brain lunged forward like a hound at a foxhunt. He peeled aside her panties and eased himself inside her, hearing his own relieved gasp as if from across the room. Moments later, he shuddered as if he'd been shot, knees buckling as he mashed her to him and spent himself. His own ragged breathing filled the room. When he could walk, he tossed their coats in front of the stove, where the heat had begun to gather, and helped her out of her dress and long gloves. He unhooked her brassiere and garter belt and unrolled her stockings slowly. She looked very young in the firelight. She lay back against the coats and shut her eyes, and now it could really begin, without a word. He moved his mouth over her body until she seemed not to breathe. When he parted her legs, she tasted like the sea, which he heard even now, a beat of waves just beyond the walls. She climaxed like someone in a seizure, and he was inside her again before she'd finished.

They slept fitfully, Dexter rising now and then to add wood to the stove. At some dark hour she woke him with her hands, touching him in the faint reddish light with such potency that he thought she must be on both sides of his skin, inhabiting him—how else could she know what he felt at each move she made? Her eyes were closed and he shut his own, drifting in a sweet agony that seemed to last hours. When at last she allowed him to finish, he left himself entirely, returning to his senses only to fall into laughter: in forty-one years of life, it had never

been better than that. And all the while, another part of him was measuring the approach of dawn, eager to be done before it came. How
much more would it take? She'd climbed on top of him, quivering like
a bowstring for his touch, and he felt himself grow hard again. There
would be no end, he thought—nothing but this, ever again. But he
knew better than to believe it.

"Anna."

The whisper pierced layers of filmy sleep and dropped sharply into
her ear. She opened her eyes. Dull light leaked through the shuttered
windows. The stove contained only embers. She was cold and needed
to pee. He'd covered them with a coarse blanket, and she felt his bare
flesh touching hers underneath it. "Anna," he whispered, close to her
ear. "I need to take you home."

She held very still, her eyes barely open. She felt afraid to move. A
memory of Nell's date came to her from the night before: his unnatural stillness. Now she felt it, too: inertia to stave off disaster.

"Are you all right?" he asked.

"Yes," she said. "Yes, I'm fine." But she was not. The dawn, which
normally brought relief from the misery of her nights, now threatened a
catastrophic exposure. Her heart beat spasmodically, and her ears rang.

He rose and crossed the room, the first naked man she had ever
seen: a towering stranger with coils of dark hair that seemed to pour
from his chest down his torso and pool around an assemblage of private parts that brought to mind a pair of boots dangling by their laces
from a lamppost. Anna had never experienced the aftermath of passion, arriving in secret to the basement hideout and sneaking away
separately from Leon. There had been no gathering of clothing in
daylight, no retrieval of a *gun*, which hung in its holster from the
back of a chair. The depravity of what had transpired between herself and this gangster appalled her. Had she been drunk? Out of her
mind? She tried to reason away panic: her mother would never know;

it was her day off from the Naval Yard—she wasn't truant or even tardy. But how would she get back inside her building in last night's clothes without giving herself away? She needed to get out of here now, before it was fully light; to pee, bathe, and fall asleep in her own bed before the new day properly began. She needed right now to be the last phase of a night already on its way to being erased.

She waited until he had his trousers on before rising unsteadily to her feet. With her back turned, she pulled on her panties, fastened her brassiere, and shimmied into her slip. She was still wearing her jewelry. One of her nylon stockings had caught on the stove and shriveled in the heat. She left her legs bare and stepped into her dress, signaling with her retreating posture that she wanted no assistance. Not that he was offering any. He seemed as distracted as she, squinting at the label on an empty liquor bottle. He picked up two cigarette butts from the floor, examined them, and let them drop. Anna buttoned her beaded cloak to the neck and pulled on her hat. Her bare legs were covered in gooseflesh.

She waited by the door while he checked his pockets. Now that they were two people in coats and hats, she felt calmer. When he joined her at the door, she smiled up at him, relieved. He held her chin in his fingers and gave her a perfunctory kiss—a kiss goodbye—before unbolting the door. Then he kissed her again, more deeply, and Anna felt a window fall open inside her despite everything—a wish to start again, even with sunrise approaching. The hunger he'd wakened in her banished every scruple—she would think about them later. And reentering the dream made her shame of minutes ago melt away.

He shot the bolt, took off his hat, and began to unbutton her coat. Anna felt how easily this could go on. On and on. How she wanted it to!

"We've met before," she said, feeling the impact of these words only as they wandered from her mouth. "You don't remember, I think."

"In the club?" he murmured.

"No. Your house."

She had his attention. His hands paused on her buttons. And even as Anna longed for him to continue, she knew she'd stopped it.

"My house."

"Years ago. I was a little girl."

He shook his head slowly, eyes on hers. "How is that possible?"

"I came with my father," she said. "Edward Kerrigan. I think he might have worked for you."

The name filled the room as if she'd sung it out. Or as if someone else had. For hearing it—her father's name—seemed to vault Anna instantly outside her debauched circumstances. Her father was Eddie Kerrigan. Everything that had happened between her and Dexter Styles seemed now to have been leading her to this revelation.

He'd no visible reaction to the name, as if he hadn't heard or didn't recognize it. He turned a gold ring on his finger, straightened the lapels of his coat. But Anna recognized in his stillness the very dread and caution she'd felt herself, on first awakening. "Why didn't you tell me before?" he asked softly.

"I couldn't find a way."

"You said your name was Feeney." He seemed less accusing than confused, as if patting his pockets for something he'd missed.

"He disappeared," Anna said. "Five and a half years ago."

Dexter Styles replaced his hat, checked his watch, cracked a shutter to look outside. "We need to get out of here," he said.

They walked to the car a distance apart. The dawn was a cold, sparkling blue. He opened the passenger door, and Anna slipped inside the fragrant interior. He shut his own door, hard, and pulled away. After several minutes of silent driving, he said, "It puts me in an uncomfortable position. Learning this now."

"Then you did know him," Anna said. "He did work for you." She realized that she had never fully believed this. The memory had too much the quality of a dream or a wish.

"I'd have told you any time you'd asked."

"Do you remember when he brought me to your house?"

"No."

"It was winter, like this. I took off my shoes."

"You can be absolutely certain," he said, "if I'd remembered any of that, we would not be sitting together in this car."

"Do you know what happened to him?" she asked. "To Eddie Kerrigan?"

"I haven't the slightest idea."

Anna watched him, waiting for him to look back at her, but he stared fixedly at the road. "I don't believe you," she said.

He braked so suddenly that the tires made a little shriek, pinching the curb of a quiet street lined with houses. He turned on her, white-faced. "You don't believe *me?*"

"I'm sorry," she stammered.

"You're the one who's been lying through your teeth. I've no idea who you are—what you are. Are you a hooker? Did someone pay you to fuck me and say these things?"

She belted him across the face, her mind a half second behind her hand, which left a red slash on his cheek. "I've told you who I am," she said, her voice shaking. "I'm Anna Kerrigan, Eddie Kerrigan's daughter. That's who I've been all this time."

She thought he might hit her back. The hands clutching the steering wheel were scarred, like a boxer's. He took a long breath. At last he turned to her. "What is it that you want? Money?"

She nearly hit him again. But the rage flashed through her and left her calm, more lucid than she'd felt in weeks.

"I want to know where he went," she said. "Or if he's alive."

"I can't help with any of that."

"Wouldn't you want your daughter to look for you if you disappeared?" she asked. "Wouldn't you expect it?"

"It's the very last thing I would want."

She was taken aback. "Why?"

"I'd want her to stay as far away as possible," he said. "To keep her safe."

He was looking straight ahead. Anna watched his pugilist's hands on the steering wheel and felt his words move through her. She threw open the door and sprang from the car with no idea where she was. She began walking down the block ahead of the car, half expecting it to pull up alongside her, to hear his voice. But Dexter Styles drove past without turning his head.

PART FIVE

The Voyage

CHAPTER EIGHTEEN

Five weeks earlier

On New Year's Day 1943, Eddie Kerrigan climbed Telegraph Hill to Coit Tower—or as close as the soldiers standing guard would let him go—to look down at the Embarcadero Piers. He made out three Liberty ships taking on cargo. They were identical, of course, but he knew that the middle one was the *Elizabeth Seaman*, where he was expected to report for duty in under an hour. Eddie dreaded this. In fact, he'd climbed Telegraph Hill in hopes that elevation, with its attendant perspective, would help to shrink his reluctance.

He'd taken the third mate's examination the previous week, over five consecutive days, in San Francisco's vast columned Custom House. Just walking up those steps—as if to a library or a city hall—had cowed him. He'd had so little schooling, read nothing but newspapers before going to sea. But everyone read aboard ships—there wasn't much else to do if you didn't play cards or cribbage. Tentatively, Eddie had begun to read, and found that it suited him. He still read slowly, but his mind proved to be like a dog waiting for someone to throw a stick so it could tumble and pant to retrieve it. He'd memorized whole portions of the *Merchant Marine Officers' Handbook* and had a nearly perfect mark on his third mate's exam.

He scrutinized the *Elizabeth Seaman* as best he could without binoculars. Booms were lowering large crates into the number two hold: aircraft, he guessed. As he watched, he was troubled by an unfamiliar vigilance—a readiness to be galled by missteps, as though he were already responsible for this ship he hadn't set foot on, even at a half-mile's distance. He chided himself: the merchant service wasn't the navy, for Pete's sake. Merchant officers hadn't so much as set uniforms. Yet now that he'd become an officer, even in the abstract, Eddie sensed that the passive tranquility he'd cultivated during five and a half years at sea was in jeopardy.

Not that he hadn't worked hard. He'd worked like a coolie—that had been an essential part of the peace. In his first jobs, on the engine room's "black gang," he'd shoveled coal, fed furnaces, and broken up fires; cleaned and lubricated the ship's scalding, sweating innards at temperatures of 125 degrees while being bludgeoned by an engine roar that had left a permanent jingle in his ears. Exhaustion had emptied his soul. After eight months he'd crept from the engine room to join the deck crew, the garish sunshine hounding him mercilessly at first. When at last his eyes had adjusted, he'd looked out and noticed the sea as if it were entirely new: an infinite hypnotic expanse that could look like scales, wax, hammered silver, wrinkled flesh. It had structure and layers you couldn't see from land. Fixing his eyes upon this unfamiliar sea, Eddie had learned to float in a semi-conscious state, alert but not fully awake. Blood broke in golden flashes inside his eyeballs. A humming emptiness filled his mind. Not to think, not to feel—simply to *be*, without pain. He remembered his old life, but those memories occupied just one room in his mind, and there were others—more than Eddie had realized. He learned to avoid that particular room. After a while, he forgot where it was.

He'd bunked with as many as twenty men on the early non-union ships, before they were barred from the West Coast in the wake of the Great Strike. Criminals, dope addicts with hypos in their seabags, amateur boxers with holes in their memories—all stacked together so snugly in their sacks that when another man coughed or farted or moaned, Eddie thought he'd done it himself. Once he'd happened upon two men locked together in a stokehold in a slick, grunting embrace. The sight revolted and enraged him. He resolved to act—

protest, find a sea lawyer and file a complaint—but by the time his watch ended, he'd ceased to care. The incident had fallen into the past, left behind with the nautical position at which it had taken place. They all had their secrets in 1937. No one talked more than men on ships, but the point of the stories they told was to hide the ones they could never divulge to anyone.

Pearl Harbor interrupted Eddie's drifting. Experienced sailors were desperately needed to transport war supplies, and he was promoted—through no effort of his own—from an ordinary seaman to an able-bodied seaman. ABs were strongly encouraged to study for the third mate's exam. For months Eddie resisted, longing to preserve the floating peace whose essential feature was his own passivity. It was no good; idleness in wartime—even a war he couldn't see—had felt like loafing. He grew bored, restless. Finally, having not spent two consecutive weeks ashore in over five years, he'd paid off in San Francisco and taken the train to Alameda for the two-month officers' training course.

Mindful of the hour, Eddie began descending Telegraph Hill. Warships crowded the bay. The hills around it were speckled with pale houses, like birds' eggs. He was disappointed to find that the view had not assuaged his anxious new vigilance. But it wasn't new. It was a relic from his old life. Eddie had forgotten what it felt like.

Thirty minutes later, he was climbing the slanted gangway from Pier 21 to the *Elizabeth Seaman*. Before he'd reached the deck, a familiar voice gusted against his ears: florid and bawling inside crisp British corners. Eddie froze on the gangway. He tried to imagine the voice issuing from another man—any other man—than the bosun who despised him. He could not. There was only one man in the world who talked like that.

On the main deck, he glanced through the tumult of booms and cargo and scrambling army stevedores for a glimpse of the bosun's dark skin. But the Nigerian was nowhere in sight, nor could Eddie hear him anymore. This wouldn't be the first time he'd conjured him up.

Outside the midship house, Eddie introduced himself to Mr.

Farmingdale, the second mate. Farmingdale's courtly manners and snowy beard gave him the noble air of a profile on a coin, but Eddie pegged him for a juicehead. It wasn't just Farmingdale's overcareful walk that gave him away—this was New Year's Day, after all, and plenty of men were tiptoeing about. It was the smell that eked from his pores, like soil mixed with rotten orange peels. Eddie felt a twinge of distaste.

In the wardroom, he presented his brand-new third mate's license to the master, the ink still wet, as it were. Young Captain Kittredge was fair-haired and striking—more like a picture star playing a skipper than a real one. Eddie felt old beside him; *was* old for a third mate. "You've come out of retirement?" the master asked, clearly thinking along the same lines.

"No, sir. I was already at sea."

The captain nodded, doubtless placing Eddie in the category of misfits one found aboard merchant ships before the war. Kittredge had that American air of bullying optimism: expecting the best and presuming he'd get it—or else. This would be his third voyage on the *Elizabeth Seaman,* he told Eddie, the first two having been uneventful island-hopping runs to the Pacific.

"She's a special girl, Mrs. Seaman," he said with a wink. "We've been making twelve knots."

"Twelve!" Eddie exclaimed. Liberties were notoriously slow; twelve knots would be flank speed. Perhaps some of the captain's buoyant American power had seeped into the ship.

A breeze sallied through three open portholes on the forward wall. Beyond them, Eddie had an impression of San Francisco's colors, blue, yellow, pink. It was a light city. In the union halls and seamen's churches, men imparted ghastly tales from the East Coast: torpedoed tankers vaporizing like Roman candles, men frozen to death at their lifeboat oars on the dreaded North Sea runs to Murmansk. It was hard to envision any of that here. Eddie's voyages in the year since Pearl Harbor had been much like the ones Captain Kittredge described:

offshore unloading, no liberty, but no apparent danger, either, now that typhoon season was over.

His third mate's stateroom was on the boat deck, starboard aft, beside the sick bay. Small and straightforward: a bed with built-in drawers, a small closet, desk, sink. But to Eddie—accustomed to living out of a single locker in a cabin with at least one other man, more often several—so much solitary space was an intimidating luxury.

Unpacking his seabag, he found a sealed envelope with *Save for later* written on the front in a neat schoolteacher's hand. It must have been placed there by Ingrid, a young widow he'd met three weeks before, in San Francisco. Feeling a twinge of baffled irritation, he set the envelope inside the desk drawer and went to the wheelhouse to begin his third mate's duties. He checked over the bell books and signal flags. Having already sailed twice on Liberty ships meant that he knew the *Elizabeth Seaman*—being mass-produced, Liberties were interchangeable down to the last oilskin locker. From the wheelhouse window, he watched the number two hold receive more of the boxed cargo he'd spotted from Telegraph Hill. They were aircraft, as he'd guessed: Douglas A-20s. The crates were stamped with Cyrillic letters.

He left the midship house and returned to the main deck. In the after part of the ship, number three hold was receiving general cargo: bags of cement, canned beef, powdered eggs, boxes of boots. Eddie climbed onto the rear gun deck and greeted the gunner on watch, painfully young and big-eared like they all were, with their crude generic haircuts. No sailor wanted the job of guarding a merchant ship, yet every cargo required a complement of navy gunners to operate the cannons and machine guns in case of attack.

As he climbed down from the gun deck, Eddie noticed that the hatch to the steering engine room, belowdecks, had been left ajar. Only officers were supposed to go down there, but the deck crew had ways of getting hold of the keys, as Eddie well knew, having done it himself. The steering engine room was an excellent place to dry laundry.

Curious to know who was behind the infraction, he began descending the ladder into the familiar greasy warmth of the ship's innards. He nearly collided with the Nigerian bosun, who was on his way up the very same ladder.

"What? . . . You . . ." the bosun sputtered, surprise and displeasure rendering him uncharacteristically mute. "Is this a deranged attempt to report for work on my deck crew?"

Eddie had the advantage of forewarning. "Not at all, Bosun. I've my third mate's ticket now," he said, taking his first genuine pleasure in the promotion.

Like most bosuns, this one disdained officers. More, he disdained former able-bodied seamen who *became* officers—"hawsepipers," as they were known. Eddie glimpsed these strains of contempt at work in the bosun's dark, expressive face. "A hawsepiper!" he remarked at last with honeyed mockery. "Congratulations, *sir!* Would this be your maiden voyage at that rank?"

"As a matter of fact, it is," Eddie said, his heart accelerating as it always did when he tried to match wits with the bosun. The man discharged words in a way that left Eddie punch-drunk. He'd an imperious accent, something Eddie couldn't get used to in a Negro. "And you don't have to 'sir' me, Bosun. As I think you know."

"Oh, I am keenly aware of that fact, *Third*," the bosun bellowed merrily. "My 'sir' was merely a courtesy intended to acknowledge and salute your breathtaking rise in the maritime hierarchy."

"Have you a reason to be in the steering engine room?" Eddie asked.

"Naturally, I have, or I would not be spending even a second of my precious time in that place."

"I'd like to come down and take a look, if you'll kindly step aside," Eddie said. "Make sure that reason doesn't have anything to do with drying laundry."

The bosun's nostrils flared. His husky build and violet-dark skin made him seem larger than Eddie, even looking up from below. He did not step aside. "Perhaps this would be an opportune point at which to remind you," he said, snapping the words like a whip, "that as third mate, and a brand-new one at that, you haven't the slightest jurisdiction over me. Which is to say, putting it plainly, you may not give me orders."

He was right, of course. A third mate commanded no one, whereas a bosun commanded a deck crew of some thirteen sailors—six ABs, three ordinaries, three deckhands, and Chips, as the carpenter was always known—and answered directly to the first mate. Eddie knew, having worked under this bosun, that he was an old-school tyrant—the sort shipping companies loved because they wrung the maximum from their deck crews while paying them a minimum of overtime. Like most autocrats, the bosun was solitary, a fanatical reader who read with a riveted attention that suggested physical engagement. While most sailors talked of their reading at chow and exchanged books to stretch their meager libraries, the bosun covered his in oilcloth and turned them facedown when anyone came near. Some theorized that they were dirty; others speculated that he read only one book: the Bible, the Koran, the Torah, or perhaps all three. His secrecy had nettled Eddie. He thought of himself as being kind to Negroes, but was accustomed to Negroes who had less than he. The jumbling of races on merchant ships had been a shock at first: it was common for white men to work under Negroes, South Americans, even Chinamen. But this bosun was not just better spoken than Eddie, with palpably more education. He'd also had a contemptuous way of looking at Eddie that brought to mind the phrase "dumb mick."

On a dare from the other ABs, Eddie had made bold once to approach the bosun and ask—with a smirk he couldn't fully repress—what he was reading. The bosun had closed his book and walked away without a word. They were crossways of each other after that. The bosun buried Eddie in make-work until his head swam from the fumes of the rust-retardant fish oil, followed by red lead paint, and then battleship gray, that he'd had to apply to every inch of the ship including the masts—normally a deckhand's job. In high winds, Eddie had swung to and fro, pointlessly plotting his revenge.

"I've a feeling, Bosun," he said now, with mounting frustration at finding his path down the ladder still blocked, "that you think I should be taking orders from you."

"I wouldn't dream of suggesting such a thing," the bosun protested, "despite knowing that a mere voyage ago, that would have been precisely the case."

"Well, it isn't the case anymore. And it won't be again, unless one of those books you've always got your nose in is preparation for the third mate's exam."

The bosun gave himself to laughter, a sound somewhere between bells and drums. "With all due respect, *Third*," he chortled, "had hawsepiping been my object, I'd have been master of my own bucket long ago."

Eddie smelled an advantage. The bosun could swagger and verbiate all he wanted, but Eddie had never encountered a Negro captain on any American merchant ship, and he doubted the bosun had, either. An awareness of this seemed to infect both of them at once. "Fine, then," Eddie said with meaning. "I think we understand each other."

"We will never understand each other," the bosun spat with loathing. He continued up the ladder, forcing Eddie backward. Eddie felt as if he'd won by playing dirty—worse than losing. He retreated onto the deck, and the bosun shouldered past him.

When at last Eddie reached the steering engine room, he found no laundry anywhere.

Later, through a door behind the galley, he climbed down to the engine room. The temperature rose as he descended through a skein of pipes and catwalks and grates and vents into the gut of the ship, although the three giant pistons that turned the screw were still.

The third engineer, Eddie's counterpart belowdecks, had an accent at odds with his name. "O'Hillsky?" Eddie asked skeptically. "Irish?"

The engineer laughed. "Polish. O-C-H-Y-L-S-K-I." He was smoking a pipe, a rarity in the engine room, it being already so hot. "You heard the rumor?" Ochylski said. "Russia."

Eddie recalled the Cyrillic lettering on the airplane crates. "That doesn't make geographic sense."

The third engineer chuckled around his pipe, and Eddie recognized a dour European humor he'd come to appreciate. "A machine can't think," Ochylski said, "and the War Shipping Administration is a machine."

"Murmansk?" Eddie asked, the name feeling strange on his lips.

"Only if they give us the arctic gear. Do you know?"

"I'll find out," Eddie said.

During the next eight days, the *Elizabeth Seaman* moved from pier to pier along the San Francisco waterfront and continued to load. Number four hold was filled with bauxite; number one hold with C rations and boxes of small arms. At her last stop, Pier 45, tanks and jeeps were placed around her battened hatches and secured as deck cargo, then lashed down with lengths of chain shackled to a padeye. The first mate, a knowledgeable Dane of about sixty, oversaw all of this, along with the bosun and his deck crew. Eddie's port responsibilities were nebulous, and he tried to steer clear of the bosun. Luckily, officers and crew ate in separate mess halls, although the food was identical. The saloon, where officers ate, had white tablecloths. Alone in his stateroom at night, Eddie eluded the echoey range of his thoughts by reading. His favorite books were about the sea, and he'd finally got his hands on a copy of *The Death Ship*, which had made the rounds on one of his jungle runs before Pearl Harbor.

On the *Elizabeth Seaman*'s last evening in port, Eddie stood on the flying bridge with Roger, the eager, nervous deck cadet. Along with Stanley, the engine room cadet, Roger had completed three months of officer training at the Merchant Marine Academy in San Mateo and now was beginning his required six months at sea. The cadets quartered together on the bridge deck, near "Sparks," as the radioman was always known.

"What sort of fellow is our Sparks?" Eddie asked. Radiomen were rarely seen; they were either in the radio shack or asleep in a cabin beside it with an alarm to wake them should an emergency transmission come in.

"He curses quite a bit," Roger said.

"Soon you'll be doing that, too."

The cadet laughed. He was scrawny and beak-nosed, a few steps short of manhood. "Mother won't like it."

"No mothers here."

"I saw something strange today," Roger said after a pause.

He'd opened the door to a storeroom and found Farmingdale, the second mate, busy at something inside it. When Roger approached, he saw that Farmingdale was tipping a can of gray paint over the mouth of a mason jar, pouring a thin stream of paint into a loaf of bread he'd wedged into the mouth of the jar. The bread absorbed the paint's viscous pigment, so that what reached the bottom of the jar was a trickle of cloudy liquid. In full view of Roger, Farmingdale lifted the jar to his lips and calmly drank this down.

"He looked angry," Roger said, "but he didn't stop."

"Imagine the state of his stomach."

"Will he be fit to sail?"

"If he can drink like that, then he's used to it," Eddie said.

"Who'll handle the navigation if the second mate is drunk?"

"I will," Eddie said, though his own navigation skills were still rudimentary. He was disgusted with the second mate for having let the cadet witness his degeneracy. "And you, kiddo. Get to work with that azimuth."

Dusk fell moodily on the city, pricks of diamond light pulsing from Telegraph Hill. The fog hadn't yet come in.

"I'll sure miss Frisco," Roger said.

"So shall I," Eddie said. "Although it turns out only sailors call it Frisco."

"San Francisco," Roger said, laying down the words in a voice that hadn't fully broken yet. "She's a hell of a town."

They cast off lines at six the next morning, January 10, and were directed by a local pilot to the degaussing range, where the *Elizabeth Seaman*'s hull was demagnetized so she wouldn't set off mines. Eddie led a fire and boat drill, safety procedures being a third mate's one clear responsibility. But the drill was perfunctory; they didn't even swing out the davits, much less lower the lifeboats. Captain Kittredge was in a hurry to sail, and the bosun seemed indifferent—perhaps inclined to minimize Eddie's domain.

When they were past the Golden Gate, the captain disclosed their destination: the Panama Canal. That meant the Persian Gulf almost certainly, from whence the cargo would be transported overland to Russia, whose infinite Red Army continued to beat back the Krauts. The *Elizabeth Seaman* hadn't been given the arctic gear required for crossing the North Sea in January, to the extreme relief of everyone aboard. The refrain "better than Murmansk" echoed through the gangways and over chow tables for the rest of that night. But Eddie felt no such relief. The Caribbean was hazardous enough, and he seethed over the halfhearted boat drill.

When he relieved the first mate of his watch at eight the next morning, Eddie persuaded him of the need for a second drill. That afternoon, the engines were reduced to standby and the order given for the abandon-ship drill: six short blasts followed by one long blast of the general alarm bell. As men began moving toward the boat deck, the bosun sprinted up the ladders and accosted Eddie there.

"*Third Mate,*" he began, smacking his lips at the utterance of the title, "are you cognizant of the fact that it has been over a year since a Jap submarine sank a merchant ship on the California coast?"

"I am, Bosun."

"Can you explain, then, why we are now undertaking our second boat drill in two short days at sea?"

"The first was sloppy. If this one is sloppy, I'll hold another tomorrow."

"You would enjoy that, I can well imagine," the bosun said with a wily smile at his growing audience—the blasts had brought all hands onto the boat deck. "After all, safety drills afford you a rare opportunity to frolic in your newfound authority!"

"Is that what this looks like to you? Frolicking?"

"Every man frolics differently," the bosun said.

Eddie caught smirks on faces around him, felt a rise of incipient laughter. The mate and master stood by. If they stepped in now, Eddie would never regain his authority.

"Do you refuse to participate in this drill, Bosun?" he asked sharply, recognizing that he'd arrived late where he should have begun.

"I would not dream of refusing!" the bosun expostulated. "On the contrary, I am putty in your hands, *Third*—we all are. Please, lead us through the necessary steps!"

It took all of Eddie's self-restraint to ignore the sarcasm and proceed. The man raised in him a welt of provocation whose itch he could barely withstand. This time, at least, all four lifeboats were lowered and boarded successfully. Eddie resolved to hold a boat drill every week, exactly as the rules stipulated, even if it brought him to blows with the bosun. He rather hoped it would.

A day out of Panama, ten days into their voyage, the *Elizabeth Seaman*'s call numbers appeared in a radio message—a highly unusual event. Sparks deciphered the message with codebooks and brought the typed result to the captain's office. They were not to go through the canal after all, but to continue south, around Cape Horn and across the Southern Atlantic to Cape Town, South Africa: a journey of some forty days. Captain Kittredge was convinced they could make better time.

There was widespread chagrin over not being able to buy Panamanian rum from the bumboats that swarmed both ends of the canal, but it soon dissolved into the monotony peculiar to long voyages. Everyone resisted this at first; they were bored, stymied, restless. But within a few days, peace overcame the ship like a sigh—the relief of knowing this was all there was, or would be, for some weeks. Men took up their sea projects of whittling whistles or making square knot belts. Eighteen days out of San Francisco, Farmingdale mastered the tremor in his hands enough to fashion two dolls out of hemp. That night, when he relieved Eddie of the eight-to-twelve watch, Eddie complimented him on the dolls and asked how he'd learned to make them.

"An old salt," Farmingdale said. "He's made five hundred sixty, if you can feature it. Keeps 'em in a storage locker at Rincon Annex."

Old salts were men who had sailed on wooden ships in their youth—sailed, in other words, when "sailing" meant actually *sailing*. "Is he still around?" Eddie asked.

"Been a couple of years since I've seen him, come to think of it," the second mate said.

"They're disappearing," Eddie said. "The old salts."

Five years ago, there had been one or two aboard most ships—palm wax, needle, and twine in their pockets. Eddie suspected that the War Shipping Administration was weeding them out.

"We've one here," Farmingdale said. "Pugh, third cook."

"Say, that's good luck!"

Farmingdale inclined his head noncommittally. He was aloof and unreadable even when sober; Eddie couldn't like him. But the presence of an old salt aboard the *Elizabeth Seaman* was profoundly reassuring. "Iron men in wooden boats," they were called, as opposed to the wooden men in iron boats of today, like Kittredge, Farmingdale, and Eddie himself. Old salts partook of an origin myth, being close to the root of all things, including language. Eddie had never noticed how much of his own speech derived from the sea, from "keeled over" to "learning the ropes" to "catching the drift" to "freeloader" to "gripe" to "brace up" to "taken aback" to "leeway" to "low profile" to "the bitter end," or the very last link on a chain. Using these expressions in a practical way made him feel close to something fundamental—a deeper truth whose contours he believed he'd sensed, allegorically, even while still on land. Being at sea had brought Eddie nearer that truth. And the old salts were nearer still.

He left Farmingdale on the bridge and entered the notes of his watch in the logbook: their course was 170 with a fresh breeze and a moderate following sea. He stopped in the wardroom for his "night lunch," a cold-cut sandwich and coffee, then filled a cup with milk for Sparks, the radioman, whose metal leg brace (polio, Eddie presumed) gave him trouble on the ladders. Eddie had fallen into the habit of visiting Sparks after his watch, as a way of putting off his solitary stateroom.

"What a lovely fucking thing to do, Third," Sparks said, taking the cup of milk.

Eddie checked to make sure the blackout screen was fully closed before lighting their cigarettes. Sparks was near fifty, elfin and slight, lashes invisible on his hooded eyes. "I'm part newt—my tail comes off and grows directly back," he'd told Eddie in his spectral Irish accent. He was homosexual—Eddie knew this without knowing how he knew. Sparks had grown up in New Orleans and gone to sea in his twenties. He was a teetotaler, unusual in an Irishman. "Ah, but I dream of this stuff," he said, gazing into the cup of milk before downing it in a cascade of voluptuous gulps. "I'll crawl across broken glass for a cup of milk like an opium addict for a pipe."

"You might like opium better."

Sparks snorted. "It's bad enough needing food and sleep and cigarettes, having to drag this fucking leg around. I can't afford a habit like that."

"I've seen cripples in opium dens."

"Sure you have—trying to forget they're cripples! How's that for smarts—you've got a brace on your fucking leg and a monkey on your fucking back, and you think you've solved your fucking problem when all you've really done is stuck your head up your arse."

As Sparks shook the cup to catch the last drops of milk, Eddie was stricken with sympathy. To be a deviant *and* a cripple, without good looks or fortune or physical strength—how had Sparks managed to endure such a life? Yet he'd more than endured; he was ever cheerful.

"Your mother must have loved you, Sparks," Eddie said.

"What on God's green earth makes you say such a thing?"

"Just a hunch."

"Well, you'd best be taking those hunches of yours and stuffing them in your ear. My ma was the ward's chief lush. She once puked in my bed trying to give me a good-night kiss! Holy mother of Christ, she was a pig, my ma, an absolute pig."

"It's bad luck," Eddie said. "Talking that way about your mother."

"The bad luck was *having* such a mother," Sparks said. "There was no living with her. Pa had to put her in a home. I did have a lovely sister, though. Lily. She used to call me her little dandelion—don't you fucking laugh or I'll nail you to the wall, you fucker." But Sparks was laughing—he was always laughing. Only the BAMS, the broadcasting for Allied merchant ships, silenced him. It came at set hours each day, Greenwich time—which was designated by the second hour hand on his radio clock. At 0300, Sparks turned the receiver from five hundred kilocycles to a higher frequency and began listening through earphones for the *Elizabeth Seaman*'s call numbers. Because Allied merchant ships maintained radio silence, the whole of Sparks's job was to listen. He went utterly still, his body inclined toward the transmitter as if he himself, or perhaps the metal leg brace, were the instrument of reception.

Eddie left him there and brought the empty cup back down to

the galley. Still reluctant to turn in, he stepped outside the door by his stateroom. The night was calm, clouds muffling a moon whose diffuse glow fluttered like thousands of moths over shifting points of sea. The ship's roll was a welcome and soothing respite from the hard intractability of land. Eddie felt nearer that empty awareness that had sustained him during his years of jungle runs from San Francisco to China, Indonesia, and Burma via Honolulu and Manila. Above the port of Shanghai, on shaded streets, he'd listened to sounds of daily life outside walled courtyards: crying babies, clanging pots. Occasionally, through an open door, he'd glimpsed a woman walking on shrunken feet with the stiff, halting poise of a flamingo.

The world's mysteries. He'd never believed they were real. Had thought they existed only in books read aloud by charitable ladies.

At last he returned to his stateroom. Without the ballast of bunkmates, he felt unmoored. Aimlessly, he opened the drawer to his desk and was startled to discover the envelope he'd placed there after signing articles on his first day. He'd forgotten it. He'd forgotten Ingrid—could hardly picture her anymore. Faraway things became theoretical, then imaginary, then hard to imagine. They ceased to exist.

Now, in the small light by his sack, Eddie opened the letter—his first in over five years at sea.

Dear Edward, it read in strong, unsentimental cursive, *The weather has been fine, though after many days of fog we would appreciate some sunshine. My pupils are planting their spring victory gardens, but I worry that they will be disheartened. The war has changed many things, but I believe plants still need sunlight to grow! The boys and I speak of you often and fondly. I have offered to take them back to Playland, but they refuse. They are waiting for you.*

The tone was measured, even bland, but the effect of these words upon Eddie was galvanic. He was flooded with the memory of seeing Ingrid for the first time at Foster's Cafeteria: a woman in a blue scarf buying a single slice of pie for her two sons, which they shared raptly and without argument. Eddie had asked her the time. She was

German, it emerged—had only narrowly managed to keep her job by denouncing Hitler and her motherland before a committee. There had been a third child, a girl who'd died in infancy. Stephan and Fritz, who were seven and eight, spoke of their sister as though she had vanished the previous week. "Baby Helen," they called her, and blessed her before each meal. Their father had died more recently, in a factory accident, but he was rarely mentioned. It was Baby Helen they remembered.

At Playland, Eddie and the little boys had ridden potato sacks down long wooden slides, getting friction burns where a knee or an elbow dragged against the wood. The fun-house floor was pocked with holes through which loud blasts of air (fired by some hidden wiseacre) were meant to lift girls' skirts. Ingrid had a horror of these blasts, and she clung to Eddie, laughing.

As they rode the streetcar back, Eddie had placed a hand on each boy's chest to steady them. He'd been startled by the sensation of their hearts scrambling like mice against his fingertips.

They were still there, Ingrid and her boys. They were thinking of him—waiting for him. Eddie felt this truth in his body like a layer of earth turning over. It was all still there, everything he'd left behind. Its vanishing had been only a trick.

CHAPTER NINETEEN

Eddie lay in his sack, half-asleep. They had entered the Roaring Forties, off Chile, and the *Elizabeth Seaman* rolled momentously. Perhaps that movement was what had awakened the old familiar rhythm inside of Eddie: a small, insistent counterpoint, like a bouncing ball.

"Are there real gangsters?"

"The pictures didn't make them up."

"Do they look like Jimmy Cagney?"

"Jimmy Cagney doesn't look like Jimmy Cagney. He's shorter than Mama."

"Is he your friend?"

"I've shaken his hand."

"Does he look like a gangster?"

"He looks like a picture star."

"How do you know a gangster?"

"Usually, the room goes a little quiet when he walks in."

"Are they scared?"

"If they aren't, then he isn't much of a gangster."

"I don't like being scared."

"Good. You won't end up kowtowing."

"Do you kowtow?"

"Have you noticed me kowtowing?"

"Do you talk to them?"

"I say hello. Some I know from long ago."

"Would you ever be on their side?"

"Not if I'd any choice."

Her small warm hand slipped inside his own. It was always there, that hand, like a minnow finding its crevice.

"Are we going to see Mr. Dunellen?"

"Funny you should mention him, toots."

"He gave me caramels."

"Mr. Dunellen has a sweet tooth. Like you."

"He's your brother."

"In a manner of speaking."

"You saved him from the waves."

"That's true."

"Did he say thank you?"

"Not in so many words. But he's grateful."

"Is that why he gave me caramels?"

"It might just be, toots."

"Did he give you caramels?"

"No. But I haven't your sweet tooth."

Anna returned to Eddie after an absence of years: her voice, the pattering quality of it, the feel of her small hand inside his. She towed him by the hand along the halls of his memory to the room where his old life had been carefully stowed away. Inside, he found everything as he'd left it.

Sunday Mass. Lydia began to cry: a strangled sound that was louder and more wrenching than seemed possible in a baby. She wasn't a baby, she was three—just small enough to remain inside the pram, where her condition was hidden, more or less. Agnes lifted her out to quiet her, exposing her swiveled form to the crowded church. Eddie's shame had the blunt force of a blow to the skull; he grabbed the pew in front of theirs to steady himself. Lydia continued to choke and howl; Father couldn't be heard. The men, wincing, pretended nothing was amiss while two wives helped Agnes from the church, one pushing the pram, the other holding Lydia's flailing legs. Anna tried to follow, but Eddie clamped his hand around hers. His surroundings felt at a sudden weird remove, as if something had ruptured in his mind. He fastened his eyes to the priest but heard only a drone.

After Mass, a group of men drifted into somebody's flat for a touch of that god-awful beer Owney Madden was brewing in plain sight at the biscuit factory on West Twenty-sixth. Eddie nipped in, too, intending to stay just a minute. The bad feeling he'd had in the church was still with him; he wanted to shake it before returning to Agnes. The fun of drinking Madden's No. 1 wasn't the taste, God knew, but trying to pinpoint what it tasted *of*: Sawdust? Wet newspaper? The pigeons Owney famously loved to breed? Children threw snowballs outdoors, moving aside for the occasional automobile. Eddie observed from the window as Anna, all of six, sprang at the boys from behind a snowdrift. Watching her made him feel well. *I have one healthy child,* he thought, *thank God. Thank God.*

Early-winter twilight had seeped into the snowdrifts by the time they hurried home through Hell's Kitchen. Eddie was weaving a little from the beer. It was later than he'd meant; Agnes would have to rush to make her call. The Follies were on hiatus since the crash, but Mr. Z. had arranged for her to be hired on another show.

"I want to play outside more," Anna informed him through chattering teeth.

"You're wet and you're cold. Take my hand."

"I won't." But she did, in her soggy mitten, first transferring something to her other hand.

"What is that, may I ask?"

He relieved her of a snowball, tightly packed, flecked with straw and manure. "I'm saving it," she said.

"Snow melts indoors. You know that."

"In the icebox."

"You'll give us all typhoid. Leave it outside on the stoop."

"Someone might take it!"

"Not likely, toots."

He opened the apartment door braced for Agnes's anger and Lydia's cries. But a peaceful scene awaited them: Lydia lay on the settee, her hair damp. Anna ran to her sister. The kitchen tub was full of water.

"She needed a bath, that's all," Agnes said, drained and ashen. He wondered how long the crying had lasted.

"You had to bathe her alone," he said. "I'm sorry."

Agnes washed hastily, using the water left in the tub. Eddie leaned over the settee and kissed Lydia's downy cheek. Whatever had broken inside him at church seemed, for the moment, to mend.

When the girls were asleep, he sat on the front stoop—they'd a ground-floor apartment in Hell's Kitchen—and smoked, oblivious to the cold. He had heard of children who were clubfoots, Mongoloids, halfwits, and gimps; who'd fallen out windows, been trampled by horses, brained themselves diving off Hudson River piers onto submerged piles. Why was this worse? He could not explain why. The alloy of beauty and contortion in Lydia suggested some gross misstep of his own. She was not as she should be, not remotely, and the shadow of what she should have been clung to her always, a reproachful twin. Often, when alone, Eddie revisited the moment when the doctor had first come to him from the delivery room: the dark look, the offer of a cigarette, Eddie's terror that the baby—a son, he'd hoped—was dead. Now, in his reimagining, the doctor delivered the very news he'd dreaded to hear that day: *I'm so terribly sorry. Your baby is stillborn.* And for a moment, Eddie catapulted into a life remade by this adjustment: they would move to California, where everything was supposed to be better! Agnes would go back to being the lazy vixen he'd wed, who'd teased him in bed with feathered fans and stabbed out her cigarettes into piles of mashed potatoes. But Eddie paid dearly for this flight of fancy when the grim facts of his life tumbled back over him. There would be no move, no change, no end to this.

He went indoors to check on the girls and add more coal to the stove. Lydia slept in a cradle in the kitchen, where it was warmest. Even breathing was a trial for her. *In . . . out. In . . . out.* The pause between her breaths seemed longer than natural, as if, having managed to exhale, she had to muster the energy to begin anew. The curious detachment Eddie had felt at Mass returned, its numbing remoteness bringing relief from his despair. He was an observer, no more, watching a man lift a pillow and set it lightly upon the face of his sleeping daughter. Her breathing slowed as she struggled to contend with this new weight. Eddie watched the man press down upon the pillow. The child's small chest bones flexed and worked above the collar of her nightdress. Her head began to move as she tried to turn her face. The man pushed harder. Eddie was astonished by her frantic efforts to find air. She would never walk, never talk, but still she groped for life—fought for it. The ferocity of her instinct forced Eddie back inside himself with the violence of a door slamming into its frame. He dropped the pillow and scooped Lydia from the cradle. He wanted to howl, but that would frighten her, so he kissed her tiny face, wetting it with tears until her eyes fluttered open and she smiled up at him. He held her, weeping softly, and rocked her back to sleep. In his mind's eye, he threw himself from a roof or under the wheels of a trolley—punishments he deserved, even craved. Suicide was a coward's choice, as much a sin as the other, yet the fantasies were rapturous. He couldn't make them stop.

When Agnes came home late that night, she glanced at Eddie and ran to the cradle as if she'd felt the brush of a wing of the angel of death. He told her calmly that he couldn't stay at home with Lydia anymore. That was the last show Agnes danced. She never returned, despite Mr. Z.'s pleas that she finish out the week. Overnight, she abandoned the work she adored—that had brought her to New York eleven years before, at seventeen, and brought them together. And Eddie, without savings or prospects, walked to the West Side piers to find the scrum of his youth.

After the morning shape-up, when the hiring boss had made his foregone choices of who would work, scores of luckless gees stubbed out their cigars and drifted dejectedly into a gauntlet of saloons, loan sharks, dope peddlers, and games of chance. Thanks to Dunellen, Eddie was guaranteed a slot from the afternoon shape if not the morning. Often he chose to pass the time in between drifting among the crowd of have-nots: Poles and Italians, Negroes, even Americans, or white men who were born here. The variety of awaiting enticements obscured their common purpose: to wring money from men who'd been unfairly denied a chance to earn any. It amazed him that Negroes showed up at all on these piers, where the only jobs they'd a hope of getting were the ones no one wanted: deep in the hold unloading bananas, for example, which bruised at a touch and were riddled with biting spiders.

It didn't take Eddie long to discern that the games of chance near Dunellen's piers were all rigged: a funny deck, loaded dice, or even—especially common with African golf, as craps were known—an apparent loser who was really in cahoots with two or three other "losers" to fleece the rest. Eddie's shock at this discovery attested to an idealism he hadn't realized he still possessed. A man who borrowed from a loan shark knew what he was getting into, and men who took dope or drank themselves stupid deserved what they got. But a man who elected to try his luck in hopes of bringing something home to his wife deserved a chance at winning. Luck was the single thing that could rearrange facts. It could open a door where there was no door. A crooked game was worse than unfair; it was a cosmic violation.

Eddie began warning Negroes away from Dunellen's games. "You'll find the play fairer elsewhere," he would say cryptically, or "Strangers don't win in that room." Always with a vertiginous sense of great risk—he was defying not just Dunellen, at whose behest he'd any work at all, but the men behind Dunellen whom he didn't know. Eddie's shifty agitation likely explained the wary reactions his warnings provoked. "I guess I'll play where I please," he'd been told, and "I suppose we can take care of ourselves." But occasionally, the men he warned would avoid the game rather than go inside. At these times Eddie was euphoric, as if he'd saved a soul.

When the shipping dried up completely, in '32, he became Dunellen's full-time lackey. Anna came along after school and on weekends, and Eddie mixed Dunellen's "errands" with trips to the Hippodrome, the Central Park menagerie, the Castle Garden aquarium. Only in Anna's company was he truly at ease. She was his secret treasure, his one pure, unspoiled source of joy.

"We're stopping here quickly, to do a favor. I'll need you to behave."

"Will you behave?"

"I'll do my best, toots."

"Who will be mad if we *don't* behave?"

"We mustn't stand out, that's all."

"What favor?"

"We're passing a hello from one man to another. But it's a secret hello."

The notion excited her. "I want to say a secret hello!"

"You can. If you give me a kiss, I'll give the kiss to Mama, from you."

Anna considered. "I want to give a secret kiss to Lydia."

"Lydia won't understand, toots."

"Yes, she will."

When the car was stopped at a light, Anna seized his head between her star-shaped hands and kissed the side of his face with utmost tenderness. Eddie felt a sting in his eyes.

"*That* kiss," Anna said. "That one is for Lydia."

At home, she watched him deliver it. Eddie did so tenderly, exactly as she had instructed. He was a bagman, after all.

Eddie knew he was sluicing the corruption by delivering the boodling payoffs that sustained it—to aldermen, state senators, police superintendents, rival pier bosses, and back again, at different times. Yet he maintained an observational stance—he wasn't really doing what he was doing; he was watching it. This distinction was essential to assuage his sense of failure and despair—the stubborn, beckoning vision of an oncoming trolley wheel. Gradually, his routes began to ramify beyond Dunellen's piers to gaming halls where Dunny had an interest but not control. There was cheating here, too, but never when a higher-up was present. That meant the cheating wasn't sanctioned from above, but a sub-racket of the dealers and game runners to increase their take without risking a suicidal move like robbing the house. It might therefore be stopped, if Eddie knew what higher-up to tell.

When Dunellen hadn't any work for him, Eddie sometimes posed as a regular player to study the crookedness, and the crookedness inside that. He imagined he was a detective—real police, not the corrupt pawns who were the only bulls he knew. He wrote nothing down. The cheating was all in his head: who; when; how; how much. Meanwhile, a larger structure disclosed itself gradually—to know who paid whom was, in some sense, to know everything. It turned out that a single man controlled much of the gaming in New York City in late 1934. The path of profits to this personage contained switchbacks and hairpin turns that only a person making and receiving deliveries could begin to track. There was always a man behind the man, and another man behind that one—all the way up to God, Eddie supposed.

Two days after Christmas, Eddie polished his shoes, brushed his hat, and trimmed it with an iridescent green feather Agnes had saved from her piecework. He paid this almighty stranger a call at Nightlight, a former speaky in the West Forties that ambushed Eddie with nostalgia when he walked inside. He must have been here with Agnes and Brianne and the other dancers, back in the time he'd come to think of as *Before*.

According to the front-of-house man, the boss was not present. Eddie said he'd wait, ordered a rye and soda, and opened his silver pocket watch on the bar. He'd been a sucker in his nostalgia, he saw; the joint played on that, its seediness manufactured, or at least aware. He sensed that gaming was taking place, watched until he found the door, and guessed at the stakes by the men and women passing through it in paste pearls and last year's hats. Nightlight's racket wasn't gambling, that was clear. It was something else—a way of making money that involved losing money on the surface.

Twenty-four minutes later, another man came along and asked whether Eddie would like to see the boss. Eddie followed him to a back room, where a gee with a Dick Tracy jaw was surrounded by wop goons. Eddie was shocked. Outside the purview of his piers, Dunellen was doing business with the Syndicate. That could only mean he hadn't any choice.

Styles sent his lackeys packing. When Eddie had taken a seat across his desk, he said, "Are you police?"

Eddie shook his head. "A concerned citizen."

Styles laughed. "What can I do for you, Mr. Kerrigan?"

Eddie laid out his discoveries game by game: location, means of cheating, approximate take. Styles listened in silence. Once or twice he interjected, "That's none of ours," but mostly, he listened. When Eddie had finished, he asked, "Why tell me this?"

"I'd want to know, if I were you."

"Of course I want to know. What do *you* want?"

Eddie hadn't expected to reach this point so quickly. He found himself uncertain what to say—what he wanted from Styles, exactly.

"I can give you something right now," Styles said. "Just about anything, in fact."

He eyed Kerrigan, searching for the weakness. Money wasn't his object, or he'd have demanded it before singing. What, then? In a mick it was usually booze, but Kerrigan hadn't the look of a lush. Nor was there much propensity for violence in those scrappy limbs, though he'd likely fight hard in self-defense. Women? Micks were famously prudish, faithful to their blowsy wives—perhaps recalling the bonny colleens they'd been before the assembly line of children, or from fear of their drunken, bellicose priests.

"Girls?" He was watching Kerrigan's face, awaiting that trigger flinch that would let him know he'd found it. "We've girls galore around here."

"I've a beautiful wife, Mr. Styles."

"So have I," Dexter said. "We're lucky."

Money, then. He was disappointed in Kerrigan; it would be less than he'd have gotten by demanding it first. "What do you call a fair price for the information you've given me?"

Eddie collected his thoughts, unsatisfied. "As I see it," he began, "you could run your business better and at the same time make it cleaner—more fair, I mean—to the men who try their luck." This sounded disingenuous, even silly. He sensed Styles's bafflement—but sensed, too, that Styles enjoyed being baffled.

"Is it your impression, Mr. Kerrigan, that I run a charitable organization?" he asked.

Eddie couldn't help but smile.

"You think like a police," Styles said. "Why not join?"

"I'd still be working for you."

Only then did Eddie understand what his object had been, coming here. He wanted a job.

"Some men find it a bitter pill to swallow, working for me," Styles said. "They don't like the change in times."

Eddie took this to mean he wasn't the first waterfront mick to come calling out of sheer desperation. "I guess that depends," he said, "who they were working for before."

Styles leaned back, sizing him up. Eddie did the same of the younger man across the desk: the phony name with a wop name crumpled just behind it, a restless dissatisfaction that registered as curiosity, energy. And underneath that, a sadness deep enough to bear its weight. Eddie saw a man he recognized and liked. He felt an affinity for Dexter Styles, whose very power derived from the fact that it was outside his scrum—in defiance of it. An allegiance purely of choice.

"It happens you're right," Styles said. "I'd like to clean up those games you mention. And I'd like to know what other leaks I've got. They've a tendency to vanish when my boys show up."

"You need an ombudsman," Eddie said. It was a word he'd

discovered years ago, in a newspaper. He'd been waiting ever since for a chance to use it.

Styles smiled, bemused. "All right, then: an ombudsman. But we can't meet here. Or be seen together."

"Naturally."

"Bring your family to my home and we'll talk some more. You've children?"

"Two daughters."

"I've a daughter, too. They can play together. Will Saturday do?"

A light rain was falling when Eddie left the Nightlight, but in his elevated state he barely noticed. He strode down Fifth Avenue, empty of everyone but the gutter snipes searching for discarded smokes. Soon he was passing the encampments at Madison Square. Fires hissed and smoked in the damp. He smelled coffee and condensed milk boiling in cans—a sweet, metallic odor that always set his teeth on edge. Normally, that smell made him cringe with awareness that John Dunellen alone—that bloated, capricious monster—stood between Eddie and the men boiling coffee outdoors.

He'd found an opening, a way out. Lydia would have her chair. And maybe, Eddie thought, dazzled by the tiny globes of rain sparkling in the trees, maybe it would help her in ways he hadn't foreseen in his gloom. Perhaps, after all, Lydia would begin to right herself.

To his original goal—granting men an honest audience with Lady Luck—Eddie gave not a thought during his wet, dark, ecstatic walk. What he felt was the sheer relief of having saved himself.

PART SIX

The Dive

CHAPTER TWENTY

Dexter had tried in vain, in the month since his disappointment with Mr. Q., to maneuver a private conversation with his father-in-law at one of their Sunday lunches. The difficulty of doing so had turned out to be an advantage; with each week, Dexter became more certain of what he wished to propose. At last, at a hunt club dinner dance, the old man caught his eye across a table strewn with half-eaten slices of baked Alaska and said, "I could do with some fresh air. Yourself?"

Dexter rose in the smoky candlelight. The orchestra had sidled into "White Christmas," wearing dangerously thin by mid-February, and he was more than willing to suspend his patrol of the fox-trotting faithful. He'd been watching for Tabatha and Grady, but what he kept seeing instead was his wife in the arms of Booth Kimball (known, in seriousness, as Boo Boo), a polo champion she'd been in love with as a girl. Boo Boo had married Lady Something-or-other and moved to London shortly after Dexter and Harriet married. Now, not having seen the man in over a decade, Dexter hardly recognized him—Boo Boo's hair had gone snow-white. "You dodged a bullet, sweets," he'd whispered to Harriet during cocktails, nudging his chin in Boo Boo's direction. To which she'd intoned sepulchrally, "Pippa died of cancer last year."

The old man led the way through the velvet blackout curtains into an arctic gale. "Fresh air," he said fondly over a lacerating wind. "Feels good." He wore a thin silk scarf—little more than a cravat—and a bowler, but he was famously, almost comically hardy. Dexter had never seen him sweat even wearing a dinner suit in dead summer. He'd a quick knifelike walk that required Dexter to stride in earnest to keep up, although he was several inches taller.

A lunar sheath of old snow encrusted the fairways, but the paths where the caddies walked were mostly clear. They followed one of these to the shore, remarking during lulls of wind on how fine Grady looked in his uniform, the terrors his departure was giving his poor mother. This weekend was his final leave before shipping out. With three other native sons in similar straits—two army, one Coast Guard—this dinner dance had become a farewell party. Cooper was queasy with fear for his son, but Dexter felt confident that not even a world war could extinguish Grady's promise.

They reached Crooked Creek, a tendril of frozen greenish sea neutered by its slog around Long Beach, through the Broad Channel, and over various marshy hassocks. Dexter would have liked to keep walking—he preferred to move as he talked—but the old man came to a halt.

"I like to be near water whenever possible, don't you?" he said, gazing into the dark. "Melville put it best: 'Nothing will content men but the extremest limit of the land'—but that's not it, I can't recall the quote. It's in our nature to seek out the edge. Even on a golf course."

"Especially then," Dexter said, and they both laughed. Among their shared irreverences was a disdain for golf—Dexter because he hadn't the patience to learn a game whose experts had imbibed it with mother's milk; the old man because he saw it as sloth masquerading as sport.

Dexter recognized this spot: it was the very one where he'd asked for Harriet's hand so long ago. That had been summer, trees buckling under loads of leaves, the freshly mowed fairways huffing up a smell that always reminded him of fresh money. Now, as he looked toward the blacked-out horizon, he found himself recalling some version of that earlier conversation.

"Your friends and my friends, Mr. Styles," his future father-in-law had remarked over gibbering cicadas, "I think it's fair to say they wouldn't like each other much."

This dire understatement seemed to flirt with humor, but Dexter took it straight. "I suppose they wouldn't have much in common, sir," he said.

"Oh, I think they'd have a great deal in common, although they might not like to admit it. Or possess a shared language with which to do so."

This extraordinary statement had silenced Dexter.

"You might think it strange, Mr. Styles, how little I care who your friends are."

"I'm . . . glad to hear it, sir."

"Harriet is nuts about you, that's what matters to me. And now you must consider very carefully how nuts you are about Harriet. She will be your one and only. That is where I draw the line, Mr. Styles. Not at your friends, not at your line of work, your reputation, your history. Fidelity. That will be your promise to me."

"I promise," Dexter said with all the careful reflection of a young man eager to keep fucking the banker's daughter he'd been fucking and have it be legal.

"I want my daughter to be happy," Mr. Berringer said, watching him with calm appraisal. "And I will be monitoring her happiness with vigor and care."

"I understand, sir."

"You don't," he said pleasantly. "You can't. But I hope for your sake that you'll keep the promise nonetheless. A promise means no exceptions. Understood?"

Of course he hadn't understood. And later, when he began to, Dexter could only marvel at the sleight of hand whereby his father-in-law had jimmied himself out of a straitjacket with enough leverage to extract promises. Houdini couldn't have topped it: his daughter was knocked up and refused to have it taken care of. Had Arthur withheld his consent, she'd have run away with Dexter: a disgrace. The old man hadn't had enough room to scratch his nose, yet he'd bargained as if the advantage were all his—intuiting with eerie perspicacity that, although criminal, Dexter was a man of his word. Monogamy was nothing short of exotic in his line of work, yet no sooner had the ice-creamy arm of a chorus girl encircled his neck than Dexter felt watched: Would this be the slip? The thin end of the wedge? It worked better than a cold shower. Afterward, he was always relieved, grateful, even. Dames were as bad as dope for turning a man against his interests. And Harriet was better-looking than all of them.

There had been the one on the train. A unique misstep—out of time and place—that had strengthened his resolve never to err again.

Now, having broken his promise a second time exactly two weeks ago on this night, Dexter was forced to consider that the old man might have brought him here to confront him with that fact. But how could he know? What George Porter had seen was nothing. And even if George suspected, Dexter's sin paled beside his own. Anyway, the doctor had became bluff and friendly again with Dexter since that night, the manly understanding between them newly enriched.

He emerged from this brown study to find the old man watching him. "You've not seemed quite yourself these past weeks," he said. "I wonder what's on your mind."

Dexter swallowed. How did the real adulterers do it? But there was something on his mind, of course—he'd been conniving for a month to bend the old man's ear about it. With relief, he began, "I feel the need of a change, sir."

"Sir?"

Dexter flushed. "Arthur."

"What sort of change?"

"Professional."

"You've quite a diversity of interests already, haven't you?"

"That's a fact. But I'm on the wrong side."

Music sputtered like a distant phonograph through bursts of glacial wind. They might have been standing at the end of the earth: a gray-black landscape of water and ice.

"Right and wrong are relative terms, aren't they, in your line of work?" the old man asked.

"I've always said so."

Arthur whistled. "It's late in the day to come down with a case of idealism."

Dexter heard his smile. "It seems to be an epidemic," he said.

"War will do that. One of many ancillary benefits."

"I want to be an honest part of what comes next," Dexter said. "Not a leech sucking blood off its back."

The old man took a long breath, something like a sigh. "It's a pity we're forced to make the choices that govern the whole of our lives when we're so goddamn young."

"If they're the wrong choices, then we have to make new ones," Dexter said. "Even late in the day."

An onslaught of wind made his eyes water, but the old man didn't so much as hold his hat. When the blast subsided, he said, "Judging by my limited knowledge of your associates and their business practices, changing sides won't be easy."

"It's already happening naturally," Dexter said. "I've legitimate interests here, in Chicago, in Florida. I've friendships all over."

"I don't doubt that. You're a likable fellow. But is your employer aware of this . . . natural divergence?"

It was the first time Dexter could recall the old man referring, singly and directly, to Mr. Q. His fleeting amazement gave way to a heady sense of convergence, as if a bridge had suddenly appeared between irreconcilable worlds. And a bridge was precisely what he needed.

"I'm certain he's aware," Dexter said. "But it's up to me to take a decisive step."

The old man was too canny not to have sensed where this talk was leading—probably he'd known from the word "professional," or even "sir." Dexter squared his shoulders and took a breath. "It occurred to me," he said, swallowing back another "sir" that rose like a bubble in his throat, "that I might bring my legitimate assets and interests to you. At the bank."

"We'd buy you out," the old man said.

"Exactly."

His father-in-law's silence seemed a good sign—a sign of serious consideration. Dexter eyed the whorls of frozen sea at his feet. His life had already changed course once in this spot—why not again?

"You're not thinking clearly, son," the old man said at last, in the same mild way he said everything. "And that worries me considerably—for your own safety and that of persons dear to me who are under your protection."

An entity deep within Dexter recoiled as if scalded, but he managed to say casually, "How do you figure?"

"You've a good life, Dexter. A beautiful family. You're known, respected—sought after. Your name is in the papers. That's double, triple what most men achieve in a lifetime. But it isn't portable. You possess a currency that cannot be used in any country besides its own."

"I don't see it."

"Then clear your head, son. Clear your head." *Son* was a diminutive; what the old man called Cooper.

"It feels terribly clear," Dexter said. "My head."

"Do you know," the old man said affably, "after the Great War, when we formed syndicates to underwrite the bond issues to build railroads and factories, we never had so much as a contract with any of our partners? Not the managing group closest to us, not even the purchasing group that sold the bonds to the public. There was no law to oversee those transactions. Trust, reputation—those were all we needed. All we had! To this day, the entirety of my business rests upon trust."

"But you do trust me," Dexter said. "You've shown that time and again."

"I trust you entirely. You'd have made a tremendous banker, Dexter. A partner, nothing less." This was a reference to Cooper, a junior in the firm unlikely to rise much further despite his pedigree. "I've absolute faith in your vision. Which is why I'm mystified by your failure to see that your reputation—your history—is prohibitive."

Dexter strained to regroup. How had he not foreseen this objection? But he had—it was the first thing he'd foreseen. He'd simply counted on the old man's power, reputation, and independence to sweep it aside.

"I never thought you cared for other men's opinions," he said.

"Personally, I don't," the old man said. "In business, I've no choice. I know exactly how far I can go. Am I saying no bank in New York would have you? Certainly not. There are banks where reputation matters less. But why? Why become a middling banker at a middling firm, forever trying to prove you've gone straight?"

"That isn't what I want."

"It's the best you'll get if you pursue this line. If I were you, I'd stay exactly where I was. Recognize the myriad advantages of your position and enjoy them. Trying to change the position midstream is likely to mean losing those advantages without gaining any new ones."

The wisdom of Arthur's words was manifest, irrefutable, yet Dexter already knew he couldn't heed them. Something had shifted inside him. "I've paid too much for my advantages," he said, surprising himself with this disclosure. He was speaking of the blood on his hands.

His father-in-law seized Dexter's shoulders in his delicate grasp. His very compactness seemed a source of authority, Dexter's comparative bulk a feature of blundering youth. "We all pay for our advantages," the old man said, with meaning. "There's not a man in this world who hasn't, and I include the priests. Every man has his secrets, his costs of doing business. It's no different in my line. Don't be fooled by the marble columns—the Romans had those, too, and they fed their prisoners to lions. There's a good deal of brutality behind institutions like mine, leavened by an equal measure of hypocrisy."

Dexter's eyes smarted, not from the wind. How he loved Arthur Berringer for believing they were alike! The old man's "brutality" was not the same as Dexter's, of course, whatever he might think. Still, there was an intensity behind the words that made him wish he could see his father-in-law's face. But darkness was the essential feature of their exchange.

By tacit agreement, they began following the orchestra sounds back toward the clubhouse. At last it came into sight: an unearthly colonnade leaking festivity into the icy lunar landscape.

"Not enough has been written about the treachery of middle life," the old man mused, his voice carrying over the wind. "Dante went to hell to escape it, and I've seen plenty of other men do the same, metaphorically speaking. Be patient, Dexter. Wars have a way of shifting the terrain into configurations we can't foresee, hard as we might try. This is no time for bold moves."

Dexter liked that word, "configuration." The tide had turned in the war, unmistakably—what the old man had foreseen last fall was already coming to pass. But a dissatisfaction of weeks—months—had accumulated in Dexter's limbs, and he needed to act. Even the wrong move was more appealing than none at all.

George Porter hovered just inside the blackout curtains, anxiously grooming his mustache. "I was wondering where you'd gone off to," he greeted them searchingly. Dexter was too distracted to reassure him.

Every Berringer except the boys away at school was present tonight, filling four tables in the crowded dining room. Dexter had been seated next to Bitsy. With poor Henry casting baleful looks at them from across the table, he'd questioned her over dinner. Yes, the baby was crying less. No, she was not as unhappy as before. Her calm made Dexter suspect that she and George had found an available nook during cocktail hour. There were plenty of those at the hunt club, as Dexter well knew from the days when Harriet had brought him here as an act of insurrection. Charm and a heavy bankroll could secure one's entrée to many places in this world, but not the Rockaway Hunting Club. Dexter's frigid reception by the old stoves and their prissy progeny had amused him back then—what did he care? They could cold-shoulder him, refuse to host his nuptials (a thing that had made the old man very angry), but he'd snagged one of their own and was swinging her hand as they walked beside the swimming pool at night, looking for a place to fuck. The fillip of collective opprobrium had summoned their lust like a knife chiming crystal; its ringing emanations filled the trees and shook in the moonlight until they could think of nothing else. Conjugal bliss had been achieved in a sand trap, behind a garden shed, under a case containing photographs and trophies from the famed steeplechase races. Eight months pregnant, Harriet had serviced him under a table-cloth during a presentation of awards for lawn tennis.

Now, however, the *configuration* had shifted. Tabby and the twins had been embraced from the start, and Harriet was a prodigal returned—welcomed the more warmly for the distance she'd traveled. Only Dexter remained outside. His own generation was friendly enough; the wives flirted with him rashly when they were tight. But the old guard treated him with a weary revile whose foremost ingredient was boredom. He was far too familiar to be shocking, but they hated him still.

Grady and the other departing boys began waltzing with their proud, frightened mothers. The boys blazed in their fine uniforms, already heroes. Dexter decided to look for Mr. Bonaventura, who ran the kitchen (even Puritans knew that when it came to food and drink, you needed a Brazilian), to discuss the source of his black-market beef. The roast had been tough; Dexter knew he could do better and liked the notion of transacting this bit of business while the Puritans danced. But even as he strode toward the padded swinging door to the kitchen, a part of him shrank from this course. It was more of the same—the same, the same—and within the span of an instant, the idea of haggling with Mr. Bonaventura over beef went from vaguely promising to wretchedly bad. He was as sick of himself as the stoves were of him.

Rooted mid-ballroom, Dexter recognized his bind: any action he'd the power to take would push him further in the direction he wished to withdraw from. There was, quite literally, nothing he could do.

Yet in that discovery, he felt a stirring of possibility. Suppose *doing* was the wrong idea. Perhaps there was something he could *undo*.

He spotted his wife leaving the ladies' lounge and caught her hand. She looked startled and pleased as he pulled her onto the crowded dance floor. A stiffness had arisen between them since the night he'd spent with Kerrigan's daughter. That interlude had been difficult to shake: the shock of learning who she was, above all, but also the smell and feel and taste of her. He'd returned to the boathouse two days later to investigate those empty bottles and determine who the interlopers had been. But no sooner was he surrounded by the props of that night—table, stove, a stocking crumpled on the floor—than he'd found himself leaning against a wall with a hand in his trousers. He'd not returned to the boathouse since. Nor had he made love to Harriet—an aberration she had accepted with surprising equanimity. Now, having watched her in the arms of the newly bereaved Boo Boo, Dexter was determined to resume their normal relations. He held her close, breathing the musky smell of her hair and feeling, in her sinuous hips, the memory of childhood horseback riding she'd long since recanted.

"Remember how we used to be in this place?" he asked.

"Oh yes."

"Let's hope it isn't like that with Tabby and Grady."

He'd meant to be funny, but she tensed in his arms. "She's sixteen."

"How old were you?"

She was no virgin when they'd met. At the time, it hadn't occurred to Dexter to demand details of when or with whom. It might have been Boo Boo, ten years older. She'd likely have married the polo champion if he'd asked, but she'd been too young and far, far too wild. Not even a father like hers could compensate. They all had fathers like hers.

"The boys are being very good," he said to conciliate.

"They're good boys," she said. "You don't credit them enough."

"I'll credit them more."

"Will you?" He felt her warm breath at his ear and knew they would make love that night. The events of the boathouse moved to the horizon of his thoughts. But they would not entirely disappear.

"If it will make you happy."

"Very happy."

The orchestra concluded with "Tangerine," from that not very good picture starring Dorothy Lamour. Family groups began fumbling into the dark. The old man, along with Cooper, Marsha, and Grady's sisters (average girls toiling invisibly in his glare), would see Grady off tomorrow at Pennsylvania Station. For the rest of them, this was goodbye.

Dexter left the clubhouse alongside George Porter, an arm around the doctor's shoulders to dispel his evident worry about Dexter's confab with the old man. George must know him better than that.

Grady seemed taller than he had even a few weeks before, his gaze nearly level with Dexter's own. Moonlight touched the brass buttons of his uniform. Dexter felt his throat tighten as he shook his nephew's hand. For all his confidence that Grady would survive, he'd an eerie intimation that he wouldn't see him again.

Tabatha threw her arms around Grady's neck and hung there, sobbing. Dexter hovered nearby, concerned that her display was unseemly. But his mother-in-law merely said in a taut voice, "They've always been so close."

Dexter tried to make her out in the moonlight. Could it be? Under cover of darkness, rogue tears had seeped from Beth Berringer's stingy eyes and now sparkled with gaudy subversion in her kaleidoscopic wrinkles.

"Grady needs to say other goodbyes, darling," Harriet admonished gently, prying Tabby away from her cousin.

Tabby ran to Dexter, and he wrapped her in his arms. "Shh, Tabby Cat," he said, holding her. "Come now. Everything will be all right."

"It won't be like this," she said. "Not ever again."

"Grady will come back healthy as a horse, I promise."

She drew away, trying to see him. "You can't promise that, Daddy."

She'd a point; he was talking out of his hat. "I can promise that because I believe it. I haven't the slightest worry about Grady Berringer: zero."

It was hooey of the highest order, yet Dexter felt the calming effect of his words as if his daughter's heart were relaxing inside his own chest. He felt the likeness of their flesh, their common smell, their way of moving. She was his own. And he was hers.

Harriet walked ahead toward the Cadillac, one arm around each of the twins. Dexter followed, still holding Tabby. No one spoke; there was only the crunch of their shoes on the gravel path. And just then, as he held his anguished daughter in the moonlight, Dexter knew what action he must take.

CHAPTER TWENTY-ONE

Anna often recalled hauling herself up the ladder on test day, triumphant. A moving picture would have ended there, with the promise that, at long last and against all odds, she'd earned the respect of the crusty lieutenant. In fact, he liked her less. He referred to his divers as "boys," "men," or "gentlemen." He fell silent when Anna passed, as if she were a black cat. She understood that her hope of pleasing him could be achieved only by quitting, and he gave her no reason to stay.

Over two weeks had passed since the test day, and she'd not been back in the water even once. The men dove often; Bascombe and Marle had worked together, patching the submerged hull of an Allied destroyer. Anna had been nominally made a rigger, meaning that her specialty was salvage: the raising of sunken objects. The *Normandie*, at Pier 88, was a salvage operation, as had been the scuttled German fleet at Scapa Flow. But there were no sunken ships in Wallabout Bay; instead, there were several thousand railroad ties that had slid from a barge a decade ago and now interfered with the passage of certain deep-bottomed ships. With the exception of Anna, those chosen to remove these ties were the biggest and least skilled of the diving class—Savino, for example, who had nailed a hole through his diving dress on test day. Anna had had to patch that hole; Savino, meanwhile, was chosen to receive welding lessons in the diving tank. There his mishaps continued; two days before, he'd shattered his faceplate on the corner of the steel panel he was trying to weld. They'd pulled him up quickly—Marle was one of his tenders—and Savino had seemed all right at first, just some pressure bleeding from his ears and nose. But inside the recompression tank, he had fallen unconscious. Lieutenant Axel suspected an air embolism, meaning that Savino had taken a breath and held it before they'd pulled him up. As the pressure around him dropped to sea level, the pressure exerted by the air inside his lungs would have mounted until a bubble was expelled into his bloodstream. It would travel through veins and arteries until it lodged in a passage too small to pass through—in Savino's case, one bringing blood to the brain. Air embolisms were often deadly, but Savino had survived. He hadn't returned to work yet.

Anna had spent today cleaning the lufer sponge filters inside the oil separators on all ten air compressors. Most of her assignments had this air of the domestic: patching diving dresses with rubber cement; rubbing neat's-foot oil onto the leather gaskets of helmets; separating hoses too long attached. She felt even further from the war than she had in the measuring shop—there, at least, she'd run errands to other parts of the Yard. Now, as she changed back into her street clothes in her locker-closet, Anna lapsed into a familiar state of hopeless surrender: she *was* weak; she felt weak. The railroad stanchions were too heavy for her to lift; Lieutenant Axel was right to keep her from them. This feeble turn of mind assuaged Anna's scathing sense of injustice; feeling undeserving was less terrible, somehow, than feeling cheated. It evoked a novel impression of herself, tentative and fragile, like the marrieds. But a roar of fury incinerated this vision like an effigy. How she loathed Lieutenant Axel—wished that *he* would disappear. Hating him infused Anna with strength. But she had to conceal her rage, absorb it, even when doing so felt like drinking bleach. The slightest infraction would be grounds for her dismissal. And then the lieutenant would have won.

Her favorite times were those when superior officers visited Building 569. In the presence of naval brass of higher rank, Lieutenant Axel looked abashed and dutiful, and Katz, his henchman, appeared starstruck to the point of paralysis. Thus reduced, they forgot their disdain for Anna. It was the only time.

Anna left the Yard with the other divers and headed for the Oval Bar. Bascombe had engineered her inclusion in this nightly ritual as deftly as he had Marle's: shortly after the test dive, his fiancée had approached Anna outside the Sands Street gate and said, in a voice touched by a head cold, "Basky wants me to go out with the boys, but you'll come along, won't you? I don't want to be the only girl."

Tonight everyone wanted the story of Savino's air embolism from Marle, who had been with him inside the recompression tank. After Savino fell unconscious, Marle said, Lieutenant Axel had increased the pressure to 120 pounds, a depth of almost three hundred feet, in hopes that the bubble would be reabsorbed into Savino's blood. Blue ink had exploded from the lieutenant's pen, spraying both of them. Marle had held Savino's legs aloft and Lieutenant Axel had massaged his hands and feet, trying to increase the circulation to his brain.

"All the time he's talking," Marle said as they washed down free bar food—intended to lure in sailors—with B&H beers. "Saying, 'You're going to be fine, son, you know how I know? You'd be dead already if you were going to die.'"

"Sounds like vintage Axel to me," Bascombe muttered, sipping Coca-Cola.

"Like a man calming a horse. Even though Savino is out cold. 'Someday you'll tell those kids of yours how you risked your life so they wouldn't have to eat seaweed and sauerkraut at Sunday dinner.'"

"Laying it on a little thick, if you ask me."

"And he brought the man back. I watched him do it. Not that this cynic will believe it." Marle flicked his eyes at Bascombe.

After forty-five minutes, Savino had regained consciousness. It had taken five more hours to decompress the chamber. When at last it was done, after midnight, Savino had walked into the waiting ambulance.

"I'm surprised Axel kept the grin off his yap," Bascombe said. "He's been dying to play hero from day one."

"That's an act," Marle said. "If he loses a diver, they'll shut him down."

"Cry me a river."

Marle shook his head. He and Bascombe were often on opposite sides, but also inseparable. Bascombe wasn't welcome in Ruby's home; her father regarded him as a drifter and refused to shake his hand. Bascombe had taken to eating Sunday supper with Marle and his parents in Harlem.

Anna caught the streetcar home with Ruby and Bascombe. Bascombe would escort Ruby all the way to Sunset Park, where she lived above her family's grocery, then return to his rooming house by the Naval Yard: an hour and a half's journey. Their engagement was secret until he could change her father's mind. Like Bascombe's campaign to join the navy after failing three eye tests, this one seemed, on the face of it, doomed. Yet he seethed with such roiling ambition that Anna half believed he would succeed. The campaigns were intertwined; were Bascombe to join the navy, he was certain, Ruby's father would see him differently.

Anna got off at Atlantic Avenue. She was alone for the first time since morning, but the isolation of weeks ago could get no purchase on her now. She was too preoccupied. She sat at the kitchen table with an evening newspaper and the unopened mail and thought about Dexter Styles. He rarely crossed her mind at work, as if the marine guards had barred his entry from the Yard. But at home she confronted afresh the certainty that he knew what had happened to her father. He'd cautioned her not to look into the matter—warned her, even.

She slid open the fire escape window and climbed outside into the hard winter air. She tried to bring her father to mind—to *see* him as she would any other man, with no relation to herself. Night after night he'd sat where she was sitting now, smoking, gazing down at the street. Thinking—about what? For all the time she'd spent with him, Anna hadn't any idea. It was as if being his daughter had blinded her uniquely, as if anyone else—everyone—had seen and known him in a way she could not.

Something was going to happen; she and Dexter Styles weren't finished yet. This inevitability turned a gyre of excitement in Anna that made her forget her father. It was Dexter Styles she longed for—not the gangster but the lover. The tawdriness of the scene she'd wakened to had blurred away, leaving only sensation. In moments, she regretted even having told him who she was—she didn't want to give him up. She went back inside the apartment to bathe and then to bed, her mother's letter still unopened. In the dark, she gave herself to memories of Dexter Styles.

Had he threatened her? Or merely warned her?

Two days later, Anna was assigned to the barge in diving dress, tending Majorne. She'd gotten this far twice without going down. Still, after days of working indoors or marooned on the West Street Pier, she was grateful just to be on the open water. Sunlight struck Wallabout Bay like the flare of a welding torch as she watched Majorne's bubbles.

"Kerrigan. Wake up!"

It was Katz, idling in the motored dinghy around a corner of the barge. She was needed. The front tender helped her lift the crate containing the weighted parts of her dress onto the dinghy, which yawed under its weight. As Katz motored through ice slurry, he explained that there was a jammed screw—as propellers were known—on the battleship that had recently been floated from Dry Dock 6 to Pier J. Allied ships were unidentified, but Anna knew from her visits to the captain of the Yard's office that this was the USS *South Dakota*—"Battleship X," as she was called in the newspapers, for security. She'd downed twenty-six Jap planes in the battle of Santa Cruz.

The battleship loomed spectacularly, shrinking everything around her, even the hammerhead crane, to an afterthought. Savino and Grollier were already at the flywheels of an air compressor on the edge of Pier J. Savino still wasn't diving since his air embolism; Grollier, who had already dived that morning, was in partial dress. Anna's job was to inspect the battleship's four propellers, locate the problem, return topside, and explain what needed to be done. Grollier, recently trained as a burner, would go down to make the repair.

"Shouldn't I make the repair if I can?" Anna asked, betraying more eagerness than she'd meant to.

"The only reason you're diving at all is we've no one else," Katz said.

She flushed. "That wasn't my question."

"Just do as you're told."

A stage—a platform lowered by ropes—had been prepared for her descent. As the water closed around her, she rediscovered the sensation of being weightless. She felt the pull of the East River's infamous currents even on the ship's lee side. Down she went through soft fronds of daylight alongside the stupendous hull. Its sheer scale suggested violence. Anna wanted to touch it. Holding a rope of the stage, she swung her body toward the ship's hull and let her gloved hand slide over its outer shell while the stage pulled her down. Her skin prickled into gooseflesh. The ship felt alert, alive. It exuded a hum that traveled through her fingers up her arm: the vibration of thousands of souls teeming within. Like a skyscraper turned on its side.

At last she made out the whorls of the after starboard screw and signaled to Katz that she'd reached it. Descending lines had been hung to help her maneuver, and she used these to float herself toward the screw. It was fifteen feet high, its five blades curved like the inside of a seashell. Anna moved among them, running her gloves along the edges of each blade to the center ring where they met. Nothing fouled them. Taking care not to foul her own lines, she climbed around the screw to the shaft connecting it to the engine. She followed this to the forward starboard screw, which had four blades rather than five. It, too, was clear. Now she gripped the forward edge of the ship's rudder—like the steel door to a bank vault—and used it to pivot around to the port side of the hull, which faced the river. Currents buffeted her, swells of passing boats. On the forward port screw, she found the problem: a rope the width of her arm had snared among the blades. It was being held tight by one of the infamous railroad ties, which dangled several feet below.

A pull from Katz. Anna pulled back. Now she was supposed to return topside so that Grollier could cut through the obstructing rope with his oxy-hydrogen torch. But why should she go back up? Why not saw through the rope by hand, using the hacksaw in her tool bag? Anna made this choice in perfect knowledge that it was the wrong one. Following rules had got her nowhere. Passing tests had got her nowhere. In the course of getting nowhere, she had given up on some larger vision in which being good and trying to please made any sense. Why not take what she could while she had the chance?

She moved around the fouled screw blades, tugging at lengths of rope. The tightest segment was near the center, a figure eight caught between the two most vertical blades. Anna removed her hacksaw on its manila cord and began to saw at this portion of rope. It was slow work. Katz signaled again, then again. Each time she gave one pull in return—*I'm all right*—and continued with her work.

Katz signaled that he was sending down a slate. Anna repeated the signal but did not go starboard to write on it. As soon as they read her findings, she would be ordered topside, already in trouble. Why not stay down and finish what she'd begun? Like a thief trying to crack a safe before an alarm rang, Anna sawed in the half-dark, possessed by a feral determination she knew was pure selfishness, bound to hurt her in the end. She didn't care. The rope began to strain where she sawed; she felt its tension pass into the dwindling number of intact strands until they quivered like fiddle strings. Then the rope snapped with a twang she could hear over the hiss of her air. Its two ends hung in the murk, hemp threads oscillating like tentacles. Anna climbed over the screw, tugging at other segments of rope, trying to redistribute their slack. The effort made her light-headed. All at once the ropes began to slip, the stanchion's deadweight lulling them gently away from the screw blades. Then all of it fell away, rope frills waving as they fluttered into the dark.

Back on the rising stage, Anna experienced a first pinch of regret. Her modest achievement, easily replicable by Grollier with his torch, shrank beside the enormity of her offense. Even before the stage had reached the pier, she saw the scar burning scarlet on Katz's upper lip. "It's done," she said quickly when he opened her faceplate. "The screw is clear."

"How dare you ignore my orders?" he roared before she could step off the stage.

"It's done," she said, swallowing. "The job is done."

"Who the fuck do you think you are? I sent down a slate and you ignored the slate."

An animal smell, like ammonia, rose from inside Anna's dress. She was afraid. "Let me off," she said.

But Katz seemed out of his right mind. "Wait until I tell the lieutenant, you lousy cunt," he bawled, jabbing his head at her so she saw gold fillings in his mouth and smelled baloney on his breath. "He'll give you the bum's rush so fast you'll see stars."

He was going to kill her; she could feel that he wanted to. She leaned backward, clutching the ropes of the stage.

"She's falling," someone screamed. "Grab her, grab her!"

The weight of the destabilized dress was too great to arrest; Anna's left glove lost its grip on the rope, and she toppled like a tree, aware that gravity was pulling her away from her feet but unable to stop her fall. She saw veering sky and must have screamed. Or maybe the screaming was Katz.

Then she hung suspended. Katz had seized her lifeline and stopped her plunge at the last possible instant, before the heels of her boots left the stage. Anna held her body rigid, trying to anchor them in place. If her shoes slid off the edge, the weight of the dress would hurtle her straight to the bottom of the bay—along with Katz, if he didn't let go. The lifeline was fastened to goosenecks at the back of her helmet and threaded through eyelets at the front of her breastplate. Gingerly, terrified of flipping over, Anna reached up a gloved hand and tried to close her faceplate.

"No. No," Katz rasped from above her. "Don't move."

Hand over hand, with shuddering arms, he began to pull her lifeline toward himself by agonizing degrees, pivoting Anna's rigid 320-pound bulk toward a vertical position. His face was scored with sweat, his eyes locked to Anna's, as if the effort were happening there. She concentrated on not bending, an imperative that caused a conflagration of pain in her back. She was afraid of vomiting into the helmet. She longed to close her eyes, but it felt essential to maintain eye contact with Katz. Slowly, gravity began to pour the weight of her dress back toward her shoes. At last she bent her knees and rocked forward, nearly collapsing facedown on the stage. Katz caught her and pulled her upright, then guided her carefully onto the pier.

Savino and Grollier led her to the diving bench and unscrewed her helmet. Anna sat leaning over her knees, still thinking she might be sick. A hush encompassed all of them. Had she fallen into the freezing bay with her faceplate open, Anna could have drowned by the time they'd managed to haul her back up. She looked at the wet gray clouds that had covered up the sky while she was below. In one way, it felt like nothing: she was here, everything was fine. But it seemed possible that she still might fall.

Katz stood apart. He ran his hands through his hair and shook his head, then walked to the gangway to speak with the sailor on watch. Grollier and Savino removed Anna's belt and breastplate and shoes. Anna clutched at familiar sounds of the Yard—motors, machinery, shouts—as if they could stop her fall.

Eventually, Katz returned, and they began loading equipment onto the truck. Anna was breaking down the flywheels on the air compressor when three naval officers approached from the ship's gangway in double-breasted blue overcoats with gilt buttons and gold epaulettes.

The senior officer was tall and trim; even his salt-and-pepper hair looked rigorous under the crisp blue hat with its gold braid. "I want to thank you, gentlemen—ma'am—personally," he said, shaking each of their hands and betraying no surprise at the sight of Anna. "Fine work, Mr. Katz. Fine, efficient work."

Katz received this praise flinchingly, as if the words were goring him. Wet snow had begun to fall, but Anna hardly noticed it in the presence of these officers. They had come from the skyscraper ship; they would sail it into battle. In touching its hull, Anna had touched the war directly for the first time—felt the vehemence of its pulse.

When the officers had gone, the gray day closed back around them. Anna felt calm, but Katz was grave and distracted. His eyes wandered to hers, and without intending to, she smiled at him. Katz smiled tentatively back. They each took half the compressor and loaded it onto the truck.

Anna was crossing Navy Street, arm in arm with Ruby, when she recognized Dexter Styles's Cadillac idling outside Richard's Bar and Grill. She had looked for it every night.

"Excuse me," she told her friends. She didn't want them to meet, or even see, Dexter Styles. "I need to speak with someone."

She crossed Sands Street, trailed by their curiosity. Dexter Styles stepped from his automobile and opened the passenger door. The familiar leather smell surrounded her.

She felt a change in him as soon as he sat beside her, an uncharacteristic quiet. The shadow of his beard was gray against his skin. He pulled away from the curb and nosed the car alongside a throng of Yard workers and sailors. Anna watched them longingly through her window. A minute ago she'd been among them, laughing with her friends. She felt as if she'd fallen down a well to someplace cavernous and bleak.

"He's dead," she said when they'd driven a block in silence. "Isn't he."

"Yes."

She swallowed. "Where?"

"I can find out."

She stared at the windshield wipers, their back-and-forth gumming the traffic lights into viscous colored syrup. The hunger for Dexter Styles was still alive in her, a field of feverish energy with no affinity for the man beside her. He was a different man, cool and withdrawn. But it was Anna who had changed. Returned. That was how it felt: as if a long, disjointed detour had delivered her at last to a familiar landscape. "Well, then do it!" she said, her voice rising. "*Find out!* What are you waiting for?"

He pulled up along an empty curb on Navy Street. The brick wall of the Yard was directly outside Anna's window. Glancing at her, he said, "You'll need your diving suit."

"I'll— What?" He was talking nonsense. When the words forced their meaning upon Anna, she lunged at his face.

Dexter Styles seized her hands with the artful speed of one practiced at disarming others. "Knock it off," he breathed. "Or I won't lift a finger."

She'd forced him back against his window. Blood oozed from a scratch she'd made on his temple. Anna breathed his familiar breath, and the appetite rose in her. She felt his heart stamping through his overcoat. Their faces were nearly touching; he was about to kiss her. She was dying for him to. But she knew that she would bite him— kick and scratch and scream her head off.

He must have known, too, because he pushed her away from him slowly, keeping her hands immobilized. "Yes or no," he said.

She took a ragged breath. "It isn't that simple," she muttered finally. "You need a boatload of equipment to dive."

He tipped his head toward the wall, still holding her hands. "How much can you get out of there?"

"I don't know. Some."

"Whatever you can't bring, I will."

His confidence affronted her. "Really. A boat. An air compressor. Hoses. A diving ladder."

"The boat is easy. I've people who can get the rest."

"You've people who can do just about anything, haven't you?"

"Just about."

"We'll need a second diver," Anna said. "Normally, there would be two, but we could get away with just one."

With a warning look, he let go her hands. "You've someone in mind?"

She tried to imagine Bascombe's reaction to such a proposal. "He doesn't like trouble."

"No one does."

Their eyes met pragmatically. They were working together, after all.

"How dangerous is it? Diving in an unfamiliar place?" he asked.

"I don't know. I don't care." She remembered being suspended under the veering sky, believing she would plunge to the bottom of the bay. It seemed to her now that she had fallen and survived.

"I care," said Dexter Styles.

CHAPTER TWENTY-TWO

Captain Kittredge brought the *Elizabeth Seaman* into Cape Town on February 25, eight days ahead of schedule, having made good on his boast by maintaining an average speed of twelve knots. He looked so picturesque, commanding the bridge with his fair hair and fine patrician hands, that Eddie sometimes imagined the *Elizabeth Seaman* as a yacht like the ones he'd watched, gathering into regattas at the foot of Long Island Sound, from the Bronx piers where he and the other protectory boys went swimming in summer. Kittredge was like a grown-up version of the youths he'd seen skylarking from Central Park with their tennis racquets and riding crops. The captain had so much luck, he'd luck to spare, Eddie told himself—enough for fifty-six men, he hoped.

Channel fever set in days before land was sighted, sea projects giving way to diffuse anticipation with no clear object. Farmingdale stowed away his hemp dolls and took to winding his watch so often Eddie was sure he would snap the gears. At last the mooring lines were brought up from the storeroom and the booms raised to discharge cargo.

After quarantine, the *Elizabeth Seaman* docked in Table Harbor to unload her cargo of bauxite and take on stores of fresh food and water. Cape Town was a favorite port, and those not assigned to port watch hightailed it off the ship at sundown: the merchant crew and navy gunners to the Malay Quarter, whose whores the port agent had specifically warned them against; gasheads like Farmingdale to the cheapest gin joints. Naval officers occupied a different sphere in port;

Lieutenant Rosen, the armed guard commander, and his junior officer, Ensign Wyckoff, were greeted at the gangway by car and taken to dinner at a private home.

Roger and Stanley, the merchant cadets, watched forlornly in their pressed academy uniforms as the navy officers were spirited away. Too inexperienced for brothels, they were uncertain where they belonged. Eddie promised he would take them to a nightclub before they left Cape Town.

Radio operators had few duties in port and often disappeared, but Sparks chose to remain on the ship. "The fuck am I going to do in Cape Town?" he asked Eddie, who stayed aboard the first night in port to keep him company. "Drag this fucking leg around, saying, 'Thank you very much, I'd like a glass of milk'? I can see their famous Table fucking Mountain right from my porthole—look, there it is, I needn't shift a limb to play the tourist. Now I can use this radio for the purpose God intended."

It had been weeks since they'd heard any news in the radio silence, and what those hushed BBC announcers had to report was mostly good: Rommel's prize tanks fleeing helter-skelter in Tunisia; the Russians surging in Kharkov; the Allies pounding Messina.

"We're winning the fucking war, Third," Sparks said. "What do you say to that?"

"Who can tell, with those voices," Eddie said. "They could say I was a dead man, and I'd think I was hearing good news."

Sparks reared back in disdain. "Third," he said. "I'd never have thought you'd be a pussy for a posh accent."

Eddie conjured the lacerating snap of the bosun's speech. "I wouldn't have, either," he said.

He climbed down through the empty ship to return Sparks's cup to the galley. The bosun was there, drinking coffee and reading. At the sight of Eddie, he stood and clapped the book shut, holding his place with two fingers. Eddie, too, was taken aback.

"I'm surprised you're not ashore, Bosun," he said.

"What conceivable reason could you have to be surprised, Third?" the bosun said sourly. Clearly, he'd not expected to see anyone, and seemed out of sorts.

"We've shipped together before," Eddie reminded him. "Then you went ashore whenever you'd the chance."

"As you did, if memory serves," the bosun retorted. "Perhaps your dizzying new stature accounts for your change of routine. But you'll note that I merely speculate. It is none of my affair what you do—or do not—with your liberty, just as it is none of your affair what I do with mine."

"Keep your shirt on," Eddie said. "I was making conversation."

The bosun eyed him skeptically, holding his place in the book. Eddie caught the surprising pink of his palm against the blue-black iridescence of his skin. When he'd worked under the bosun, those flashes of pink had mesmerized Eddie like a flutter of wings.

"*Making conversation* has its uses, I will grant you," the bosun said. "In the present case, however, the explanation strikes me as disingenuous for the simple reason that it ignores our unwavering acrimony. We are, as it were, beyond *making conversation*. Ipso post facto, your statement cannot be taken at face value."

"Do you talk this way to everyone?"

"What can be the purpose of your question, Third?" the bosun erupted, losing his bookmark and throwing up his hands in frustration. "Do you intend it rhetorically or literally?"

"Literally," Eddie said, not entirely certain of the difference.

"Very well, then. You are a literal man, Third, and I will give you a literal and, if you will permit me, bracingly candid response." The bosun took a step closer and lowered his voice. "I do *not* talk this way to everyone. Men so far outside my intellectual scope do not normally crave extensive and repeated interactions, as you do. Your reasons for persisting in this effort elude me, I confess. I could speculate, of course, but that would be a fool's errand—in part because it would imply that our inner lives had the slightest modicum of solidarity—which I more than doubt—but also because it would indicate that I care one jot about what moves and motivates you, Third, which I do not."

Eddie lost his way early on, but he knew he was being insulted. Blood rose to his face. "Fine, then," he said. "Good night."

He turned and left the galley, taking scant satisfaction in the bosun's visible surprise. Eddie felt like a whipped dog but knew he'd only himself to blame. What did he want from the bosun? He didn't know.

The next afternoon, he left the ship with the cadets to explore Cape Town. It was larger than Eddie had expected, a real city crouched under the earthen gaze of Table Mountain. The cadets bought chocolate and satsuma oranges. Eddie bought Player's Navy Cut cigarettes and smoked them as they walked along Adderly Street, a grand thoroughfare lined with columned buildings. He knew within twenty minutes why the bosun had stayed aboard. Negroes were kept apart from whites in every sphere: buses, shops, theaters, picture houses. Eddie was accustomed to seeing Negroes treated badly—on the West Side piers, wops were regarded as Negroes and Negroes as something worse. Still, he was shocked when a policeman asked an elderly Negro lady to leave a bench where she'd stopped to rest with her shopping bags. The imperious bosun would never set foot upon the soil of such a place. Still, Eddie had to admire a man with enough self-restraint to resist touching land after forty-seven days at sea, purely on principle.

After dark, he brought the cadets to a nightclub he'd heard Lieutenant Rosen mention at chow that morning. As Eddie had hoped, Rosen himself was there, along with Ensign Wyckoff, and they invited Eddie and the cadets to their table. Rosen was a handsome Jew, a reservist who worked in advertising. Wyckoff looked at least a decade younger: a pudgy, freckled enthusiast. Elatedly, he described to Eddie a tour of wine vineyards that he and Rosen had made that afternoon with their South African hosts. They'd watched the grape harvest, and Wyckoff had purchased two cases of wine.

"Wine?" Eddie said. "You're pulling my leg."

Wyckoff was serious. After the war, he hoped to become a wine merchant.

"I've never cared for wine," Eddie admitted, although he did like champagne mixed with Guinness—black velvet, they called it.

"I'll change your mind, and that's a promise," Wyckoff said, already in the salesman's mode.

A large orchestra was playing "White Christmas," which mingled strangely with the smell of ripening citrus. Mulatto girls sat with Allied officers at their tables and danced with them. These weren't prostitutes or even B-girls, who were charged with encouraging sailors to buy them drinks. More likely they were clerks or shopgirls. What money changed hands would be a gift, not a fee. Eddie had partaken of many such arrangements over the years, but found himself observing the present scene with disdain. Then he realized why: he was picturing it through the bosun's eyes.

The day before they were to sail, Farmingdale failed to report for duty and could not be found. The *Elizabeth Seaman* couldn't sail without a second mate, so she missed the convoy she was to have joined through the Mozambique Channel, a stretch of sea between Madagascar and the African coast where many Allied ships had been lost to Nazi submarine wolf packs. Farmingdale turned up three days later in the army stockade, his offense so grievous that the army refused to release him until the *Elizabeth Seaman* was ready to cast off lines.

On March 9, military police delivered the second mate to the gangway, and he was summoned directly to the master's office. For all Kittredge's pretty-boy looks, no one could say he didn't let Farmingdale have it. If there was one thing this captain could not abide, it was being left behind. Now a laggard, the *Elizabeth Seaman* was forced to sail independently on an evasive course—twenty degrees to the right for ten minutes, then twenty degrees to the left, then back to her original course for ten minutes more, and so on—not only at night, when U-boats were most active, but all day. They sailed toward the Mozambique Channel with davits swung out, ready to lower the lifeboats if their ship should be hit.

Farmingdale was a pariah. For two days, he came late to chow and sat with the cadets at their small table. He wore a quixotic smile, as though his isolation were a rare privilege. On the third day, Eddie tried to signal forgiveness when Farmingdale relieved him of the morning watch. Eddie made a point of greeting him warmly, even giving him a conciliatory pat as he relayed their course and position. But Farmingdale heaved an impatient sigh at these transparent efforts and stared off, stroking his snowy beard as though it were a secret trove of strength.

That afternoon, Sparks received a second direct radio message for the *Elizabeth Seaman,* and their course was altered. Shortly before midnight, at a rendezvous point fifty miles northeast of Durban, seventy-seven ships materialized around theirs as if through divine intervention. An immense effort was required to maneuver the *Elizabeth Seaman* into her station without colliding with other ships, all of them blacked out except for a faint light at the stern. Eddie stood with the captain on the flying bridge, working the engine room telegraph to communicate speed and direction to the engineers below. He couldn't help ascribing almost supernatural powers to Kittredge. His American good luck had come to their rescue. Eddie had craved such luck all his life—reached for it every way he could. Perhaps having luck meant you didn't have to reach.

The convoy course was transmitted in Morse code by blinker signal lights that operated like venetian blinds. From the commodore's ship in the middle of the first row, the signal was passed backward along each column of ships, a process that took nearly thirty minutes to complete. Then, as one invisible mass, the convoy set a course of forty-three degrees toward the Mozambique Channel.

At sunrise, during general quarters, Eddie gazed out alongside the mate at an ocean studded by nearly eighty ships arrayed in a vast design with the ritual splendor of chess pieces. "That is beauty like no other I've seen," he said.

"Prettier near the middle," the mate said, chuckling, for their station was perilously close to one of the "coffin corners" most vulnerable to U-boats. It didn't matter. The convergence was so spectacular, so monumental in its scale and span, that being part of it made Eddie feel invincible. He saw ships' flags from Portugal, Free France, Brazil, Panama, South Africa. On the Dutch freighter to starboard, two children scampered among linens billowing from a wash line. Apparently the ship's master had fled Holland with his family to escape the Nazis.

Fifteen smaller, faster escort vessels—destroyers and corvettes—flitted alongside the expanse of ships like police horses at a parade. While a convoy couldn't stop for a disabled ship, an escort vessel would stay behind and help to rescue its crew. This fact, more than any other, relieved Eddie.

Only one man aboard the *Elizabeth Seaman* was unhappy with the new arrangement: her captain. Convoys had to run at the speed of the slowest ship, and because this one included a Panamanian coal burner, they were held to eight knots. "We made better time zigzagging," Kittredge groused to the chief engineer, who sat to his right at chow.

After midnight, when Eddie was relieved by Farmingdale (still wearing his whimsical smile), he found Wyckoff, the naval ensign, waiting outside his stateroom with a bottle of wine. "We'll drink it outdoors," he said. "It's a perfect night. Where you drink wine matters as much as the wine itself."

They sat on the number two hatch cover. The night was cool and clear, a rolling sea just visible under a paring of moon. Eddie couldn't see the ships around them, but he perceived their density, five hundred feet away fore and aft, a thousand feet abeam, all nosing together through the swells like a spectral herd. Eddie heard the cork leaving Wyckoff's bottle, caught a tart, woody smell of the wine. The ensign poured a modest amount into two enameled cups. "Don't drink it yet," he cautioned as Eddie lifted his. "Let it breathe."

The Southern Cross hung near the horizon. Eddie preferred the southern sky; it was brighter, denser with planets.

"All right. Now," Wyckoff said after several minutes. "Take a sip and move it around your mouth before you swallow."

It sounded loopy, but Eddie did as instructed. At first there was just the ashy pucker he'd always disliked in wine, but that flavor yielded to an appealing overripeness, even a suggestion of decay. "Better," he said with surprise.

They drank and looked at the stars. After the war, Wyckoff said, he hoped to find a job planting grapes in the valleys north of San Francisco. There had been vineyards there, but the dry agents had burned them during Prohibition.

"What about you, Third?" he asked. "What will you do after the war?"

Eddie knew what he wanted to say, but waited several moments to be sure. "I'll go back home to New York," he said. "I've a daughter there."

"What's her name?"

"Anna."

These syllables, which Eddie hadn't uttered aloud in years, seemed to crash together like a pair of cymbals, leaving behind a ringing echo. Abashed, he looked away. But as the seconds passed without reaction from Wyckoff, Eddie realized how unremarkable his disclosure was. Nowadays, most men on ships had left other lives behind. The war had made him ordinary.

"How old is she?" Wyckoff asked. "Your Anna."

Eddie took a moment to calculate. "Twenty," he said with surprise. "She'll have been twenty just last week."

"Grown-up!"

"I suppose twenty is grown-up."

"I'm twenty-one," Wyckoff said.

CHAPTER TWENTY-THREE

There were nights in the Mozambique Channel when the escort vessels dropped depth charges, filling the air with a tingling crackle. The general quarters bell rang and rang, bringing all hands on deck, and the convoy zigzagged for long stretches. Eddie stood on the flying bridge, raw-eyed, trying to maintain the *Elizabeth Seaman*'s station among the rows and columns of turning blacked-out ships. When he collapsed into his sack, he slept fitfully, Anna prowling his thoughts like a restless spirit.

"I want to go with you."

"Children aren't allowed, toots."

"I used to go."

"These are different places."

"I used to go *lately*."

"I'm sorry."

"Did I change?"

"Well, you're bigger."

"Did I get bigger suddenly?"

"Growing isn't like that. It's gradual."

"Did you suddenly *notice* I was bigger?"

"I may have."

"*What* did you notice?"

"Please, Anna."

"*When* did you notice?"

"Please."

After a long pause, she said, in a harder voice, "I'll punish you back."

"I don't recommend that."

"I'll be idle."

"That's punishing yourself."

"I'll eat too many sweets."

"You'll end up like Mrs. Adair, without teeth."

"I'll dirty my clothes."

"That's punishing Mama."

"I'll be a floozy."

"Pardon me?"

"I'll be a floozy. Like Aunt Brianne."

Eddie slapped her face. "Don't you ever. Say that again."

Anna held her cheek, dry-eyed. "Then let me come with you."

After seven days, the convoy emerged from the Mozambique Channel without having lost a ship. Waves of vessels began peeling away—some west, to Mombasa, others east to Ceylon and Indonesia. The *Elizabeth Seaman* remained in a smaller convoy of eighteen ships and four escort vessels. There was still the drag of the Panamanian coal burner, now stationed directly in front of them. Several times each day, when the burner cleared her pipes, fine grains of soot settled over every inch of the *Elizabeth Seaman*. Captain Kittredge flicked them from his sleeves and fulminated over their glacial progress. As they plowed the calm, intensely blue waters of the Indian Ocean, Eddie observed the master's mounting impatience with equally mounting curiosity. Kittredge was unpracticed at being denied the things he wanted. How would he stomach weeks behind the coal burner?

Eddie never found out. Before they reached the Seychelles, a flag signal indicated that the convoy was to scatter. Ships began moving away from one another in a slow, dreamlike version of birds startling.

So languorous was their progress that at first it seemed they would never fully leave one another's sight. Yet within the span of three hours, even the coal burner had faded away.

As Dexter Styles's new ombudsman, Eddie visited roadhouses, casinos, restaurants, poker games. He assumed the guise of a visiting out-of-towner with money in his pocket; in early 1935, nobody turned that man away. If he chanced to meet someone he knew, Eddie greeted him warmly, bought him a drink, and left soon after. He went back the next day. He needed more than one visit to see beyond the surface of a place, and Styles gave him plenty of cash for expenses. These were the only bags Eddie still carried.

At first he met Styles every couple of weeks at a boathouse on Manhattan Beach to detail his findings. Crooked games were his bread and butter, but he observed other things he correctly guessed would interest Styles: a chef pimping out cigarette girls, dope-addicted card dealers tipping games for a fee, fairies he suspected of being blackmailed.

"You're reaching, Mr. Kerrigan."

"Isn't that the job?"

"Don't invent stories to divert me."

"I wouldn't know how."

At the end of each visit, Styles gave him another two or three addresses. "Shouldn't you write these down?"

"No need."

"You're that smart, eh?"

"I'm not a Harvard man, if that's what you mean."

Styles laughed. "If you were, I'd chuck you out."

"You know the expression," Eddie said. " 'Don't write if you can talk, and don't talk if you can nod.'"

Styles was delighted. "A mick said that."

Eddie winked.

He told Dunellen he'd found work at a theater, as he had before the Depression—a world too distant from Dunellen's own for him to realize how far-fetched this story was. He seemed relieved to have Eddie off his payroll, their tangled history stymieing the full expression of Dunellen's ruthlessness. He bequeathed Eddie's bagman duties upon the next desperate man, O'Bannon, then bewailed the hash he made of the job.

"He doesn't have your touch, Ed," he whined at Sonny's, where Eddie still made a point of appearing with some regularity. "Banny walks in a room, all eyes are on him. He dropped an envelope at Dinty Moore's, you fucking believe that? Greenbacks spilling out . . . you'd have thought that dough had leprosy, how fast everyone backed away, so they tell me. The waiters got rich. I told him, 'Banny, one more like that, I'll toss you off the pier myself. You can tell it to the fishes.'" Dunellen roused the slag heap of his corpus into a long-suffering shrug. "But his wife is going blind, and they've five little ones . . . I can't leave him high and dry." He swung his hard little eyes heavenward, then checked his loogans stationed at the door.

"You're too good, Dunny," Eddie said, all but laughing. "Too, too good. But mind yourself, friend: the world will try to take advantage of that soft heart of yours."

"Speaking of, Ed." Dunellen lowered his voice. "I took your advice about the wop."

Eddie wasn't sure which wop he meant, so many having offended Dunellen. "And . . . ?"

"I made a deal. With Tancredo."

Eddie remembered now: Dunny's middle lightweights. Tancredo had been putting the screws on him in order for them to fight.

"Humbled myself to that wop on bended knee. Let him trample my face right in the fucking mud."

Eddie listened with concern. Dunellen prostrate was a vision he could see ending only in violence. Then a soft smile played at Dunellen's lips. "Best advice I ever got."

"No kidding," Eddie said, exhaling.

"My boys are winning, Ed," Dunellen said with the blushing air of a man imparting secrets. "They're bursting with life. All they needed was a chance, a fair shake."

"Glad to hear it, Dunny."

"We'll do anything for our kids, ain't that right, Ed? Get walked on, spit on, shit on, pounded into a pulp. It's all worthwhile if it makes them happy."

Masochism didn't suit Dunellen; Eddie wanted it to stop. "Sure, Dunny," he said. "But don't let it go too far. Look for your opening and get the hell out."

Dunellen nodded, watching Eddie gravely. They were back inside the deeper story that was always between them like buried treasure: riptide, panic, rescue. Swimming parallel to shore, looking for a way back. At the same time, Eddie was explaining why he'd thrown Dunellen off—*fucked him*, Dunny would surely say if he'd a whiff of whom Eddie was working for now. The precise alignment of these several spheres made Eddie feel as though he could see in every direction at once.

"Tancredo doesn't have to know," Eddie cautioned. "Should never know. Look to yourself."

Dunellen nodded, listening.

Eddie borrowed the Duesenberg and drove his family to a medical supply store in Paramus, New Jersey, where Lydia was fitted for her chair. The effect was transformative: at nine, she joined the vertical world for the first time. She sat at the table for meals. Agnes took her on walks. Anna leaned beside her at the window, watching sparrows peck at bread crumbs she'd placed on the sill. From behind, Eddie saw no obvious difference between them.

Once, when Agnes was changing Lydia's diaper, the iceman drove away without waiting. Eddie bought his wife an electric icebox outright, not on layaway—he'd done with the lie of possessing things you didn't own. For days, neighbors traipsed through the kitchen to admire this luxury, Lydia grinning at them from her new chair.

The icebox emitted a sullen drone that kept Eddie awake. When at last he fell asleep, he dreamed of unplugging it.

"You must thank Mr. Dunellen for me," Agnes said.

And: "What would we do without the union?"

And: "My, but we're lucky, Ed. Look at everyone else."

She said such things often, and Eddie smiled and murmured assent. But he detected a false bottom in his wife's effusions, a hidden chamber containing all she was leaving unsaid. Agnes knew her way around. She couldn't have failed to notice his longer hours, the fact that he rarely borrowed the Duesenberg, never took Anna with him. Yet apart from anodyne exclamations at their good fortune, she acknowledged none of this. Eddie took a morbid pleasure in observing his wife's disingenuousness. But at night, when he held her in his arms and searched her careworn face, he could find no treachery in it.

Styles sent him to Albany, Saratoga, Atlantic City. He liked to know every particular of an operation, as though Eddie were a moving-picture camera. They never used names; it was Eddie's job to fix on the key detail of a man that made him recognizable. Scars were easy. But there was always something: over-brilliantined hair; a particular ring; trousers puddling at the ankles; a bearlike walk. Girls were harder. "Blond," "brunette," and "pretty" were about the best he could do. What mattered were the men they came with.

Eddie marveled at how accurately Styles had diagnosed his deep indifference. "You're my eyes and ears," he often said, and Eddie liked the description. He was a channel for facts, nothing more. He relayed whole conversations without knowing who'd had them. And even when he came to know, inevitably, in the course of two years, he hadn't any point of view. *It's nothing to do with me,* he would tell himself. *It happens the same, whether I'm there or not.* Consequences were not his business.

"You're a machine, Kerrigan. A human machine," Styles marveled. It was a compliment. With Eddie as his eyes and ears, Styles could be anywhere, everywhere. He'd only to be curious.

Gradually, Styles's curiosity reached beyond the businesses he controlled to rivals within the Syndicate, even associates. In January 1937, Eddie brought his cardboard please-don't-rain suitcase to an Eastern Airlines ticket office on Vanderbilt Avenue. There he boarded a limousine with several other men to Newark Airfield. He was going to Miami to watch a man Styles wanted to know about. It was his first airplane ride.

At the airfield, Eddie removed his hat and ducked through the hatch of a silver airplane, his heart flailing. When everyone was aboard, the propellers swarmed outside the windows, and the plane staggered down a runway between snowy fields, accelerating into a breath-catching instant when its wheels parted from land and it hurtled aloft like ash in an updraft. Through a porthole, Eddie gaped at a toy replica of New York City: tiny cars on tiny streets; houses and trees and ball fields inlaid with snow; and then the sea, a sheet of beaten pewter—still infinite, even from this height. The engine buzzed in his ears. A woman wept beside him, hands clasped in prayer. Looking down at the heedless expanse of the earth, Eddie felt on the verge of a great discovery.

The airplane made stops in Washington, D.C., Raleigh, Charleston, Jacksonville, Palm Beach, and at last Miami, where an eye-level moon dropped silver onto a velvet black sea. The air smelled like honey. Even at the airport, Palm Beach style was on vivid display: white dinner jackets, pale silk shirts. By nine o'clock Eddie had Styles's man in his sights: he sat at the rear of a casino, ashen-faced, heavy-lidded, looking more like an accountant than a fight promoter. Eddie tried to break even at a roulette wheel while memorizing the sequence of visitors to the man's table. Thus engaged, he took a while to register that the girl leaning against him at the roulette wheel wasn't doing that by mistake. He added her drinks to his tab with an idea of repaying the effort she'd already made. Or so he told himself. By the time his mark left the casino, Eddie's decision to bring the girl to his hotel room seemed already to have been made.

He woke at sunrise to an unfamiliar perfume on his sheets. Disgust and desolation closed around him. *It doesn't matter,* he told himself. *Men do it all the time. No one will ever know.* But these bromides made him feel as though he were being soothed by a idiot. He left the hotel and paced the cement-colored sand, flicking cigarette butts into the surf. His only relief came from telling himself that it wasn't really *him* with the prostitute. He was Dexter Styles's eyes and ears, no more. "I'm not here now," Eddie said out loud more than once, the phrase providing, each time, a burst of analgesia.

That night, at a poker table that afforded a different slant on his mark, Eddie found his attention riveted by a familiar gait: the walk of a woman with corns carrying too many groceries. John Dunellen. He shambled through the casino with a limp Eddie hadn't seen before—but he hardly saw Dunellen nowadays. His presence here so astounded Eddie that he forgot to turn away for several moments. For Dunellen in his element, that would have been too long, but he was far from his element now. He hobbled to the table Eddie had been watching—Tancredo's, he realized, perhaps had already known—collapsed onto a chair, and bowed his great head in a masque of abjectness that Eddie could hardly bear to witness, even covertly. How had his old friend been brought so low? The meeting was insultingly short; Tancredo dismissed Dunellen with a curt nod whose disregard made Eddie flinch. Dunellen tottered to his feet and staggered away, lurching among gaming tables with such wobbling instability that Eddie thought he might crash down on top of one, scattering chips and chairs. Eddie dreaded this, knowing he would have to sit by and do nothing.

As Dunellen approached the distant exit, his limp softened, and Eddie caught a gleam of pleasure in his face. In that instant Eddie realized, with a spreading, dizzy delight, that he'd overlooked the mockery in his friend's performance. The limp was phony. The suppliance was phony. Dunellen was laying it on thick, almost too thick—but then Eddie had been fooled. Dunny hadn't rolled over for the wops, bless his mean, flinty heart. It was all a ruse, playacting as a means to some other end. He'd taken Eddie's advice and found his opening. And more surprising than the spectacle of Dunellen's charade was the joy Eddie took in seeing him pull it off. How he loved Dunny—wanted him to win! He wished he could run to his old friend and kiss his pendulous cheeks.

In his report to Styles, Eddie made no mention of Dunellen.

Eddie confessed at a church where he'd never been so the priest wouldn't know him, and was given a rosary's penance. Too easy. Despair wrapped him in its black cloak, and the trolley wheel rolled again through his thoughts. What was the point of anything he'd done, or was doing now, if it led to cavorting with prostitutes? It had all been a means to an end—but what end?

Instinctively, habitually, he turned to Anna. "Toots, I've a taste for a charlotte russe," he said on a Saturday when Agnes was out with Lydia. "How about you?"

"I don't care for them, Papa."

"What? You used to love them."

"Too sweet."

Taken aback, he scrutinized Anna, seated at the kitchen table surrounded by her schoolbooks, with a sense of not having looked at her carefully in some time. She was fourteen, tall and lovely, but less specific than she'd once been. More like the women he struggled to describe to Dexter Styles.

"Come with me anyway," he said. "Order something else."

Anna rose and put on her coat. As they descended the stairs, Eddie detected an air of sufferance about her, as if there was something else she preferred to do. He was mystified. Anna always wanted to come with him! She'd fought so hard when he'd stopped including her in his work. That had been a while ago, of course—going on two years, he realized with a shock, counting up the months since he'd begun working for Styles. Eddie had presumed all along that he and Anna could revert to their old arrangement whenever he chose. Now, for the first time, he doubted this.

They sat at the counter at White's. Anna ordered a chocolate soda; Eddie stuck piously to charlotte russe, which Mr. White brought him from the window case. While they waited, he lit a cigarette and handed her the coupon from inside his packet. She looked at it oddly, then said with a disbelieving laugh, "Papa, I don't collect these anymore."

"No? What about all the ones you saved?"

"There were never enough for the things I wanted."

"There might have been by now."

She looked at him curiously. "Why do you care?"

He didn't care. He wanted *her* to care. "It seems a waste."

"You would have smoked anyway," she said. "Or did you smoke extra for me?" She smiled at him fondly, indulgently: a woman's smile.

Eddie felt a deep stirring of unease. "When did you stop collecting them?"

She shrugged, a gesture he disliked.

"Recently?" he asked sharply.

Her face shuttered. "No. A long time ago."

An elfin ghost appeared suddenly at Eddie's side: his lively little Anna. Where was that garrulous sprite inside this languorous, indifferent girl seated beside him, disciplining herself not to look out the window? It was Eddie's job to perceive such things. Whom did she want to look for?

Mr. White slid her chocolate soda across the counter, and they ate in silence. Eddie could think of nothing to say. His mind would only go back—to the snowball, the secret kiss. He wanted to ask Anna if she remembered those times, but was afraid she would not—worse, that they meant nothing to her.

And what about all the other days? The hundreds of other days they had spent together; why could he not remember those?

"You were right about the charlotte russe," he said at last. "It's too sweet."

Afterward, they stood outside the drugstore. Anna said she was going to Stella's, but Eddie sensed an untruth and began to sweat, despite the cold. Something had changed about Anna, permanently, fundamentally—he was certain of it. He'd looked away from his daughter—looked where Styles paid him to look—and she'd gone astray.

The ghost sprite leaped and jumped and swung Eddie's hand. She turned her face up at him, chattering: hours of meandering talk, thoughtless as a dog's wagging tail, back and forth, back and forth.

Eddie gazed into Anna's large dark eyes under their heavy lashes, trying to find that little sprite. But he'd looked away for too long, and the sprite had vanished. In her place stood a girl who hardly remembered him, wanted only to get away.

Dunellen was shot fifteen times from a moving automobile outside Sonny's shortly after midnight. April 1937, three months after Eddie had seen him in Miami. Naturally, there were witnesses—Dunellen didn't so much as take a leak by himself—but none would say a word. He'd had enemies galore, rivalries over hiring and pier control, but those feuds had simmered for years without serious issue. It was a wop-style execution.

He hung on for three days in the intensive care ward at Saint Vincent's. Bulls came and went, but they never expected to get a word out of Dunny, even if he'd somehow managed to snap out of his coma and speak around the tube bisecting his throat.

The protectory scrum gathered by twos and threes in the hospital lobby, all forty or thereabouts, with thinning hair and missing teeth. Eddie sobbed in their arms. "You knew him best," they affirmed. "You were his favorite. No wonder; you saved his life. A man doesn't forget." Eddie craved these testimonials, but they provided only fleeting solace. He felt as if he'd shot Dunny himself.

He recognized Bart Sheehan instantly, although he hadn't seen his old friend in twenty years. Sheehan still had his hair, half-gray and in need of cutting. He looked like a man who lived in shirtsleeves. "You saved us once, Ed," he wept, his black-Irish face riven by grief. "Pulled us out of the waves. I wouldn't be here today, God is my witness."

Being dead did not hinder Dunellen from presiding over his own two-day wake, his silhouette like a pile of ore commanding the room from an oversize coffin. Under powder and pancake makeup, bullet holes were visible in his temple and forehead and neck. His wife, Maggie, howled inconsolably but garnered little sympathy. Her voluble grief—like her habit of yanking her husband out of bars prematurely—was widely construed as unwillingness to "let Dunny have a bit of fun."

Eddie was able to talk more calmly with Sheehan at the wake. His old friend was a widower, three kids, still living in the Bronx with his unmarried sister.

"You're a lawyer, so I hear," Eddie said.

"State attorney's office. You, Ed?"

"Oh, this and that."

"Tough times," Bart said, mistaking Eddie's vagueness for unemployment. "I'm lucky I work for the state."

"Is it like being a copper, what you do?"

"Cleaner," Bart said, and they laughed.

A tidal wave of mourners surged into Guardian Angel Church on Sunday morning for Dunellen's funeral—many still drunk, the rest hungover. Eddie heard whispers down the block: *Joe Ryan is in the church.* What better testament to Dunny's power than having the most corrupt kingpin of them all, president of the International Longshoremen's Union, present at his funeral?

Agnes clutched Eddie's arm. A bagpiper played on the church steps, and he felt tears come again. "What will this mean for us, love?" she asked with such an anxious look that Eddie realized she must have understood less than he'd thought. Perhaps nothing at all.

"We'll be all right," he mumbled.

Sheehan found his way to Eddie's other side, and they walked arm in arm up the church steps. Inside the door, Eddie leaned close to his old friend's ear. "The kite had it, a while back, you were looking into the Syndicate," he whispered.

He felt Sheehan's recoil of surprise. Guardedly, he whispered back, "There's truth in that."

"I might be able to . . . contribute."

Bart turned a skeptical eye upon Eddie. "What do you know about it?"

"I know everything," Eddie said.

CHAPTER TWENTY-FOUR

Twenty minutes south of the Red Hook boatyard where they'd met, the ancient man everyone referred to as "the skipper" began making noises that seemed to approximate speech. Leaning against the outside wall of a tiny wheelhouse, his ravaged face aimed skyward as if someone were jerking him backward by the hair, he moaned and keened at the spattered stars—more stars than Anna had ever seen, even from the dimmed-out shore.

"Earile . . . smolf . . . skynech . . ."

She turned to the skipper in alarm at each anguished utterance. No one else seemed to take any notice, with the exception of the helmsman: a tall blank-faced individual who ticked a wheel infinitesimally in response to each ejaculation. But he seemed less a human being than a lever the skipper was turning with his mind.

It was eleven o'clock. The night was clear, the temperature forty-five degrees—warm for early March—the moon pronged and low. Searchlight beams prodded the night sky for aircraft. The harbor was crowded with invisible boats. Occasionally a towering shape bore down upon the lighter, and the skipper yowled at the helmsman, who steered them out of harm's way nimbly as a butterfly, to be jostled by a violent wake. The Statue of Liberty was a dark silhouette, a single faint light at her flame.

Even the skipper fell silent as they approached the Narrows, the entrance to the Lower Bay, patrolled by Fort Hamilton to the east and Fort Wadsworth to the west, on Staten Island. Dexter Styles said he'd "had a word" with someone at the Coast Guard who would make things right should the lighter be stopped, but no one wanted that. For perhaps ten minutes, the only sound on the lighter was the churn of its engine. Anna wondered if the draft would be shallow enough to pass over the submarine nets, then realized that the gate must be open. They had followed other ships—a convoy perhaps—into the Lower Bay. Horns and sirens grew fainter, and she felt rising wind and chop. Dexter Styles's five "goons" (Bascombe's word) leaned over the gunwales, holding their hats. They'd been brought along to turn the flywheels of the air compressor, but their presence on the lighter had an ominous effect.

Only Marle and Bascombe continued to work, inspecting and preparing the air compressor Dexter Styles had arranged to have on board. It was a Morse Air Pump No. 1, identical to the compressors at the Naval Yard. They had anchored it to the bow, and now they cleaned its air reservoirs, oiled the piston rods, and lubricated the pump shaft handles with a mixture of oil and graphite. They'd had surprisingly little trouble removing a pair of diving crates from the Naval Yard—each containing a two-hundred-pound dress—along with six fifty-foot lengths of air hose, a loaded tool bag, two diving knives, and a spare-parts tin. It was almost too easy, they'd crowed when Anna had met them outside the Red Hook boatyard. So many divers had been commuting to the freshwater pipeline that the marine guards barely took note when they hauled the equipment through the Marshall Street gate onto a small flatbed truck Marle had borrowed from his uncle.

Beyond the Narrows, the lighter turned east, and soon the Parachute Drop's faint silhouette materialized to the left, along with skeletal shapes of the Wonder Wheel and the Cyclone. Then it turned south, then west; then Anna lost track. She thought they might be heading out of New York Harbor into the Atlantic. How deep would she have to go down?

Dexter Styles stood at the back of the boat, a hand on his fedora, his grim mien heightening Anna's dread. They'd exchanged hardly a word on the drive to Red Hook, and she'd stuck close to Marle and Bascombe ever since. Their merriment kept her foreboding at bay. She had approached them squeamishly about the project, afraid they would laugh in her face or telephone the police, but it seemed that diving for a body at the bottom of New York Harbor—they never asked whose—was exactly the sort of crackpot adventure that had been missing from both their lives. Anna had felt compelled to remind them of the possible risks and pitfalls, but none of it registered in their dancing eyes—or perhaps the risks and pitfalls were the point.

When at last the lighter began to slow, Anna removed her coat and shoes and pulled a set of woolens over her jumpsuit and a warm night-watch cap onto her head. She wriggled inside the canvas dress without assistance while Bascombe and Marle tested the helmets and air hose couplings. The moon laid a faint feathery path toward them across the water. The helmsman undertook a series of adjustments and corrections until at last the skipper emitted a howl that made Anna's scalp prickle, and the engine was silenced. The lighter's two sailors, dungarees black from the coal they'd been heaping into a furnace belowdecks, began to lower the first of two double anchors, one at each end of the lighter, that would hold it stationary.

"Have you any idea where we are?" Anna asked her friends.

"Search me," Bascombe said.

"Staten Island," Marle said. "Southwest shore."

"I knew that," Bascombe said. "I was testing you."

Their laughter had a defiant edge, as if sustaining their exuberance had become a strain. They dressed Anna: first the shoes, laced and buckled; then the helmet cushion. These steps were so deeply ingrained by now that performing them made their alien surroundings seem recognizable. Breastplate; bib; studs; collar; washers. When everything was on except the hat, Marle summoned the goons to the compressor's flywheels. They began turning them zealously, elbowing each other aside in a show of indefatigability. Dexter Styles watched all of it from a distance, his face a mirror of Anna's anxiety. She avoided looking at him.

When both anchors were taut and the boat stationary, Marle took a sounding. The rope's wet knots indicated a depth of thirty-nine feet, a soft bottom of sand and mud. Then Bascombe and Marle heaved the descending line, with its hundred-pound weight, over the starboard side of the boat, close to the diving ladder. Anna and Marle helped Bascombe into the second dress—just the canvas, without the weighted parts. Her friends' ebullience had flattened, and they proceeded now in workmanlike fashion. Anna sat on the diving stool wearing everything but her helmet. "I must speak with Mr. Styles," she said.

He was beside her a moment later, kneeling to meet her eyes. His own looked cavernous.

"What am I looking for?" she said.

"You know what."

"I mean what else."

It took a moment. "Ropes, I'd imagine. A weight of some kind. Possibly a chain."

Raising her voice to Marle and Bascombe, she said, "I'm ready."

She rose from the stool and stumped to the ladder. They screwed on her helmet and attached the air hose and lifelines to its goose-necks, testing her air. Marle pulled the lifeline under her right arm and the air hose under her left, and secured them to the metal eyelets on the front of her breastplate. As she was about to mount the ladder, Bascombe peered at her through her open faceplate, his narrow eyes engaging hers with unusual directness. "I don't like it," he said.

"I'm sorry."

He snorted. "Hell, I'm not the one going down."

"What could go wrong?" she said, which got a laugh.

He sealed her faceplate, and a cool chemical hiss of air filled Anna's mouth and nostrils. She descended the ladder backward, then held the descending line and let the harbor swallow her. The current was tremendous, a pull with the force of the ocean behind it. Recalling Lieutenant Axel's lesson on currents, she positioned herself so the water pushed at her back, pressing her against the descending line rather than separating her from it. Down, down she slid. She'd assumed that diving at night would be no different from diving in Wallabout Bay, with its poor visibility. But it turned out that the bay's muddy opacity was something she'd *seen*. Here, there was no difference between opening her eyes and closing them. This made for an eerie dislocation, as if she were sliding toward nothing or floating in a void. When at last she reached the bottom, she clutched the line and blinked into the dark, wondering if she'd come down too quickly. A pull on her lifeline steadied her, and she pulled back. The current was milder at the bottom. Anna shut her eyes and immediately felt calmer. Here was a blindness she could tolerate.

She took a sixty-foot circling line from her tool bag and bent it to the descending line, just above the weight. Then, recalling a trick Lieutenant Axel had taught them (strange how well she'd listened, even with Bascombe muttering in her ear), she wedged her gloved fingers under the edge of the weight and flipped it over, so now her searching line was pinned underneath the weight and would slide more closely over the harbor floor. She looped the other end around her right wrist and walked away from the weight until the line pulled taut. Then she set down her tool bag to mark the beginning of her circle, lowered herself onto all fours, and began to crawl over the harbor floor in a clockwise direction, dragging the radius of circling line from her wrist. Immediately, the rope met with swells in the harbor bottom. At first Anna felt compelled to investigate each interference, but gradually, she was able to distinguish objects from topography. She kept her eyes closed and tried to forget the immensity around her, her own tiny solitude within it. Divers who'd worked on the freshwater pipeline from Staten Island spoke of wrecked ships on the harbor floor, hundred-year-old oyster beds choked with monstrous shells, eels fifty feet long. These apparitions seemed to flicker just beyond the reach of Anna's fingers. She calmed herself with the thought of

Marle holding her lifeline and air hose, gathering them in and letting them out as she moved. They could haul her up at any time. Four sharp pulls were all it would take.

Dexter watched his boys powering the air machine like figures on a clock. He was struggling, as he had from the start of this ride, to do the single thing he was worst at: nothing. His idleness made everything around him register on a scale from irksome to intolerable: Anna's cohorts holding her ankles to guide her feet into the massive diving shoes; the Negro's hand under her chin while they attached the harness, or whatever the hell it was. Their insularity made him envious—not just of the men but all three of them. They were working together, two men and a girl, with evident ease. Even after the diving suit was on and she no longer looked like a girl, he was resentful of their shared knowledge, their nomenclature and expertise. As they helped her backward into the harbor, Dexter took his first cigarette in five years and placed it between his lips. Enzo darted from the shadows in the nick of time to light it.

Smoking woozily after his long abstinence, Dexter pulled a chair alongside the skipper's and tipped back his head in solidarity with the ancient's palsied neck. A stroke. Even in the cold, a sheen of sweat coated the skipper's face. Dexter was near enough to smell the tomato juice he drank more or less constantly (slopping it liberally onto his clothes)—for ulcers, he said, though it seemed to Dexter that so much tomato juice might well be the ulcers' cause. There it was, in a tin pail at his side. A riot of stars flashed overhead.

"Who could've guessed, Skipper," Dexter said. "That we had all these stars right over New York City."

The skipper gave a cough, unimpressed. He was a New York skipper, accustomed to navigating by landmarks and shore lights. The stars had confounded him. But when it came to the harbor, its winds and currents and tricky passes, he knew every bump and hole, the whereabouts of eddies neglected by the currents—places where objects would sink and not wash ashore. And he knew how to find those places again, or so he claimed.

"Come now, Skipper. You'll get used to the stars."

A bark of contradiction, which Dexter understood to mean that the war would end, the lights would go back on, and the New York sky would resume looking as it had.

"You're right, of course," Dexter said. Then, very softly, "Say, you're certain this is the place?"

The skipper barked his umbrage at the very question.

"How can you know, when everything looks so different in this dark?"

The mariner tapped his temple below the white cap he always wore aboard, its starched cleanliness a bizarre contrast to his tomato-streaked squalor. "Nothing moves," he said, startling Dexter with the abrupt clarity of his speech. "In here."

"I see."

Soon restlessness overtook Dexter again. He considered trying to speak with Nestor, the helmsman, but that was hopeless. Once garrulous, Nestor had clammed up some years back after receiving a fright. Instead, Dexter approached the front of the boat, where his boys were sweating at the air machine. One of the Naval Yard men was there, a sour-faced towhead whose disapproval was thick enough to butter bread. His eyes were fixed on two gauges at the front of the air machine.

"They turning those wheels fast enough?" Dexter asked him.

"So far."

"Oh, they won't let up."

"They'd best not."

A provocation. Its touch was like an electric current, so bracing and welcome that Dexter refrained from pointing out to the mug right then and there who was boss. He went instead to the other Naval Yard man, the Negro, who stood at the opposite end of the boat near the diving ladder. The lines attached to Anna ran through his hands into coils at his feet. His eyes were fixed on the water.

"What are you watching, exactly?" Dexter asked.

"Her bubbles," the Negro said, not moving his eyes. "See them breaking? The current carries them; she isn't necessarily right in that place." He seemed friendly, neutral, difficult to read the way Negroes often were—except to other Negroes, he supposed.

"How do you know where she is?"

The Negro held up the cords in his hand. "I let these in and out as she moves, so there's never too much slack. That way I can feel her signal pulls."

"Is it dangerous? What she's doing?"

"Not if we all do our jobs right."

They watched the bubbles, a pale boil on the harbor's inky surface. "Your partner," Dexter said. "Why has he a diving suit on?"

"There's always a second diver in case the lines get fouled. Or something else goes wrong."

"Who'd watch the air machine dials if he went down?"

"Are you volunteering, sir?"

Dexter laughed, impressed. In four simple words, the man had managed to both establish a jocular familiarity and assure Dexter that he understood exactly who was in charge. A diplomat.

"Can the one machine make enough air for two divers?" Dexter asked.

"They're designed to. At the Yard, we use one per diver, but this one tested well for efficiency. With those gentlemen at the wheels, we'd get the maximum."

Dexter smiled, having finally received the compliment he'd been fishing for. "Say, suppose the machine should stop working?" he said. "What then?"

"No reason for that to happen," the Negro said evenly, but Dexter sensed a new wariness in him. "Even so, she'd have about eight minutes of air left inside the dress. More than enough to get her topside."

A signal must have come through the cord he was holding, for he jerked it firmly several times, waited, then jerked again. Then he walked backward along the gunwale toward his partner at the bow, letting out slack as he went, eyes still fixed to the bubbles. After a brief conversation, the towhead left the air machine, lifted the weighted line, and walked it quickly to the bow of the lighter, not far from the air machine. Dexter sidled up to the Negro, who explained that "the diver," as he referred to her, had made a complete sweep around the line without finding anything. Now she would begin a second circle in a new location.

"This could take forever," Dexter said. "How long can she stay down?"

"Two hours free and clear. Longer, and she'll need to decompress on the way up. We've only a bosun's chair for that, but we'll manage it." The Negro glanced at his wrist, where Dexter saw three watches strapped. "She's been down thirty-eight minutes."

"I'd like to go down," Dexter said. "And help her search."

The suggestion was pure impulse; a verbal essay that was more an expression of general impatience than a proposal. But the moment Dexter uttered the words, his mind locked around the idea. "I'm serious."

The Negro inclined his head politely. "Have you ever dived before, sir?"

"I'm a quick study."

"With all due respect, from a safety angle, it would be out of the question."

"Nothing is out of the question," Dexter said amiably, "as long as there's someone to ask the question."

The Negro watched the bubbles. Dexter waited, knowing the man was too polite to ignore him for long. Sure enough, he resumed in a gently reasoning tone, "We had two weeks of training before we went down."

"And yet there was a first time," Dexter said. "You hadn't done it, and then one day you had."

The Negro cocked his head, trying to read him.

"Today is that day for me."

The white diver watched the air machine gauges, giving no indication that he'd heard this exchange. Dexter moved closer to him and cleared his throat. He spoke softly, so that the diver could hear him but the boys turning the flywheels could not. "I'd like to take that suit off your hands and go down myself."

"That's not the way these things are done," the diver muttered, eyes on the dials.

"They can be done any number of ways," Dexter said. "Like all things."

The man didn't glance at him.

"I'd like to help, is all. It will save her time. And you're needed up here."

"You'd be no help whatsoever."

"Say, now, that hurts my feelings."

"Just a risk and a distraction."

"Is it air you're worried about? Having the one machine supply two people?"

"Among other things."

"If there's trouble, cut me loose," Dexter said. "I'll float to the top. I'd have eight minutes, right?"

Now he had both divers' attention. "Your size?" the Negro said. "Less."

"Do it anyway."

The white diver made a dismissive noise. "That's no favor to us if we end up with your body on our hands."

"There wouldn't be a body."

The men exchanged a glance. "How do you figure?" asked the Negro.

"Skipper," Dexter barked. The mariner jolted as if a pan of water had been tossed in his face. "Come on over here, would you?"

The skipper hobbled over painfully, like a squashed insect.

"I need you to reassure these gentlemen of something," Dexter said. "If I should happen to croak while diving in this harbor, can you guarantee that they would be free and clear to walk away? No entanglements with the law, the coroner, or the postman?"

The skipper nodded, breathing hard. Dexter wasn't entirely sure he'd understood.

"With all due respect," the Negro said, "bodies can't just disappear."

"Ah, but they can," Dexter said. "They do. You're in a different world right now, my friend. It may look like the one you know, may smell like it, sound like it, but what goes on here doesn't carry over. When you wake up tomorrow, none of this will have happened."

They were staring at him as if he'd gone unhinged. How to explain the workings of the shadow world in a way that would persuade them? He didn't have to, of course, but Dexter always preferred argument to brute force. "I'm saying we've different rules," he said. "Different practices. What can't happen in your world can in mine. Including bodies disappearing."

"Where does our diver fit in?" the Negro asked. "What if something happens to her?"

"Nothing happens to her," Dexter said. "That we all agree on. But I'm different. I'm like . . . a reflection. A shadow." He was reaching for something he'd not articulated before and didn't fully understand.

"That's a lot of pretty talk," the white diver said, looking at Dexter head-on for the first time. A hard face, tipped inward. "In my book, there's but one world, and without oxygen, none of us lasts in it for long. Amateurs trying to play hero are a pain in the neck, but the chumps who let 'em muck things up are to blame for whatever goes wrong. I'm telling you no, pal. I will not equip you to dive in that harbor."

Dexter took a long breath. "I've tried reasoning with you," he said. "But it doesn't seem to work."

"Ain't a word of reason in what I've been hearing."

"I'm giving you an order: take off that diving suit."

"I answer to the U.S. Navy. Not to you."

A burst of rage made Dexter's nerves fizz. "The U.S. Navy isn't here right now," he said softly. "At least I don't see them."

"Oh, they're here. They control this harbor. They're all around us."

Dexter turned to the Negro. "Does your friend have a screw loose?" he asked just loudly enough for the towhead to hear. "Does he not understand that my boys will shoot him through the head and throw him overboard for fish food as soon as they'd step on a cockroach?"

Though he hadn't raised his voice, a charge passed over the boat, distinct even through the wind. Enzo loped over eagerly. "We got trouble, boss?"

"I don't know," Dexter said, watching the Negro. "Have we?"

Who better than a Negro to recognize when the world had cut him off at the knees? Calmly, he went to his partner's side and spoke into his ear. Dexter caught phrases:

". . . not that hard if he . . ."

". . . fact that Savino could . . ."

". . . navy does it routinely . . ."

Dexter knew he'd won; the Negro was in charge. Sure enough, he returned to Dexter's side and said, "We don't want trouble, sir. Not at all."

"Neither do I," Dexter said. "That's why I'm giving your partner one last chance to sidestep the part where I scare him so badly he shits his pants. I assure you, it's not pleasant."

The color had drained from the white diver's face. Reflexively, he glanced at the dials on the air machine. Dexter imagined he was inside the man's mind, undergoing the compression on his skull that he must feel. He disliked knowing what another man felt.

"Holy Christ," the white diver said to his partner, his voice dry with horror.

"I don't see him here, either," Dexter said.

When Anna received a signal that a second diver was coming down, she wondered if she'd mistakenly requested him. Then it occurred to her that something had gone wrong—beyond the obvious fact that the descending line had been moved three times (the last around to the lighter's other side), and she'd found only a broken barrel and a tree stump. She kept crawling while he descended, then felt him lift the circling line and follow it toward her, forcing her to rise. Instinctively, she opened her eyes, but of course saw nothing.

She recalled having learned in class that two divers could hear each other underwater if their helmets touched. Bascombe was taller than she'd expected, and she had to tug a little on his arm to make him stoop. She pressed her helmet against his and said, "Why are you here?"

The reply was distant, tinny, like a radio playing under a blanket. "Dexter," she heard.

"What about Dexter?"

"That's me. I'm Dexter."

She thought fleetingly that Bascombe was playing a trick, but couldn't imagine him joking at such a time. "That's impossible."

"Apparently not."

"It's—dangerous," she sputtered.

"The gentlemen above made that clear."

She had a fractured intimation of the ugliness that would have preceded Dexter Styles's replacement of Bascombe in the diving dress. Her mind swerved away; she needed to stay calm. "Can the compressor make enough air for both of us?"

"Are you breathing all right?" he asked.

She took a long inhale, which steadied her. She'd heard that the navy sometimes put men directly into the water in diving dress as the first step in their weeding-out process. The air coming into the hat was cool and dry, and her head felt clear. "Yes," she said. "I've enough air. And you?"

"Never better."

There was truth in this. Once he'd adjusted his air valve as the Negro had instructed, lifting the harness from his shoulders, Dexter had felt an unaccountable exhilaration while being pulled by the heavy shoes through the mighty, pressing dark. It was as if some mammoth effort he'd not been fully aware of having made was about to pay off at last. He could breathe. He could breathe and walk on the bottom of the sea.

"I'm afraid we won't find anything," he heard her say. "How do we know this is the right place?"

Her voice was faint, like a long-distance telephone connection. The result was that singular mix of intimacy and distance that Dexter often felt over the telephone, when a person far away seemed to whisper directly into his thoughts. "We'll find him," he said, his own voice booming by comparison. "The skipper knows. He's here."

This utterance confused Anna; the skipper was here? The voice that arrived through the helmets was leeched not just of volume but of any trace of feeling. It sounded the way a machine would sound if one could speak. Yet the words lingered. *He's here.* A clear image of her father came to her suddenly: rising from the water at Coney Island after one of his morning swims, his body dripping, shining. A wink and a wave to the startled lifeguards who'd come on duty after he'd gone out, a rub with the Turkish towel he'd left beside Anna on the sand with his clothing and billfold. The radiant bliss that rose from him after those swims, as if he'd shaken off a sorrow that was with him always.

"I'm here," she said softly. "I'm here, too."

Dexter Styles pressed his helmet to hers. "If you've another rope, we can hold it between us and cover more ground," came the mechanical rendering of his voice.

"I have."

Taking his gloved hand, she led him back to her starting point of a few minutes before, where she'd left the tool bag. Inside was a thirty-foot rope with a lanyard at each end. She slipped one over her free wrist, the left, and the other onto his right wrist, below the wristband. Pressing her helmet to his, she said, "Walk away from me until the rope is taut, then crawl in the direction you feel me crawling. Your helmet should always be higher than your body; don't let it drop."

"All right."

He did as instructed, getting awkwardly onto his knees when the rope tensed. He felt the soft harbor floor through the rubberized fabric of the diving suit. He lowered his gloves to the earth, taking care to keep his head up—though he'd forgotten to ask what would happen if he did not. Crawling felt grotesquely unnatural—when had he last crawled, for Christ's sake? But the rope tugged at his wrist, and crawl he did, tentatively at first, afraid of dropping his head. Each slight resistance of the rope made him believe they'd found something, but he came to recognize these as bumps and tufts of plants on the harbor bottom. Gradually, the primal nature of the motion emptied his mind. He was crawling in the dark. Crawling in the dark. He was crawling. Crawling. After a while, he could not remember why.

The obstruction, when it came, lay along the outer rope conjoining Anna to Dexter Styles. She unhooked the inner circling line—the one holding her to the weight—in order to crawl toward him. Only then did she recognize the flaw in her plan: the rope she was letting go was their only link to the boat. She remembered her first dive—the confusion of wandering, disoriented, underwater. Even in the comparatively luminous and shallow Wallabout Bay, a three-inch manila rope had been impossible to find. In the worst case, Marle and Bascombe could haul her up by her lifeline. But could they haul up Dexter Styles?

Finding no alternative, she let go the inner line from her wrist and crawled along the outer rope to the obstacle: a heavy chain attached to a block of concrete. She felt Dexter Styles crawling from the other direction and then in the water beside her. She turned on her flashlight, its sallow glow awakening perhaps two feet of murky bay. The chain's three-inch links were slippery with plant life, as if they hadn't moved in a long time. Anna doused the light, frightened of what else she would see. She touched her hat to Dexter Styles's and said, "What do you think?"

"That looks right," came the faint reply.

The foreboding she'd felt all night moved very close. "I'm frightened," she said, adopting the same monotone that his voice acquired in its passage through the two hats. This flat delivery had the odd effect of checking whatever emotions she might have felt. Only the words were left.

"Why did they kill him?" she asked.

"It's what they do when they're crossed."

"Was he a criminal?"

"No."

"Why did he cross them?"

"Only he knows that."

"I'm going to search without the light."

She felt him rise to his feet, perhaps to give her privacy, or from a disinclination to know what she found. The chain was coiled and doubled back to such an extent that it had assumed a solid mass. Tentatively, Anna began to loosen the folds of chain and probe among them. An enormous padlock affixed several links together and attached them by a padeye to the block of concrete. Anna wedged her fingers among the links, searching for something organic: fabric, leather, bone. She hadn't any memory of what her father had worn the day he didn't come back, but surely there had been a suit, a necktie, a hat. Shoes. She felt a pressure at her breastbone like a dark egg, its contents horror and revulsion. Anna dreaded these sensations, yet she craved a discovery that would unleash them: some proof that he hadn't gone away. Had never left her. Anna's need for this certainty drove her gloved fingers through mud and sand and slippery links of chain. But she found no shoes, no fabric, no bones. Could all of that have been carried away?

Flagging, she reminded herself how close she'd already come. Her presence here was miraculous; her only chance. This recognition catalyzed a frenzy of new digging. She swore under her breath the way men swore at the Yard: *Damn it! Fuck it!* She dug until she was distracted by the glow swarming behind her eyelids. She tried opening her eyes to dispel it, then realized that her eyes were already open. The glow was coming from outside—from the water itself. It intensified as she dug: metallic orange, purple, green, colors that weren't exactly colors, like the hues of a photographic negative she'd once seen. They rose from the newly exposed earth and shimmered in the water around her.

Anna tugged at the laces of Dexter's dress until he crouched. He rested his helmet against hers. "What the hell is that?"

"Phosphorescence. Live things in the water." She had learned about it in diving class.

He began digging, too. The phosphorescence glowed around them in a cloud, dimly illuminating Dexter Styles in the water beside her. Warmth radiated from under her fingers, under the sand. She located a small round object stuck fast inside a buried link of chain and began working at it with her crude gloves, trying to dislodge it without snapping the tiny chain that held it fast. At last she freed the disk and turned it over in her hands. More metal; she was disappointed. There was a nub or a bolt along one rounded edge. Then, with an icy shock, the object became legible: a pocket watch. Anna cried out, the sound boxing her ears inside the helmet. She lifted the watch to her faceplate. Dexter Styles was still digging, and in that incandescence she barely made out the familiar engraving of a stranger's initials.

Her father's watch.

She began to cry. Even through her gloves, she felt the faint indentations of the engravings. JDV: Jakob De Veer, the man who had helped her father when he was a boy. Clutching the watch, she sobbed until the humidity inside her helmet began to daze her. She turned up her air and opened her spitcock to flush out helmet and dress. Still weeping, she pressed her helmet to Dexter's, knowing that he would hear only the mechanical echo of her words, nothing else.

"I found him," she said. "He's here."

By the time they began looking again for the cord they'd slid down, Dexter had long felt the need of more air. Crawling was harder than walking, had left him light-headed and rubber-legged. Holding the rope taut between them, they walked slowly in the direction where Anna believed the vertical line would be. Mercifully, they hit it.

Dexter waited at the bottom while she ascended. With his hand on the line, he felt her pause partway up to decompress a few minutes; then a jerk as she passed from line to ladder. Then nothing. The line went still in his hand, and Dexter felt only the currents muscling him. Carefully, he turned the air knob on his helmet clockwise just slightly, as the Negro had instructed. He took voluptuous breaths, the pleasure of gorging himself on that hissing air like guzzling cold water in a towering thirst. His light-headedness passed, leaving his senses sharp. He was alone at the bottom of the sea. The extremity of his position mesmerized Dexter. He'd always liked the dark, but night was the only version of it he'd known until now. This was the primeval dark of nightmares. It covered secrets too atrocious to be exposed: drowned children, sunken ships. He let go the line and took a few steps away, imagining himself cut off and alone in this forsaken place. Something long and smooth slid along the envelope of his diving suit—an eel? A fish? He felt the possibility of panic.

But what visited Dexter instead, as he stood alone in the throttling dark, was his first clear memory in years of Ed Kerrigan. An ironic asymmetrical smile from under the brim of his hat. Always a good hat, an excellent feather. The man knew how to dress. Holding down his hat in the wind as they'd walked along Manhattan Beach. How Dexter had liked him! Kerrigan's accommodating manner; his quick, unshowy way of getting things done without letting on what it cost. A mick. There had been an understanding between them, Dexter had felt that instinctively. Later he'd wondered: understanding of what?

Kerrigan's cipherlike nature had been essential to the job. He could go anywhere, find out anything. Through him, Dexter had tasted freedom from the constraints of time and space. He could appear where he was not supposed to be, listen to what he was not permitted to know. *Proximity*—that was what Kerrigan had granted him. Omniscience.

Invisibility. And Dexter had grown accustomed to it—dependent upon it. He'd been far too comfortable, too greedy for the flow of facts, to consider that access, like all things, had its price.

In Dexter's line of work, men who broke the rules egregiously were taken for a ride, as the parlance went. Everyone knew what had happened, and they were rarely mentioned again. Certainly Kerrigan had understood this.

Then why? Here was the question that had dogged Dexter in the years since his erstwhile employee had sung and paid the price: *Why* had he done it? Money? Dexter had paid him well—would have paid more, had Kerrigan asked.

Now, having seen the man's lowly home, his crippled daughter, Dexter understood the reason even less. Why risk getting snuffed when his family needed him so badly? Why take the chance that someone—the healthy daughter, perhaps—might investigate?

There were no answers. Just the man, smiling his uneven smile as he looked out at the sea. "Not a ship in sight," he'd said once, his reticence giving so little away that Dexter couldn't tell if the news was good or bad. He'd looked out, and it was true: there was not a single ship.

Dexter seized the cord he'd come down on, looped his right arm and leg around it as the Negro had advised, and opened the air valve to inflate the diving suit. Sure enough, he began to rise as if by magic. For a euphoric moment Dexter felt godlike; he was flying, floating, breathing underwater—all things a human could not do. A sense of blinding comprehension assailed him. *Yes,* he thought, and then cried it aloud: *"Yes!"* An essential thing was clear to him at last, one that underlay everything else. He was gaining velocity, the diving suit ballooning uncontrollably as he flew up the rope, forcing his arms rigid so he couldn't touch the dials on his helmet or even hold the rope any longer. He hardly cared; he was too enthralled. *Of course,* he thought, distracted from the rocketing speed of his ascent by the need to seal in his mind the crucial thing he'd finally understood.

His blown-up form shot to the surface fifty feet from the lighter. Marle bellowed at the goons, two of whom ran to the gunwale and began yanking at his lifeline. Bascombe kept his eyes on the compressor gauges, cursing fantastically. A mood of panicked concentration imposed harmony upon their motley ranks, all of them moving as one. Anna descended the ladder, bootless in her dress, and waited as the goons yanked Dexter Styles toward her, facedown and spread-eagled. He looked dead. When he was beside her, she tried to flip him over, intending to open his faceplate, but Marle bellowed for her to leave him.

"We need to get him on deck," he said. "If he loses pressure, he'll sink."

It was true—in her fright, she hadn't been thinking. She helped as best she could to shove his bloated form over the gunwale onto the deck, where two goons caught him under the armpits and two more backed them up. Anna leaped over the ladder and crouched beside him as the men turned him over. Water poured from his diving dress around her feet. She opened his faceplate with shaking hands. His eyes were glassy, wide-open.

"Can you hear me?" she said.

He blinked, then grinned. A tidal wave of relief nearly toppled all of them.

"Did you . . . hold your breath coming up?" she asked, recalling the air embolism.

"Of course not," he said. "Your friend the Negro warned me not to."

PART SEVEN

The Sea, the Sea

CHAPTER TWENTY-FIVE

It was only when Dexter returned to his automobile outside the Red Hook boatyard that he had the ease and solitude to revisit his discovery. The Cadillac's fragrant leather seat received him like a pair of arms, and he settled exhaustedly into its embrace. A trying dispute had followed his "blowup," pitting him against not just the Naval Yard men and Kerrigan's daughter but also his own boys and even the skipper. These unlikely bedfellows were united in the belief that he should go back to the bottom and rise again slowly, with stops along the way, so as not to get the bends. Dexter waved them off. He felt fine, no pains anywhere—in fact, he felt damned good, considering he'd muffed the dive and had to be fished out of the harbor like a rag doll by the very men he'd forced into submission earlier. He hardly cared. Behind all of it beat the tattoo of his discovery. He was aware of it through each step of dismantling their voyage, all the way to the end, when he shook hands with Kerrigan's daughter and her colleagues and noted without rancor that the men met his eye as equals.

He'd chanced upon his favorite hour: a premonition of dawn without any visible sign of it. He started the car to warm it, then let his mind turn at last to the revelation that had bombarded him during his ascent. But the flash of comprehension, of illumination, was all he could remember.

Dumb with surprise, Dexter returned to the moment of discovery: rising through the dark water faster, then faster still, the friction of the rope making a hot stripe through the middle of his gloves. Meanwhile, dawn leaked under a rim of Brooklyn sky and a hush fell on the harbor, lighters and tugs and freight-car floats falling briefly silent in the sudden faint light like strangers in an elevator.

Had he really forgotten?

He could still get home before sunrise. This wish—to make today ordinary, like any other day—hardened into urgency. He pulled away from the curb and accelerated through Sunset Park and Bay Ridge, racing against the sun. The stakes seemed to rise as he drove, until he was convinced that if he could just begin at the usual time, in the usual place, something would have been repaired. Success hinged upon rhythm and timing, like the old game of sidearming pennies under moving streetcars. You had to know exactly when to release the penny to get it through.

A pointed brightness had gathered above the Flatlands by the time he reached Manhattan Beach. He'd beaten the sun. He was breathing hard, unaccountably relieved as he entered the silence of his home. He heated the coffee Milda had left, poured himself a cup, and drank it on the porch with the wind in his face, exactly as he'd imagined. The sun rose humbly, scattering weak light over the sea. The dawn minesweepers reminded him of custodians waxing a lobby floor. A procession of ships shouldered past each other beyond Breezy Point. Gulls hung stationary, like kites. All of it felt salubrious, as if his proximity to the sea had rubbed everything—Kerrigan's daughter, the dive, even his revelation—into insignificance.

He wondered if Tabby might join him. She'd done little besides mourn and mope since Grady had shipped out nearly three weeks before—a bereaved widow of sixteen. Dexter would have missed his nephew, too, had he not been so relieved to be rid of him.

He refilled his cup twice and drank coffee until sunlight laid bare his need for sleep. He descended to his sunken bedroom, picturing Harriet dreaming in their bed and longing for her—for his wife specifically—in a way he hadn't in weeks.

He found the blackout shades raised in their bedroom. The resulting slash of brightness affronted him after the gentle murk he'd anticipated. He heard running water from behind the bathroom door. Saturday. Why on earth was she up so early?

He was on the verge of rapping on the door to pose that question when something made him wait. He went to his dressing room, removed his piece and locked it up, released his socks from their garters, and unfastened his cuff links, which he'd worn beneath the diving suit. When the bath taps had been turned off, he called through the door, "You're up early, darling."

"I've a bridge game at the club," she called back. "Tabby's coming, too."

Gently, he turned the doorknob but found it locked. The twins had a habit of bounding into rooms. "Is she awake?" he asked.

"She spent the night at Lucy's with some other girls. A Carmen Miranda party." He could hear her washing. "They make headdresses out of fruit and hang curtain rings from their ears and dance to 'South American Way.' As I understand it."

This onslaught of bright detail had the same off-putting effect as the sunlight. "I'm surprised she has the spirits for it," he said at last, through the door. "With Grady gone."

"Oh, I think she's getting over that."

He heard her rise from the tub. A few moments later, she opened the bathroom door in her satin coral peignoir, expensive smells lazing in the steam behind her. Dexter had met Carmen Miranda when *Down Argentine Way* first opened, and she could not hold a candle to his wife. He approached Harriet, aroused by the beads of humidity gathered in her hairline. She brushed past him into her dressing room, closed the door partway, and flung her peignoir over the top. For a second time, Dexter found himself making conversation through a slab of wood. "Since when does Tabby play bridge?" he asked.

"Felicity's got her hooked on it."

"Felicity."

"Booth's daughter."

"Ah." He lowered himself to the bed in his trousers and shirt-sleeves. The sun jabbed his eyes. "You didn't mention Boo Boo."

"I told you days ago. We're playing a rubber and having lunch, and then I'm driving the girls to the Squibb Building to wrap coats for Bundles for Britain."

Something about this litany of plans had the airtight quality of an alibi. Dexter lay back on the bed and waited for Harriet to emerge in the sporting ensemble she usually wore to the club. She appeared in her new "capote" scarf-hat with mink along the face, presumably for the mirror—she wasn't leaving yet.

"I'm glad Boo Boo is putting our gasoline to good use," he said.

"Booth."

"You call him Boo Boo."

"I know him better."

"And getting to know him better still. Using my gasoline."

"You're a fine one to talk."

Dexter sat upright. She was throwing open windows, letting in wind, along with more sunlight. He left the bed and moved close to his wife. He took both her hands in his, interrupting her flurry. "Harriet," he said. "What can you possibly mean by that?"

She avoided his eyes. "I need to pick up Tabby."

"What are you thinking?" He was holding her hands, waiting for her to meet his eyes. *Let it come,* he thought, whatever it was she'd guessed; let them put it to rest.

"I'm *thinking* that I want a cigarette."

"What else?"

"The car may need gasoline."

"What else?"

"You're strange today, Dex. You're making me nervous." At last she returned his gaze from within her oval of mink.

"What else?" he asked softly.

"You're restless. Unhappy. You've been for months."

"What else?"

"Isn't that enough?" she asked, impatient. But she held his gaze.

"Only if there's nothing more."

"You're off your game. Father said so, too." She broke away, took a cigarette from the silver case on her bureau, and placed one between the bright stripes of her lips.

"Did he," Dexter said, lighting it with her onyx lighter.

"I wasn't supposed to tell you that," she said through a stream of smoke. "You drove me to it."

"Your father said that?"

"Promise you won't tell him."

"I won't." He sat back down on the bed, trying to manage his extreme disquiet. That the old man had thought along those lines— that was nothing. Dexter had as much as told him so. But the fact that it had been said aloud in Harriet's presence—discussed—was a horse of a different color. It implied a family conversation of which Dexter had been the topic.

He breathed Harriet's smoke, craving one himself. "When?"

"Just in passing."

"Recently?"

"I don't remember. Forget it."

"Like hell you don't."

From his first meeting with the old man at the hunt club years ago, their communication had been forthright and direct. Under what circumstances should Dexter need to be discussed? He felt injured and wanted his wife not to see it.

"Why don't you come with us?" she said, sitting on the bed beside him.

He scoffed. "To play bridge with Booth?"

"Tabby can play. I don't have to." She'd taken his hand. There was a skittering avoidance about her eyes.

"You're nervous," he said.

"You used to like going there."

"Why are you nervous?"

"I hate to see your feelings hurt, that's all."

"I'm just tired."

He was uncertain what was happening between them—whether it was something important or nothing at all. He would know only when he'd slept.

He stood and began pulling down shades. Harriet crushed out her cigarette. "I'll lie down, too," she said, moving close to him and spreading her long fingers over his chest. He felt their cool slenderness through his shirt. She'd taken off her hat, and her auburn hair fell loose.

"I thought you had to go."

"Tabby won't mind if I'm late."

Her smile had a downward tilt that made it look naughty. How he'd always adored that smile! Dexter breathed the smell of her hair and felt a trickle of distrust. She was a pretty stranger standing too close, making a jittery effort to seduce him. He thought: *I will never touch this woman again.*

"You go ahead, baby," he managed to say warmly. His sudden revulsion for his wife felt dangerous—a poison that would remain inert only until she perceived it.

He lay with eyes shut and listened for the front door. When he knew she'd gone, he slept a parched, fitful sleep. He woke at noon, as usual, washed, dressed, and readied himself to go to Heels's place. Although his head ached, he felt saner. What had gone wrong with Harriet, exactly? Nothing so bad, it seemed now.

As he was taking his coat from the front closet, he sensed, or heard, someone else in the house. "Hello," he called.

A faint reply: the twins. It was Saturday. Dexter climbed the stairs to their room and thrust open the door without knocking, moved by a habitual wish to catch his sons unaware. Their startled faces shamed him. Phillip was struggling into a shirt; Dexter glimpsed the gash of his appendix scar and experienced heartbreak so profound that he lurched toward his son with a notion of embracing him. The boy turned wary eyes upon him. "Are we in trouble?"

"No," Dexter said. "No. Goodness."

He'd been avoiding their bedroom for weeks, protesting the redundant prizes they were bent on winning in pointless contests. But the room had been transformed since his last visit. Now the roller skates, bugles, accordions, and slingshots were nowhere in sight. "Say, what happened to all your loot?"

"We brought it to Saint Maggie's," John-Martin said.

"For soldiers' children," Phillip added.

Once again, Dexter found himself chasing events that seemed to have run away from him. A vision of the importunate deacon, hands outstretched to receive this windfall, wafted through his mind. "When?"

The boys consulted each other. "Lately," John-Martin said.

"You mean recently?"

"Recently," they agreed.

A narrow table had been introduced between their beds, converting them into a pair of workbenches. John-Martin sat upon his, facing a spread of balsa wood, rubber cement tubes, waxed paper, and Bluejacket instruction pamphlets.

"Airplanes?" Dexter asked.

"Why does everyone think that?" John-Martin huffed.

"Ships," Phillip explained. "We've just begun." After a pause he added, "Recently."

Dexter noticed for the first time that the challenging snap of John-Martin's tone was exactly offset by the caress of apology in Phillip's. Was that new? "Why not airplanes?" he asked.

Both boys stared at him; he'd missed something obvious. "Grady," they said.

"We're going to sea ourselves when we're sixteen," John-Martin said with a show of carelessness.

"If you give your permission," Phillip said. "And the war is still on."

Dexter felt the boys' quick brown eyes appraising his reaction. Clearly, they'd been more aware of the collective Grady worship than he'd supposed. "Sixteen is awfully young," he said.

"We'll be ready."

"If we stop monkeying."

"We stopped last week!"

"Except for this morning."

Their window faced the sea. From habit, Dexter's eye sought the parade of ships past Breezy Point. "Look," he said. "Here comes a tanker."

"The porch has a better view," John-Martin said.

"You watch ships from the porch?" Dexter was surprised; he had never seen them do it.

"When no one is home," John-Martin said.

"Which is a lot," Phillip put in.

"Let's go look," Dexter said. "I like to do that, too."

The telephone rang as they were descending the stairs, and Dexter picked up the extension in the front hall. Heels. "Everything all right?" Dexter asked.

"Frankie Q. telephoned the Pines early this morning," Heels said. "He mentioned some kind of activity at the boathouse. You might want to take a look on your way over."

A telephone call from a son of Mr. Q.'s was unusual. "Someone was in there a few weeks ago," Dexter mused.

"Frankie seemed . . . surprised that I didn't know where to find you," Heels said. "I told him ours was a marriage built upon trust."

Dexter laughed. "What did he say?"

"Dead silence."

"All right. I'm leaving now."

The twins were side by side at the porch rail. John-Martin handed him the binoculars. "Take a look, Pop," he said. After a moment he added, "Sit down."

"It will steady your hands," Phillip explained.

"Aren't they steady?"

"They're shaking."

Dexter never had a tremor. He wondered fleetingly whether he should have gone back down to the harbor bottom, as everyone had begged him to.

"Mine tremble, too," Phillip reassured him.

Dexter braced his elbows on the porch rail and looked through the binoculars. The boys draped thoughtless arms around his shoulders. He was aware of a bodily love for them, an affinity in their bones. Harriet would be pleased by this scene; he was fulfilling a promise. He waited, letting his eyes blur against the binoculars, putting off the moment of telling his sons he must go.

Dexter smelled a rat before he'd even reached the boathouse. It was a setup—he knew this without knowing how he knew, and was pleased to find his faculties still alert, despite the shaking hands and a raw, bright ache behind his eyes. Normally, he would have rounded up a few boys to bring with him, but the tip had come from Frankie Q.—in effect, from Mr. Q. himself. That meant this wasn't a setup in the usual sense; it was theater. Dexter would have a role to play, and Mr. Q. knew there was no need to prepare him in advance. Dexter liked to think on his feet.

He parked a block away, flicked dust from his new oxfords, straightened his tie, and walked to the boathouse. A black sedan was parked right out front, dead silence within. The whole thing phonier than a surprise birthday party.

His pleasure tapered off abruptly when he shoved open the door and found Badger playing at cards with two hoods. Dexter had kept only a vague eye on his erstwhile protégé since the kid had brought his numbers game into two of the minor clubs. Now Dexter took in his painted necktie, pearl stickpin, and Borsalino hat. Badger had prospered since his arrival in New York. Yet apparently, there was still more he needed to be taught.

Badger and his crew were fresh; they'd washed, shaved, drunk their morning coffee. That was strange. If they weren't here last night, then whom had Frankie Q. seen in the boathouse?

"Badger," Dexter said. "Pleasure."

"Have a seat," Badger said with the crisp magnanimity of a man who believed he was in charge. Dexter let this go. He gazed upon Mr. Q.'s callow relation and waited for the offenses to mount. Badger's boys melted into the walls, and Dexter took one of their chairs.

"Drink?" Badger asked. A bottle of Haig and Haig sat on the table.

"Thanks just the same."

"Say, it's not friendly to let a man drink alone."

"Then don't drink."

Dexter leaned back in his chair and crossed his legs, both to exhibit his relaxed state and to place his ankle holster within easy reach. In the act of crossing them, he experienced what they called déjà vu: sitting across from Kerrigan in this same boathouse, watching him cross those marionette legs of his. He'd been seated where Dexter was now. But Kerrigan had taken the drink.

"I'm all yours, Badger," Dexter said. "Tell me what's on your mind."

"I go by Jimmy now."

"No kidding?"

"Badger was Chicago. Jimmy is New York." He gestured, left versus right, clutching the cities like two grapefruits.

There had been no fear in Kerrigan, though he must have had an inkling of what was coming. Dexter could smell a man's panic a room away: an animal odor, part skunk, part sex. Some men were aroused by it, erections straining at their trouser buttons as their victims wept and begged. But Dexter felt only relief when Kerrigan raised his glass with a steady hand, smiling his cockeyed smile. "To better days," he said, a standard of the decade. Dexter found he couldn't meet his friend's eyes as they drained their glasses.

"I thought you were nuts for Chicago," he said to Badger.

"Why, sure, it's a fine place for amateurs."

He was hopeless: a boy in knickers parroting a moving-picture hood. A walking target. "You grew up," Dexter said, managing a sober look. "Jimmy."

Thus acknowledged, Badger became expansive. "You put me out of your automobile a few months back, you might recall."

"Vaguely."

"Best thing you could've done."

Dexter grew alert. Fawning was an anesthetic, nearly always a prelude to something less pleasant.

"You taught me not to talk so much," Badger said.

"Is this your way of saying thanks?"

"I suppose it is."

"Well, I'm touched. And now tempus fugit. I've an appointment to keep."

"It can wait."

Dexter gave him a long look. "You don't tell me when to go, Badger," he said slowly. "I tell you."

"Jimmy."

Dexter stood, impatient to move things along. As expected, Badger's boys slunk in front of the door and looked up at him with rods in hand, seasick expressions on their faces.

Now must come the inspiration that Dexter had always managed to provide in like interventions over the years. How to restore order and authority—chastise, humble, and correct—without dealing mortal injury? A damaged finger, sure. A broken ankle. But nothing more serious.

Dexter smiled at Badger. "I asked before what I could do for you," he said. "You can't answer without the heavy artillery?"

"I want to teach you something, too," Badger said. "Return the favor, so to speak."

The drink had hit Kerrigan instantly—his slenderness, perhaps. He'd looked startled, then disoriented; then he'd just sat, gazing at Dexter in cloudy silence. Dexter hadn't bothered to feign surprise. The look between them was all the conversation they'd needed: no recriminations, no explanations. The rules were clear to everyone. Kerrigan's head hit the table not five minutes after he threw back the shot. Something about the set of his shoulders made Dexter think he might sit back up. He waited, watching his friend's slow breaths while wood ticked in the stove. Only when he'd shaken Kerrigan's shoulder and felt his body threaten to slide to the floor in that gelatinous sleep of dope addicts did Dexter rise from his chair and rap on a window to summon the skipper and his boys, who were waiting in the boat.

"You think there's no one above you," Badger said.

"Everyone but God has someone above him," Dexter said. "That doesn't make it you, Badger."

"Jimmy!" Badger roared, slamming both palms on the table. "How many fucking times I have to tell you? Does hobnobbing with picture stars make you soft in the head?"

"Badger suits you better."

He'd blasted his way out of rooms full of rods, God knew. But not in a while. He'd been younger, quicker on his feet, a few pounds lighter, without much to lose if the curtain came down early. Here, survival wasn't the question; instruction was the question. Setting an example without killing anyone was the question.

"You think I can't touch you," Badger said. "I see it in your face."

"You've no idea what I think." But it was true. Badger could not.

An incongruity returned to Dexter: the call from Frankie Q. had come in the wee hours, when Badger was still getting his beauty sleep. How had Mr. Q. known Dexter wouldn't come to the boathouse right away? Might he have gotten wind of what Dexter was doing instead?

If that was so, then he'd read the situation backward: *he* was the one to be taught a lesson, and what Mr. Q. wanted from him was not instruction but apology. The amateurish setup was for his own protection: keep it in the family, avoid a public reprimand or any real danger. Dexter's failure to consider this possibility was an uncharacteristic lapse—perhaps a consequence of his throbbing head. Had the dive blunted his thinking? It was obvious now how this was supposed to go: he would grovel to Badger, and word of his groveling would reassure Mr. Q. as he unswaddled his grapevines when the weather turned. Dexter would carry on as before, on a tighter leash. Badger would be Jimmy, his equal.

All of that lay in one direction, predictable as sunrise. And in another lay something less distinct: an unfathomable landscape, flickering and dark, full of glowing dust. A mystery.

Mr. Q. was an old man. A very old man by now.

Dexter was tired of groveling. He'd been groveling most of his life. And the fact was, he didn't have to. He knew that, and so did Mr. Q.

With a swiftness he hadn't known he still possessed, he grabbed the throat of one of Badger's boys in each hand and squeezed until he felt cartilage snap. They fired wildly. One must have hit Badger, because someone shouted, and the room was full of pain. Then Dexter was on the floor clutching his belly, recalling that the Negro had warned him about stomach cramps.

But he hadn't the bends. Badger had shot him in the back.

The kid loomed over him, his face suffused with the lurid wonder of someone gazing into a bonfire. Dexter knew then that his murder had been sanctioned. But how? By what radical reordering of the world had such an act become feasible? The answer arrived with cold certainty: his father-in-law had forsaken him. The old man had cut him loose.

Badger stood above him, gat raised and ready. Like any garrulous killer, he wanted his victim to hear him out before he finished him off. As long as Dexter appeared to listen, he would live. He fastened his eyes on his assailant's face while the contours of what had happened revealed themselves like parts of a building through fog: George Porter had blabbed preemptively, out of fear of being exposed. The channel Dexter had yearned for between the old man and Mr. Q. had come into being— perhaps had existed for years. And both men had done with him.

Badger spoke eagerly, apparently flattered by Dexter's captive interest. Dexter didn't hear a word. He slipped the confines of his skull like a boat sliding away from a pier when her lines are cast off. Soon he found himself on open water, the wet night in his face. The skipper was beside him, erect and commanding, the stroke not having felled him yet. Kerrigan lay crumpled on the bottom.

"Will you remember where we are?" Dexter asked the skipper.

"Always do."

"Suppose they tell you not to."

The skipper lifted his hands, raw and knotted as newborn calves. "They own these," he said. Then, tapping his skull, "Not this."

Dexter's boys wrapped the chain around Kerrigan and fastened it to the weight. No one wanted him floating to the surface in the April thaw. Now, having seen that chain, Dexter knew that nothing of his friend remained inside it—not a bone, stitch, hat, or shoe leather. This irregularity filled him with hope. His discovery of the night before returned to him with effortless clarity: rising through the dark harbor, he'd felt his own edges dissolve, and a surge of current had leaped from inside him toward a glowing intimation of the future. What he was trying so hard to do, he'd already done! He was American! The lust and yearning that seethed in his veins had helped to fashion whatever was to come.

"You're smiling," Badger said. "You know something I don't?"

Keeping his eyes on Badger, Dexter sank into the pause that followed, dividing it in half, then in half again, determined not to arrive at its opposite shore. He fell into the stillness, dark enclosing him like the harbor water, while on the open boat he helped his boys hoist Kerrigan's chained and weighted body up to the gunwale and tip it over the side.

Eddie held still just long enough that anyone watching from the boat would see him disappear. Then he commenced the spastic writhing he'd been practicing in his mind's eye from the moment he began to feign unconsciousness—tentatively at first, half expecting Styles to jump to his feet and ask what the matter was. Eddie had had an inkling of what might be in store, and come to the boathouse armed with a few tricks from his vaudeville days: razors in the lining of his trousers, a lock pick nestled between his jaw and gum. He'd been afraid of swallowing the pick while pretending to drink, but in the event, he hadn't had to pretend. Styles had looked away, and Eddie had flicked the shot over his shoulder.

He'd left his affairs in order, the second bankbook open on the bureau for Agnes, who knew nothing. That had been his sole condition to Bart

Sheehan: his wife must never know, even if the worst should happen. Especially then. Knowledge invited action, and Eddie was resigned to be remembered as the worst sort of rat rather than risk Agnes training her single-mindedness on the question of who'd done him in. Too hazardous. Men walked out on their families every day—miscreants he'd always said should be jailed. Yet, if murdered, Eddie would be remembered as such a man. So often did he remind himself of this fact that at times he was surprised to find he was still alive, still at home, where his presence had become superfluous. He'd mattered once to Anna, but not anymore. It might relieve her to be rid of him.

The weighted chain hurtled him downward at such a clip that he thought his skull would be squashed by the water's pressure like a walnut under a boot. His writhing freed up a leg, then an arm, and at last the chain and weight divested themselves of his person and continued their rush to the bottom. Nobody chained an unconscious man with the care they would use on a man who was fully awake.

He began kicking madly in his stocking feet, pumping his arms and reaching toward what he prayed would be air, but it was water, still water, until he thought he must have swum the wrong way by mistake. His heart slowed and his legs grew heavy as unconsciousness groped him with its blunt, furred touch. At last he broke through, gasping weakly. It was then he came closest to drowning, for he'd no strength left. He lay on his back under a yellowish night sky, moving his hands like fins to keep afloat. He breathed and breathed, and the buoyant salt water saved him.

It was a long time before he'd enough strength to look for a shore. It wasn't Brooklyn. He began to swim, a soft edge of summer still in the water. Eddie swam long after his last resources had been spent, like scooping at an empty container in hopes that more would somehow be inside, *a little bit more, a little bit more, a little bit more,* and miraculously, there was just enough each time for one more stroke.

He washed up on the southern shore of Staten Island, near a small dock. A fisherman had stayed out longer than usual chasing a school of bass, which was why there was enough light for him to see a man's body left by the tide in the muddy shallows. He assumed it was a corpse and dreaded the long walk to the nearest telephone to report it, but when he tied up his boat and looked again, he saw that the body was shaking.

His wife drew a bath and added boiling water until the temperature was barely warm. They lowered Eddie in, and the man held him under the armpits while his wife heated kettles and warmed the bath gradually, over hours, until it verged upon hot. When at last Eddie stopped trembling and color returned to his cheeks, they dried him, greased him with lanolin, swaddled him in feather blankets, and laid him on a pallet in front of the stove. The fisherman pressed his ear to Eddie's heart and found its rhythm stronger, more regular, than before.

Eddie woke into a fever, looked for a familiar face, but saw only a woman with a gray stripe at the parting of her hair. Sometimes there was a man whose fish-smelling hands touched Eddie's forehead and chest. Eddie raved at these two—they'd stolen his pocket watch. They spoke of bringing him to a hospital. *No,* he murmured. *No!* And forced himself not to mention the pocket watch again.

When the fever broke, he sat upright on a kitchen chair, wrapped in a blanket made of feathers. Harlan, the fisherman, poured each of them a glass of clear spirit that tasted like rye bread. His grandson did schoolwork at the table by the stove. Harlan was Norwegian, born here. As a boy, he'd fished with his father to supply the lobster palaces, Rector's and Café Martin, Shanley's, the fishermen entertaining one another with gossip about the outsize appetites of Diamond Jim Brady and Lillian Russell: fourteen lobsters between them one night, and the lady had to remove her corset. Eddie listened with his own story ready—*I fell off a ship*—but the question of why he'd been in the harbor never came. He understood. Knowing another man's trouble made it yours, and Harlan was barely getting by, fishing to feed his family and trade with his neighbors for eggs and apples and milk.

With each new day, Eddie felt the mounting pressure of his life, so nearby. His mind was too weak to fathom what should happen next.

They would have to flee New York—but go where? To Agnes's people in Minnesota, who disdained him? He would perish in that muddy land of bawling animals hundreds of miles from the sea. To some place where they knew no one? Eddie found himself clinging to the forms of convalescence, closing his eyes and trying to sleep.

But Harlan knew. "You are well," he said. "Tomorrow you will tell me where to take you."

At sunrise he ferried Eddie to the West Side docks. A freighter from Brazil was just out of quarantine, hundreds of eager men waiting for the morning shape-up, scratching, smoking, gagging over the river. With Dunellen gone, Eddie no longer knew the hiring boss. It was September 1937.

He hung back, hands in the pockets of the loose-fitting trousers Harlan had bequeathed him, a cap pulled low over his eyes. The *Sea Cow*'s rusty hull raked the pier like a cur rubbing her scrofulous hide against a tree. A tramp ship with no set route, she grudgingly extruded her cargo of melons and rubber and coconuts. She'd an air of lazy complacency, like an old whore who knew she'd cornered the market. When the morning's unloading was done, Eddie walked up the gangway as he'd watched any number of criminals and gasheads and dope fiends do over the years, always marveling at what kind of desperation might lead a man to take such a step. His was a shady hire, no articles to sign, and the job was coal passer: lowliest of all engine room positions. But as Eddie descended the slippery ladders into the ship's broiling nether parts, he counted himself lucky. That was how much he dreaded going home.

CHAPTER TWENTY-SIX

Three days after the convoy scattered—nerve-racking days of cloudless skies and mild seas that required zigzagging day and night until the captain's frustration roiled throughout the ship—the barometer began, mercifully, to drop. Sparks typed up the daily weather report and brought it to Captain Kittredge in his office. A major storm was predicted. Eddie heard the master's whoop of celebration all the way from the wheelhouse.

By general quarters, the sky had clouded over, and there was a strong breeze. The captain advised the first mate that they would end the evasive variant of their course, although the storm wasn't due until early next morning.

"Even with the sea still calm, sir?" the mate asked.

"For exactly that reason," Kittredge said. "Dirty weather will slow us down again; this is our chance to make up some time."

During Eddie's eight-to-midnight watch, the *Elizabeth Seaman* performed her usual magic, steaming along at twelve knots. The barometer continued to drop, and the doors were closed and dogged to keep swells from breaking into the midship house. Farmingdale relieved Eddie at midnight, along with Roger, the deck cadet, who now stood watches with Farmingdale. Eddie and the first mate had concocted this change; since Cape Town, neither of them trusted the second mate.

By the time Eddie was ready to turn in, the ship was rolling on a rising swell. He climbed to the bridge a last time to check on Roger, who had been seasick and terrified while the *Elizabeth Seaman* negotiated the Roaring Forties. "I know you don't like rough seas," he told the cadet. "Just remember, U-boats don't, either."

"I've changed," Roger told him with shy pride. "I've my sea legs now, like you said."

Eddie saw a difference in the cadet—Roger had shaken off his gawky imbalance and looked taller, or perhaps he'd actually grown in the course of this voyage. Eddie stood beside him and looked out. The rising wind had swept away the stratus clouds and was blowing in towers of cumulus. A quarter moon appeared patchily, as if blinking Morse code. Eddie crossed to the port side of the bridge, where Farmingdale was, and felt the second mate stiffen. His palpable discomfort, along with the importunate moon, gave Eddie a feeling of unrest. Farmingdale gazed out, but it was hard to know what—or *if*—he saw. The binoculars hung at his neck.

"May I have the glasses, Second?"

Farmingdale handed them over. Eddie climbed up to the flying bridge and walked all the way around the smokestack, binoculars pressed to his eyes. The moon vanished behind clouds, and the rolls of ocean were barely touched by light. Two points abaft of the port beam, he saw a straight dark edge. Eddie blinked and lowered the glasses, then raised them again. It was still there: a straightness one didn't find in nature. It had to be a conning tower—the raised structure of a submarine—yet disbelief plucked at Eddie even as he shouted down the ladder at Roger, "Get the captain. I'll ring for GQ."

Captain Kittredge was on the bridge in an instant. He elbowed Farmingdale aside and held the glasses to his eyes. Then he barked at Red, the AB at the helm, "Hard right." To Eddie, now at the engine room telegraph, he said, "Full speed. Give me all the revolutions you've got."

Eddie communicated the order to the engine room and felt corresponding vibrations under his feet as the engineers opened the throttle. The AB turned the wheel hard. The general quarters alarm had brought everyone on deck, and men hurried to their gun stations in their Mae Wests, as life vests were affectionately known. Using the flying bridge's sound-powered telephone, Lieutenant Rosen ordered the five-inch stern gun to fire at the conning tower. A blast tore through the windy dark, and the tower submerged unscathed. Still, U-boats could make only seven knots underwater. The *Elizabeth Seaman* would outrun it easily.

Eddie stood by, ready to operate the telegraph. Suddenly, Roger was yelling into his face. The cadet pointed, and Eddie saw a second conning tower fully exposed, three points off the starboard bow. The hard right had brought them toward it. At that same moment an explosion shook the ship. Hatches blew open, and overhead booms crashed onto the deck. The *Elizabeth Seaman* shuddered, and her stack disgorged a ball of flame whose orange blaze illuminated everyone on the decks and then floated, crackling like a giant dissolving sun, over the sea. There was a reek of burning oil followed by deep silence as the ship's engines went still.

Eddie charged down ladders through the dark midship house toward the engine room. The emergency lights on the bulkheads illuminated if you gave them a quarter turn, and he twisted a few of these as he went, oil dust collecting in his mouth. He found smoke pouring from the engine room door. Ochylski, the third engineer, staggered from it, bloody and drenched in oil. "The boiler blew," he panted.

Eddie pushed past him, sliding down hand rails, his feet hardly touching the ladders. But he couldn't get to the engine room deck; the flames were too high. No one on watch down there would still be alive. He ran to his stateroom, threw on his Mae West, and seized his abandon-ship package and flashlight. He heard the forward three-inch cannon firing, along with the rear five-inch, and imagined the U-boats diving to evade the blasts and then being churned by the rising sea, unable to fire again. On the boat deck, he tied his bag containing clothing, sextant, cigarettes, brandy, and his *How to Abandon Ship* pamphlet—inside his own boat, number four. The davits were already swung out, but Eddie hesitated to unlash the boats in gale winds when there was no order yet to abandon ship. As long as the fire was contained belowdecks and the *Elizabeth Seaman* stable, they would be far safer riding out the storm aboard than in the lifeboats.

The second torpedo seemed to explode against Eddie's sternum. It must have come from the first U-boat, or possibly a third they hadn't seen, for it hit below the waterline on the port side, aft of the midship house, between the number four and five holds. It was followed by a juddering rumble deep inside the ship. Eddie had never heard this sound, but he knew it was the noise of the ocean invading the *Elizabeth Seaman's* holds. Almost immediately, her after end began to list toward the sea. Captain Kittredge gave the abandon-ship order, and a dreamlike atmosphere ensued, confusion magnified by the darkness and the roll of the sea, which cuffed broadside at the dead ship like a cat trying to rouse an exhausted mouse. Pugh, the ancient third cook, was still at his twenty-milimeter-gun station on the flying bridge. Eddie took the old man's arm and urged him to his lifeboat, number two—he'd memorized the boat lists. On the bridge deck, he looked in at Sparks, who was stuffing codebooks into the perforated metal suitcases that were supposed to sink them.

"You need to get to your boat," Eddie said. "Number one."

"What's your fucking hurry, Mac?" Sparks asked with a laugh. "None of these arseholes has answered me yet; I'm going to send the SOS one more fucking time." The radio, now on auxiliary power, looked conspicuously alive on the burnt-out ship. Eddie offered to carry the emergency radio to the captain's boat for Sparks. The radioman kissed his cheek. "Bless your fucking heart, Third," he said.

Eddie grabbed the bulky emergency radio from the wheelhouse. He felt as if time had fanned open sideways, allowing him to move laterally as well as forward, so that any amount of activity became possible even as the slant of the *Elizabeth Seaman's* decks grew more pronounced. On the crowded boat deck, he placed the radio in lifeboat one, the captain's. Across from it on the port side, the mate's boat had already launched: two men rowing, the rest crouched at the bottom to stabilize it in the heavy swells, which shoved the boat back against the hull of the ship. The bosun knelt at the tiller, and even through the gale, Eddie heard his bellowed commands and knew that boat two would get away.

Where his own boat should have been, he found Ochylski, his second-in-command, standing by the falls looking down. The boat had been released empty and now bobbed uselessly on the *Elizabeth Seaman*'s lee side.

"What the hell happened?" Eddie screamed at the third engineer over the wind.

"She just . . . went down," Ochylski said. His face was deathly white under a sheen of fuel oil, empty-looking without his pipe. He'd gone into shock, Eddie thought—perhaps had released the boat by accident.

"Never mind," he said, trying to suppress his habitual need to find the guilty party. Double-ender lifeboats were commodious, and there was more than enough room for everyone in the two remaining. Directly across, on the port side, Farmingdale's boat was being lowered into heavy seas, a gaggle of men preparing to scramble down the falls once she was waterborne. Boat one, the captain's, was about to be lowered. Eddie stood in the driving rain. He experienced a strange reluctance to leave the *Elizabeth Seaman*. Through the soles of his feet, he felt underwater explosions as seawater poured down her passageways and struck the hot boiler. In occasional gusts of live ash from her stack, he made out the deck cargo they'd worked so hard to load and secure: the Shermans, the jeeps. So much effort and worry and expense. It seemed like not enough to emerge with just their lives.

A thought came to him: Sparks. The radioman was assigned to boat one, the captain's, but when Eddie scanned the crowd of men waiting to slide down the falls, he didn't see him. He ducked back inside the midship house, now tilting at a crazy angle, and climbed to the bridge deck. He found Sparks in his chair, inert as his radio, and yanked him onto his feet.

"Leave me the fuck alone," Sparks said weakly.

"Come on, you gimpy little shit." Enraged, Eddie slung Sparks onto his back and hauled him slowly down the ladder to the boat deck.

"Interfering bastard," Sparks muttered.

All four lifeboats had gone, and the boat deck was empty. Through the downpour, Eddie saw the stern of the *Elizabeth Seaman* submerged halfway to her mizzenmast, waves breaking over her rear gun tub. On the lee side, a pontoon raft had released automatically from its slide rack and now floated by the deck. Still carrying the radioman on his back, metal leg brace cracking his heels, Eddie fumbled down a ladder to the main deck and began stepping sideways down a grade worthy of San Francisco, taking care not to slip on the slick iron deck. He carried Sparks to where the raft floated, pulled it toward him by its painter rope, and half rolled, half threw Sparks over the gunwale onto its wood lattice. As Eddie was vaulting over the rail onto the raft, he heard a thundering disturbance overhead: cargo was tearing loose from the ship's nearly vertical bow deck. Tanks and jeeps snapped their chains and tumbled end over end like boulders, crushing booms and masts, caroming over the midship house and smashing onto the after deck in explosions of metal parts, before flinging themselves into the sea. Eddie tried to cut the painter holding the raft to the ship, certain he and Sparks would be crushed by the onslaught. But it was wire rope, and even his bowie knife couldn't hack through it. The *Elizabeth Seaman* shrieked and shivered in an agony of tormented steel as Eddie scrambled to retrieve the ax that was secured to each raft. But before he could chop again at the painter, the ship's doomed bulk discharged an aching, burpy, primordial groan and slid under the sea, pulling their raft down with her. Eddie and Sparks were left in the water. He seized the radioman around the chest and braced himself for the vortex, a body memory of holding boys at Rockaway Beach coming to him suddenly. "Hold your breath," he shouted to Sparks. But no vortex came. The sea bubbled and frothed where the ship had been, pushing Eddie and Sparks away.

Eddie peered around wildly for the lifeboats, but in rain and darkness and high swells, he couldn't see any. He made out a cluster of red lights from Mae Wests: another raft, possibly, crowded with men. Holding Sparks around the chest, Eddie lay on his back and kicked to propel them toward it. The radioman was so slight, a bird-like assemblage of bones and flesh without even a coat, much less a life vest. Eddie felt the sea convulsing underneath them as the ship plunged. The surface was covered with oil—he tasted it, felt it in his eyes and nostrils. He kicked and paddled, checking occasionally to see that he was still moving in the right direction. Eventually, someone hauled him out, still clutching Sparks. Eddie lay on the raft, unsure whether Sparks was alive. When at last he opened his eyes, he saw Bogues, a navy gunner, beside him. "You're a hell of a swimmer," Bogues said.

Eddie began to retch onto the raft's latticework timbers. Sparks was retching, too, which presumably meant he'd survived. Even as Eddie heaved up oil-smelling vomit into the oil-smelling sea, his mind was straining, sifting: Bogues had been on Farmingdale's boat, number three. Why was he on a raft? Had three gone down? The raft was composed of identical nine-by-twelve-foot wood-timbered lattices with steel flotation drums sandwiched in between. Eddie hooked his arm around a timber and held on. The swells were enormous, but the ship's oil slick kept them from breaking and allowed the raft to slide over their crests. Eddie kept raising his head to look for the ship, but nothing marked the spot where seven thousand tons of welded steel loaded with nine thousand tons of cargo had floated thirty minutes before—not a depression, not even a patch of effervescence, to recall the magical girl who'd carried them halfway 'round the world.

From Bogues, who lay beside him, Eddie gleaned that lifeboat three had been broken against the side of the ship by the swells. Everyone had made it to the raft except the injured engineer, who had disappeared in the waves. "Ochylski went under?" Eddie said in alarm. But the gunner didn't know his name, and Eddie refused to believe it was Ochylski. He pictured the third engineer holding a bight of lifeline that ran around the perimeter of the raft, smiling sardonically at their predicament. With Eddie and Sparks, there were twenty-nine of them aboard, Bogues said—four more than the raft was built to hold.

Now the storm set upon them in earnest, trying to suck them from the raft as if they were bits of food caught between its teeth. In flashes of lightning, Eddie counted bodies with the cringing hope of a gambler after a roll—four sevens—yes, plus himself: twenty-nine. The raft scaled swells so mountainous that he feared it would be pitched backward end over end, flinging men away and drowning Sparks, whom he'd lashed to the timbers with his belt. Each time, the raft managed to slide over the crest and skid down into the trough to begin another climb. After a while, Eddie stopped counting men and felt for Sparks's leg brace with his foot. The arm he'd fastened around the planks stiffened as if in rigor mortis. He no longer could tell up from down. At times a tense, fragmentary sleep overcame him. Luminescence flared from the sea: plankton, Eddie knew, having encountered this phenomenon in the Pacific. Now their glow seemed an emanation from the ocean floor: the *Elizabeth Seaman* and other lost ships, hundreds over centuries, signaling up from the deep.

Morning brought a dirty light on a high confused sea. The worst of the storm had passed. Six of their number had vanished: the first cook; the AB called Red; a gunner; a wiper; a messman; and Pelemonde, a dreamy ordinary who had been a favorite with the deck crew. Bogues was still there, along with Farmingdale, the two cadets, and a mix of naval guardsmen, ordinaries, firemen, and Sparks, who had been fixed in place by Eddie's belt. Pugh, the old salt, had somehow held on. *Iron men in wooden boats.* For a long time the group hardly spoke, absorbing the loss of their shipmates. For Eddie that included Ochylski, who was nowhere to be found.

Farmingdale was the highest-ranking officer, which put him in command of the raft with Eddie as his second. For all his reservations about the second mate, Eddie was glad to have the ship's navigating officer on board. Better yet, Sparks reported that his SOS signal had been answered, meaning there was a good chance of rescue when the storm subsided.

At midday, with rain still falling on and off, someone spotted between swells a distant lifeboat riding low—perhaps overcrowded. They broke out the raft's oars, and Eddie made an oarlock for each by twisting a bight of lifeline around it—a trick he'd learned from his pamphlet. A gunner and a fireman rose onto their knees and took an oar each, men anchoring them fore and aft. When they managed to get close enough to see the boat more clearly, they found it empty and swamped. It must be Eddie's boat, number four—the one that had gone off prematurely. This was excellent luck. Compared with a pontoon raft, a lifeboat was a palace: 297 cubic feet of shelter, equipment, and supplies, not to mention a sail and a tiller. Eddie's abandon-ship package would be tied inside, containing a sextant, blankets, and extra waterproof rations. The cigarettes would likely be soaked, but the bottle of South African rum would be more than welcome.

They lashed the raft to the boat, and men took turns boarding and bailing. To Eddie's confusion, the boat was marked number two—the first mate's—yet there was a sack tied in the very spot where he'd tied his own. Mystified, he pried open this sack and found it crammed with books bloated by seawater into a sodden mash. With a twitch of fear, he understood: only one man in the world would rescue from a sinking ship a sack containing just books. And he'd last seen the bosun at the tiller of the first mate's boat, number two, which had gone off first.

He explained his findings to Farmingdale. "There were seventeen men on that boat, with life vests," Eddie said. "We must search for survivors."

Farmingdale made a skeptical gesture, but Eddie persisted to a chorus of agreement from the other men. Farmingdale shrugged and remained on the raft, recalcitrant, while the rest of them prepared the boat for a search. Pugh, the old salt, pronounced the wind still too high to raise a sail. A set of oars and oarlocks had been lost from the lifeboat, but the spares were stowed. They would row in a square, a thousand strokes in each direction, blowing the whistles on their Mae Wests every five strokes. Everyone, including Farmingdale, moved from the raft onto the boat, but they left the raft attached, unsure how many survivors they might find. Eddie carefully opened the steel cylinder containing emergency food rations and distributed a portion of pemmican and two malted milk tablets to each man, along with six ounces of water from the jug—the contents of which had been changed just four days earlier—in an enamel measuring cup.

Eddie's ears began playing tricks as soon as the rowing began. Every pause seemed full of human-sounding cries, but they completed the eastern portion of the square without sighting anyone. They turned south with fresh rowers. Three hundred strokes in, several men heard a faint whistle, and Roger gave a shout from the bow. Abeam to port, Eddie made out an intermittent fleck of what looked like flotsam. As they rowed toward it slowly on the high seas, he saw that it was the bosun and Wyckoff lashed together. Carefully, they extended oars to the floaters and hauled them over the side of the lifeboat. Both men lay at the bottom, shivering violently, then lost consciousness. Sparks removed his leg brace and spread himself on top of the waterlogged pair to warm them.

At sunset, the sky swung open like a hatch, revealing an exotic cargo of pink and orange. They had searched the remainder of the day but found no one else. The swells began to moderate, and Eddie distributed another round of rations. Wyckoff and the bosun were able to eat and drink, although Wyckoff said little and the bosun not a word. Eddie found it eerie to have his nemesis be so silent. It was like having the bosun's ghost on board.

As darkness fell and the weather calmed, everyone's spirits rose. The discovery of the lifeboat virtually assured that they were in range of where the *Elizabeth Seaman* had gone down; help would likely reach them the following day. The best course now was to keep a sharp lookout and stay with the current, which rescuers would take into account when choosing where to search. They lowered the sea anchor, a cone-shaped canvas bag, over the bow of the lifeboat to fix them to the current. They left the raft attached, to make themselves more visible to planes. Then they set watches and took turns sleeping huddled together at the bottom of the boat on life preservers, or sitting on the thwarts with their heads against the gunwales. Eddie made a notch with his jackknife on the thwart where he slept, marking the passage of twenty-four hours away from the *Elizabeth Seaman.*

They woke shivering, heavy dew on their sodden clothing. Eddie distributed rations of food and water. As the sun rose, Wyckoff told them that a rogue wave had overturned boat two in the storm, sending all seventeen men into the sea. Everyone had managed to stay with the boat, clinging to the lifelines on its gunwales and waiting for a chance to flip it back over, when a shark had attacked the second cook. Some men swam away in panic at his screams; others, including Wyckoff and the bleeding man, scrambled onto the overturned boat. This proved an error, for when another wave righted it, they were tossed into a frenzy of sharks. Wyckoff had been spared somehow. He could hardly swim, but his Mae West had kept him afloat. At daybreak he caught sight of the bosun, who swam to him. They had been trying to reach the swamped lifeboat ever since.

Eddie kept his eyes on the bosun as Wyckoff spoke, wondering what kind of terror it must have taken to silence such a man.

When the sun was up, they raised the lifeboat mast, and Eddie ran up the yellow flag that was among the boat's emergency provisions. Shortly after noon, they spotted a plane flying low. Everyone screamed and jumped from boat and raft, waving their shirts—except the bosun, who sat quietly at the bottom of the boat. The plane flew away, apparently not having seen them, a blow that left all of them spent. Still, no one doubted that the plane had been searching for survivors of the *Elizabeth Seaman,* and hours of daylight remained. Four men stood every watch, one facing each direction. Eddie grated his eyes against the line of horizon. It seemed always on the verge of yielding up a ship, but hours of warm, clear weather—perfect rescue weather—passed without any further sightings.

By sunset the men were baffled, grumbling, hungry. What was the matter with those fucking planes? Were blind men flying them? Eddie said nothing. He was wishing Kittredge were there. It was impossible to imagine a rescue plane bypassing their lucky captain.

The bosun sat vacantly at the bottom of the boat. "Some help you were, lazy bastard," Farmingdale chuckled with a glance at the others. Eddie sensed he was trying to provoke the bosun into speaking, as if that might change their luck. Eddie wondered if it might. "We know you can talk," Farmingdale needled him. "Third knows better than anyone." He cast a sly look Eddie's way—an invitation. Eddie gave a neutral smile.

On their third dawn, the wind was no more than a breeze. Farmingdale thought they should ride the current one more day before setting sail for land. They sighted a ship far away, but their leaps and cries did no good. In the last of the daylight, they prepared to begin sailing the next morning toward Africa's long sandy coast. The *Elizabeth Seaman* had sunk a thousand miles due east of Somaliland. Farmingdale estimated that the current had taken them north, which would make the distance to land even shorter. Sailing with a good westerly wind, they might make landfall in fifteen days or less. The combined rations from the raft and lifeboat—supplemented, hopefully, by fishing and more rain—should be enough to sustain them that long. And they might still be rescued on the way.

Night fell cold and hard. They lit flares at the same time from boat and raft, and continued their watches, hoping to spot a neutral ship with her running lights on. Eddie sat on a thwart, unable to sleep. He thought of the ocean as it looked on pilot charts, crowded with depth contours and shipping lanes and arcs of current. There seemed no relation between those images and the emptiness surrounding him now. Overhead was the extravagant canopy of stars that had so astounded him when he first went to sea, a shimmering excess like the inside of Ali Baba's cave. Viewed from the deck of a ship, that sky was a spectacle reserved for those privileged enough to see it. Now the stars looked random, accidental—like the sea itself. Anna had stopped coming to him in his dreams; he'd traveled beyond her reach. Eddie understood that he had passed through another layer of life into something deeper, colder, and more pitiless.

He made a third notch in the thwart.

CHAPTER TWENTY-SEVEN

After the dive, Anna turned Lydia's bed on its side so it leaned against the wall. She closed the door to her parents' bedroom, moved the kitchen table into the front room, and dragged the radio there, too. She wanted the apartment to be different, to mark the change she felt—the weight of her discovery.

Her father's pocket watch leaked seawater for several days. When it dried, its hands were frozen at ten past nine. Cupping her palm around its lozenge of weight gave Anna a surge of strength, of protection. It was a relic from an underworld she'd visited once, under perilous conditions, purely in order to retrieve it. She slept with it under her pillow.

Within days of the dive, she knew that she wanted to leave the apartment. Girls weren't allowed in the rooming house where Bascombe lived. There was a YWCA near her building, but it had a waiting list—and anyway, she wanted to be closer to the Yard. There were rooms to let along Sands Street; she'd seen the odd handwritten card in the window of a bar or uniform shop. She wondered if it might be possible to rent one of those rooms without anyone finding out she was living there. But the wrong kinds of girls did such things, and the danger of discovery was too great.

One evening she chanced upon Rose leaving work. As they walked arm in arm through the Sands Street gate, Anna mentioned her dilemma—rather, a version of it in which her mother had to return to the Midwest to nurse an ill sister, and naturally Anna couldn't live alone. Rose clapped her hands: her mother's tenant, a newlywed, had decided to follow her husband to a naval base in Del Mar, California. There would be a room to let in their apartment, on Clinton Avenue! Anna agreed on the spot to take it.

Since she was earning enough money to keep the apartment and rent the room at Rose's, Anna decided not to mention her move to her mother or aunt. It required too much explanation. She and Brianne met less often anyway, and usually at a picture theater. As long as Anna collected the mail every couple of days, even the neighbors weren't likely to miss her.

She bought a large cardboard please-don't-rain suitcase (as her father used to call them), filled it with clothing, toiletries, and Ellery Queens, drank what was left in the milk bottle, and wrapped the butter in a dish towel. She sat once more at the table where it seemed now that she'd spent the better portion of her life—eating, sewing, cutting paper dolls out of butcher paper. The fire escape cleaved the sunlight into slabs, each swarming with dust like the glittering mica flecks in the water of Wallabout Bay. The building felt heavy and still. In the kitchen, she ran her hands over the tin-lined sink where she and her mother had bathed Lydia until she was too big to fit inside it. She looked into the mirror where her father used to shave. Then she left the apartment, locking the door behind her.

Descending the six flights, she half expected a curious neighbor to intercept and question her. But no one came or even—that she could hear—shuffled to a peephole. Perhaps everyone was still asleep. She stepped into the softening air of late March and noticed strangers on the block. A man carried a suitcase, hurrying, looking up at numbers chiseled over doorways. He was arriving.

Anna's new bedroom was at the back of Rose's apartment, facing a tree that looked as if it were lifting barbells. An old man on a horse cart delivered butter and milk. Rich people once lived on Clinton Avenue, and the biggest houses had their own stables, empty now, some used for automobiles. Two of Rose's brothers were in the army, but the youngest, Hiram, was still at home, and he covered his school-books in the same licorice-scented oilcloth Anna had used as a child to cover hers. She adored this new home.

Some evenings, she met Rose outside their old shop and they rode the Flushing Avenue streetcar together, sharing an evening newspaper. Only a few weeks ago, Anna had watched Rose from outside this same streetcar, feeling she might drown in her solitude. She touched the pocket watch.

On afternoons when she dived, she worked later, and Rose knew not to wait. Those evenings, Anna went to Sands Street with the other divers. She was careful to suck a peppermint on the streetcar back to Rose's, not wanting to smell of beer when she said good night to Rose's parents.

Living with Rose made it awkward to spend time with Charlie Voss, who was still Rose's supervisor. Anna went to his office to explain after the marrieds had gone home one evening.

"I understand, of course," he said. "It's a shame."

"I'll miss you, Charlie."

"You'll stop by now and then?" he asked. "When the coast is clear?"

"I promise."

Leaving the Yard after work, she still looked for Dexter Styles's automobile on Sands Street—always with a throb of disappointment when she didn't see it, followed by relief.

Two weeks after her harbor dive, while she was waiting for the other divers to get their food at the Oval Bar, Anna opened her *Herald Tribune* to glance at the encouraging headlines she was coming to expect: Rommel barely hanging on in Tunisia; the Russian army forcing the Germans back toward Smolensk. When she flipped the paper over, her eye caught on an item at the lower left:

MISSING NIGHTCLUB OWNER FOUND DEAD
BULLET-RIDDLED BODY LEFT NEAR
ABANDONED RACETRACK.

Anna stared at the photograph. Although she was not aware of reading, words seemed to crawl inside her: *A two-week search for missing nightclub impresario Dexter Styles ended in gruesome tragedy on Sunday, when Andrew Metuchen and Sandy Kupech of Sheepshead Bay, both ten years old, discovered his body near the vestiges of the old racetrack . . .*

She pushed the newspaper away and took a sip from her beer. She watched the divers around her wolfing down bay mussels and pigs in blankets. Her head felt like a balloon floating several feet above her body. She heard breaking glass and realized she was falling.

They brought her to with smelling salts. She lay on her side, sawdust under her cheek. Ruby's face hovered just above, her smeary eye makeup close enough to Anna that its floral sweetness sickened her. She vomited and tried to stand. Eventually, Bascombe and Marle hoisted one of her arms around each of their necks and helped her up. They walked her out of the bar past smirking sailors who presumed she was drunk.

The cold street air was a relief. Anna walked with her eyes shut, relinquishing most of her weight. It felt like sleepwalking. Something awful had happened in the bar, but she'd escaped. After many twists and turns, they were indoors again, and she recognized the briny burnt-rubber smell of the diving dresses. They'd brought her to the recompression tank.

Marle got in with her. "Any pains?" he asked, setting the dial. "What about before you fainted?"

"It isn't the bends," she told him, and then remembered what had made her faint. Her hands began to shake.

"Who was your tender?"

"Katz," she said through chattering teeth. "But I wasn't down too long."

"He was the one wearing the watches."

She vomited again.

When her recompression was complete, Marle unscrewed the door to the tank, and they stepped back out. Bascombe and Ruby were waiting. Bascombe gave Anna a long look through his narrow silver eyes, and she wondered whether he'd seen the headline. They hadn't spoken again about their illegal dive beyond noting that the equipment smuggled from the Yard had been returned without incident. Anna had been afraid her friends would avoid her after that night, but it was the opposite: now the bond between them felt familial and complex.

Marle agreed not to record Anna's symptoms or recompression in the diving log if she promised to go directly to the hospital and have her vital signs checked. A marine guard ferried her up the hill on his motorbike. She described to an intake nurse what had happened, and was told to wait. The newspaper headline floated in Anna's mind preposterously. It couldn't be true, but it exhausted her to keep discounting it.

A naval nurse woke her eventually; she'd dozed in her chair with her head against the wall. By her wristwatch, it was after nine. The nurse looked hardly older than Anna, a blond chignon tucked behind her cap. She took Anna's temperature and administered the blood pressure cuff with a look of pure concentration that Anna admired. With a small bright light, she peered inside Anna's eyes and ears. She held a cold stethoscope to her heart and noted each result on a clipboard.

"Everything looks fine," she said. "How do you feel?"

"All right," Anna said. "Just tired."

"The doctor wanted me to ask whether you're married."

"No," Anna said, surprised. "Why?"

"If you were, he would recommend a pregnancy test. Some girls faint early on."

"Ah."

"He thought you might have taken your ring off to dive."

"Did you . . . give me the test?"

"No, of course not. I would have to draw blood."

"It isn't necessary," Anna said.

She left the hospital, stepping between square white columns down a shallow flight of steps that faced the grassy oval where she and Rose had given blood the previous fall. She lingered in the shadows, fixing her eyes on a pale columnar sculpture she remembered from that day.

It had an eagle on top. She hadn't had her monthly since joining the diving program—two months. She'd assumed that diving itself was the reason, and had been relieved, dreading the complications. This new interpretation arrived not as a possibility but as a certainty.

Anna returned to the apartment to find Rose's father in the front room, reading the *Forward* by his green glass desk lamp. She thought she saw a flicker of disapproval—or perhaps just concern—at her tardy, disheveled state. In her own room, she lay in bed with her hands over her belly and stared at the tree outside her window. She reminded herself that she didn't know for sure. But she did know. She was in trouble, at long last.

The next morning she left early, without eating. She placed the pocket watch in her purse with an ominous sense that she'd reached the limit of its protective powers. Riding the streetcar to Flushing Avenue, she was stricken with nausea compounded by monstrous hunger. At a cafeteria on the corner of Flushing and Clinton, she joined a legion of Naval Yard workers lining up for eggs, hash browns, coffee, and dry toast—there was a freeze on butter and other "edible fats." She felt steadier after having eaten, and walked the rest of the way to work. She stopped at Lieutenant Axel's office to say good morning. He was always the first to arrive.

"Kerrigan," he called. "I was hoping you'd turn up. Come in a minute." When she was standing before his desk, he said, "I've five new trainees coming in today, don't know their elbows from their asses. What have you scheduled?"

"Tending in the morning, diving in the afternoon."

"All right if I send these dopes along and hope they learn a thing or two by watching?"

"Of course, sir."

The change in her relations with Lieutenant Axel had happened perhaps three weeks before. From one day to the next, he seemed to grow accustomed to Anna, as if the attrition of habit had caused the scaffolding of his prejudice to crumble spontaneously. It was a stunning, almost magical reversal, and although it had begun before Anna found the pocket watch, she felt as if the watch had catalyzed the transformation. Now she found herself cast in the unlikely role of favorite—*pet*—as if the animus between herself and Lieutenant Axel had been converted into intimacy. He spoke to her in shorthand, and she understood it. His disparaging remarks about girls were compliments to Anna, for she was not like other girls. "Do me a favor, Kerrigan," he'd told her the week before. "Cover up your hair on the barge, or we'll have every birdbrained secretary on the goddamn Yard pounding on our door."

"They might not want to dive, sir."

"Probably true. There aren't many as crazy as you. But I'm warning you, if they start turning up in droves, it'll be your job to send them packing."

"Unless they're any good," she'd said. But the lieutenant merely snorted, as she'd known he would—wanted him to, it seemed to Anna later, when her disingenuousness shamed her.

"Get a feel for the new men," he told her now. "Tell me if any stands out. And Kerrigan." He lowered his voice, glancing at the door. "Rattle them a little. You know what I mean. Separate the men from the boys."

She left his office feeling buoyed by the flattery and guilty for enjoying it. She put on her work clothes and went outside to the pier. Sunlight poured through the building ways, and she closed her eyes, letting it warm her face. The pressure of her problem began to ease, like a fresh blow that had finally ceased to ache. The solution was obvious: diving would put an end to it. Trouble like hers was incompatible with this work; her monthly would come. That afternoon she had cramps while inspecting the hull of a torpedoed destroyer, five trainees observing her from the barge. She worried that the diving dress would be soiled—luxurious fretting that made her smile in the privacy of her helmet. When at last she asked Greer to stand guard at the restroom, she was incredulous to find she'd been wrong.

Each morning she awoke convinced that her trouble would end

that day. By evening she was too exhausted to dwell on the fact that it hadn't. The weather warmed enough that she and Rose began walking home along Clinton Avenue from Flushing rather than take a second trolley. On Friday, which was Sabbath for the Jews, Rose and her family lit two candles after supper and gathered around the table with a loaf of bread. While they added extra blessings for Sig and Caleb, in the army, Anna issued her own fervid prayer: *Please let my trouble end.* Unless her trouble ended, all of this would shortly disappear: the candles, the bread. Rose and her family. There were other kinds of homes where girls in trouble went to live.

In a separate chamber of Anna's mind, a clock had been set in motion. If the diving failed to work, there was another way, but you couldn't wait too long. Two weeks after her faint, Anna opened her eyes one morning and thought, *I have to do something.* She'd no idea how to begin, but the answer came as if she'd been planning it all along: She would find Nell. Nell would know what to do. Nell had done it herself.

After work, she took the subway to Union Square. Old men who'd fought in the Great War were playing chess in their heavy coats, pins and medals affixed to their hats. "I've Heard That Song Before" played on a portable phonograph, and teenagers were holding each other in their coats, dancing to the music. Watching them, Anna was stricken with longing. She had danced that way with boys at Brooklyn College, but she'd never felt as innocent as these teenagers looked. She had always been hiding something. She was hiding something now.

Twenty-one Gramercy Park South. It was uncanny how Nell had made her repeat it.

At the mention of Nell's first name—still the only name Anna had—a doorman in a gray military-looking uniform went to a wall switchboard and plugged in a cable. Anna touched the pocket watch. She'd hoped that Nell would be at home preparing for the evening, and it seemed she was right. An elevator man ferried her to the eighth floor and released her into an alcove containing two paneled doors facing each other across a gush of red roses whose breadth was amplified by a mirror hanging just behind them. Anna's wan reflection startled her. She was pinching color into her cheeks when Nell emerged from the left door wearing a satin peignoir whose lapels effervesced with tiny white feathers, like soapsuds. She seemed to take a moment to recall who Anna was; then she threw her arms around her, holding her cigarette away so as not to burn her. "How are you, darling?" she cried. "I haven't seen you in ages, you naughty thing. Where have you been hiding?" Anna made a neutral murmur to each shrill utterance, and in the course of this back-and-forth, something settled in Nell. She drew away, narrowing her eyes at Anna. "Come in and tell me what's wrong," she said.

Anna returned to Gramercy Park early Sunday morning. She and Nell walked to Park Avenue, Nell's sharp heels striking the pavement like nails being hammered. Her peroxided hair appeared blanched in the morning sun, and there were blue shadows under her eyes. She'd become a person who looked best in artificial light.

When they were seated in a taxi, Anna returned to the topic of price softly, so the cabbie wouldn't hear. She'd no notion what the procedure would cost and was hoping she could pay over time.

"Hammond is paying," Nell whispered back. "I told him it was for me."

"Suppose he finds out?"

"Believe me," Nell said, "he owes me."

"Thank you," Anna breathed, but the phrase seemed hardly sufficient. "And for coming with me. I never expected it."

Nell shrugged. There was something curiously impersonal about her ministrations; Anna was fairly certain she would have done the same for any girl who came to her in trouble.

"You heard about Dexter Styles," Nell said.

Anna fixed her gaze on the blur of tall gray buildings outside the window. "I saw it in the paper," she said. "Horrible."

"No one talks of anything else."

"Do they know who did it? Or why?"

"There are a thousand rumors. Some people say it was the Chicago Syndicate. They're more ruthless than the New York one, supposedly."

"Why would they kill him?" Anna asked.

"There's an investigation, but no one will talk. Unless they want the same treatment."

"Maybe Dexter Styles talked."

Nell considered this. "But why?" she said. "People say he was three quarters legitimate. Seven eighths! Why risk all that?"

"Had he children?" Anna knew the answer, but she wanted to keep the conversation going. It relieved her to talk about Dexter Styles.

"Twin sons and a daughter. Stunner of a wife—society girl, rich family. He'd the world by the tail, that's what everyone thought."

"It's so sad," Anna said, and felt a welling of sorrow. She fixed her eyes on the window, afraid that Nell would know.

"People were crying at the club," Nell said.

His death was shared by many—by hundreds, Anna thought, and felt herself dissolve into their midst. She had known Dexter Styles much less than those others. Hardly at all. Yet darts of memory pierced her resolve: the feel of him in her arms; his hoarse whisper. And what she was going to do now.

The taxi brought them to the corner of East Seventy-fourth Street, just blocks from Dr. Deerwood's office. The coincidence dazed Anna. It had just gone April—they would have been bringing Lydia for her next appointment in a matter of weeks. She wondered whether Nell's doctor might be in the same building as Dr. Deerwood, the same office—whether he might actually *be* Dr. Deerwood. Chilly sunlight flooded the intersection; pigeons crowded the air. Nell put on a pair of dark sunglasses, like a picture star. Her pale wool coat had epaulettes of gold braid on the shoulders. Church bells began to ring.

"Where is the office?" Anna asked.

"Down the street. He doesn't like taxis to stop outside on week-ends. It draws attention."

They walked toward Madison Avenue. Anna's head ached, and she wished the bells would stop. In the middle of the block, Nell turned to a row house with striped awnings and sculpted hedges. Down a small flight of stairs, a rectangular brass plaque read DR. SOFFIT, OBSTETRICS. Nell pressed a buzzer and a door-pull released, admitting them to a waiting area akin to Dr. Deerwood's in its sumptuousness, although the decor was different. This office had silvery wall-to-wall carpeting and a crescent-shaped couch upholstered in gray velvet. Anna began to sweat. The church bells seemed to ring inside her head. "I wish they would stop," she whispered.

Nell jumped. "Who?"

A faint chemical odor hung on the air as if, behind the carpet-ing and velvet, there were a hospital room. And there must be. You couldn't have an operation on a crescent-shaped couch.

"I was nervous, too, my first time," Nell said. She sounded ner-vous now.

"How many times has it been?"

"Three. Well, two. This would be the third."

"What about after?"

"You'll be drowsy," Nell said. "Crampy. But fine, really. By the next day you're good as new."

Anna hadn't meant that, exactly, but it hardly mattered. Mingled with her fear was an accumulation of hope, familiar from years of bringing Lydia to Dr. Deerwood. The doctor would come. The doctor would come! Magazines had been fanned precisely over a lacquered coffee table: *Collier's, McClure's, The Saturday Evening Post.* Nell opened a copy of *Silver Screen,* and Anna looked over her shoulder at the blondes: Betty Grable, Veronica Lake, Lana Turner, all of whom once seemed like possible versions of Lydia. Anna fixed her eyes on the door that led from this room to the next. The door was uphol-stered. A beautiful door. She found she was clutching Nell's hand.

"It doesn't hurt," Nell said. "He gives you chloroform and you go to sleep." She was looking at a feature about movie stars' hairstyles—rolls, waves, curls—but her eyes didn't move on the page. Anna sensed her wish to be done and away. Soon the doctor would come. Dread and longing churned in Anna's stomach.

She was staring at the door when it opened. Dr. Soffit was younger than she'd expected—that was to say, younger than Dr. Deerwood. He was tall and sandy-haired and wore a wedding band. He greeted Nell warmly and shook Anna's hand with a gentle earnestness, looking into her eyes. He led them through the upholstered door into a room that was less hospital-like than Anna had feared, with small paintings of fruit hanging from moldings. A high bed was covered with white sheets. In an adjacent room, Anna removed her slip and pulled a soft cotton smock over her brassiere and panties. Her flat, muscular belly seemed to mock the proceedings. Suppose it wasn't even true? Suppose she wasn't in trouble after all? *How could she know, without the test?*

Or had they given her the test?

Nell sat in a chair beside where Anna's head would go. "Miss Konopka won't see anything," Dr. Soffit said. "But she'll be right beside you, holding your hand while you sleep. Won't you, Miss Konopka?"

"You bet I will," Nell said. She seemed relieved to have the doctor there.

Konopka. *A Pollack,* Anna heard in her father's voice, and began to cry. She lay back on the table, legs straight in front of her, clutching her hipbones through the sheet. Nell lifted one of Anna's hands and pressed it between her own, which were trembling. "In thirty minutes this will be done," she said, but the gravity of the moment had burned off the layers of pretense that usually swirled around Nell, leaving her exposed in a state of raw urgency. "He's getting the chloroform now. Then you'll go to sleep."

"Try to relax, Miss Kerrigan," Dr. Soffit said.

He was behind Anna, out of sight, his voice indistinguishable from Dr. Deerwood's. Anna lurched upright, trying to see him. Her heart kicked in her chest.

"Relax," Dr. Soffit said gently. He sat down beside her, holding something in his hands. The doctor would come. The doctor had come! He was here to make everything right.

But it wasn't Dr. Soffit who came to Anna then; it was her sister. With an immediacy she hadn't experienced since the night with Dexter Styles, she recalled Lydia's milky, biscuity smell, the softness of her skin and hair. Her coiled, unfinished state. The fluttering insistence of her heart. And hovering around her always, like gossamer, the dream of who she might have been.

The dream: a running, beautiful girl, knees flashing in the sun. A girl glimpsed from the corner of the eye. It seemed to Anna now that she might bring that girl to life.

The doctor placed a cone over her mouth. Sweet fumes issued from it, a concentration of the chemical odor she'd detected in the anteroom. "No," she said.

Nell leaned over her, and Anna saw her own terror mirrored in the eyes of her friend. The fumes touched her brain, a sleepy shadow gathering like a cloud on the verge of discharging rain. She imagined leaving the doctor's office with no one, with nothing. A void inside her where something had been.

The running girl. The dream.

"No," she said again, to Nell. "Make him stop." But the cone muffled her voice, and she couldn't hear herself.

Somehow Nell understood—perhaps she read the meaning in Anna's eyes as they rolled back inside her head.

"Wait," Nell said sharply, and lifted the cone from her face.

CHAPTER TWENTY-EIGHT

Eddie worried that being confined to just the lifeboat, without the raft to spread out on, would feel impossibly cramped. He worried that Farmingdale would resist letting Pugh take charge of the sailing. He worried about how far they would have to deviate from their course to stay with the wind; whether they could make four knots using the sail; and he worried, above all, about rations: whether they should continue drinking three six-ounce allotments of water each day or cut one out; whether Sparks's fishing would ever yield a bite; whether they might somehow navigate toward an island, as the captain and mate of the SS *Travessa* had done in 1923. Those gentlemen had sailed two lifeboats seventeen hundred miles across the Indian Ocean, but they'd had instruments and charts. Eddie had only a compass.

What he hadn't considered, as he sat awake the night before they were to sail, craving a cigarette—just one, or better yet, fifty—was that the wind would die out.

On their fourth dawn, the air was hot and still, the sea like a sheen of sweat. The gunners wanted to row for the sake of doing something, and Farmingdale agreed, which forced Eddie to point out, as respectfully as he could, that rowing would waste energy and resources to no purpose. They were at least a thousand miles from the African coast—not a rowable distance. Other men joined Eddie's plea, and Farmingdale relented with the show of waggish whimsy that Eddie was coming to recognize as his way of confronting defeat.

They let it be a lost day, a day to rest up before sailing the next. Men not on watch avoided the sun by lying under the spray curtain in the lifeboat, or under the boat cover, which they spread out like a tarp on the raft. At night they set off the last of their flares and maintained their watches. The cold kept waking Eddie. He thought he felt a wind, a spray of surf, but it turned out he was dreaming.

The next day was the same, and the next. The only bearable hours were in the early morning, when the sun sucked the dew from their boat and fell deliciously on their chilled bodies; and the evening, when a first intimation of cool salved their scorched limbs like the touch of a nurse, before cold set in and made them cling to each other, shivering under the lifeboat's six blankets. Eddie distributed rations during these lulls, and all enjoyed a fleeting contentment. Clearly, they had drifted into the equatorial, a zone where the trade winds could not be relied upon to move a boat. These calm spells never lasted long, Pugh assured them, a day or two, rarely more. But each windless day felt like ten. Their discouragement was compounded by occasional zephyrs for which they raised the sail, full of hope, only to have the wind die twenty minutes later. They were consuming rations they would need if they were ever to have a chance of making land. Their best hope was to be picked up by another ship—pinned, as they were, like a specimen to silk. They saw three more ships at a distance. Each time, they screamed and hollered and jumped, then collapsed and lay as if dead. There were no more planes; they were too far from land. The early rescue planes would have come from a ship.

On the third windless day—the sixth since the *Elizabeth Seaman* went down—they agreed to cut their rations by a third. Eddie's dungarees were already slipping over his hips. He'd tightened his belt three notches. They talked about food in the florid detail with which protectory boys had talked about sex, and for the same reason: talk was all they had.

Without the midday ration to look forward to, they toppled into lassitude. Ostergaard, an AB, lay asleep in the sun for hours, pushing away whatever cover they tried to force upon him. By evening he was feverish from sunstroke. Roger had taken first aid, and tended to the AB with wet bandages and calamine lotion from the boat's first aid kit. The AB begged for water so piteously that Roger and Eddie each forfeited half the evening ration to double his. The next morning, Ostergaard had vanished from the lifeboat. Eddie, who'd slept on the raft along with several others, found it difficult to believe that none of the thirteen men aboard the boat had seen or heard the AB go over. He eyed them with suspicion—especially Farmingdale. While he distributed the morning rations, Eddie felt men scrutinizing *him,* as if they suspected him of playing favorites or taking more than his share. Morale was crucial to lifeboat survival, Eddie knew, and they were lacking the surest morale boosters: booze and cigarettes. But Farmingdale, their leader, was largely to blame. Rather than keep the peace, he was one of the most captious, especially toward the bosun. That same morning, he blocked Eddie from giving the bosun his portion of condensed milk.

"No talkee, no eatee," Farmingdale decreed, looking around for participants in the hazing. "We'll see how long he stays mum."

When Eddie tried again to hand the bosun his share, Farmingdale seized his wrist. "You're soft, Third. He was never soft with you."

"We need every man strong," Eddie said.

"He doesn't move a muscle. Doesn't matter if he's strong or weak. Doesn't matter if he's here at all."

He was offering Eddie a role in a provocation that would satisfy the collective need of a scapegoat. Not a man aboard the *Elizabeth Seaman* had failed to see the bosun humiliate Eddie. Now the bosun was a broken man, the last vestige of his pride his apparent indifference to their present conversation. Eddie had always wanted to best the bosun, but the prospect of doing so now, in allegiance with Farmingdale, repelled him.

"Leave him alone, Second," he said severely, and handed the bosun his milk.

Farmingdale looked from Eddie to the bosun and back again. The whimsical smile played at his lips. "I see how it is," he said.

From that moment forward, Farmingdale began to follow Eddie— if one man could be said to "follow" another in their constrained circumstances. Wherever Eddie was, the courtly, snowy-haired second mate was directly beside him. It was a hostile pursuit—a surveillance—beneath which Eddie sensed Farmingdale's fear that Eddie might turn on him and persuade others to do the same. The prospect, which hadn't occurred to him before, began to tempt him.

That afternoon, he cut off the dangling end of his leather belt and gave it to Sparks, who had been using a rag to bait the lifeboat's hook and line. With the leather as bait, Sparks managed to hook a small tuna just before sundown. Eddie helped him wrestle the fish alongside the lifeboat, and Bogues drove his hunting knife into its heart. Eddie leaped overboard and helped to get a line around its tail, and they dragged the fish over the gunwale onto the boat. Farmingdale sliced it into portions, which they distributed using a method whereby a man with his back turned chose the recipient of each. There was enough for each man to have two large portions, and the liquid inside the fish quenched thirst as well as hunger. Afterward, the distrust among them seemed to melt away. They lit the kerosene lamp and talked into the night about what they would do after the war. When everyone had fallen into a sleepy, sated silence, the bosun touched Eddie's bicep, gestured at the fish carcass lying on a thwart, and spoke so softly that no one else heard. Eddie doubted it himself a moment later.

"Good," the bosun said.

After three more days, windless except for the cruel, teasing zephyrs, hunger and thirst returned with redoubled viciousness. They pulled buttons from their clothing and sucked them to waken their saliva. Eddie's tongue lay in his mouth like shoe leather; he would have liked to cut it out. On day six without wind, Hummel and Addison gulped seawater with such luxuriant bliss that Eddie had to shout at the others not to do the same. By evening both men were hallucinating, and Hummel was dead the following morning, his stomach distended. When they'd rolled him into the sea, Addison informed Eddie that Hummel had left him his rations, as a last will and testament. When Eddie replied that it was not in Hummel's power to do so, Addison came at him with fists raised. Farmingdale was beside Eddie, as usual, but he did nothing to fend off Addison; it was the gunners who held him back. He was dead by evening. Before moving onto the raft to sleep (Farmingdale following to snore at his side), Eddie made another notch in the log of days he was keeping on the lifeboat thwart, with a special mark for each man who had died.

On the seventh day of no wind—tenth overall—Eddie lay on the raft at sunset, savoring the fragment of relief between the agony of heat and the agony of cold. He felt wind on his cheek for several seconds before the sensation registered, and even then he assumed it was another dream of wind. For days they'd moved only just enough to keep the kinks out of their knees, and all of them were slow to react. But this was unmistakably wind—a squall that had appeared so suddenly that the sluggish lookouts failed to note it. There was a collective shout of jubilation. On the lifeboat, Pugh and others pulled in the sea anchor and began preparing the sail. Already the sea was growing choppy. Bogues leaped back onto the boat and began seizing other men's hands to pull them from the raft so it could be released. As Roger was pushing off from raft to boat, the painter connecting them snapped, and he dropped into the sea, smacking his face on the lifeboat's gunwale as he fell. Bogues lowered an oar for the cadet to grab, but Roger seemed to panic, and flailed back toward the raft. Eddie jumped in and lifted him onto it. The cadet's face was a garish white, cut along one cheekbone.

The raft, meanwhile, was being blown away from the boat with remarkable speed—it hadn't any draft. Bogues tried to toss Eddie another line, but it kept falling short. They gave up when a downpour began. Farmingdale appeared immobilized. Eddie ordered the men still on the raft to swim to the boat in pairs, so those on board would have time to pull them in. To his surprise, he saw the bosun helping to lift swimmers from the waves, his first activity since they'd rescued him.

Farmingdale refused to swim. Eddie meant to go last with Roger, who lay on the raft with eyes closed, bleeding from the gash on his face. "All right, Second. I guess you'll bring up the rear," Eddie told him when the rest had gone. To Roger he said, "You needn't swim, but you must help me swim. Can you?"

The cadet nodded. The distance between boat and raft was only fifty feet but widening by the second. As Eddie was about to lower himself into the rain-pocked water, Farmingdale seized his shoulders and yanked him backward into the middle of the raft. He was begging incoherently, not in his right mind. Eddie slapped his face hard to bring him around. "You can swim, Second. What's the matter with you?" he shouted.

Farmingdale punched Eddie in the jaw, and they began to struggle on their knees, wrestling on the raft's slick latticework in the driving rain. Eddie felt the raft skidding over waves like a child's balsa boat. Each time he managed to glimpse the lifeboat, it was farther away. He sensed the anxious gazes of the men on board—Sparks, Wyckoff, the bosun—a skein of connection so alive that it seemed to collapse the distance between them and light the falling dark.

Eddie managed to work his bowie knife from his pocket, intending to cut Farmingdale's throat. The second mate wrested the knife from his hand and flung it into the sea. Then he hefted his bulk on top of Eddie, immobilizing him so Eddie saw nothing, felt nothing but the sodden, foul-smelling mass of the larger man pushing him down. Roger roused himself and tried to pull Farmingdale off. When at last the second mate rolled away with a groan, Eddie could hardly see the lifeboat. He began to weep, sobs of rage and frustration at the knowledge that his compatriots were lost to him; that the log of days—his record of incidents and occurrences—was lost, too. He threw back his head and opened his mouth, letting rain wet his throat for several minutes. Then he looked again. He could still see the lifeboat—see, or thought he saw, the men's eyes fixed upon him. Eddie told himself that the boat was reachable. He could swim that far, even in the confused sea—perhaps even carrying Roger. It was possible. But the very passage of this thought through his mind seemed to awaken the second mate's nervous attention, his horror of being left behind. Eddie understood then that his only hope was to dive in alone, faster than Farmingdale could catch him. He would have to leave the cadet. No one would question such a move; it was a matter of survival. But his mind veered away. He couldn't leave Roger to Farmingdale.

As he strained to see through the dark, Eddie noticed what appeared to be a swimmer. He rubbed his eyes and looked again. No. Yes. A lone head bobbing among the swells like a cork. Bogues? Who else would have the strength and guts to do it? And why? Roger noticed, too, stared and pointed as the shape grew closer. When at last the swimmer reached the raft, Eddie was stunned to see that it was the bosun. He and Roger pulled him aboard. The bosun spent a moment recovering himself and then rose to his feet, somehow managing to balance on the pitching raft. He unhooked a lifeboat ax attached to his belt by a lanyard, lifted it over his head, and brought the ax down through Farmingdale's skull, which cleaved and broke like a dropped plate, spilling brains and blood on the raft's timbers. The bosun took Farmingdale's pocketknife from his belt and shoved his body over the side of the raft, where it disappeared into the waves. A swell washed away the pulpy smears.

All of this transpired in under a minute. Eddie would have thought it a hallucination except for the fact—the immeasurable relief—that Farmingdale was no longer with them on the raft. Within an hour, the rain had stopped and it was entirely dark, the sky clear and moonless. In the distance Eddie saw a smudge of light: the lifeboat's lantern. The raft hadn't oars, nor any way to signal to the boat. They had stripped it of everything of value: food, water, compass, anything else that might have helped to keep a man alive.

It had rained hard and long enough that the water in their clothing was only brackish. They squeezed every drop into each other's mouths and tried to sleep. Eddie woke often, awaiting first light in hopes of spotting the lifeboat. When dawn came at last, the boat was not in sight. They stared at the empty ocean. Eddie was sick with fright but did his best to behave as if their dire circumstances were merely a setback.

The bosun touched his throat and shook his head miserably.

"I know," Eddie said. "I miss those beautiful sentences."

The bosun cocked his head, indicating disbelief.

"I mean it," Eddie said. "Now that they're gone, I want them back."

The bosun gestured at himself. "Luke."

"No. To me you're the same bosun you ever were. Isn't that right, Roger?" But Roger just stared at the sea.

The bosun opened the rations hold and found the boat cover stuffed inside it; they had been using it for a sun shield the day before. He pulled the broken painter from the water and began working the two together to some purpose.

"He's making a sea anchor," Eddie explained to Roger, trying to engage the cadet. His cheek had swelled grotesquely, shutting his right eye. The wound was deep and red. "We're better off fixing ourselves to the current," Eddie went on. "Until there's a wind in our favor, it's more likely to bring us to land. Good thinking, Bosun."

The bosun cut him with a sharp, familiar glance that roused in Eddie a cavalcade of words: "I know, it's an outrage that an ignoramus like me should dare to compliment a vastly superior seaman like yourself, Bosun, especially on your thoughts, for God's sake, but you're speaking pig latin over there, so I've no choice but to try to read your mind—vastly unequal to that task though I surely am."

The bosun gawked at him. Even Roger looked up. Never in Eddie's life had he spoken this way; he felt as if the words were being routed from the bosun's mind directly through his own throat. He loved the tumbling rush of language coming easily, the unfamiliar pleasure of sheer utterance.

The bosun grinned for the first time since they'd pulled him from the sea. Eddie had always felt too much the victim of that smile to acknowledge the crescent beauty of its perfect white teeth.

He used Farmingdale's knife to begin a new log of days on the raft's edge. He began at day one, for already their time aboard the lifeboat seemed unreal and full of ghosts. In their new life, the wind was high, the water heavy and black. There was no buffer from the elements—wind, sun, and rain groped and clawed them at will. The stars and moon seemed proximate and unguarded, like bits of shell or sparkling rock that Eddie could crawl among when he chose. They saw night rainbows. By day, Eddie and the bosun scanned the horizon for ships and for their own lost lifeboat. On the second day, two flying fish landed on the raft, which the three of them shared, sucking every fiber of meat from the soft bones, then grinding the bones between their teeth. On the third day, another squall eased their thirst, but they had nothing in which to store the rain.

Since he'd hit his head on the lifeboat, Roger had grown dim and confused. The eye on the injured side of his face remained shut, and the swelling increased. Eddie tore off a strip of his shirt, soaked it in seawater, and pressed it to the wound. There was nothing more he could do. The gash began to fester, its red aureole spreading over more of Roger's face. At night he shivered wretchedly, and Eddie and the bosun locked their arms around him from both sides to try to warm him. Each sunset, Eddie made another notch in the edge of the raft: four days; five days. Roger whispered about his Welsh corgi pup; about the eighteen dollars he'd saved from his paper route; about a girl named Annabelle whose breast he'd touched through her Easter sweater. He called for his mother. Eddie pressed his parched lips to the boy's face and whispered, "We love you, my darling; everything will be fine." He would do anything to bring the boy peace. He'd witnessed such love for a child somewhere, but he couldn't recall where or when.

On the sixth night, Roger lay livid with fever, huffing shallow, frantic breaths. Eddie and the bosun twined their arms around him from both sides. At last the boy let out a long gasp and went still. They held him until all the warmth had left him. When the sun rose, they gently rolled his body into the sea. But Eddie refused to believe he was gone, and kept reaching for him.

And now he adapted to yet another life in which the lively cadet moved among the legion of ghosts he couldn't reach. Scorching sun, frigid nights, the press of their grating, unconquerable hunger. Eddie felt his body devouring itself, an agony like gnawing teeth. They lay prone upon the raft, too weak to look for food or ships, occasional brief squalls relieving their thirst. Eddie was skeletal and frail; he couldn't remember the last time he'd urinated. He was a corpse, little more, yet even as his body failed, his thoughts whirled with elastic new freedom. Eddie understood what he'd seen in the opium dens of Shanghai: people draped and torpid, but their minds must have ranged as his did now, careening through clouds of sound and color like a spirit unleashed.

The bosun's visible shrinking mirrored Eddie's own, their wild hair and beards a mockery of their withdrawing flesh. The bosun was less afflicted by the sun, which lacerated Eddie's skin through his tattered garments. His only relief came from floating in the sea. At least once between sunrise and sunset, he shook off his paralysis enough to lower himself into the water, clinging to the sea anchor line. Only at these times did Eddie escape the assault of gravity, which leaned on his frail bones like a heel grinding him onto pavement. The pleasure of floating, of being submerged, was worth even the stinging aftermath of salt drying in his sores. The bosun helped to pull him back onto the raft; Eddie hadn't the strength. They never spoke. For long spells they lay side by side, gazing into each other's eyes. Eddie regretted having missed the chance to ask his friend about Lagos and why he'd gone to sea, whether he was Catholic, his best memories and worst. It was too late for stories. They had left language behind, even the root language of the sea.

Once, as they lay on the raft in daylight, Eddie became aware of a gentle weight beside them. He opened his eyes and saw an albatross, white and awkward, her massive wings folded at her sides like artists' easels. The bosun was asleep. Using some vestige of strength, Eddie slashed at the bird with the pocketknife, trying to slice her head from the neck. The albatross dodged him easily, rising a foot or so in the air and settling back down. She cocked her head, watching him curiously with her bright black eyes.

The next day Eddie lay shivering although the sun was hot. The bosun held and tried to warm him. "Good man," he said, and Eddie recognized a version of his own endearments to the dying cadet so very long ago. He wanted to object, to correct the bosun with a range of facts that faded into colors before he could force them into language. Eddie hardly moved, hardly breathed, conserving the last of his energy, slowing things down nearly to the point of death in order to live another hour. He would die to stay alive, to savor the sensuous gallop of his thoughts toward some truth he hadn't yet perceived. He no longer knew if it was day or night, whether he was alone or with the bosun. He recalled his younger daughter—her mind locked inside a body condemned to still-ness. His discovery of their likeness pierced Eddie with such intensity that he cried out, although no sound came. Mashed against the raft, longing to float, he remembered Lydia in her bath, her relief and laugh-ter at the pleasure of lying suspended in the warm water. But Eddie had turned away, appalled by her misshapenness. And for the first time, the only time, the crime of his abandonment assailed Eddie, and he cried out, "Lydia! Liddy!," his harsh choked voice shocking him as he groped for the child he had abandoned—the family he had abandoned.

Eddie lay stricken, Lydia's name like a coin in his mouth. Then a light, wafting sound filled his ears, a voice he dimly remembered—not Anna's, certainly not the bosun's, but one that spoke in a bubbling, giddy rush, a lolloping prattle like the chattering cheerful nonsense of birdsong. Eddie broke away from the body on the raft and followed this sound to its source as if it were music drifting from an open window. He stopped to listen, straining to catch hold of the chuckling babble like two hands clapping to capture a bright ribbon snapping in the wind. He was following Lydia, and she was breathless, she was laughing, her words coming not in sentences so much as waves, a language he'd once discounted but now, at last, could understand, *Papa Anna run Mama see the sea Mama clap Anna see the sea Papa kiss Anna run to see the sea the see the sea the sea the sea theseatheseatheseatheseatheseathesea*, the words becoming a monotone, a simple back-and-forth, the plucking of a string, the beating of a heart: his heart, her heart, one heart. Here it was, the truth that underlay all the rest, like stirrings from the bottom of the sea. And only now did Eddie feel the bosun's arms still around him—he'd been there all the while, had never left. "Coming soon," the bosun said. "Coming soon, my friend. Almost done. God is with us yet."

PART EIGHT

The Fog

CHAPTER TWENTY-NINE

"You might have given it a bit more thought beforehand!"

Nell, hissing in the morning sunlight a block from Dr. Soffit's office. If not for the mothers and children wandering Central Park in their church hats, she would have been shouting.

"Thank you for stopping him," Anna said.

"I shouldn't have. You'd be all done by now, and that would be that. We could even—" She glanced toward Fifth Avenue. "We could probably still go back."

"No. Please." It felt to Anna as if the pleasure she took in breathing the cold dry air had nearly been lost to her. "Please, no."

"Stop saying that!"

Anna grasped her friend's arm, feeling something close to love for this cranky, glamorous protector. "Thank you, Nell."

Nell stiffened, then relaxed. Anna's effusions of gratitude seemed gradually to appease her. Or perhaps Nell's outrage had begun to bore her, compared with the interesting new shape Anna's trouble had assumed. "So. You're in it to the bitter end," she said softly. "You'll have to go away. But I'm warning you: the good places cost an arm and a leg."

"I've some money saved."

Nell laughed. "Darling, the money comes from *him*. You tell him straight: if he wants his nice life to continue without conversations between you and his wife that are likely to make things pretty hot around the house, he pays. Simple as that."

"He's gone."

Nell cocked her head. "Nobody's gone until they're dead. Find the fiend and make him pay or you'll end up with the nuns, which I don't advise," she said. "Nuns are not fond of our type. I've that on good authority."

"I mean he's—gone." Spurred by Nell's incomprehension, she found herself adding, "Overseas."

"Ah, a soldier. Why didn't you say so?"

Anna hadn't any answer, but none was required; Nell had fallen into thought. "It was a *stolen interlude*," she reflected, uttering this phrase as though it placed Anna's predicament in an entirely new category. "You were living in the moment and so was he. No thought of consequences."

". . . True," Anna allowed.

"But say, why spoil your figure and waste a year of your life when you can be done in thirty minutes? Unless . . . if he shouldn't come back . . ."

"He won't. I'm certain of that."

She'd gone too far. Yet the absurdity of her statement was somehow lost on Nell. "In that case, the child can carry on his line," she mused. "Even if nobody ever knows it's his. In a way, *he'll* still be alive—you'll have kept your soldier alive by bearing his child. That's what you're thinking!"

Anna was actually thinking that Nell in the role of romantic was awfully like an imposter. Clearly, her friend had been listening to too many love serials. But Nell's habit of posing questions as if they were answers was proving convenient.

"The nuns, then," she concluded. "You'll grin and bear it for a year. And they'll find him a good Christian home."

"Or her," Anna said.

After supper, Anna sat with Rose and her family in the front room and listened to Mozart on the gramophone. Rose's father was absorbed in his *Forward*; her mother crocheted another square in the tablecloth she was making to celebrate the safe return of her sons. Hiram did his homework. Little Melvin rolled his wheeled horse over the sofa and eventually over Anna, beginning at her thighs, rolling it up her arm, over her shoulder, and then, when she didn't object, over the top of her head.

"Don't be a monster, Melly," Rose said.

"I like it," Anna said. The rounded edges of the horse's wheels kneaded her skin and scalp pleasantly. Everything felt pleasant in this fragile, precious life she had made. In the days and weeks that followed, her contentment billowed into rapture. The trees on Clinton Avenue flashed into flower overnight. Anna swung her arms as she walked underneath them, thinking, *Soon I won't see these trees anymore, or hear the creak of their branches.* She helped Rose's mother sew her crocheted squares together. "You'll be with us, Anna, when we use this tablecloth," Rose's mother said. "You're part of our family—and your mother, too, when she comes back from nursing her sister." Anna thanked her, filled with a teetering delight that arose from proximity to disaster. If Rose's mother knew her secret, she would cast Anna out of her house. But she didn't know—she'd no idea! No one had!

And so Anna swilled the dregs of a life that was already over—yet still, by a miracle, hers to enjoy. She craved lemonade. When everyone had gone to bed, she squeezed lemons into cold water at the kitchen sink, adding sugar she'd bought with her own ration coupons so it wouldn't be missed. The sweet-tart concoction gave her shivers of pleasure. She guzzled it in her room while the tree outside her window splayed its new leaves like poker hands. It was impossible to resist waiting one more day to dismantle this sweetness. Just one! And then one more! But the days added up, and soon it was May and she'd no more plan than she'd had in March. A slight bulge appeared in her lower abdomen, but this was easy to conceal; at work she wore her baggy jumpsuit or the diving dress, and the men had grown as indifferent to her physical person as they were to each other's. Rose's mother credited her own excellent cooking for helping Anna to "fill out" what had been, in her view, a gaunt frame. She began packing lunches for Anna without charging extra.

Now that she'd learned to weld and burn, Anna's diving work included hull patches and screw jobs, working alongside other divers on mats pulled taut beneath battleships. The vast hulls ticked and hummed under her hands. Never had the enchantment of weightlessness been greater. She hung from screws and let the current waft her heavy shoes. At times she still wondered if her trouble might end naturally this way, but she no longer expected such a reprieve; nor did she want it, exactly. When Bascombe organized the divers to give blood to the Red Cross, Anna demurred at the last minute, pleading a stomachache.

A crew of *Normandie* salvage divers visited the Yard from Pier 88, in Manhattan, and Lieutenant Axel chose Anna to lead the tour of his diving program. Her photograph was printed in the *Brooklyn Eagle*. LADY DIVER SHOWS NORMANDIE SALVAGERS BROOKLYN STYLE, the headline read. Anna was smiling in the picture, hatless in her jumpsuit, the wind blowing her hair from clips. Within a day of its appearance, the image seemed an artifact from long ago. She kept it beside her bed and looked at it every night before going to sleep. *That is the happiest I will ever be,* she told herself. Yet she could enjoy that happiness one more day—like waking from a dream of bliss and being allowed, briefly, to resume it.

"What in hell shall I do without you, Kerrigan?" Lieutenant Axel remarked one evening as she hosed off diving dresses.

Anna was wary. "Why should you have to, sir?"

"Russians have broken the Caucasus Line. We'll have Tunis and Bizerte in a matter of days. Soon enough, the boys will be back here looking for their jobs."

"Oh," she said with relief. "That."

"I'll be out on my ass before you can say Jack Robinson. Back in my dory, waiting for the catfish to bite." He screwed up his eyes at her. "What'll you do, Kerrigan? Hard to see you tying on a frilly apron."

"Thank you, sir."

He cackled. "Wasn't meant as a compliment, but you're welcome just the same."

If he knew her secret, he would cast her out. But he didn't know. A stolen, perilous joy.

Anna's duplicity pained her only when she was writing to her mother. Her newsy accounts of Naval Yard life felt like an alibi, and she considered spelling out the truth—it would be easier by letter. But the news would crush her mother, and she would blame herself for having left Anna alone. There would be no one for her mother to confide in; if Anna's aunts or grandparents were to know, Anna would never again be welcome in their house. Another blighted child. She couldn't bring more shame upon her mother, who had lost so much.

On the first Saturday in June—Anna's day off that week—she stopped by her old building in the morning to fetch the mail while Rose and her family went to Shabbat services. Leaning in the vestibule, she noticed an airmail envelope with exotic stamps amid the usual letters and V-mails. Her own name was penned across the front in a crimped, slanted cursive that looked jarringly familiar. Her father's, she would have sworn.

Anna climbed the six flights to her old apartment for the first time since her move, aware of her heavy tread on the stairs she'd once flitted up like a dragonfly. The apartment smelled like an old icebox. Anna slid open a window and brought the mysterious letter outside onto the fire escape. Her father's pocket watch was in her purse— proof absolute, from the bottom of New York Harbor, that he wasn't alive. Yet she knew the letter was from him. She knew.

He'd written in a faint scattered hand from a hospital in British Somaliland. He'd been rescued at sea twenty-one days after a torpedo sank his ship. He had been with the merchant marine since 1937. All of this washed through Anna's brain and back out, leaving it empty. He was in poor health, unsure when he would be well enough to return. *I miss you girls terribly and long to see you again,* he'd written, with the address of a postal box in San Francisco.

Anna sat so still, for so long, that sparrows began to puff and squabble on the fire escape rungs at her feet. Her father was alive, had always been alive. Despite the apparent impossibility of this fact, she didn't feel surprise, exactly. More a sensation of falling headlong, dangerously, with no inkling where the fall would stop. She clutched a fire escape rail in each hand. Carefully, as though the building were moving around her, she climbed back indoors. The sun had withdrawn to the windowsills. It must be almost noon. In the kitchen, she found the pencil her mother kept nailed to the wall on a string for her shopping list. Anna flattened her father's letter onto the counter and scrawled over it, *LYDIA IS DEAD,* so that the lead tore through the paper. Then she went to her old room, lay on her bed, and fell asleep.

When she woke, she knew by the light that it was afternoon. It no longer felt possible to return to Clinton Avenue. She needed to act. She turned on the radio, sat at the kitchen table, and tried to think. Who were the nuns Nell had spoken of, and how did one find them? Had they a telephone? It seemed too late to go back to Nell; whom might she turn to? Strangely, Charlie Voss came to mind, although she'd hardly seen him since moving to Rose's. Instinct told her that Charlie might be sympathetic, but she'd no way of knowing and couldn't afford the risk.

The Roy Shields Show came on, a program she'd often listened to with Aunt Brianne. The mere thought of her aunt was enough. Of course. Anna's virtue and good sense were as axiomatic for Brianne as for her mother, but disillusionment wouldn't break her. Nothing could break Aunt Brianne.

If she telephoned her aunt and left a message, she would have to wait, and Anna felt incapable of waiting. She decided instead to go directly to Sheepshead Bay, even without an address, and telephone her aunt from there. Brianne had always used a postal box; her residence changed often, and at times she hadn't had one, depositing trunks full of furs and feathers, occasionally pieces of furniture with Anna's parents. Anna glanced at the pile of odds and ends on her bureau. Sure enough, she had saved one of the cocktail napkins her aunt had brought for Lydia's funeral lunch. *Dizzy Swain, Emmons Avenue, Sheepshead Bay.* She would begin there.

Consulting the Seamen's Bank transit map pasted inside the kitchen cupboard, she saw that the BMT went directly to Sheepshead Bay. Anna left the apartment and walked to the subway.

She'd gone to Sheepshead Bay with her father, on "errands," and recalled a jumble of rotting docks and small fishing boats. He'd taken her to a shanty where several men at a counter leaned over their bowls like animals at a trough. While her father conducted his business, the proprietor had brought Anna her own bowl of chowder. She remembered the taste: creamy, buttery, full of fish. Her stomach creaked at the memory.

Emmons Avenue looked wider than she'd expected, its homey scramble of docks replaced by a series of monumental piers slanting identically into the bay. She crossed to a cafeteria on the north side of the avenue and held up the cocktail napkin to the cashier, who had dyed black hair and a mustache that looked pasted on. "Do you know this place?" she asked.

"Why, sure," he said. "Straight east on Emmons. You can catch the trolley a hundred feet from here."

Anna gazed from the trolley window at coasties milling in the late afternoon—the eagle insignia on the officers' caps was gold, not silver, meaning they were Coast Guard rather than navy. Across Sheepshead Bay, family homes gave way to military buildings—this must be the Maritime Training Center her aunt had spoken of. When Anna got off the trolley, she might have been on Sands Street: crowded bars, a photo studio offering twelve poses for sixty-nine cents. MADAME LAROUSSE: CARDS, OUIJA, CRYSTAL. She spotted the Dizzy Swain a block over, its sign a replica of the lovestruck shepherd holding a cocktail shaker.

The Swain was much like the Oval Bar, its reek of beery sawdust enriched by the smell of seafood. It was dense with un-uniformed men she guessed must be merchant sailors. The place seemed beneath her aunt's level, yet there was Brianne, right at the bar! Anna rushed toward her, but it turned out that her aunt was behind the bar—she was the barmaid! Anna froze in confusion, half expecting Brianne not to know her, so otherworldly was the encounter. But her aunt let out a whoop. "Why, it's high time! Seems I have to open up the *Brooklyn Eagle* if I want to catch a glimpse of my niece. Two weeks without a phone call, not to mention I've left three messages at White's, and they haven't seen hide or hair of you. Are you hungry? Chowder for my niece, Albert, and don't skimp on the clams."

The bluster of cheerful accusation left Anna stammering apologies. Albert, whose Adam's apple protruded further than his nose, seated her at the bar and brought her a bowl of steaming soup. She crumbled in a handful of oyster crackers and took a spoonful. She shut her eyes: fish, cream, butter. It was the soup she remembered, only better—better for being in her mouth at that moment. It warmed the reaches of her belly and radiated out to her limbs. She had a curious sensation as she ate, as if a fish from the soup had swum against the interior of her stomach. When it happened a second time, she wondered if the chowder was giving her indigestion. But it wasn't that. A live thing had moved inside her.

Her throat closed, and she set down her spoon. For the first time, terror ricocheted through Anna at the catastrophe she had allowed to befall her. She'd distracted herself for nearly two months—believing somehow that there would still be an avenue of retreat. Now the disaster confronted her nakedly. She was ruined.

Brianne joshed with the sailors and filled their glasses like a slatternly den mother. Anna hardly heard. She was watching an impassable distance open between herself and everything she loved: working underwater; Marle and Bascombe and the other divers; Rose and her family. The photograph in the *Brooklyn Eagle:* a good girl; a smiling, innocent girl. But Anna was not that girl. She was a corrupt interloper bluffing her way through her life.

She finished her soup without tasting it. The creature didn't stir again, but she felt it coiled inside her: a darkness she'd hidden since childhood, now in animate, corporeal form. Only her father had guessed at her deviousness and low morals; he alone had sensed what she'd become. His disenchantment with Anna had driven him away. She had always known this.

Her aunt was beside her, a hand on her shoulder. "Francine has agreed to start early, so we can go upstairs and have a nice chat," Brianne said. Anna thanked Francine, whose expression resided wholly in her freckled décolletage, and followed Brianne out of the Dizzy Swain. They took a side door into a stairwell whose carved oak banister seemed a relic of better times. They climbed to a wain-scoted hallway scented with onion and boiled potatoes. The puzzle of her aunt's circumstances distracted Anna. How did the Lobster King fit in?

After a second turn of stairs, Brianne fished a key from some aperture in her bust and opened a door. Anna followed her into a room whose one window admitted indirect light. Her gaze caught on furniture she recalled from her childhood: a red upholstered chaise; a Chinese screen; a coat stand that looked made from cursive. The room's walls and ceiling seemed to contract around the furniture, making it appear outsize and too tightly packed. Her aunt turned on lamps, revealing a small sink, a gas ring with a coffeepot, a drying rack strung with girdles and brassieres.

"Does the Lobster King . . . live nearby?" Anna asked.

"He's gone," her aunt said, inserting a Chesterfield between her lips and lighting it with a device shaped like Aladdin's lamp. "A louse like all the rest."

"So . . . you haven't any friend?"

Brianne drew on her cigarette, then balanced it carefully in an upright silver ashtray. "I've many friends, but they're females," she said through a gust of smoke. "Except my landlord, Mr. Leontakis. He owns the Swain. A Greek," she added, as if in apology.

She lowered herself onto the red chaise and tapped the upholstery beside her. Anna's legs wobbled as she sat. Brianne pressed Anna's sweating hands between her own, which were stubby and soft. *My one bad feature*, she used to say of her hands. *Thank God it's not my face.* Anna looked in her aunt's eyes and realized that she'd guessed.

"When did you last have the curse?" she asked.

"I can't remember."

"Roughly."

"This happened on February the ninth."

Brianne whistled. "I knew I should have visited more often."

It was her sole expression of regret. When she spoke again, it was to pose a series of practical questions with the warm impartiality of a doctor. Anna answered in a monotone. No, she'd not been surprised or taken advantage of. No one else knew of her condition. She did not care to name the father, nor would she see him again. She presumed she would give up the child but was not entirely certain.

"You need to make that decision now. Today," Brianne said. "Those two choices lead in opposite directions."

If she was going to give the baby up, it was simply a matter of deciding where to have it. Brianne knew several places, all with nuns. "Prepare to gorge yourself on crow," she said. "Followed by fat slices of humble pie. Confess, repent. Confess, repent. They'll make your head spin."

"How do you know?"

There was a pause. "Everyone knows," Brianne said.

If she wanted to keep the baby, she would need to marry immediately. This notion wrested a laugh from Anna. "Who would want to marry me, Auntie?"

"You'd be surprised," Brianne said. The most common motive was unrequited love. "A man who wouldn't have a chance if it weren't for your trouble might be willing to raise another man's child as the price of having you."

When Anna assured her aunt that no such suitor existed, Brianne introduced a second possibility, this one involving men who were "different." "That can work quite well," she said. "And a kind of love can develop over time between husband and wife."

"*Different?*"

"Homosexual. You know, pansies."

Anna did know of such things, but only by hearsay. "How on earth would I find a man like that?"

"There are more around than you might think."

Anna frowned, shaking her head, but an image of Charlie Voss floated inadvertently to mind. Was it possible? Or was desperation making her reach?

"I might know one," she said. "But what if I'm wrong?"

"Do you like him? Does he like you?"

"Very much."

"Bingo. There's your answer. Assuming he has a decent job."

"But how would it happen?"

"Prospects, rather. Everyone has a job right now."

"I can't just come out and ask."

"You'll see him tomorrow morning, urgently. Seek his council over your predicament and leave it to him to make the offer, if he's so moved."

"And then?"

"You marry immediately, privately. Normally, you would go away together to cloud the time line, but with this stupid war, you'll have to leave the marriage date and the child's birthday vague and fix them later on. Your child—children if you have more—will have a father. That's the main thing: they'll be legitimate."

"Do people really live that way?"

"I know several couples. Usually in the suburbs, Long Island or New Jersey. The man commutes to the city, rents a pied-à-terre, and stays over for work a couple of nights each week. Separate bedrooms. It's like living with a girlfriend, except it happens to be your husband."

"It sounds so grim," Anna said.

"*Grim?* Look at you now."

"I'd rather be alone than live like that."

Brianne placed her cigarette on the silver stand and gathered herself into an icy tower of rebuke. "Oh, you'll be alone, all right," she said. " 'Outcast' would be a better word, and your child branded as a bastard. Let me tell you something, dearie: the world is a closed door to an unwed mother and her illegitimate child. If you have that baby and fail to marry, you'll lead the life of a shadow, and so will the brat. Why you didn't come to me when we could have fixed this, I'll never know, but you're too smart to be stupid, Anna. Think about your homosexual friend—possibly homosexual friend. If you're lucky enough to get a proposal out of him, it may be your best chance at happiness. If you want to keep the baby."

Anna saw that she must give the baby up. She would have to go away, but afterward she could resume her present life. She took a quick inventory of what would await her: a rented room; a job she would lose when the war ended. Friends who would scatter. Nothing, in other words. Her life was a war life; the war *was* her life. There had been another life before that—her family, the neighborhood—but everyone from that time had died, or moved, or grown up. Its last vestige had been the odd dark magic of her father's death.

"I need to walk," Anna said, standing suddenly. "I need to think. I need to be alone."

"Oh, no," Brianne said, rising from the chaise with a groan. "You've been alone too long, that's quite clear. We don't have to say a word, but I'm not leaving your side until we've a clear plan."

They walked east on Emmons Avenue. The sun had set, rinsing the sky in pink. Anna smelled the bay, its oily piers. Clusters of seagulls hopped at the shore like white rabbits.

"Papa is alive," Anna said, breaking a long silence.

Her aunt glanced at her. "You thought otherwise?"

"I've had a letter. He's been sailing with the merchant marine."

When Brianne failed to evince amazement at this unlikely turn, Anna whirled on her. "You knew about this?"

"I'd an inkling." Then, preempting Anna's explosion, she said, "How else do you think I've had the money to help you and your mother? Working at that greasy spoon?"

"But . . . the Lobster King."

"There is no Lobster King. Oh, come now, don't look so flabber-gasted—that story was phony as a three-dollar bill. An old bag like me with a fancy man? I'm flattered you believed it."

Anna was beset with rage. She stopped walking and shrieked at her aunt, causing passersby to turn and peer at them. "You never told him about Lydia! He thinks she's still alive!"

"I've never had an address," her aunt said mildly. "Not even a postal box. He sent a money order twice each year, told me to spend a bit on myself, and give the rest to Agnes."

"I wish he was dead," Anna shouted. "I liked it better."

"If wishing could make men die, there'd be nary a live one left."

As suddenly as it had gathered, Anna's anger shrank into disgust. "Do you hate him, too?" she asked when they were walking again.

Brianne heaved a sigh. "He's my only brother," she said. "Who knows, the war may knock some sense into him. Wars have been known to do that."

"You said the war was a joke. Boys poking each other with sticks."

"The men who *make* the wars, yes. But the ones who fight, those beautiful kids . . . they're innocents."

"Papa isn't a soldier, Auntie—he's with the merchant marine!"

"And they're not soldiers, too?" Brianne countered hotly. "They take every risk without a hope of glory: no medals, no five-gun salutes. In the end they're just merchant seamen, hardly more than bums, from the world's point of view. They're the real heroes, I say."

There was no mistaking the tremor in her aunt's voice. Heroism, apparently, was the one thing Brianne didn't find ridiculous.

"Papa is a hero? Is that what you're saying?"

Brianne said nothing. Anna thought of her father's letter: the torpedo, the raft, the hospital. She would tell her aunt, but not now. Her mind was finally beginning to work, as if rage had scorched a path through her thoughts.

They had reached a part of the waterfront blocked by military fencing, and turned back. Neither said a word the whole way. When they'd climbed the stairs to Brianne's room and hung up their jackets, Anna asked, "How much is left of the money Papa sent?"

"Two hundred dollars, more or less. Why?"

"I've a plan."

Her aunt poured a glass of Four Roses and offered it to Anna, who declined—even now, she couldn't bring herself to drink in front of her aunt. They returned to the chaise, and Brianne lit a cigarette and twirled the whiskey in her glass.

"I'm going to take a train to California," Anna said. "On the way, I'll put on a wedding ring and a black dress. I'll arrive a war widow and move near the Mare Island Shipyard and work there as a diver. I think I can get a transfer from the Brooklyn Yard."

Brianne snorted. "You realize a Pullman sleeper to California costs a hundred and fifty dollars."

"I've five hundred forty-two in the bank and three hundred twenty-eight in war bonds. And I'll ride coach."

"Not in your condition!"

"Auntie, I've been welding under thirty feet of water!"

"You'll be poor," Brianne said. "Destitute."

"I can sell my war bonds."

"You'll wind up on the streets."

"Don't be ridiculous."

"Who can you depend on? Who do you know in California?"

Anna laughed harshly. "Well, if I'm desperate, I suppose I could write to Papa," she said. "I understand he's a hero nowadays."

After "Shore Dinners" at Lundy's famous restaurant, followed by slices of huckleberry pie, Anna changed into an old satin negligee of her aunt's, stained under the arms. Brianne arrayed herself in a matronly housecoat of brushed rayon, buttoned to the neck. They lay together in her four-poster, buffeted by gusts of Saturday-night revelry from the Swain. Anna remained wide awake, staring at the ceiling fixture with its base of sculpted plaster roses. She was electrified by her plan—by the relief of finally having made one. She assumed her aunt had fallen asleep and so was caught unawares by her voice in the dark.

"About the father . . ."

"No, Auntie."

"One question."

"*No.*"

"You needn't answer. I'll know just by asking."

"You won't know anything."

"Was he a soldier?"

Anna said nothing.

"Those uniforms," her aunt said, with a chuckle. "Who can resist?"

CHAPTER THIRTY

"A letter won't do a goddamn thing, I'm afraid," Lieutenant Axel said. "Should, but it won't."

"It's supposed to act as a transfer," Anna explained. "From the Brooklyn Naval Yard to Mare Island."

"A transfer is bullshit, if you'll pardon my French. It'll take forever to come through, like everything in this stumblebum place. What I'll do—" He peered up at her across his desk. "I'll telephone long-distance and speak with the man in charge."

"Why, thank you."

"I'm likely to know him already, if he's done any real diving." He wore his bad-news face, but without the elfin pleasure that normally twinkled at its edges. "Sit down, Kerrigan."

Anna sat, nervous. Now that her every move was aimed at propelling herself to California with reputation intact, the fear of discovery hounded her.

"There's an unfortunate fact you've been protected from, working for me. But I can't protect you out in California." He took a long breath and leaned toward her confidingly. "Many of the old boys are—are backward in their thinking. They won't want a girl in their diving program. Might snigger at the very idea."

He regarded her gravely, and Anna grew confused. Could the lieutenant be kidding? Engaging in uncharacteristic self-mockery? Or was it possible he'd forgotten their beginning?

"Of course, you aren't like most girls," he said. "We both know that."

"It's hard to know what most girls are like," Anna murmured.

"Point is, I'll need to have the conversation man-to-man: *Hire this girl. She'll work like two fellows.* If I send you out there with just a letter, he'll assume I've low motives for writing it. That's an ugly truth that I'm sorry to be the bearer of, Kerrigan, but it's how their minds work."

Anna listened in wonderment. "I see."

"Man-to-man: *This ain't some dizzy blonde who likes to chum it up with the lads,* because that's what they'll think. You're shocked, I see that, but the world can be an ugly place. *She's the best goddamn diver in my unit, so wipe that smirk off your map and put her on the payroll, for Pete's sake.*" His cheeks flamed as he faced off against the base suppositions of his imagined interlocutor. "We've a war to win, god-damn it! We need the very best men out there—uh, people. I've a Negro working for me, Mr. Marle. Happens to be my best welder. Do I mind that he's a Negro? Hell, I'd take a giraffe if they sent me one that could weld underwater like he can."

His vehemence bent Anna's memory. Had she exaggerated the lieutenant's harshness early on? Been oversensitive? She could no lon-ger recall. "Do you think you'll persuade them?" she asked.

"I've an idea of their language, I suppose, the way their minds work. Enough to communicate."

"Thank you, sir."

He was quiet a moment, observing his folded hands on the desk. "That's the first thing," he resumed more calmly. "And the second is: the Pacific is lousy with sharks. I'm told you can watch great whites gobbling seals in the Frisco Bay like candy dots. May I ask what you intend to do about it?"

Just twelve days elapsed between Anna's announcement that she must join her mother in California and her departure. During that time—or rather, after work and during her one day off in that time—she gave notice to her landlord, boxed and mailed her mother's clothing and linens, put the furniture into storage, closed her account at Williamsburgh Savings, and sent her balance by telegraph wire to the Bank of America in Vallejo, California. She visited Lydia's grave, promising to send for her sister when she was situated. Bascombe, Marle, Ruby, and Rose (whose family was bereft at the prospect of Anna's going) all offered to help, but she couldn't risk accepting. A more radical tale had been required to explain her departure to her mother and neighbors: after a two-week courtship, she'd been whirled off her feet straight to the altar and now was following her new husband to the Mare Island Naval Shipyard. She bought a wedding band at a pawnbroker's and slipped it on each time she entered her old block. The fabrication required a giddy, breathless delivery that exhausted Anna more than any amount of packing or lifting. Even writing it out in letters to Stella, Lillian, her mother, and the neighborhood boys in the service drained her. She doused the stationery in rose-scented toilet water and strewed exclamation points. Lying to her mother was hardest, but it was only temporary—a way of establishing the story for her family in Minnesota. Anna would tell her the truth when they saw each other.

She named her husband Charlie. *Lieutenant Charlie Smith!!!!!!*

Sustaining two incompatible falsehoods required not just vigilant precision in the donning and doffing of her wedding band but the enforcement of an absolute separation between her old life—her mother and neighborhood—and her present one at the Naval Yard. It meant not saying goodbye to Charlie Voss, whom Anna doubted she could lie to, face-to-face. She would write him from California.

Over a final round of beers at the Oval Bar, she gave her friends the address of the Charles Hotel in Vallejo. She promised to kiss the Pacific shore for Bascombe and mail a palm frond to Ruby. For Marle, who hoped to move to California after the war, she promised to find out which places were friendliest to Negroes. Then she hugged Ruby, shook the hands of sixteen divers, and walked to the Flushing Avenue streetcar for a final supper with Rose and her family.

Brianne arrived by taxi at noon the next day. Rose and her father had left for work, so Rose's mother saw Anna off, exclaiming at the quantity of luggage already in the taxi: two cartons, a valise, an overnight case, a cosmetics case, and a large trunk—all Brianne's. Her aunt's involvement in Anna's move had escalated from promising to see her off at the station, to accompanying her as far as Chicago, to going with her to California on her way to visit friends in Hollywood, to staying in Vallejo long enough to help her settle in, to remaining through the birth because who could leave a girl at such a time, to a revelation that had wakened Brianne from deep sleep (by her own report) and jettisoned her from her four-poster bed: she was sick to death of New York, pining for California weather, and long overdue for a permanent move there. She had stored her furniture alongside Anna's.

Rose's mother held up little Melvin, and they waved together as the taxi pulled away. Anna saw that she was weeping. The silvery trees along Clinton Avenue shook in a coal-scented breeze tinged with chocolate. When they were out of sight, Anna leaned back against the taxi seat and shut her eyes. An unnatural energy had propelled her through the many steps leading up to this departure. Now that those steps were complete, her excitement collapsed into emptiness. She had never wanted to leave and didn't now.

Brianne wagged a hand-painted Chinese fan, liberating an odor of stale powder from inside her dress. Anna felt a throe of revulsion. She didn't want to go—especially not with this musty old woman for a companion. She rolled down her window and let the breeze box her face. The cabbie took a left on Flushing and drove west alongside the Naval Yard—past Building 77, from whose high windows Anna had looked down at the ships in dry dock; past the Cumberland gate and the officers' mansions with tennis courts behind them. On a hill above the smokestacks, she glimpsed the gabled yellow commandant's house.

The driver turned right at Navy Street, and they passed the Sands Street gate and Building 4, where Nell had worked. Anna felt physical pain in her chest and throat as they approached the Yard's extreme northwest edge. Building 569 was just across that wall! An ordinary day, perfect diving weather! She felt as if she, too, were across the wall, lugging equipment onto the barge with her friends and, at the same time, driving away from them forever. The separation was violent—a rending expulsion. Anna seized upon landmarks as if clawing a hillside to stop her slide: the Woolworth Building! The old Seaport piers! The harplike spokes of the Brooklyn Bridge!

Across the East River, the Naval Yard became visible again, the *Missouri*'s dark shape looming through the building ways. The battleship was ahead of schedule; already people were machinating about which seats they would try to get for her launching. The most coveted spots were inside the building ways, and Charlie Voss had promised Anna one of these. She wondered if she might somehow return to Brooklyn for the *Missouri*'s launching; to miss that would be like not having been at the Naval Yard at all.

As it turned out, Anna did watch the launching from inside the building ways—on a newsreel at the Empress Theater in Vallejo, California. It was late April 1944, three months after the launching took place. Anna watched the reel so many times that the ticket-taker began letting her in for free; she never stayed to watch the feature. The battleship's mountainous jutting stern dwarfed the camera's perspective, making the sailors waving from her fantail look minuscule. The ship's sponsor was Margaret Truman, the nineteen-year-old daughter of a Missouri senator. She cracked a champagne bottle against the hull with a report like gunfire, but Anna had already had it from Marle, who'd proved a reliable and detailed correspondent, that Miss Truman had needed three tries to break that bottle. *We all said, "Kerrigan would have done better,"* he wrote.

As soon as the bottle broke, men began knocking away the wood stays that held the *Missouri* in place. In a matter of seconds, the "largest and most powerful battleship ever built" was sliding down the ways with a silken ease that owed much to the fact that whatever shrieking resistance had accompanied her slide was replaced, on the newsreel, by marching band music and the rousing voice of the announcer: "The *Missouri* is symbolic of the ever-growing strength of the United States Navy." Men held their hats and ran after her, but the ship was past their reach—even as her stern slid down the tracks, her bow had already made its splashing entry into the East River, which parted around her with the ease of a cushion receiving a cat. And then she was floating away, her bottom half submerged, as though she had never been on land in the first place. It was like watching a creature being born, growing up, and moving irrevocably away, all in under a minute.

The taxi turned west at Forty-second Street, toward Grand Central, sunlight stuttering through the sieve of the Second Avenue El as they drove underneath it. Then skyscrapers blocked the sun, their abrupt shadow like the sudden louring of a storm. Newspaper vendors bawled out the headlines:

"American planes down seventy-seven Jap fliers in Guadalcanal!"

"Biggest Pacific air battle yet! Only six U.S. planes lost!"

"Let's have a look at your ring," Brianne said.

Anna had gone to a pawnbroker on Willoughby Avenue, near the courthouse, intending to buy the cheapest ring she could find. But she'd lingered, trying on one with pinprick diamonds set in fourteen-karat gold, another of brass filigreed with a pattern of leaves. The longer she looked, the more critical the decision seemed to become. This was her wedding ring, after all; she would have to wear it every day. Why choose a dented copper oval that would stain her finger green? As Anna deliberated, studying the rings, she had a sudden, lucid impression of Dexter Styles, his restless proximity. She imagined him dismissing the pinpricks: *A diamond should be big enough to see. No telling brass from gold, if you keep it polished.* She chose the brass filigree.

"Not bad," Brianne said, running her finger over the leaf pattern, which Anna had burnished just that morning. Then, with a wink, "Your soldier has good taste."

Brianne splashed toilet water into her cleavage as they approached Grand Central. Soon she was flirting with the young Negro redcap.

He caught Anna's eye and they shared a smile at her aunt, pushing fifty, still reeking of Lady of the Lake.

The rush of uniforms through the smoky concourse verged upon turmoil. The trains were overcrowded. Brianne had had to use "all my wiles" to acquire two tourist sleeper tickets from Chicago to San Francisco on short notice; Anna suspected the feat had entailed bribery, not flirtation. Moving through bands of hazy light that angled from the lunette windows overhead, she felt the taint of her failure begin to lift. There were girls everywhere: WAVES, WACS, mothers tugging children by the hand. There was nothing unusual about Anna's departure; she was one tiny part of a migration.

They took facing seats beside a window aboard the Pacemaker to Chicago. Six more people squeezed in alongside. Relieved of the need to hide her condition, Anna relaxed, letting her sweater fall open so her belly protruded. Apparently, that was enough to tip a balance, for she sensed her fellow passengers prising apart her circumstances until they located her wedding band. The satisfaction of their curiosity was like a sigh. There was magic in that ring. She was offered a fan, a newspaper, a glass of water. So much power in one slim band.

Conversation was trickier. Everybody knew someone in the navy, and Anna's vague replies about Lieutenant Charlie Smith only invited further questions. She solved this problem by reading: first the *Times*, then the *Journal American*. Then Ellery Queen's *The Tragedy of Z*.

Softly, she asked her aunt, "Have you brought the dress?"

"Several," Brianne said. "Each one lovelier than the last. But no need for that yet." She whispered into Anna's ear, "Enjoy a week of marriage before you go into mourning."

The flotilla of warships along the Hudson River winnowed as the Pacemaker rushed north. This was the same route Anna had taken on trips to Minneapolis with her mother and Lydia, but she didn't recall those trains moving so fast. The Pacemaker roared over crossings, laundry flapping in its wake like frightened starlings. Soldiers prowled the corridors, playing cards and flicking their cigarettes out of windows. The train's speed roused a tingle of anticipation in Anna. She gazed from her window: town after town flung wide, then folded into vanishing. Trains going the opposite way passed with a punch.

She woke from a nap to find they'd reached Schenectady, early-evening light honeying the brick factories along the tracks. Back in Brooklyn, she would be leaving the Naval Yard with Rose by now, perhaps drinking beers at the Oval with the other divers. Already the sensation of being ripped from her life had relaxed into an ache. Sheer distance had done this. A letter mailed from Schenectady would take a day to arrive in New York; telephoning would involve multiple coins and interruptions from an operator. She'd gone far away.

Anna and Brianne repaired to the dining car as the sun was setting on Syracuse. They reviewed their plan in whispers over chicken cutlets: Lieutenant Axel had secured Anna's job at the Mare Island Naval Shipyard, where she would dive until her condition became impossible to hide. Then she would take a leave, have the baby, and return, a widow, when she'd found someone to care for the child. "I'm hoping Mama will come," she said.

Brianne looked miffed. "Something wrong with present company?"

Anna laughed. "You hate children, Auntie."

"Not all children."

"You call them brats."

"I've been known to be rather wonderful to certain exceptions."

Anna cocked her head. "Would you want to care for a baby?"

Somehow it had become a proposal. Anna watched her aunt consider, the dramatic lines of her face settling into a rare look of contemplation. "It may be the only thing left that I haven't done," she said.

By Rochester, all that remained of the day was an orange blaze on the western horizon. Planted fields sent a tang through the open windows. To the right spread Lake Ontario, purple-black. Anna pictured Rose and little Melvin curled in her bed, Rose munching walnuts as she finished a last chapter of her Jack Asher mystery. Bascombe would have brought Ruby home by now, harbor noises crowding the night as he rode the streetcar back to his rooming house. Anna pictured all this with wistful resignation; so quickly, she had consigned that life to the past. Its telescopic fading was the price of hurtling forward into whatever smoldering promise issued from that orange blaze. She hungered toward it, longing for the future it contained. As the train roared west, Anna bolted upright. She had thought of her father. At last she understood: *This is how he did it.*

CHAPTER THIRTY-ONE

Eddie sat on a park bench across from the Empress Theater and eyed its doors, waiting for Anna to emerge. She was watching a newsreel about the USS *Missouri*, a battleship built at the Brooklyn Naval Yard, where she'd worked for nearly a year before her marriage.

He'd wanted to come inside with her to watch, too, but she'd put him off. "You were gone," she said. "It won't mean anything to you."

"May I wait?"

"You can do whatever you want."

Eddie was encouraged. So far, this visit was an improvement over his first, last October, when he'd taken the electric train from San Francisco and rung the buzzer of a bleak apartment after dark. He could hear the baby crying, and the sound instantly brought him low. He was on the verge of slinking away when the door opened and there she was—Anna, grown up—peering out at him. "Papa," she said softly, and Eddie thought he saw wonder in her face, mixed with astonishment—but it may have been just astonishment. He was astonished by the pale, dark-eyed woman in the doorway, her long hair falling loose over a dressing gown.

She slapped his face with such force he saw stars. "Don't ever come back here," she said, and shut the door quietly—so as not to scare the baby, he later thought.

His second visit was in January, after a three-month run to the Gilbert Islands as second mate—his first voyage since the *Elizabeth*

Seaman, owing to lingering stomach problems. He came while Anna was at work that time, to see Brianne and meet "the little gentleman"—as his sister was fond of calling the burly, fierce-eyed infant who gazed at Eddie reproachfully from a basket.

"What did his father look like?" he asked, eyeing the baby. "Have you a photograph?"

"No," Brianne said heavily. "All of that was lost in the valise that went missing on the train."

It was Eddie's good fortune that Agnes wasn't caring for the baby. Agnes had walked off the family farm last June, according to Brianne, shocking her dour relations to the same degree she had by up and running to New York at seventeen. She'd hitched a ride into town and volunteered with the Red Cross. Now she was overseas, working as a nurse's aide. Her letters were too heavily censored for Brianne to know where she was, but Agnes had mentioned forests. Europe, they guessed.

Eddie watched the baby kicking like a restless cub. "Poor little devil," he said.

"He isn't poor in the least," his sister retorted. "There was never a little gentleman so spoiled and adored."

She seemed bizarrely at ease, feeding and burping the tyke as though he were her very own, not a rumor of booze in the house. His sister's transformation from aging tart to fussing nanny seemed almost instantaneous, like the flick of a kaleidoscope.

"Say, where were you hiding your mothering tendencies all those years?" he asked.

"I wasn't hiding them, I was wasting them," she said. "On rats and louts more babyish than this one!" She swooped the cub into her arms and smattered his face with kisses until he guffawed. "Come, brother dear," she said. "Hold your grandson."

Eddie reached for him gingerly, fearful of hurting him. But the sturdy infant cleaved to him with such tender resolve that Eddie felt as if he were the one being held.

"Now now," Brianne said. "Only the baby is allowed to cry."

At the end of that visit, Eddie had gone to the Mare Island gate to wait for Anna. By then he'd done some reconnaissance and knew which road she would have to take from the shipyard up to the bungalow she and Brianne had moved into, among other Mare Island workers.

He stood back from the road among a thatch of eucalyptus trees, pungent leaves dangling around him like sickles. Anna appeared after the general rush, laughing with another girl. Her athletic walk was so like Agnes's that he felt disoriented; which was he looking at? Anna bade her friend goodbye and quickened her pace, cheeks flushed under her hat. She looked awfully happy for a girl newly widowed. But then he supposed she'd known Lieutenant Smith for too short a time to miss him very much—especially with the little gentleman to come home to. Watching his daughter approach, Eddie had felt an annihilating emptiness, as if he'd died on the raft after all and returned as a ghost. He nearly stepped from the shadows just to see his presence register in her face, to know that he was really there. But that would dash her high spirits. So he stayed hidden and let her pass.

It was enough, he told himself after that, to know that she was happy. That all three of them were happy. It should have been enough, but it was not. At the urging of his paramour, a term Ingrid used laughingly (a widowed schoolteacher being the last thing one pictured), he had returned this afternoon to try again. He'd completed another run, this time to New Guinea—part of a force pressing the Japs farther back toward their homeland in hopes of prompting a surrender. He'd been reunited with Wyckoff on that voyage, and they'd drunk another bottle of wine on the deck, under the stars. Eddie was developing a taste for the stuff. The warm Pacific breeze lapping at their faces had made the agonies of the *Elizabeth Seaman* seem no more substantial than a nightmare.

Pugh, the indomitable old salt, had steered the lifeboat all the way to British Somaliland, with Wyckoff, Sparks, Bogues, and the rest still alive and in passable health upon arrival. Captain Kittredge's boat had been picked up long before, with all hands accounted for. That meant that roughly half the *Elizabeth Seaman*'s merchant and navy crews had survived the wreck. The War Shipping Administration had a policy of immediate duty for shipwreck survivors—to keep them from spreading their horror stories, so the rumor went. All were back on ships except Pugh, who had retired to live with his daughter, and the bosun, who still could not speak in his old way. He'd returned to Lagos, where Eddie had promised to visit him after the war. They exchanged frequent letters, addressing each other as "brother," and Eddie found, to his morbid satisfaction, that his own writing style was reduced to a schoolboy stutter beside the bosun's extravagant prose.

Anna did not see her father when she left the theater, and assumed he must have gone. She felt a beat of distress until he rose from a bench across the street and waved. She waved back, surprised by the intensity of her relief. By the time he reached her, she was angry again and wanted to send him away. But what was the point? Clearly, he intended to return and keep returning. She couldn't hit him every time.

As they walked together up the hill toward her bungalow, Anna sensed how much he'd changed. He was older, his face creased, hair gone silver, but that wasn't it—in fact, his scrawny handsomeness was the most familiar part of him. He'd shed a brooding abstraction that seemed, in its absence, to have been his most singular trait. That and the smell of smoke. But he no longer smoked, and there was a disconcerting calm about him. He'd been so near death at the time of his rescue, Brianne said, they couldn't find his heartbeat.

Her father had become a stranger: a man she was meeting for the first time and sizing up as she would anyone. Anna dimly recalled having wanted to see him this way, but the fulfillment of the wish left them with little to say to each other. He knew nothing of her life; could not appreciate, for example, the delight she'd taken in a letter she'd received from Marle just yesterday:

An angel smiled down on our friend Mr. Bascombe: the navy has accepted him. Before he took the train to boot camp in Great Lakes, Illinois, Ruby's mother cooked him supper and her old man raised a glass to his health. Apparently it's true that "The uniform makes the man." Wish I could tell you more, but B. was reticent as ever, couldn't even get the menu. Bldg 569 isn't the same without him.

"You know about Mama," Anna said to break the silence.

He nodded. "Those soldiers are lucky to have her."

Anna missed her mother, who had joined the Red Cross just after Anna's move to California, before she announced her pregnancy. Her mother still believed in the doomed Lieutenant Charlie Smith. Anna wondered now if she would ever tell her the truth—whether it would even matter by the time the war ended. One thing was certain: Rose had been wrong about the world becoming small again. Or at least it would not be the same small world it had been. Too much had changed. And amid those shifts and realignments, Anna had slipped through a crack and escaped.

"She'll be a nurse when she comes back," she told her father.

"She's been a nurse for many years," he said.

They paused to catch their breath at the top of the hill. The Mare Island Naval Shipyard was arrayed below them at the foot of San Pablo Bay, a peninsula studded with piers along a channel full of warships. Anna loved being able to look down upon it every day before work and know which ships had sailed overnight and which new ones had berthed. She owed her job to a miracle, for by the time she and her aunt had settled in Vallejo, she'd felt too pregnant to dive. She worried it might harm the baby. She and Brianne had taken jobs at a diner—Brianne as a waitress, Anna as a cashier—and waited in a cramped, dingy apartment for the baby to arrive. It had been an awful time.

Last November, six weeks after Leon was born, Anna had finally presented her transfer documents at Mare Island. By then, Lieutenant Axel's telephone call was long forgotten. But it turned out not to matter; three *Normandie* salvage divers were employed at Mare Island now, and one of them—a supervisor—had been on Anna's tour of the Brooklyn Naval Yard. All three remembered her photograph from the *Eagle.* She was given a job at eighty dollars a week, and now worked underwater most days.

"Funny you've so many destroyers," her father said, looking down at the Yard, "with so few convoys out of the Golden Gate."

"Just four," she said.

"Six."

Anna looked again. "You're confusing your ships."

He pointed, counting. At three, she stopped him. "That's a mine-sweeper, Papa."

He took a long look, then turned to her, smiling. "I stand corrected."

The fog had begun its creeping advance, a lone tendril leading the way from the Pacific. Foghorns lowed in the distance. They sounded deeper and louder than the foghorns Anna had heard all her life. But then, this fog was different, solid-looking enough to mold with your hands. It gushed in overnight, engulfing whole cities like amnesia.

Ahhh Ohhhh

Ahhh Ohhhh

The ships were calling to avoid each other, but it always sounded to Anna as if they were lost, seeking companionship in the depthless white. The sound stirred in her a foreboding she couldn't explain. At night, wakened by the foghorns, she reached inside the basket where Leon slept, searching for the rampant patter of his heartbeat.

"Look," her father said. "Here it comes."

She was surprised to find him watching the fog. It rolled in fast: a wild, volatile silhouette against the phosphorescent sky. It reared up over the land like a tidal wave about to break, or the aftermath of a silent, distant explosion.

Without thinking, she took her father's hand.

"Here it comes," she said.

ACKNOWLEDGMENTS

I was heartened, during the years I spent circling *Manhattan Beach*, to know that if nothing more came of the endeavor than the pleasure of having researched it, I would count myself lucky. The good times began in 2004 at the New York Public Library, where I was a Fellow at the Dorothy and Lewis B. Cullman Center for Scholars and Writers, led by Jean Strouse. There, librarians Rob Scott and Maira Liriano helped familiarize me with the historical dominance of New York City's waterfront—a feature of the landscape that had mostly escaped me in many years of living here.

At the Brooklyn Historical Society, I stumbled upon a rich wartime correspondence between Alfred Kolkin and Lucille Gewirtz Kolkin, who met while working at the Brooklyn Navy Yard. In 2008 I had the opportunity to accompany ninety-year-old Alfred Kolkin back to the Yard along with his daughters, Judy Kaplan and Marjorie Kolkin.

At the Brooklyn Navy Yard, I was embraced and encouraged by Andrew Kimball, Eliot Matz, Aileen Chumard, and the extraordinary Daniella Romano, a guardian angel of this project. We collaborated with the Brooklyn Historical Society on an oral history of the Brooklyn Navy Yard. Under the expert tutelage of oral historian Sady Sullivan, I was able to assist in interviewing a number of our subjects: Ellen Bulzone, Don Condrill, Lucille Ford, Mary and Anne Hannigan, Pearl Hill, Sylvia Honigman, Alfred Kolkin, Helen Kuhner, Sidonia Levine, Audrey Lyon, Antoinette Mauro, Giovanna

Mercogliano, Robert Morgenthau, Ida Pollack, Charles Rockoff, and Rubena Ross. I've incorporated details from some of their stories into *Manhattan Beach*. I also benefited from Andrew Gustafson's Navy Yard tours (and subsequent help) through BLDG 92, the exhibition and visitor center of the Navy Yard, whose advisory board I had the honor to serve on. Bonnie Sauer at the National Archives gave me physical access to the collection "Photographs of the Construction and Repair of Buildings, Facilities and Vessels at the New York Navy Yard (1903–1945)."

My awareness of the link between ship repair and deep-sea diving began with an article by Robert Alan Hay, a civilian World War II diver at the Brooklyn Navy Yard. Two more guardian angels, MSG MDV Stephen J. Heimbach and James P. Leville (Frenchy), Sergeant Major, retired, dressed me in a two-hundred-pound Mark V diving dress at a reunion of the United States Army Diver's Association, where I was fortunate to be their guest in 2009. I'm obliged to World War II Army divers James D. Kennedy and Bill Watts for sharing their stories; some details of Mr. Kennedy's remarkable history appear in this book. My several talks with the first female U.S. Army deep-sea diver, 1SG Andrea Motley Crabtree, U.S. Army retired, were essential to my understanding of the challenges of being a female diver. Gina Bardi, Diane Cooper, and Kirsten Kvam at the San Francisco Maritime National Historical Park gave me access to rare technical diving books and a trove of historical diving artifacts. Staten Island diver Edward Fanuzzi shared a few of his harbor secrets.

The wartime experiences of merchant mariners caught my attention via two narratives, Herman Rosen's *Gallant Ship, Brave Men* and Harold J. McCormick (USNR)'s *Two Years Behind the Mast: An American Landlubber at Sea in World War II*, both of which inform *Manhattan Beach* directly. Repeated visits (and one short voyage) on the SS *Jeremiah O'Brien*, an operational Liberty ship and museum in San Francisco, introduced me to a group of World War II veteran mariners whose memories and knowledge were crucial to this effort:

Radio Operator Angelo Demattei, Deck Officer James Rich, Engineering Officer Norm Schoenstein, and Naval Armed Guard S1c John Stokes. In New York, I relied heavily upon Joshua Smith, interim director of the American Merchant Marine Museum at Kings Point, for reading lists and fact-checking.

For additional waterfront knowledge, I'm indebted to Joseph Meany's excellent monograph on New York Harbor during World War II. Richard Cox, director of the Harbor Defense Museum at Fort Hamilton, provided a tour. The McAllister family of McAllister Towing & Transportation, whose tugboats have plied New York's waters since 1864, was immensely generous—Brian McAllister with his World War II–era memories, and Buckley McAllister with present-day knowledge and harbor excursions.

For small-boat expertise and fact-checking, as well as numerous reading leads, I'm beholden to John Lipscomb. For naval fact-checking, I am grateful to Vice Admiral Dick Gallagher, USN retired. Economic historians Charles Geisst and Richard Sylla did their utmost to help me understand banking in New York during wartime. David Favaloro of the Tenement Museum provided an excellent tour and much knowledge. Alex Busansky shared legal advice.

I'm lucky to have been writing about a period that exists in living memory, and I vastly appreciate the longtime New Yorkers who shared their personal histories with me. The painter Alfred Leslie, with his crystalline recall, granted me several meetings. Also illuminating were Roger Angell, Don and Jane Cecil, Shirley Feuerstein, Joseph Salvatore Perri, and Judith Schlosser. Marianne Brown at the Condé Nast Archive provided access to a wealth of periodicals from the war years.

A bibliography would be tranquilizing, but a few books were critical. *Paddy Whacked: The Untold Story of the Irish American Gangster*, by T. J. English, and *On the Irish Waterfront: The Crusader, the Movie, and the Soul of the Port of New York*, by James T. Fisher, were both pivotal to my portrayal of Eddie Kerrigan's waterfront. John R. Stillgoe's

Lifeboat is a deeply original meditation on small-boat survival. The Center for Fiction provided a reading list of early-twentieth-century fiction set in New York City.

A series of smart and resourceful people helped me with my research. Sara Martinovich worked with me while a student at DePauw University. Peter Carey at the Hunter College MFA program bestowed *three* Hertog Fellows upon me, beginning in 2005: Jeffrey Rotter, Jesse Barron, and Sean Hammer, all fiction writers in their own rights. Meredith Wisner, professional researcher extraordinaire, provided exhaustive period knowledge.

The Corporation of Yaddo granted me a vital last-minute residency.

I would be nowhere without my readers: Monica Adler, Ruth Danon, Genevieve Field, Lisa Fugard, David Herskovits, Don Lee, Melissa Maxwell, David Rosenstock, and Elizabeth Tippens. Their insights and queries made the book immeasurably better.

My agent, Amanda Urban, is a true partner. She and her team at ICM and at Curtis Brown—Daisy Meyrick, Amelia Atlas, Ron Bernstein, Felicity Blunt, and many others—are the best of the best. My editor, Nan Graham, put enormous passion and hard work into this manuscript.

Thanks to my mother and stepfather, Kay and Sandy Walker, for their love.

Thanks to my husband, David Herskovits (again and always), and to our sons, Manu and Raoul, for making my real life so much fun.

Finally, I'm grateful to my brother, Graham Kimpton, 1969–2016, who taught me the necessity of "gunpowder" in any work of art, and whose wisdom and love reverberate through me every day.